Whistlin' Dixie

IN A NOR'EASTER

Whistlin' Dixie
IN A NOR'EASTER

Lisa Patton

Thomas Dunne Books

St. Martin's Griffin ❧ New York

THOMAS DUNNE BOOKS.
An imprint of St. Martin's Press.

WHISTLIN' DIXIE IN A NOR'EASTER. Copyright © 2009 by Lisa Patton. All rights reserved. Printed in the United States of America. For information, address St. Martin's Press, 175 Fifth Avenue, New York, N.Y. 10010.

www.thomasdunnebooks.com
www.stmartins.com

The Library of Congress has cataloged the hardcover edition as follows:

Patton, Lisa.
    Whistlin' Dixie in a nor'easter / Lisa Patton.—1st ed.
        p. cm.
    ISBN 978-0-312-55660-0
    1. Women—Southern States—Fiction. 2. Hotelkeepers—Fiction. 3. Bed and breakfast accommodations—Fiction. 4. City and town life—Vermont—Fiction. I. Title.
    PS3616.A927 W47 2009
    813'.6—dc22

                                                            2009016845

ISBN 978-0-312-65889-2 (trade paperback)

10 9 8 7 6 5 4 3

To Michael and Will, my true pride and joy.

And to each and every single mother:
Go after your dream, no matter how unattainable it may seem.

In memory of Josiah David Berger and
Melanie Ann Orpet Winand

Whistlin' Dixie

IN A NOR'EASTER

Prologue

No one ever told *me* you can't bury somebody up north in the wintertime.

So when my little fifteen-year-old Yorkie, Princess Grace Kelly, decided to pick New Year's Eve to go to doggie heaven, we had a problem. My handyman Jeb had the nerve to tell me that Gracie would have to wait in a shoebox on a garden shed shelf until spring, or the Thaw, as the Vermonters call it. I told him, in no uncertain terms, that I could never make Gracie do that and his solution was simply not an option. I mean, the least I could do was give her a proper burial with a funeral and all, after dragging her 1,473 miles away from home, *in her golden years* no less, to a place where teeteeing outside was not an option for her. The first time I ever set her down "to go" on top of the four-foot snowdrift outside our door at the inn, she was nearly buried alive.

The first thing you need to know about me is that I am not a pushover. I'll admit to being a little naïve, *maybe*, but I am no doormat. My girlfriends thought I was a huge doormat, but moving all the way to Vermont changed that forever.

Anyway, here I was living in subzero Vermont, but bound and determined to get Gracie into that ground. The night before Jeb informed me about this Yankee oddity I had called my best friend Virginia to give her the news about Gracie's passing. My nose was completely stopped up from crying when I dialed her number at two thirty in the morning, my time.

"Gracie's gone," I wailed into the phone as soon as she answered.

"What'd you say? I can barely understand you."

"PRINCESS. GRACE. KELLY. IS. *DEAD*," I screamed.

"Gosh, Leelee, you scared me. I thought something terrible had happened."

"This *is* terrible."

"I know, I know. I'm sorry. When did it happen?"

"She took her last breath in the middle of New Year's Eve dinner at the inn. The busiest night of the whole year. *It's all my fault!*" I sobbed.

"It's all *what*? You're gonna have to blow your nose."

I reached over for another Kleenex and honked into the phone. "I said . . . it's all *my* fault!"

"What do you mean? Gracie was *old*, Leelee. It was her time."

My bottom lip started to quiver. "*She hated it here*. And that's only the beginning. Not only did Gracie just drop dead out of nowhere, but four of my guests at the inn caused a blackout in the middle of dinner."

"You're kidding!"

"I wish I was." I sniffed a few more times. "Then—to top it all off—this couple showed up just before midnight to check in to their room. *I didn't have a room for them, Virginia.* I overbooked the inn by mistake and there wasn't a room to be had in all of southern Vermont."

"Wha'd you do then?" Virginia sounded scared for me.

"I did the only thing I could do. I made room for them."

"Oh my gosh, Leelee, this would only happen to you. Don't tell me they bunked up with y'all."

"It's a long story. Have you got an hour?"

"I've got all the time in the world, but before you get started I wanna know one thing."

"Okay, what?"

"When are you gonna finally give up this ludicrous notion of being the only Southern belle innkeeper in the state of Vermont and *come home*?"

"I'm always thinking about home, Virgy. Always."

Chapter One

A Wonderful Hot July Evening

MEMPHIS, TENNESSEE

Memphis is my home. It always will be no matter where I live. In the South we have a tendency to be possessive of our hometowns. A Memphis girl can marry a Birmingham boy, raise her family there, and live out the rest of her days in Alabama. But when her obituary runs in the *Birmingham Post-Herald*, it will still claim Memphis as her home.

The only other place I'd spent any time at all was Oxford, Mississippi. Going to college at Ole Miss was more like "a four-and-a-half-year vacation," according to Daddy. But the point is, I had no desire to ever leave my home again. I was perfectly happy.

Memphis gives me a peaceful feeling just thinking about it. Downtown sits way up on a bluff overlooking the Mississippi. The city itself is as flat as a pancake, which makes it the most beautiful place in the world to watch the sunset. Pinks, reds, yellows, and oranges streak the sky and you can watch the entire fireball melt into the cotton fields of Arkansas right across the river.

When you drive down parts of Poplar Avenue with the windows rolled down and smell barbecue cooking, it's impossible not to turn into Corky's or Little Pig's for a sandwich. Daddy would order his "white pig strictly lean." I order mine the same way all because of him.

If you come to Memphis it would be well worth your while to visit in the springtime. Azaleas and dogwoods color the town white, pink, and red as far as the eye can see. It's nice and warm, with the temperature hovering between seventy-five and eighty-five degrees. I know people say the summer is sweltering, but it never bothers me.

Probably our biggest brag is Elvis. Everybody over the age of thirty has some sort of an Elvis story, whether it's driving by Graceland and seeing him in his front yard or knowing somebody who knew one of his stepbrothers personally—or even still, knowing someone who went to his doctor, Dr. Nick. Elvis drove a truck for Daddy once before he was famous. That's our claim to Elvis fame.

I fell in love with a Memphis boy when I was sixteen years old and married him eight years later. I first had a huge crush on him way back in the tenth grade. Baker Satterfield hardly knew I was on this earth until my bosoms finally popped out our senior year in high school. I went from an A-cup to a D-cup in nine months. No wonder I attracted his attention.

At our graduation party Baker spent most of the evening trying to flirt with me. He ignored his date and threw popcorn at me and pinched my butt, very sneakily, every chance he could. But too bad for him. I had a date with one of his best friends, Jimmy Hudson. Jimmy Hudson didn't ignore me and I *certainly* didn't ignore him. When we weren't talking or slow dancing . . . we were making out. I'd have one eye shut and the other slightly open trying to see if Baker was watching us. Without fail, he'd be boring a hole right in our direction. So I'd lay it on extra thick. I'd start giggling at whatever Jimmy said and run my hands through his hair or kiss him playfully on the neck.

You should have seen the way I gloated when I got home that night, just thinking about finally having one up on Baker Satterfield. It served him right for overlooking me just because my chest was flat. Baker told me later that he spent four frustrating years at the University of Tennessee dreaming about my newly blossomed bosoms.

We met up again after college graduation, and two years later his dreams were nestled right next to him every night in Memphis. As far as I was concerned they could stay nestled that way forever. But when Baker decided to chase another dream, my life was transformed almost overnight from an unswerving line onto a collision course at the Indy 500.

The evening Baker shared his new dream with me occupies a permanent place in my memory. He was in a terrific mood, like he'd just hit a hole in one on the back nine at the country club with all his buddies watching. He was whistling and snapping his fingers and sliding his loafers across the kitchen floor as he helped me clear the dinner table. Normally he would have had the remote control in his hand by this time, flipping through the channels for any show remotely connected to sports. He never actually sat down to watch until the kitchen was clean. He'd stand in front of the TV like he was pausing just to get the score. "I'll be right there, honey. Hold on. Scores up next," he'd shout from the den. But I always knew what he was doing.

I was an all-sports widow. What really gets me is there is never a break from sports. In the summer it's baseball, which slides into fall, overlapped by football, which passes into basketball before anyone has a chance to breathe. Football and basketball run side by side for a while, and as if that's not enough, golf has to iron its way in between the two every Saturday and Sunday afternoon.

But this particular July night, he never even turned on the TV. He took Gracie out for an evening stroll instead of opening the back door and letting her run outside for her final potty break. I was reading to the girls when Baker returned from the walk and popped his head into their bedroom.

"Honey." There was a hush to his voice. "Come on out to the porch when you're done. I'm making peach daiquiris."

"Peach daiquiris. Yum. What's the occasion?"

"No occasion, really, I just thought you'd be in the mood for a daiquiri, as hot as it's been lately."

"Can I have one, too?" Sarah, our not-quite-five-year-old, said, perking up.

Baker stood in the doorway and blew her a kiss. "Not tonight. It's already past your bedtime. But I'll make a special one just for you tomorrow night."

"But I want one *today*, Daddy." She sat straight up with a pout. Sarah takes after her father—thick and wavy dark hair and indigo eyes.

"Tomorrow. Look, your sister is already asleep, and if you don't go fast Mr. Sandman will be visiting Isabella before you." Two-and-a-half-year-old Issie was on the side of the bed next to the wall, already conked out.

Sarah plopped back down, buried her face in her pillow, and put her arm around me.

"'Night, Sarah," Baker said, in a teasing way. When she wouldn't answer him he turned to me. "I'll meet you outside when you're done."

"I'll just be a few more minutes."

Baker gave me that look. That incredibly intoxicating sexy look, his "I want you" look, and walked out of the room.

We settled on the back-porch swing, swaying back and forth to the croaking rhythm of a toad. Hundreds of lightning bugs danced all around us and the neighborhood dogs chatted with one another in the distance. The daiquiri was sweet, just the way I like it, not too much rum, and with little pieces of peach still large enough to chew.

"Honey," Baker said, breaking the silence, as he twisted my curls with his fingers, one at a time, and leered at me with his gorgeous sapphire eyes. "You know what I want? I want our girls to grow up in a place where people still leave their doors unlocked and their car keys in the ignition."

"Mmhmm." I rested my head on his shoulder and pulled my legs up under me onto the swing. "We could move down to Collierville and have room for horses and maybe even a fishing pond for you. Sarah's been begging for riding lessons. Lots of the girls in her class are taking."

I could already see it—nineteenth-century white farmhouse, long driveway, pond on the right, barn on the left, horses running around and daffodils sprinkled everywhere.

"Yeah, but even better, we could own our own business and have four months out of the year off. I wouldn't have to travel, and I could help you out a lot more with the girls." Baker had his arm around me by now, running his hand through my long strawberry-blond hair.

"That sounds good, baby, but what insurance company closes four months out of the year?" I asked, still sipping on my daiquiri.

Baker's tone plummeted to that voice he gets when he's locked in the bathroom with the Sunday paper and doesn't want to be disturbed. He moved his arm and looked at me dead-on. "I'm *sick* of the insurance business. In fact, I'm downright miserable in the insurance business. It's boring. All I ever do is work, and I'm fed up with spending only two hours a day with my children. Sarah and Isabella are almost five and three, and I feel like I barely know them."

I should mention he talks with his hands. Well, we both do, but at this point Baker's arms were swinging all over the place. "I'm thinking big—something completely different and radical. I say we should get the hell out of here and move somewhere new and exciting like . . . like . . . Vermont!"

"Baker, please. You've been reading too many Orvis catalogs." Baker has a storeroom off the garage to house his abundant supply of fly-fishing gear, plus every show Bill Dance has ever starred in on video.

"No, I have not been reading too many Orvis catalogs. Vermont is a wonderful state, and . . . you're right, it does happen to have some of the best trout fishing in the country. But, there's virtually no crime at all in Vermont. The way I see it . . . it's the perfect place to live and raise a family."

He might as well have been talking about Yugoslavia—it was just as foreign to me. "Vermont. *Vermont!*" I bolted straight up from my relaxed position. "You can't be serious?"

"I've never been more serious in my life." With that Baker leaped off the swing, almost upsetting my daiquiri, and ran into the house. Before the swing even had a chance to slow down, he was bolting back out the door with his briefcase in one hand and a fresh daiquiri in the other. He plopped back down on the swing, put his drink on the floor beside him, and placed the briefcase on his lap, unsnapping the locks. The briefcase popped open and lying right on top was the latest copy of *North American Inns* magazine. He grabbed it, licked his right thumb, and started flipping through the pages. In the back of the magazine one of the pages was dog-eared.

"Get ahold of this!" Baker said. He read aloud, with such intense emotion you'd have thought he was auditioning for the role of Hamlet.

> *Located in a village setting near two major ski resorts, Vermont's premier restaurant/inn is for sale. Circa 1700s, the Vermont Haus Inn has nine guest rooms, most with private bath, seven fireplaces, gracious lawns, twenty acres and historic stone walls. This magnificent opportunity includes operating a full-service, high-gross world gourmet—acclaimed restaurant, along with a lifestyle that most people can only dream about.*

He looked over at me with a sanguine face before continuing.

> *Mint, mint condition. Superb owners' quarters. Owners retiring. Price reduced from $555,000.00 to $410,000.00. A must-see for anyone serious about owning a quaint Vermont country inn. Ed Baldwin Agency, 10 Hill Street, Fairhope, Vermont. 1-802-CALL-ED-B.*

He dropped the magazine on his lap, sat back in the swing, and let out a euphoric sigh. "What do you think, honey?" Baker was beside himself with joy. "Look at all we could have in Vermont"—he thumped the page with the back of his hand—"just by selling our house here! Twenty acres, an inn, *and* a business for not much more than the price of this house."

I was stunned. It was the only time in my life that I can honestly say I was truly speechless.

Baker used this lull in the conversation to advance to Exhibit B. He must have stopped by the bookstore on his lunch break, because three picture books on Vermont were the next items to emerge from his briefcase. He started flipping through the pages and showing me the pictures. "Look, Leelee, aren't these beautiful? Have you ever seen trees come alive like this? Remember that time you told me you had always wanted to take a trip to New England to see the fall foliage? Think what it would be like to live there and see it *every year*."

I'm frozen. No, I'm just not hearing him correctly.

"I've always wanted to own my own restaurant. You know that. I've managed two or three of them. There's nothing to it. And you said yourself that waiting tables was one of the most fun jobs you've ever had."

"Baker," I said, springing back to life, "I was in college when I waited tables. Yeah, it was fun. But that's only because Jay Stockley worked there, too. He was president of SAE and I had a big, fat crush on him. Waitressing was not *work*. It was a way to flirt with Jay Stockley."

Baker was so busy looking through the pages of that Vermont book, I wondered if he was even listening to me.

I put my hand alongside his cheek and turned his head around to face me. "I couldn't even tell you if Vermont is the little state on the right or the little state on the left, way up there at the top of the map. All I can tell you about Vermont is they make good maple syrup there."

"Leelee . . . please," Baker said in his know-it-all voice, and looked down again at the pictures.

"What would your *daddy* say?" I had to dig deep, scramble for anything that might knock some sense into him. "He's owned Satterfield State Farm for *how* many years?"

"Who cares? I never wanted to go into the insurance business in the first place. *Never*. My dad decided that for me the minute he saw something hanging in between the legs of his newborn baby."

I considered what he said, and kind of saw his point.

"I'm *bored*, Leelee. It's time to see the world!"

"Okay, but can't we just *travel* the world? Do we have to move?"

"Have you any idea what it feels like to wake up every morning, take a shower, shave my face, eat a bowl of cereal, then drive across town to work, where I sit at the *same* desk, in the *same* office, and look at the *same* old-woman secretary who's constantly telling me, 'I have more seniority than anybody else in the entire office except Mr. Satterfield *Senior*.' Then she looks over at me like she's got something big on me. I don't give a shit how long she or anyone else in that office has been there."

"Well, it helps with our lifestyle." I was always careful when it came to talking about Baker's income. It wasn't his fault he didn't have family money. Daddy's the reason we had what we had—a beautiful home that I'd spent over a year decorating, and a ski boat that was docked at Pickwick

Lake, giving us hours of pleasure in the summertime. Dare I mention that my husband was a sportsaholic with a golf and fishing habit that could have bought us a house to go with the boat on Pickwick Lake.

"But it's driving me crazy in the process." Baker was hanging his head now, with his hands on either side of his temples, his eyes closed. If there's one thing I hate, it's to see a grown man in agony. I put my arms around him and pulled him over toward me so his head was resting on my shoulder.

"I don't want you to be unhappy. I'm happy when you're happy. But moving all the way to . . . to . . . Yankeeville, I don't know. I just don't know about that."

"Honey, look, will you just go with me to see the place? You might fall in love with Vermont. Tell me you'll think about it, baby, please." He was giving me that look again. And this time his hand was working its way up one leg of my shorts.

I reached over, pushed it away, and looked him in the eye, my nose about two inches from his nose. "I'll think about it. But that's all. And don't bug me. I'll let you know when I'm finished thinking about it."

"I'll get you those diamond earrings."

"Are you bribing me, Baker Satterfield?"

"And so what if I am?"

"I cash in on bribes, that's what. Now will you please go get me another daiquiri?"

"They're good, aren't they?"

"Delicious. But making my favorite daiquiri is not going to make me move to a place where the people talk like their noses are stopped up." I stretched out my legs on top of his.

"Just consider it. That's all I'm asking."

"All right, all right. I'll do that much. I'll consider it."

He cut his eyes over at me and smirked. What Baker knew—and what I knew—is that once he got me to consider something, he was usually home free.

His glass was empty by this time also. Stopping the motion of the swing with his feet, he rose. "I'll be back." He leaned over to kiss my lips. Just before entering the house he turned around. "By the way, it's the little state on the left. Vermont borders New York, not Maine."

"Oh, thank you, Mr. McNally."

"You're welcome, Miss O'Hara."

"Would you go on and get my daiquiri, please?"

Falling asleep that night was rough. I lay in bed for hours, staring into the darkness, my husband sound asleep beside me. I wanted to please him. I loved and adored him. And I had for over half my life. But my goodness, this was a tall order. Leaving my home—Memphis, Tennessee—for a place where I had never even stepped foot? Not Birmingham, not Atlanta, not Oxford, Mississippi, even. Baker was talking about moving all the way up to a place where I didn't know one soul. And, as I would later find out, was a heck of a lot farther away than I ever imagined.

Chapter Two

When I awoke the next morning, after very little sleep, I found myself smack dab in the middle of a Folgers moment. The scent of my favorite morning aromatherapy was wafting down the hall from the kitchen to my bedroom, arousing me away from any desire to linger under the covers. This was a landmark moment, too: the first time Baker had ever used the coffeepot. When I heard the sound of his slippers shuffling against the hardwood of the hall and two little giggle-boxes following along with him, I lifted my eyelids just enough to peek through my lashes and out the bedroom door. I could make out the image of Baker, stooped over—carrying something—and Isabella and Sarah on either side of him. They walked slowly down the hall and right up to my side of the bed.

Baker whispered, "Okay, girls, on the count of three . . . one, two, three."

"Surprise, Mommy!" they all chimed, in unison.

I popped open my eyes to see my little girls jumping up and down and clapping their hands with excitement. "Breakfast in bed! What a surprise. Thank you, girls."

"Say thank you to Daddy, too," Sarah said. "He made the food part. I folded the napkin and put on the fork and spoon."

"I did, too!" added little Isabella, distressed that her sister had not included her in the deal.

"Thank you, Daddy. What's the occasion?" I teased him with a wink.

"Can't a man make breakfast for his wife without her becoming suspicious of his intentions? Hey, a good innkeeper needs to know how to make a knockout breakfast." Baker began pointing to each item on the tray. "Here you have your gourmet coffee, cream and sugar. And your fresh-squeezed orange juice. Over here—pancakes with *real* Vermont maple syrup . . . and finally, fresh blueberries and cream."

"Innkeepers really do knock themselves out, huh?" I sat up and propped the pillows behind me. Sarah crawled up on our antique four-poster canopy bed—my great-grandmother's bed—and flipped on the TV with the remote.

"Breakfast is very important at an inn." Baker placed the tray on my lap. "It's the meal that keeps people returning to the same B and B year after year. That and the hospitality of the innkeeper." Issie raised her arms and Baker lifted her onto the bed, where she nudged her way in between her sister and me.

"I can see that." I hesitantly sipped a taste of Baker's maiden cup of coffee. "I certainly wouldn't want to spend my money on a place where the innkeeper wasn't friendly, kind of like I wouldn't want to go back to a place where the coffee is so thick it sticks to the sides of my mouth." I couldn't help making a sour face.

"Okay, so my joe needs some improvement." I watched him disappear into the bathroom and reemerge wearing only a white towel that was wrapped around his waist just below his belly button. "How do you like the pancakes?" he called from the door.

"I always love your pancakes."

The bathroom was located directly off our bedroom. Even though his back was to me I could see his face in the mirror and I watched him lather his cheeks with shaving cream. There was something so gorgeous about him when he was shaving—his dark hair contrasted with the white cream and his blue eyes twinkling in between. "You'd make a wonderful innkeeper." He raised his voice a little to be heard over the sound of the TV.

"I would?"

"Yeah, you would. You're friendly and you're nice to everybody. That's exactly what it takes."

I knew he was right about the innkeeper part but dead wrong about something else. "I probably would make a good innkeeper but you're forgetting something pretty important. I'm not the greatest cook in the world."

He stopped shaving and walked over to me. *Your body is as beautiful as it was the first day I saw you in your bathing suit at Linda Yoder's pool party, fifteen years ago.*

"So what? That's no big deal. You can cook breakfast, can't you?"

I shrugged my shoulders and nodded in agreement with him.

"Listen. This inn I'm looking at is a four-star restaurant. The evening meal is prepared by a *real* chef. You know, culinary trained and all." Those arms were just a-waving all over the place and he still held his razor in his hand. "Remember when I was the assistant manager of the Copper Cellar near campus in Knoxville?"

"That was before we were married, remember?"

"We had a basic menu—nothing too fancy—and the check averages weren't even that high. But that place made a fortune. The spot I'm looking at in Vermont is a fine dining restaurant with *high* check averages." He turned and headed back to the sink. "I'm jumping in the shower. I'll talk to you more about it when I get out."

It had been a long time since I had seen him that happy.

After he had showered and dressed he walked back into the bedroom to finish knotting his tie. He stretched way across me and kissed Sarah and Isabella. He kissed me, too. "What are you doing today?"

"Taking Sarah and Issie to Mother's Day Out. Then I'm going to Seessel's to pick up some groceries, planting the rest of the lilies that Virginia gave me, and . . . meeting the girls for lunch at twelve thirty." Actually, this last appointment was not scheduled, but it would be; we had much to discuss.

"Well, tell them hey, and have fun. I'll call you after I talk to him."

"Talk to who?"

"Ed Baldwin. The Vermont real estate guy."

"Oh yeah."

No sooner had he reached the back door than the phone was in my hand. I wasn't sure who to call first—Virginia, Alice, or Mary Jule, my three very best friends in the whole wide world. *Wait 'til they hear what my husband is cooking up now,* I thought. Nothing he did would ever surprise them. They had all known Baker as long as I had.

Thank goodness it was Wednesday. All my friends' children were with mine in Mother's Day Out on Wednesdays. It would be no problem getting everyone to meet me at the country club for lunch. I didn't reveal the reason for this little emergency get-together on the phone. I only said that I had something *big* to tell them. They'd think I had found out some major scoop about who was sleeping with whom, or maybe they'd think I was pregnant again. But there was *no way* they would have guessed *this* news.

I dropped the girls off at the church, floated through Seessel's, and drove back home all inside a cloud. I could not stop thinking about the night before. It was the strangest feeling. Surreal almost. Did my husband actually come home and suggest that we up and move to *Vermont*? A place that I couldn't locate on a U.S. map with 100 percent certainty to save my life.

As soon as I got home, and still in a fog, I headed straight outside to plant my lilies. I love to garden. It's my special time with myself. My mind breaks into heavy problem-solving mode. It's also my time to talk to God. Something about digging my fingers through His rich soil keeps me in touch with who's truly in control.

I could already feel my mind shifting into gear when I picked up the shovel and slammed my foot down onto the foot ledge, hearing that first crunching sound of the ground breaking. *He must be out of his mind for considering a move to the North.*

Never in my wildest dreams would I have ever believed that I'd have to decide whether or not to leave Memphis, Tennessee. Heck, no one left Memphis by choice. Almost everyone I knew was *born* in Memphis, just as I was. Virginia, Mary Jule, Alice, and I were even born in the same hospital, we started kindergarten together on the same day, and I bet we've gabbed on the phone almost every day since. I couldn't imagine ever moving away from them. We were closer than sisters.

We watched our childhoods fly into adolescence and our teens revolve into our twenties. From double-seat panties and ponytails to pimples and pom-poms, these girls and I were joined together at the hip. If our parents only knew how many times we snuck out in the middle of the night together. There's not a one of us who can't recall the exact boy who gave each of us our first French kiss. Our daddies strutted us down the aisle at the country club debutante ball, the winter of our freshman year in college. All of us share the same collection of taffeta bridesmaid's dresses and dyed-to-match pumps. When every one of our babies was born, we took over the waiting room at Baptist Hospital and held a hen party for as long as it took the new arrival to show up. You couldn't give me one million dollars for the trunk of memories we share.

I'm convinced going to an all-girls school for thirteen straight years is the reason we're so thick. According to a certain group of people it was the finest all-girls school in town. It had been around since the late 1800s and generations of old-money families filled the pages of the yearbooks. Miss Jamison's School for Young Ladies. That was actually the name of the school when it started way back in 1882. I don't think they changed it until 1970. Then, to keep up with the evolving times, the name was shortened to The Jamison School. We had to wear short white gloves whenever we went on a field trip, and curtsy to the teachers when they walked in the room. Chewing gum meant an automatic Saturday School, and if you were caught sitting on a desktop you might as well start marching yourself straight to our principal's office, where Mrs. Carrington would remind you that Miss Jamison's young ladies did not sit on desktops.

Virginia and I roomed together every year at Ole Miss. We both pledged Chi O, and when we got to move into the sorority house our bunks were right next to each other. Once we graduated and moved back home, we found a house to rent and Alice moved in with us. Mary Jule was already engaged. Al Barton stole her heart in college and they were married the June after graduation. She was also the first to have a baby and we all made over that child like Fred and Ethel did over Little Ricky. Now she's got three more babies and I wouldn't be surprised if she went for a fifth.

The grinding of the city garbage truck distracted me from my thoughts. I had planted twenty-five lilies and mulched nearly all of them, losing all track of time. It was noon already. I dashed inside the house, stripping my clothes as soon as I hit the door, and dropped them in little piles all the way to the tub. There was hardly enough time for a bath. But I was hot and dirty and Daddy would have had my hide if I ever showed up at the Memphis Country Club looking like a filthy ragamuffin. Daddy never left the house unless he was impeccably dressed in a beautiful suit tailored especially for him, a monogrammed shirt of the finest Egyptian cotton, and matching overcoat and hat.

If Daddy were still living, Baker would have never brought up this loony idea in the first place. Daddy was very protective of me. After all, I was his only child. He was commanding and overbearing, but completely in love with Mama and me. When Mama died, he became even more sheltering. Baker steered clear from him as much as he could.

Alice swears if it weren't for Daddy, Baker never would have gotten into the Memphis Country Club. I'd never tell Baker that, though. He thinks he got in because he was a great football player. He received a full-ride scholarship to UT and played tight end all four years under Johnny Majors. Hardly a week goes by that I don't hear about the touchdown he made at the Sun Bowl. But either way, we're members.

Driving to the club that day felt strange. I kept looking around at all the trees in the yards and the houses that I had driven by a million times. So familiar, yet I had never taken the time to study the surroundings. Now I was noticing it all—the perfectly manicured lawns in Chickasaw Gardens, the monster live oaks, and the unique architecture of each house. This was my hometown and I had been taking it for granted for thirty-two years. Why in the world should I leave a place where my pediatrician was still in practice and now taking care of my own two little girls? Even the old druggist at Walgreens was still filling my prescriptions. I wouldn't be surprised if he remembered when I had the chicken pox.

Baker cannot take all this away from me, I thought. *It's my life, too. I'm tired of how he tries to run everything and give me no say-so.*

That's it, I thought, *I'm not going. I'll just tell Baker tonight that I've thought about it long enough and I'm not going. Case closed.* But, there was only one problem with my decision. Baker had a bridle around my heart with a rein that steered me in one direction—his.

When I got to the club, I hightailed it into the Red Room and found everyone seated at one of the round tables near the back. The main reason we went there for lunch was that it was the only place we could all charge our lunches to our husbands. And before that, it was the only place we could all charge lunch to our daddies. I slithered into the only available seat, fifteen minutes late—as usual.

Alice was bobbing up and down in her seat like a dang Mexican jumping bean. "I can't stand it anymore, Leelee. What's this all about? Mary Jule and I were on our cell phones the whole way from home to the club trying to figure it out."

"You're the one dying to figure it out, Alice, I'm not having a cow to know like you are," Mary Jule said. Her blond bobbed hairdo had a little flip in the back.

"Calm down, everyone. I hate to disappoint." I leaned in closer to them. "But I have no gossip. Y'all might as well prepare yourselves. This news is about me."

Now all three of them were wide-eyed.

I searched for a good way to break it to them, but nothing would come out.

"Yeeeess . . . ," Alice said, and swept her hand as if to say, out with it.

After another long pause I finally let the words flow. "Baker . . . wants to move . . . to *Vermont!*" I watched all three of them gasp at the same time. "To buy an inn."

"AAAAHHHHH!" Alice squealed loudly, causing the next table of women to look over at us. "*Vermont!* Where in the hell is that, anyway?" In one motion, she tossed her long, freshly weaved blond hair behind her shoulder and slid a Virginia Slims regular out of its pack.

"That's just what *I* asked him," I said. Then I relayed the whole story, beginning with Baker's unusually good mood, the peach daiquiris, the *North American Inns* magazine ad, and finally the breakfast in bed bit.

Virginia was silent, but her furrowed brow let me know she was giving the situation serious thought.

"Just tell him you're not goin'." This was Alice's simple answer to my complex dilemma. "Why didn't you tell him to go on without you? He's the one who's so unhappy, not you."

"You know I could never let him do that." I threw my head back and sighed.

"Why not? If Richard ever came home with a lamebrain idea like that I'd tell him to have fun, call us every week, and be sure to set up a direct deposit account for his paycheck at First Tennessee Bank. And *that*"— she paused for effect and flipped her French-manicured hand in the air—"would be the end of that."

"I've got it!" Virginia said, like she had solved the problem. "I'll go home and tell John, who can mention it to his father, and once he does that, I'm sure his father will be happy to call Mr. Satterfield." (John's father and Baker's father had been tailgating near one another at Neyland Stadium in Knoxville for years.) "We'll just nip this crazy idea in the bud before he has the chance to take it one bit further." She tore open a melba toast and smeared it with butter.

"No, Virgy. Thanks, but . . . I couldn't let you do that. I'd feel like I was betraying Baker."

"*Betraying* Baker? You would not. But have it your way; it was just a suggestion." The light blue V-neck tee she was wearing looked so pretty next to her brunette hair. Virginia's always hated her figure because of a few extra pounds, but we all think she's beautiful.

"This is just wrong. I'm surprised at Baker," Mary Jule said. "He has never, to my knowledge anyway, ever let on to Al that he's unhappy. And Al tells me everything."

"You're in a mess," Alice blurted out before I could respond to Mary Jule. "All I can say is thank God it's not me. I wouldn't move up north for all the tea in China."

"Why not?" I asked, now strangely taking Baker's side. "Maybe you would if you could see how beautiful it is. Baker showed me the pictures last night, and I have to admit it's perfectly gorgeous up there."

"So is Jamaica, but you'd never move there, would you?" Virginia wanted to know.

"No, I mean probably not," I said.

"Then why on earth would you consider moving to Vermont?" Alice looked over at the other two for backup. Virginia raised her eyebrows and Mary Jule shrugged her shoulders.

I paused a moment before answering her, honestly giving her question serious thought. "I guess to make Ba—"

"Baker happy," Virginia interrupted, finishing the sentence for me. "Believe me, you do that enough. Don't you see that? Think back to your wedding. You didn't want to get married in the Catholic church. You wanted to get married at Grace St. Luke's. But you did it anyway, because Baker wanted you to." She threw her arms up in the air and sat back in her chair. I could tell she was getting riled up at Baker. It had happened many times over the years.

"That was actually Mr. and Mrs. Satterfield who insisted on that," I told her. "You know how Catholics are about marriage. I don't think Baker really cared all that much."

"But you still did what *he* wanted. How about your honeymoon? Would you call a trip to Montreal to see some *car race* a honeymoon? Not to mention the long layover in New York with just enough time to make it to a Yankees game. I still don't know why you didn't tell him to drop you off at Saks." Virginia ripped open another melba toast and glanced around for the waiter.

"It was my *honeymoon*. I didn't want to be away from him. And for y'all's information Montreal is a very romantic city. There's a whole lot more going on there than just that car race. We stayed at a fabulous hotel, went to great restaurants. Baker even shopped with me some. I had a good time," I said, studying each of their faces for any sign of support.

Obviously they were in unanimous agreement with Virginia.

"All right. I get the message. Y'all think I'm crazy. But try to put yourselves in my place for a minute." I took a long sip of the Coke my friends had already ordered for me.

Mary Jule jumped to my rescue. "I don't know, Leelee, it's a tough call, but if Al really wanted to move as much as it sounds like Baker does, I think I'd have to go. I'd support him." She glanced at the other two before folding her arms in front of her.

"Really?" I was thrilled to finally have a backer.

"Yeah, I think I would." Her head nodded up and down nervously.

"Now you've both lost your minds," Alice said, disgusted with the two of us. She turned to Mary Jule. "You mean to tell me if Al came home from work one night and announced that he wanted you and the children to up and move to *Vermont* you'd go—just like that? No problem?"

"Well, I'd think about it first, just like Leelee's doing."

"Come on, Mary Jule, you would not," Alice told her.

Mary Jule looked back at me with a look that seemed to apologize in advance for what she was about to say. "He probably would never ask me to do it, so it's not something I'd have to worry about." Once she saw the disappointment on my face she tried to recover. "But I suppose I'd go if he asked me."

Alice chimed in again. "That's just it, you know he'd never do it, so it's easy for you to say you'd go."

"Well . . . that's true. Leelee, I guess it is hard for me to put myself in your shoes. Alice is right. Al would never leave Memphis, nor the Memphis Country Club, if his life depended on it."

All at once I felt like they had driven me out to a secluded pasture and left me to find my way back alone. "I know it's hard for y'all to imagine ever moving away. Believe me, it's blowing my mind, too. But y'all know how I am. It's hard for me to say no to anybody—especially Baker."

"All I can say is I tried to get you to marry Michael Barkley in college," Virginia said, and turned to the group. "But Fiery was waiting on someone who never gave her the time of day." (Virginia nicknamed me Fiery way back in seventh grade. It was the red in my hair.)

"Virginia Murphey, Baker did so give me the time of day . . . once we got home from Ole Miss."

"I'm not trying to be mean. It's just that I feel like Baker always gets everything on his terms. Baker knows you'll move to Vermont. You've spent a lifetime catering to his every whim."

"And now . . . he's making me mad," Alice interrupted Virginia and hit the table with her palm. "It's not *his* money he's spending."

Mary Jule winced. Alice's the only one who could get away with a statement like that.

"My problem is," I said, ignoring Alice's comment, "I don't know how I'll ever tell him no."

"Here, I'll help you." Virginia was all too happy to oblige. "Open your mouth and press your tongue to the roof of your mouth and say nnn-nooooo."

"Nnnooo," I repeated. "Very funny."

"I'm serious. Now go home and practice it on Baker," Virginia said.

"Just don't tell him we told you to," added a worried Mary Jule.

"As if he won't figure it out," said Virginia. "Whenever she says no to him for anything, he knows right where she's getting her fuel. Can we order now?"

Alice raised her arm and motioned for the waiter's attention.

When we were leaving the club after lunch, Virginia lagged behind and pulled me into the bathroom. "We were hard on you, weren't we?"

I nodded.

"You know we'll all support you in whatever decision you make. But I do wish you'd at least try and tell him no. I'd miss you so much. I can't imagine what it would be like without you here."

"Me neither." We stood there for a long time hugging each other.

I placed my hand on the doorknob and turned back around to face my dearest friend. "Do me a favor?"

She nodded.

"Say a prayer for me?"

Virginia stood a moment, comforting me with her eyes. "You're gonna need it, friend. You're *really* gonna need it," she said, and we both turned around to leave.

Chapter Three

"Wha'd you tell him?" Virginia was on the other end of the line, dying to get the scoop, when I answered the phone at exactly 8:05 the next morning. She knew Baker was always gone by eight o'clock. "I can't wait another second. What happened last night?"

There was no point in prolonging the inevitable. "I told him I'd go up to the inn. *For a visit.*"

"You what!"

"It's just a visit. I never said I'd *move.*"

"What happened to 'no'? Couldn't get it out?"

"Couldn't get it out."

"Fiery, you're as good as gone. Dear God, I can't picture you as a Yankee."

"You can stop trying to picture it, Virginia, because I'll never be one," I told her.

"You will be if you move up to the North with them." I heard her hold out the phone and fall into hysterics. "I was just thinking about you," she said, barely able to catch her breath, "coming home for your first visit and talking like Fran Whatever-her-name-is on that obnoxious babysitting show."

"*The Nanny*? Yeah, right."

"That's it, *The Nanny*. I can just hear you now, 'Hieee you guyeeez.'"
Her nasal intonations sounded right on.

"Real funny. Oh, hold on a minute, would you? My phone is beeping."
When I clicked over to catch the incoming call, it was Baker. He must have
called me the second he put down his briefcase.

"Hey," he whispered. "Is it there yet?"

"Not yet."

"Okay, just checking. Call me right when it comes."

"I told you I would, now relax." I said good-bye and clicked back over to
Virginia. "He's about to jump out of his skin."

"About what?"

"This buyer's prospectus that's coming from Vermont. Some real estate
agent is supposedly FedExing information on the property to us this morning. Baker's coming home for lunch to look at it so he wants me to call him
as soon as it arrives."

"He wasted no time, did he?"

"Not really."

"Gotta go fix breakfast. Bye, Fran," Virginia teased, and hung up.

On time, Baker's Eddie Bauer Explorer zipped up the driveway. I watched
him through the kitchen window as he sprung out of his car and hurried
inside.

"Leelee," he called, the minute the door swung open.

"It's in the living room," I said, reading his mind. The FedEx man had
rung my doorbell at exactly 9:00 A.M., with a bulging envelope addressed
to MR. AND MRS. BAKER SATTERFIELD.

Baker dove into the living room, and didn't resurface for a half hour.
Every few minutes, though, I could hear little gushes of delight spewing
from his lagoon of euphoria. "Wow, would you look at this place—it's even
got a slate roof!" And, "Fifteen minutes from *two* ski resorts—*NO WAY!*"
When he finally did decide to pop back up for air, I heard him calling,
"Leelee, come here. Tell me what you think about it."

I took my time drying my hands on a dishcloth and then moseyed off to join him. "It's attractive," I said, walking up next to the chair where he was sitting, hovering over the inn brochures.

"Is that *all*?" he said, looking up now. "All you can say is 'it's attractive'? This house looks like it belongs on the cover of *Country Living*! It even has a slate roof. There's an antique barn, and twenty acres of land. And look, here's the most incredible part. Did you see this?" He was swiftly pointing his finger up and down on the picture. "This aerial view of the property shows a *river running right through the middle of town*, within walking distance of the inn!"

All of a sudden, Baker sprung up from his seat, raised his right arm, and started casting with his imaginary fly rod.

"Baker," I said, trying to make eye contact with him between casts, "I'm trying to be excited about this, really I am. But this whole thing has taken me completely by surprise. It's happening too fast. I mean, we have a beautiful home right here, don't you think?"

He didn't answer me.

"Baker, *Baker*," I cried, "are you *listening* to me?"

Finally he stopped fishing and sat back down in the chair. "You know I think this house is beautiful. You've done an incredible job with it. But you could make any old house look like this one. Wouldn't you love to do it again?"

"I don't know. It takes forever for the fabrics to come in and then longer for the curtains to be made. The painters never show up when they say they will. I've just now started enjoying this house."

"I know you love it, honey, but you could love any house. You never know until you try. Let's just take a trip up to Vermont and take it all in." He threw his line in again off the right side of the chair.

"I already told you I would."

"I know, I'm just trying to get you to be excited, that's all."

"What would make me *excited* is that pair of diamond earrings you've been promising me." I pulled my hair back into a ponytail. "See? Wouldn't my ears look much nicer with shiny diamond studs?" I batted my eyes and posed.

He squinted his eyes and studied my ears. "I just might be able to ar-range something." Then he arched his back over the left arm of the chair, pretending he was fighting the world-record lunker, and never gave up until he reeled the sucker in.

Baker went back to work after lunch, pouting a little because I wasn't doing cheerleading jumps around the house over the prospect of us buying an inn, with a slate roof, in a foreign corner of America.

Virginia and her three stopped by around 3:00 P.M. It was a scorching, Memphis-in-July day, so we each grabbed a few little Cokes, the green-bottled kind, from my fridge and headed out to the porch. All five children barreled out behind us in hopes of being the first one to ride on Sarah's Little Tikes train.

Virginia and I sat down on the swing together, and tilted our heads back so we could feel the wind on our faces from the high speed of the ceiling fan. I shut my eyes while she leafed through Ed Baldwin's précis of the ideal life in Vermont.

"It *is* pretty. I have to admit that," she said, when she was finished read-ing. She closed the packet and slipped it between the cushion and the arm of the swing. "He's really going ahead with this, huh?"

I exhaled an exasperated sigh. "I guess so." The loose hair around my face swirled around from the draft of the fan.

"What's gotten into him?" Virginia reached around and pulled her thick, shoulder-length dark hair into a ponytail, twisted it around, and tried to get it to stay in a bun.

"Beats me. He's talked about moving and doing something different. But I've never taken him seriously. He's never gone this far. Can you be-lieve he'd even *want* to get that far away from UT football?"

"I've been thinking about it and yes, I can believe it. His whole identity is UT football. Now that that's over—and he's no longer a *star*—he's dying to get out of town. He knows he can't ride that wave forever."

I paused before answering. "I see what you're saying, but to move all that way—just to feel good about himself?" Bless Baker's heart. He was so proud of his football prowess.

The ringing of the telephone interrupted us and I reached down to grab my cordless, which was on the floor underneath me. A stranger's voice was on the other end of the line.

"Leelee?"

"Yes."

"Ed Baldwin calling from Vermont."

How does he already know my name? "Oh, hi, how are you?" I looked over at Virginia, pointed to the phone, and then over to the prospectus beside her.

"Fieeene," he said, sooo Yankeeish. "Just fieeene. I wanted to make sure you had gotten the material I sent you and Baker on the Vermont Haus Inn."

"Mmmhmm," I answered. "Yes, we did." I glanced over at Virginia and rolled my eyes.

"Good. Well then, when will you be arriving in Vermont to tour the property? I'll make your arrangements on this end."

He caught me totally off guard. "I haven't really thought that far ahead, Mr. Baldwin. We only received it a few hours ago."

"Actually, the weekend of August fourth would work well for me. Do you guys have any prior commitments for that weekend?"

The nerve of this man. "I . . . I'm not really sure, but I can check my schedule and get back with you," I said, with a tinge of irritation.

"I don't mind holding. Take your time."

I'm not believing this. "All right," I said, miffed. I put my hand over the phone and whispered to Virginia, "You're not gonna believe this guy." Then I hustled into the house, obeying this total stranger. My calendar was blank on that day but it was still two weeks away. I never planned that far in advance.

"Mr. Baldwin?"

"Yes?"

"I don't have anything on my calendar for that weekend *right now.*

There's a *chance* we may be able to make it up that weekend, I suppose." I motioned to Virginia to share the phone with me so she could listen to this Northerner's voice.

"Good, it's settled then, I'll call you back when I've secured your accommodations."

Unbelievable. "But I haven't confirmed it with my husband yet."

"He seemed quite eager to see it when I spoke with him on the phone. It sounded to me as if he wanted nothing to stand in his way."

"Oh . . . well, I wasn't aware of that." I didn't know what else to say. He obviously wasn't even picking up on the fact that I was peeved.

Virginia mouthed the words "hang up" and made a phone slamming motion with her hand.

"I'll check to see if the Vermont Haus Inn is available. It stays booked up months in advance, you know. I'll let you know ASAP. Talk to you soon, Leelee. Good-bye now."

"Bye." I hung up the phone, sat back in the swing, and looked at Virginia. "Well, I've *never*!"

Virginia shook her head in disgust. She wasn't used to people just barging in and taking over, either. "Damn Yankee!"

"I just agreed to fly up to Vermont on the first weekend of August. I can't believe I just did that."

"You should have told him that you'd have to get back with him. You're *way* too nice, Leelee."

"I *tried*, Virginia, really I did. He just railroaded right over me. Why is it that I always find myself in these kinds of situations? Do I look like I have train tracks branded on my forehead?"

"Of course you do. No, really I think you just have a hard time saying no because you want everyone to like you. I hate to say it, but Baker does it to you, too."

"I know and I'm sick of it. He wants to make all my decisions for me. Daddy did that, too. You know what?" I said, standing up, now in a take-charge mood. "I'm going up to Vermont and if I don't like it I'm gonna tell Baker he can go without us."

"Atta girl! And hey, you never know, Baker might get up there and hate it."

"Fat chance. He discovered a river running right through the middle of town—about a block from the inn. That boy will be in trout-fishing heaven. It wouldn't surprise me in the least if he decided to wear waders on the airplane."

I had no say-so in my own life. Thinking back on it, Daddy started all this. I never placed my own restaurant order until Baker became the head of my household. Daddy always ordered for me. In fact, if he was entertaining a group of my girlfriends, he would order for all of us. When it came to Mama, he insisted upon her waiting in the car until he came around and opened her side. My grandmother never went out to Sunday lunch after church without an orchid from Daddy pinned on her dress, and he certainly never let a woman, no matter who she was, pay for one thing. He took pride in taking care of the women in his life. A quintessential Southern gentleman—that was my daddy.

But if that's the way gentlemen are supposed to be, why was I feeling so vulnerable?

Chapter Four

Just fourteen days after Baker first announced his aspirations of becoming an innkeeper, a Northwest Airlines flight 727 touched down in Albany, New York. Aboard was one starry-eyed Southerner who was ready and willing to defect to the other side without so much as a glance over his shoulder. Another Southerner on board with him was anything but willing, and as the wheels of the jet screeched to a stop, I had to force myself into a cheery mood.

We knew Albany to be the state's capital. That's it. Nothing else. Neither of us had even traveled to a single state in all of New England—unless New York City is considered part of New England.

"It's about a two-hour drive from Albany," Mr. Baldwin had informed us over long-distance. "I'll meet you around one P.M. at the Sugartree Mountain base lodge. That gives us just enough time to grab lunch and do a little sightseeing before our three o'clock tour of the Vermont Haus Inn." Ed Baldwin had come through with his promise of making all the arrangements. All Baker and I had to do was pay for everything.

When we set out toward Vermont in our rental car, Baker agreed to let me be navigator. Navigating is one of the few things he admits that I do better than him. It was a perfect day—eighty degrees, blue sunny skies, a gorgeous drive—and I had a happy Baker all to myself. No TVs, no scores, no golf clubs. Not even a fishing pole.

I could see the mountains in the distance as we approached Vermont. I was a little puzzled. "*Those* are the *mountains*?" I asked Baker. "They seem smaller than the Smokies—are they?" I had been picturing the massiveness of the Rockies.

"Maybe, I don't know. But who cares?"

"I'm not trying to be negative, honey, I just think of mountains as being vast with snowcaps . . . that's all. I mean, I've heard people ski out west in some places well into the summer and I've also heard that the skiing in the Northeast is icy."

Baker whipped his head around and snapped at me. "Who told you that?"

"Alice. Actually Richard told her."

"Richard doesn't know what in the hell he's talking about. He's never skied in Vermont. The skiing here is just as good as anywhere. You'll see."

The moment we crossed the Vermont border, about an hour from the airport, I started to perk up. The billboards had disappeared. In New York, a billboard looms at you every quarter mile like a buzzard inspecting roadkill. The contrast made Vermont look like a much prettier state. Black-and-white cows, the Ben & Jerry's kind, were grazing on either side of the road. A dairy farm sat on top of a hill with an old-fashioned silo, and the wildflowers scattered out for miles in the pastures. I had to admit it was a charming place after all, and I decided right then and there to make the best of the trip.

Just before the Bennington city limits, on the left, I saw my first Vermont inn. It was a stately mansion sitting on a large, manicured lawn, with black-and-white-striped awnings covering several of the windows. The sign out front read FOUR COLUMNS INN. *It's a shame we aren't looking to buy that place*, I thought.

Bennington was adorable. Bungalow-style homes, window boxes brimming over with healthy, vibrant flowers, and a town square with the usual businesses. A tall monument poked into the sky from the center of town. I read on my map that it was erected in remembrance of the Battle of Bennington, fought during the Revolutionary War.

On the way between Bennington and Fairhope I got a thrill that made the whole trip worth it. If I had been looking down at my map, navigating for one more split second, I believe I would have missed it. There, on the right-hand side of the road, was the most extraordinary road sign I had ever seen.

"OH MY GOSH!" I shrieked.

Baker swerved our rented Blazer over to the right like he was trying to avoid hitting something in the road. Gravel on the shoulder kicked up underneath the tires and spit off to the sides.

"DID YOU SEE THAT? GO BACK!"

"What? See *what*? *Damnit*, Leelee, are you trying to get us both killed? You scared the shit out of me. What is it?"

"That sign back there. Didn't you see it? It said *moose crossing*. Turn around, Baker, please. I want to get my picture made in front of that sign. Virginia and them are gonna die! Turn around."

"Okay. I'll turn around. But I don't want to be late for our appointment." I knew he didn't want to turn around at all, but he was trying to be extra nice.

"Why didn't you tell me I was gonna get to see a moose? I've never seen a moose *in person*. I can't wait."

I jumped out of the car and Baker hopped out to take my picture. "Smile," he said. I stood right next to the sign and put my arms around it. It was the most unbelievable road sign *I'd* ever seen and I knew my friends would feel the same way.

"You never told me they have mooses here," I said to Baker as we were getting back in the car.

"Well, to be perfectly honest, I didn't know that, either. And it's 'moose,' Leelee."

"I knew that." *Know-it-all.* I hate it when he corrects me.

Baker just shook his head and for the rest of the trip up the mountain to Sugartree, I never took my eyes off the side of the road, hoping against all hope that I might spy a real, truly live moose.

We turned into the Sugartree Ski Resort on time, at exactly 1:00 P.M. . . . BST (Baker Satterfield Time). After parking the car we followed the signs to the base lodge where we were to meet Mr. Yankee himself. When we walked in the front door I looked around at the rustic décor set amid large woodsy murals painted on the walls. It had a quaint feel like I was stepping into a Swiss postcard. Baker stopped at the information desk to ask a young girl the way to the dining area. She told us to go down the hall and that we would run right into it.

Our toes were barely in the room when Ed Baldwin came barreling right up to us. "Baker and Leelee?" he inquired. "Ed Baldwin. I'm glad you made it. How was your trip?"

"Great," Baker answered, smiling widely and pumping Ed's hand.

"Are you guys hungry?" he asked.

"Starving," Baker and I both answered at the same time.

"Good, why don't you two grab a table and I'll go through the line and get you something to drink for starters."

"I'd love a Coke," I said.

"Make that two," Baker added.

"Should I make yours a diet?" Ed looked straight at me.

"The real thing's fine," I answered, with a fake smile. *Do I look like I need to be on a diet to you, a-hole?*

"I'll be back in a flash."

When Ed walked away, I shot Baker a look that could kill. He closed his eyes, waved his hand back and forth, and shook his head, like, please, Leelee, not now.

So I just swallowed it, crossed my arms in front of me, and decided to soak in the surroundings instead.

A large moose head (I was getting closer) hung over a massive stone fireplace, which had benches in a semicircle around it. No doubt this was the gathering spot for winter skiers to warm their frosty noses and toes.

When Ed returned with our Cokes, he swung his leg over the bench and sat down opposite Baker and me.

"So," he said, placing the Cokes down in front of us. "You guys had no trouble with my directions, I hope."

"None whatsoever. We came straight here. Leelee's a great navigator," Baker said, and smiled over at me. When I took my first sip, I could tell right away it was Pepsi. I hate Pepsi. But I never said a word.

Ed Baldwin was quite the inquisitor. He questioned us on our occupations, asked if we had any children, inquired about our heritage and how much money we had in the bank. He wanted to know all about Baker's daddy's insurance company and why he would want to leave his position. The one thing he didn't quiz us on was the extent of our restaurant background. Baker never picked up on this, but I did. *Slick, very slick.*

"It's a perfect day for a chairlift ride," Ed said, when we had finished our lunch. "What do you say we ride to the top and get a better look at the Sugartree valley? You can get a terrific view of the region from the top of the lift."

"Sounds great," Baker said.

Baldwin ushered us out of the lodge. Baker took hold of my hand and the three of us strolled over to the lift. It had been years since Baker had actually held my hand in public. *Who does he think he's trying to impress?*

While Baker and Ed chitchatted about the skiing industry, I focused on Ed Baldwin—the pushy man. He was tall and lean, I'd say around forty-five years old, and wore a pair of wire-rimmed sunglasses. Whenever he opened his mouth to talk, I had to stop myself from staring at his teeth—well, actually his veneers. Bless his heart, he must have used a bad dentist because they were a little on the thick side.

His hairline was receding and what was left of his dark hair was streaked with gray. His dress was conservative—khaki pants, a white golf shirt, and a pair of Timberland hiking boots. The only thing New Englandy about him at all was his accent and the Patagonia fleece vest he wore (*in the summer*) over his shirt.

On the ride to the top of the mountain, Ed informed us that Vermont had the lowest crime rate of any state in the country. Baker jabbed his elbow into my arm as soon as he heard that. I was sitting in between the two guys, and the fourth chair was empty. I wished I had been on the outside because they were the ones doing all the talking. Besides, I was dead set on finding a moose.

Ed went on to talk about the wonderful public school system in the area, the reasonable property values, the abundant wildlife, and, of course, the fresh mountain air. "Skiing is part of the public school curriculum," he said. "Our kids get out at noon on Tuesdays, and the school buses transport them here to Sugartree to ski for the rest of the day. They have a blast. As a matter of fact, my children have become competitive racers."

"That's neat," I said, thinking that might be something I'd like the girls to take up.

"They went to a high school over on Stratton Mountain, about thirty minutes away, called the Stratton Mountain Ski School."

"Do they get any studying in?" Baker chuckled a little when he asked.

"Oh, sure, but they ski every single day."

"Do they accept girls?" Baker wanted to know.

"Of course, are you kidding? It's coed. Several of the Stratton Mountain Ski School graduates have gone on to become members of the U.S. ski team."

"I've heard the skiing in the Northeast is icy," I heard myself saying. Baker jabbed my arm again.

"Well, that's debatable. Folks out west don't like to admit that Vermont has some pretty nice conditions here. In my opinion—and I don't speak for everyone, mind you—skiing in Vermont is as good as any mountain out west." He *sounded* convincing. But then again wasn't that his MO?

"Have you ever seen a moose?" I bent down to look at the thicket of evergreens below us.

"Yuup, when you live here, you see them quite often. They're all over the place."

"Are they on *this* mountain?" I perked right up.

"Well, sure."

"What about on the side of the road?"

"Sometimes, or they could be in a field—just keep your eyes peeled. You'll see one." (I didn't find out until much later that really spotting a moose is about as likely as spotting a freckle on your own fanny.)

"What about tornadoes and earthquakes?" I asked. *There's bound to be something wrong with Vermont.*

"Nuup, we don't have to worry about earthquakes and tornadoes around here. The mountains protect us from tornadoes and, to my knowledge, there are no fault lines anywhere close."

"Then what *is* the downside to living here?" I asked. *Somebody needs to ask this question.* "There must be something—a stinky paper mill perhaps, or contaminated rivers?" I knew Baker was about to kill me, but wasn't it my job to play devil's advocate?

"Oh no, my dear lady, not here. Vermont is protected. There's a domineering group of environmentalists who practically control the legislation in this state." Conveniently for him, the chairlift came full circle and into its base just as he finished his sentence. "Well, it's about that time. Why don't you guys hop in my car so we can all ride over together."

Once we got to his Subaru station wagon, Ed invited Baker to join him up front. I slid into the backseat. *He's no Southern gentleman*, I told myself.

It was a short ride to Willingham just down the mountain. When Ed took a sharp turn, a DVD came sliding out from underneath Baker's seat and landed next to my foot. Three naked girls were on the cover wearing nothing but old-fashioned nurse caps. I thought about kicking *Naughty Nurses* back under the seat but decided to leave it out in plain view instead.

As we drove into town, we crossed a river with white water. Baker turned around and glanced back at me with a wink. Ed told him it was the Deerfield River and of course it had trout in it.

Straight up a hill, about a block from the river, Ed turned on his left blinker. "It's the moment you've been waiting for." He glanced over at Baker and then craned his neck back at me. Ed pulled in, crept down the driveway, and parked his car on the side of a white picket fence. Baker flung his door open and jumped out. I tiptoed out of my side. At last, the Vermont Haus Inn and I were face-to-face.

I recognized it immediately from the pictures. It looked as if it could have been a big farmhouse at one time. The not-so-fresh whitewash on the outside was still passable but the green paint on the shutters was peeling in a few places. A wonderful old slate roof of coral, blue, and light green made a basket-weave pattern that, when mixed with the afternoon sunlight, gave a warm, inviting feel to the place. Two dormer windows peeked from the right side of the roof and a large front porch, perfect for rocking chairs, stretched all the way across the front of the house. To the left of the porch was a front door, which opened into a small enclosed area.

The flowers in front of the porch were stunning. Not at all like Southern gardens; there were many flowers I didn't recognize. No azaleas or hydrangeas, gardenias or rhododendron. It resembled a European garden. I couldn't help noticing that there were no shrubs, like boxwoods or hollies, up close to the house. (I found out later it's because they'd never survive the winter due to the snow and ice that crashes down upon them from the roof. That should have been my first clue.)

We walked through an arbor with blue morning glories tangled up in the overhead lattice to reach the front door. I looked over at Baker and he was smiling, full of anticipation, unafraid and adventurous. Goose bumps started to crawl all over me and they weren't the good kind. More like the kind you get from panic.

"Are we ready?" Ed beamed from ear to ear.

"Ready as I'll ever be," I muttered under my breath.

Ed opened the front door and then stepped aside to let Baker and me proceed in front of him. I put one foot into the foyer and drew straight back, like I had just dipped my toe into the waters off the coast of Iceland. God as my witness, if smells could kill, I would have keeled over and died right there on the spot. It smelled like a mélange of musty upholstered furniture, garlic, and propane gas, on top of a profusion of BO. I don't know about anyone else, but I would *never* let my house smell like that. *Pee-you*, I thought, *haven't they ever heard of potpourri?* I stepped inside anyway.

A beautiful, intricately carved staircase spilled into the foyer from the second story. But due to the horrendous stink, it was hard to take notice of its real beauty. Daddy would have never made it past the foyer. He would have turned around and left as soon as the first whiff of air breezed through his nostrils. Daddy liked to brag he had "the keenest olfact'ry senses known to man." If there was one thing Daddy had no tolerance for, it was houseitosis.

I was trying my hardest to catch Baker's eye. On purpose, he was not looking anywhere near my direction. Totally grossed out, I decided to take the tour breathing through my mouth only.

"The parlor seems like a logical place to start," Ed began, and walked over to the front window.

"Was this house ever a residence?" I asked, exerting every bit of effort I could muster to not turn around and run.

"Yuup, you're absolutely correct. It was built in the late seventeen hundreds by a gentleman by the name of Harold O'Shaunessey. He built it for his young bride."

"Is this where the guests hang out?" I glanced slowly around the room.

"Indeed it is."

I couldn't help but wonder where the guests were. Ed Baldwin told us we couldn't stay at the Vermont Haus Inn because it was full. Full of what—*ghosts*?

The parlor was decorated with mismatched, worn-out furniture and lots of cluttery knickknacks. Probably every issue of *National Geographic* for the last twenty years lined the built-in bookshelves along with hundreds of paperback romance novels and wineglasses. There was a beautiful fireplace in the center of the room but the wide-board pine floors were badly worn. There were no rugs on the floors at all. The place was ragged and tattered. *How do people live like this?* I thought. I couldn't imagine actually opening my doors to the public with this shabby décor.

After the parlor, Ed showed us the dining rooms—four small, intimate rooms with only four tables in each. All the tables had candles, carnations, and red linen tablecloths. I liked the screened-in porch the most, which was used for dining as well.

If I had to rate the inn at that point, I would have given it an eight on architecture, a two on décor, and a big fat zero on aroma. For Baker's sake, I tried to picture my furniture and curtains, my paint colors, my wallpaper, and my uncluttery knickknacks in the Vermont Haus Inn. Even though I could almost see it, I still had my doubts if we'd ever be able to de-stink the place.

Next stop on the tour was the upstairs—to see the guest rooms. Nine of them to be exact. But we saw them so quickly I didn't have time to notice much. I did notice, however, that just like the downstairs, the upstairs would need a total overhaul. I'll say it right now, I certainly wouldn't have paid more than thirty dollars a night to sleep in one of those rooms. To me the Vermont Haus Inn resembled an old college dorm rather than a quaint country inn.

But there was a nice sitting room upstairs with a large fireplace and a few of the bedrooms had fireplaces. At least there was something to work with, *if* Baker ever talked me into moving.

The kitchen was next, a daunting sight when you aren't used to the commercial kind. It was like walking into a chrome store. Big sinks and ovens, three refrigerators, a huge Hobart commercial dishwasher, and several large steel pots and pans hanging from a rack near the huge eight-burner gas stove. A gigantic pot rested on top of one of the eyes, near bubbling over. Ed said it was the chef's famous stock—whatever that meant.

I was particularly, *mostly*, interested in finding the "superb owners' quarters" Ed boasted about in his *North American Inns* magazine ad and I couldn't rest until we moved in that direction.

At last we moseyed out to a dining area right outside the kitchen. Ed walked over to a door that had been nailed shut. "Actually this door leads into the apartment." He pushed a dining table out of the way to get over to it. "But the owners prefer to keep it nailed shut to ensure their privacy. I've been telling the potential buyers that it could be reopened to have easier access from the inn. It's just a matter of preference."

"Can we see it now?" I asked.

Baker shot me a look. "Only if it's convenient. Leelee's just excited," he said.

"You're in luck, Leelee," Ed said, in a rather annoying way. "It's our next stop. Follow me outside, you guys."

To get to the apartment, we had to exit via the screened porch into a lovely garden full of pink climbing roses, hollyhocks, lilies of various varieties, fresh herbs, and other perennials I didn't recognize.

Fresh air at last.

On the way to the owners' quarters, Ed explained it had originally been an old barn. It was common in New England, back in the 1700s and 1800s, to butt the barn to the house. That way people wouldn't have to be exposed to the elements when they brought in their firewood or milked their cow.

The door to the apartment was left unlocked and Ed stepped back to let us walk in before him. Once again, the odor was the first thing that hit me, and sure enough I had to go back to breathing through my mouth. This smell was mustier than the smell in the inn, though, more like the inside of a cabin at summer camp. The BO was stronger, much to my dismay, but the garlic was not quite as pungent.

Nothing could have prepared me for what I was about to see.

We entered the superb owners' quarters into a small sitting room with walls painted a dark burnt orange, and that color led up the stairs. Just off the sitting room two doors were open wide and from where I was standing I could make out the size of each bedroom. I tried holding back my shock but couldn't. My eyes widened and my jaw dropped. I tried to breathe but a sudden gasp sucked the air out of my lungs. When I poked my head into the first room, which had curtains for doors and hooks for clothes rods, the only furniture I saw was a pair of twin beds with one small end table in between.

"Excuse me, Ed. Is this the master?" I swallowed in an effort to hide the panic in my voice.

"Indeed. Actually they're both masters. The owners are brother and sister and they each have their own."

"And these are they?"

"Yes, ma'am. Nice, huh?"

No, they're hideous. And I need a microscope to find them.

The walls of the bedrooms were papered with a 1960s floral covering to match the chocolate brown windows and doors. *I hate chocolate brown.* I could flat forget about ever fitting Great-grandmother's bed in either of these two cubbyholes.

Ed zipped us through the bottom floor so fast and seemed to be engaging Baker in conversation so much that I got the feeling both of them were daring each other not to look at me.

When we got to the top floor, I was a tiny bit relieved. It was quaint, actually, with a nice size combination den and kitchen. A Franklin stove sat in the middle of the room, and that, I imagined, was a nice thing to have in the winter. The ceiling was vaulted and the enormous posts and beams of the original barn were exposed. The kitchen cabinets were painted black, though, which along with the burnt orange walls, and the drawn curtains, made me feel like I was at a Halloween party.

This room was overcrowded, too, with beds and other odd furniture. A lime green Naugahyde chair sat right next to a magenta flowered chair, which sat on top of a yellow shag rug. Ed went on and on about how lovely the place was and what mint condition it was in. *Maybe this is just one of the differences in Northern people and Southern people,* I couldn't help but think.

When Ed went downstairs to use the restroom and Baker could no longer avoid me, he whispered in a low voice, "I know what you're thinking."

I cocked my head to the side and forced a phony smile.

"Come on, honey. Try and look beyond all this. Remember what our house looked like before we started the renovation? We can have this place looking like a million bucks."

"Did you see those bedrooms? My college *dorm* room was bigger than that. And curtains for closet doors? Baker, you know I hate chocolate brown! It's gonna all have to be painted before I even consider it."

"Painting is easy." Baker reached out and tried to grab my hand.

I walked over to the window and pulled back the curtain.

"Can't you see *our* furniture in here?" he said. "The cabinets and the rest of the woodwork painted white? Take those curtains down and let the sunshine in. You'll love it, I promise."

With extreme caution, I eyed the room again and decided I had had enough. I started for the steps and Baker followed right behind me. As we made our way back down the stairs, with no handrail and green indoor-outdoor carpet under our feet, I couldn't help but think about my house back home. The one I had spent nearly a year remodeling, the one that had my very favorite wallpaper in the dining room with tropical plants and birds all over it. Over three thousand square feet of living space and Baker and Ed wanted me to trade it in for what appeared to be less than eight hundred!

Ed headed out the front door, sensing, I'm sure, that he might lose the sale if we tarried too long in the superb owners' quarters. I headed straight out behind him and right over to his car. He and Baker continued to chat while observing the outside of a little cottage with turquoise shutters in the middle of the garden.

On the way back up the mountain I stared out the backseat window of Ed's car, with my foot on top of *Naughty Nurses*, forcing myself to keep an open mind. But that malodorous old house was not my idea of a home. The thought of waking up there every morning was downright depressing. Baker and I were due back there for dinner in a few hours to watch the restaurant in motion. *Maybe I could accidentally lose the car keys when we get back to our motel*, I thought. *Then, we'd never make it back!* I knew that was pointless, though. Baker would simply call Ed to pick us up and then I'd have to endure even more of his Yankee malarkey on into the evening.

When we made it to our car, Baker thanked Ed for his hospitality and told him we'd be in touch. Thank goodness Baker didn't invite him to join us for dinner.

We made it back only five minutes late for our eight o'clock dinner reservation at the Vermont Haus Inn. We were seated on the screened-in porch. I had hoped we would be able to sit out there. It overlooked the perennial garden, but more important, it meant I'd have fresh air to breathe. I realize now I should have paid more attention to the fact that a space heater was cranking away in the corner of the porch taking the bite off the evening air. The *summer evening* air.

The hostess who showed us to our table was cute, but I honestly felt like she was a lot friendlier to Baker than she was to me. As she handed him his menu, I could have sworn she gave him a sultry look—right in front of me. Baker never acted like he noticed so I never brought it up. My copy of the menu had no prices on it. The last time I'd seen one of those was at Antoine's in New Orleans with Daddy.

Ed had told us the Vermont Haus Inn was the premiere restaurant in the Sugartree region. Rolf Schloygin was a renowned chef in Vermont. His clientele was loyal, mostly in the fifty-plus range, probably due to the higher prices and old-timey food. I say old-timey food because as I glanced over the menu, which was classic French, I noticed some appetizers that were completely foreign to me. Eggplant caponata? Vitello tunato? And something called *head cheese*? I was familiar with some of the other items like herring in sour cream, frog legs provençale, and escargots maison, but it didn't mean I would ever *order* one of those.

"I'm not all that familiar with these appetizers," I said to Baker, careful not to berate the menu. (What I *wanted* to say was, these appetizers aren't that appetizing to me, but instead I zipped my lip.) "What do you think I should order, honey?"

"Why don't you order the soup, or the prosciutto with melon? Can you believe this menu? Is it wonderful or what?" Baker gloated over it like he would his golf score. Baker thought everything about Vermont was wonderful by now.

Within ten minutes the waiter made it over to our table. "*Bonjour*," he said, and then a big smile. No conversation. He just very politely looked at me and said, "Madame?"

"Hi, how are you?" I smiled back at him.

He just kept on smiling.

Baker nudged me under the table with his knee. "I think he's ready for you to order."

"Oh, pardon me. Okay, I think I'm going to try the soup du jour, please. What kind is it this evening?" I looked up from my menu.

"Soup es vichyssoise."

"That will be lovely, and for my entrée I'll try the duckling with cherry sauce."

"And I'll have the escargots and the beef Wellington, medium rare," Baker said. "And please bring us a bottle of your, let's see now, ahhh . . .

how about a bottle of your Châteauneuf-du-Pape cab." Baker knows wine.

"*Merci*," the waiter said, and dashed off. The poor thing was running around like a chicken with his head chopped off. For some reason, he was the only one taking all the orders. I felt sorry for him, really.

Halfway through our appetizers, Helga Schloygin—Rolf's sister—stopped by our table for a brief introduction. She took me by surprise. Big-boned and very, very tall, Helga stood probably six feet, and she looked to be in her early sixties. Helga had gray hair that she brushed straight back off her face and wore twisted up in a tight bun. She had a hard-looking face, which bore not one trace of makeup. Reading glasses hung from a chain around her neck and her clothing was oddly preppy. She wore a pair of navy blue pants, a white button-down oxford cloth blouse, and navy blue flats.

"Hello," she said. "I am Helga Schloygin. Proprietor of Vermont Haus Inn."

Baker stood up. "Hi, Helga, I'm Baker and this is my wife, Leelee."

I smiled at her. "It's nice to meet you, Helga."

She grinned and gave us both a firm handshake. "Vhere are you from?"

"Memphis, Tennessee," Baker told her.

"I see. How long have you been vorking in ze restaurant business?"

"I was in management during college," Baker said. "But I'm in the insurance business now."

She turned to me. "Vhat is *your* job?"

"Baker and I have two young daughters. My time is spent with them."

"I see." Even with her heavy German accent I detected she was a smoker. Her voice was gravelly and had a slight wheeze to it.

"These vater glasses are filled too high," she barked to the busboy at the next table. "Excuse me, ve are vedy busy. I am needed in the kitchen."

"Oh sure," Baker, who was still standing, said. "Thanks for stopping by."

She nodded and was off.

"Helga has a strong personality, don't you think?" I said to Baker after he sat back down.

"She's German. All Germans have strong personalities."

"Oh. Well, how was I supposed to know that? It's not like I have a lot of German friends."

Baker rolled his eyes and changed the subject.

At the end of the dinner, which I have to say was delicious, Rolf Schloygin himself came out to greet us. When he walked up to our table, we knew right away he must be the chef by his white jacket and billowy hat. A bushy white beard and red cheeks made him look like Santa but I'll bet the red in his cheeks was probably from high blood pressure. After all, he was huge. I would say he weighed in at just under three hundred pounds but oddly enough he couldn't have been more than five-foot-six. Something must have gotten crossed in their family gene pool, I thought, considering his sister was a half foot taller. The man must have been pushing seventy; no wonder he was ready to retire.

"Hello, you must be ze Satterfields." Rolf extended his hand to both of us.

"Yes, we are," Baker said, and kept his seat. "This is my wife, Leelee."

"A pleasure to make your acquaintance," he said, and then turned to me. "You have lovely hair, my dear."

I gave him a bashful smile. "That's so nice of you to say. Thank you. And I think your food is equally as lovely."

"Vell, thank *you* vedy much." *His* accent was intriguing and I found myself actually warming up to him. "How do you like Vermont so far?"

"I'm in love with it. I can't think of anything I don't like about it," Baker said, and raised up his arms.

Rolf chuckled. "I'm sure you could find *some*zing." Bless his heart, he absolutely reeked of perspiration. But at that point I was used to the smell. I always thought Daddy was being sarcastic when he said Europeans must use a different kind of deodorant than us.

"Baker is enchanted to say the least. Are you through cooking for the evening?" I asked him.

"No, not quite. I am only dropping by to velcome you to Vermont Haus Inn. I should get back, *r*really. Thank you vedy much for coming."

"You're most welcome." Baker stood up to shake Rolf's hand again. "Love the place."

"I hope you come back soon." Rolf took off his hat to bid us farewell and

I was surprised to see his nearly bald head, with only a scattering of long white hairs slicked straight back. Rolf Schloygin could have rivaled Edmund Gwenn in *Miracle on 34th Street* for Santa any day of the week.

"*His* personality's not so strong," I informed Baker when Rolf walked away.

"Sure it is. He's just a better salesman."

On the plane ride back to Memphis, Baker went back over all the reasons why Vermont was the perfect place to live and raise our family. He reasoned that life is short and you only go around once. Why not take a leap of faith and do something different. So, in his ever-present persuasive manner, Baker actually managed to convince me that moving to Vermont was the best thing we could do for ourselves, and especially for Sarah and Isabella.

North American Inns magazine—the publication that would change my life forever. If it hadn't been for that magazine, or Ed Baldwin who placed an ad in that July issue, or if it hadn't been for the owners of the Vermont Haus Inn who wanted to sell it, where would I be today?

Mama, who had been raised in Greenville, Mississippi, used to tell me when I was a teenager, "It's a woman's duty to follow her husband." Of course, the only place Mama ever had to follow Daddy was from the Mississippi Delta to Memphis, Tennessee. Big whoop-de-doo. If Mama were still alive, would she have really told me to follow Baker all the way up to the North?

It's a definite that Daddy wouldn't have. I can just hear him now: "Why in the Sam Hill would you want to leave God's country and move all the way to the frozen wastelands of the North? I've given you life on a silva platta right here in Memphis, Tennessee."

Poor Daddy, I'm sure the ground around him just rumbled and quaked when that moving van pulled up in front of our house. He had been gone only a year and here I was digging up my roots and spending *his money* on a dream that wasn't even mine.

Chapter Five

When our former principal, Mrs. Carrington, got up to address the crowd—all dressed up in Sunday clothes—everyone instinctively stopped the chatter to give her their undivided attention. Everyone but me, that is. To think I was sitting at a luncheon, given in my honor, to bid me farewell was an out-of-body experience to say the least.

"Ladies, ladies, may I have your attention, please?" Mrs. C. announced into the microphone on the small podium at the front of the Red Room, and peered at us from over her reading glasses. I couldn't believe she still wore those on the tip of her nose. She had not changed one bit and it felt like we were back in school. Out of habit, everyone at the luncheon who went to the Jamison School respectfully stood up for her. I know she got a big kick out of it because she responded according to custom: "Young ladies, you may be seated," and everyone laughed out loud. Alice had come up with the idea of inviting her and Virginia thought it would be a hoot to have her emcee the luncheon.

"We know why we are all gathered here today. But it's quite hard to believe we have to say good-bye to one of our own. Most everyone in this room, just like me, has known Leelee Williams Satterfield since she was a little girl. It is an honor and a privilege to stand up here today and give a toast to her past, her present, and her future." Her voice climbed and she held her tea glass high in the air.

Everyone raised their own glasses and Mrs. Carrington added, "And remember, we expect you back home for many, many visits."

I can barely feign a smile.

Seated right next to me was Kristine. To this day I think of her as my true mother. She came to work for us when I was only six months old and she worked for Grandmama for ten years before that. She knows more about Daddy's side of the family than Daddy did. When I was little I couldn't pronounce my *R*s so Kristine became Kisstine. In time I dropped the *-tine* and changed it to *-issie*. Now, because of me, almost everyone she knows calls her Kissie.

The clapping seemed to last forever until Mrs. Carrington interrupted to say, "And now we have a very special treat for you. Some of Leelee's best friends—and may I just take this opportunity to say some things never change—have gone to great lengths to entertain us all. Ladies, the stage is all yours." She motioned her arm toward the back of the room.

The old familiar music of *The Bob Newhart Show* came out of nowhere and all heads turned around to see Alice, Virginia, and Mary Jule marching up the center aisle in between the tables. Each one was wrapped up in a heavy red plaid jacket, a lumberjack hat with earflaps, a scarf, gloves, and big chunky boots. Sticking out underneath the jackets were long peach-colored taffeta dresses. My bridesmaid dresses—only now with the added bonus of hoop skirts underneath. *Very funny, girls.* For their bouquets, they each carried Log Cabin syrup bottles with dead flowers poking out of the tops. As they made their way to the front, they pulled out handfuls of fake snow from their coat pockets and proceeded to throw it around the room. My guests were brushing it off their clothes and picking it out of one another's hair while the three nincompoops laughed hysterically. One thing was for sure about my best friends. They weren't going to make any bones about the fact that they thought this whole Vermont idea was ridiculous and each one of them was ready to kill Baker Satterfield.

Once they got to the front of the room they stood side by side with the edges of their hoop skirts touching. "Raise your glasses for a toast," Virginia bellowed out to the crowd. All three pulled the dead flowers out of their Log Cabin bottles and raised them in the air. "To Leelee, the soon-to-be Yankee."

That earned her some laughs from around the room. After they set their syrup bottles on the floor, Virginia ran over to the side of the room where a pile of red and blue pom-poms lay. She dramatically threw two to each girl and then bopped back to her place in line. They huddled together and then came out cheering.

Virginia yelled out first. "Give me a V."

"Give me an E," shrieked Alice.

"Give me an R," shouted Mary Jule.

"Give me a *mont*," all of them hollered together. "What's that spell?"

"Cold weather," Alice yelled.

"*What's that spell?*" Mary Jule belted out at the top of her lungs.

"Snow," Alice answered, and then screamed, "WHAT'S THAT SPELL?"

"Maple syrup!" Virginia shouted.

Virginia and Alice dropped down on all fours. Mary Jule climbed on top of their backs and raised her pom-poms in the air. "Yaaaaay, Leelee! Hope you and Baker are practicing your Northern accents." Then she climbed back down and they doubled over and laughed uncontrollably. Most of the people at the luncheon giggled and the rest forced a smile. *Y'all are somewhere between nuts and ridiculous.*

"Don't be mad at us, Leelee, we really do love you," Mary Jule said, and then looked straight at me and mouthed the words "I'm sorry."

Alice got herself together and took the microphone. "Okay, y'all, oops sorry, I mean *you guys*. In all seriousness, our best friend has decided to move far, far away to somewhere up there." She pointed up to the sky and shook her finger. "Much to our horror, but *whatever*. But to show you how much we love you, Leelee, we've put together a toast."

I'm thinking they rehearsed it for hours, because their delivery was in perfect time and by memory. They alternated verses and recited the last one together.

Here's to Leelee, our faithful, forever friend
From K through college, hours we would spend
Gabbing on phones, they grew out of our ears
Staying up all night talking, after too many beers.

A crazy cohort, a character, a damsel in distress
Part Lucy, a lot Daddy's girl, Leelee you're a mess
A lover of laughter, she's got a truly infectious giggle
Don't sit with her in church, or you'll be in a pickle.

We all love our music, whatever would we do
Without the Beatles or the Stones, and the Beach Boys, too
"Turn up the radio someone!" She never misses a chance
To twist, jerk, or pony, Leelee's always ready to dance.

Gracie is her third daughter with whom she's obsessed
Come on now, Leelee, may we humbly suggest
A person she is not, though you treat her as such
A fur coat for a dog? Now that's a tiny bit much.

She's a wonderful mother, a happy devoted wife
Baker and the girls are the true loves of her life
Never did we expect to see our best friend go
Life won't be the same, we'll be missing you so.

Although you're moving far away from here
You'll never be a Yankee, not in a million years!
You're a real Southern belle from Memphis, Tennessee
With a heart that—GOD FORBID—will never stop whistlin' Dixie!

After the applause from the toast died down, and I got up to give each of them hugs, the girls took their seats at my table. Mrs. Carrington pulled down a projector screen, dimmed the lights, and closed the curtains. Everyone sat back to watch the "This *Was* Leelee Satterfield's Life in Memphis, Tennessee," video. The Beatles' "In My Life" began in the background. "There are places I remember . . ."

Kissie reached over and took my hand in hers. Her heart had been broken in two when I told her the news. The last thing she wanted was for me to leave Memphis, although she, like Mama, ascribed to the notion that a woman's place is with her husband. "Ooooh, baby," she said, "why Baker wanna git so far away from home? You not s'pose to live anywhere takes your family three days to travel. I'll sure 'nuf miss you when you're gone." *Not as much as I'll miss you, Kissie, not nearly as much.* When my first little baby picture came on the screen Kissie looked over at me and the tears were already in her eyes. That's all I needed to see, and through the rest of the video I never turned off my own faucet of tears.

With each picture that flashed I started reminiscing about what home meant to me. There were Mama and Daddy all dressed up in front of our church with Mama holding me in my christening gown right next to my grandparents. Daddy and me at the father-daughter dance, Mama and me baking cookies.

Pictures flashed of Kissie lighting my birthday candles and Kissie fixing my hair at my wedding. There was Kissie holding Sarah and Isabella as newborns. She had been there for me during every milestone of my life. And here I was right next to her—all eighty years of her—with her old veined hand in mine. My sweet Kissie looked gorgeous all dressed up in her cream Sunday suit and hat to match.

There were pictures of my age-seven dress-up party where Alice was Florence Nightingale, Virginia was Huck Finn, and Mary Jule was Mary Poppins. I, of course, was a ballerina. I'll never forget that pink tutu Mama made me wear with itchy sequins on the bodice and the straps. Kissie put my hair up in a tight bun, and when I saw those photos I could still feel the hairs around my temples pulling, and smell the Adorn Mama sprayed all over my hair making it stiff to the touch. I can still see her now covering my eyes with her left hand and spraying with her right. All I wanted was to be Glenda, the Good Witch of the North, but Mama *made me* be a ballerina.

I looked around the room and everyone was engrossed in the video. Mary Jule was seated on the other side of me and I leaned over and whispered in her ear. "Can you please kidnap the girls and me?"

She put her arm around me and whispered, "You know I would if I could."

I had forgotten all about the picture of Mary Jule and me standing in front of the Mid-South Coliseum, age eight, holding up Monkees posters. I remember our mothers going outside during the concert to smoke after the screaming had finally gotten to them.

Next up was a picture of Alice and me around ten years old, all dressed up in our English riding habits and holding up ribbons in our hands. Alice was sitting on the other side of Kissie. I leaned over and whispered, "Why did we give up horses?"

"Cheerleading," she said, and leaned back in her seat.

Then came a picture of Virginia and me at the sixth-grade science fair when we won the blue ribbon for hatching chickens in a homemade incubator. That event marked our big debut in the *Memphis Commercial Appeal* with the caption reading: "The first chicken was christened Columbus after another famous first."

The very last picture was of Baker, Sarah, Isabella, Princess Grace, and me on the back porch of our home looking like we were the happiest family on earth. I remember when the picture was taken. We *were* the happiest family on earth.

I had no choice but to follow my husband. Baker is a good husband. He let me have children. He doesn't get mad when Gracie poops in the house. He lets me shop for clothes wherever and whenever I want. Sure we have issues just like everyone else but nothing so terrible a little romp in the sack can't fix. He always wants to make love. My friends hardly ever do it these days. Lots of women tell me their husbands never want them anymore. Mine wants me.

I was Mrs. John Baker Satterfield, a name I had wanted since the tenth grade. I'd show him a devoted wife. I'd be right at his side in Willingham, Vermont. One day, I knew Baker would finally come to his senses, drop the dream of being an innkeeper, and take me home! I was sure of it.

Our family picture remained while the music faded into silence. Within moments the applause returned and everyone resumed their conversations.

I sat frozen in the dark of the warm, familiar room, unable to move my eyes away from the screen.

Chapter Six

Baker was leaning on a post in the gate area when the girls and I got off the plane, just three weeks before Christmas.

"Daddy!" Sarah yelled when she spotted him. She and Isabella ran to Baker and he scooped them both up and twirled them around. He leaned in to kiss me while holding one girl in each arm.

I reached up and touched his face. *God, he is beautiful. He takes my breath away . . . still. No wonder I moved all the way to Vermont.*

"I missed y'all," he said. "How was the flight?"

"It was good, and the girls were *so* good. They colored most of the time and we read stories the rest." Sarah wriggled down out of Baker's arms and hunted through her Barbie backpack to show him her coloring book.

Baker and Princess Grace had left two weeks earlier in his Ford Explorer, pulling my little BMW behind on a trailer. He wanted to meet the moving van and get a head start on the restaurant operations and the apartment renovation. As we walked toward the baggage claim Baker chatted me up a blue streak. The only people he had been keeping company with were two locals he had hired to help him with the painting.

"I can't wait for you to see all the work I've done. The place looks fantastic." He grabbed a cart on the way over to our baggage carousel. "And the staff can't wait to meet you. Remember the French waiter we met when we were here before? Pierre?"

"Yeah."

"You'll just love him. You mark my words, he's gonna be a granddaddy to the girls."

"So, is there still snow on the ground?" I asked, deliberately changing the subject. "We wanna build a snowman, right, girls?" They both jumped up and down and squealed.

"Is there still *snow* on the ground? This is Vermont. There's a ton of snow on the ground. It's everywhere." The girls and I watched as Baker grabbed the first of our many suitcases off the belt.

"Well, I didn't know. For all I know it could have melted already." I was talking to his back.

"Ed Baldwin was telling me"—he grunted while lifting my suitcase—"the snow stays around all the way to spring." He hurled it onto the cart and turned around quickly for more bags. "Aren't the girls lucky? Remember how he said that skiing is part of the public school curriculum?"

I nodded my head, but I was more interested in making sure all our bags made it.

"I've met all kinds of people who say it's one of the greatest things about living here."

"Well, I've always wanted to buy them cute little snowsuits." Living in Memphis there had been no point. We were lucky to get a dusting.

"Hey, guess what?" Baker said, as he stacked the last suitcase onto the cart, which was loaded up to his chin. "I've already got your winter pass to Sugartree. Innkeepers get free passes to the mountain for selling lift tickets. Just one of the many perks of innkeeping." He labored over the weight of the cart as he awkwardly maneuvered it toward the door. "Wait 'til you see the skis I've got my eye on."

"Let me guess, they're black with trout painted all over them."

Baker rolled his eyes, but I shrugged it off. I was used to it.

As we journeyed north from Albany toward Vermont, I saw that Baker was right. There was snow everywhere. Curiously, no one was driving slowly, and the streets were completely clear. There were big piles of snow all along the sides of the highway, though, like someone had pushed it over to the side and left it there.

I saw my moose sign again but didn't ask for a stop. It just made me excited all over again. *Where will I be when I spot my first moose?* I wondered. *Are they shy like deer? Is there a better time of the day to see one?* I hadn't been this thrilled about wildlife since the days of Mutual of Omaha.

"Have you seen a moose yet?" I asked Baker.

"Not yet."

"What does a moose look like?" Isabella asked from the backseat. Her curly strawberry-blond hair was wild and free; she had pulled out her ponytail holder hours earlier.

"Oh, they are big, baby girl, with big ole antlers. They kind of look like horses but they're much, much larger. And Mama can't wait to see one. Let's watch for *moose*, everybody." I cleared my throat to get Baker's attention. He would never have to correct me on that one again.

We had settled on a price of $385,000 by the time the negotiating was all over. The CPA we hired made a determination based on the Schloygins' last five years of gross income. With the additional expense of a mortgage *and* a chef's salary, we could not afford to pay a penny more.

Ed Baldwin was elated when he called with the news. "Do you realize what a concession this is? The Schloygins have lowered the price by nearly two hundred thousand dollars! And would you like to know why?"

"Why?" I asked.

"The only people they want to continue their legacy are you and Baker. They've had other offers, higher ones I might add, but they feel like you guys are the best people to carry on their tradition. They've even agreed to hold your mortgage for the first year. By then you'll be established, and acquiring a loan from a local financial institution should be no problem."

"I don't know what to say," I told him.

"Just say you'll take it! I'll fax you guys the revised copy of the contract right away."

"This is all happening so fast. I'll need to run it by Baker," I said, in a panic and trying to buy a block of time.

"Of course. I'll be in the office all afternoon. Call me back as soon as you've spoken with him. Oh, and one more thing, I've taken the liberty of sending roses to Helga, from all three of us. You can pay me back when I see you at the closing."

I won't even tell you what Daddy would have said about that.

Of course Ed was thrilled. He had both sides of the contract. We didn't even have the sense to enlist the help of our own real estate agent to act on our behalf. *My, how we learn from our mistakes.* Naturally we were the best people to carry on the Schloygin tradition. We had a hefty down payment— two hundred thousand Daddy-dollars to be exact— a wife who knew absolutely nothing about the restaurant business, *and* the Schloygins were holding the mortgage. If we failed, they got their inn back *with interest* and all the renovations we planned to do, plus an extra two hundred grand to add to their nest egg. What did they have to lose?

Ed had convinced us that Rolf could teach Baker to be a gourmet chef in a year. All we would have to do was hire him to continue as the executive chef, and let Baker train as his sous-chef. "Keep everything just the way it is for one year," Ed said. "The customers will never know anything has changed. There's no point in risking the loss of the loyal clientele." Ed added one more piece of good news. "Helga has agreed to stay on as hostess and bartender to train Leelee."

When I arrived at the Vermont Haus Inn that frosty mid-December night, I not only had a new house, I had a new occupation. I was the owner of a four-star restaurant and the boss of four full-time employees and eight part-time employees. And . . . I was an aspiring martini mixer!

The inn looked completely different now. No more lush gardens of lovely flowers waltzing in the warm summer breeze. Instead, snow—and heaps of it. The stars were so close it seemed like if only you could climb to the top of the highest tree, you might could reach up and pluck one out of the sky. The moon looked bigger and brighter than the moon in Tennessee, which made the snow look even prettier. I had only seen this much snow one other time, on a Young Life ski trip to Colorado my junior year, and I got butterflies in my stomach just looking at it.

The girls were half asleep when we carried them inside. They would have to wait to get their first glimpse of our new winter wonderland.

There's the smell again, I thought as soon as we walked in the front door. I had already accepted the fact that deodorizing would be my toughest challenge. The second thing I noticed was total disarray. Our furniture from home was everywhere. When we bought the inn, it came completely furnished. Baker and I had loads of furniture as well, especially after Daddy died. Now we had two houses full and it was strewn all over the place, along with 150 boxes piled high to the ceiling. The sight of it all was overwhelming.

"Ignore all this," Baker said, when we walked through the front parlor. "We'll get it done. You can start unpacking tomorrow and get this place just like you like it."

I stared at the boxes and then over at Baker. "I can't unpack all this by myself."

"I'll help you. No need to worry."

"It's not the inn I'm worried about. It's our apartment that's been keeping me up at night."

"It'll get there. One step at a time."

Issie poked her head up off my shoulder. "Where's Gracie, Daddy?"

"She's back in our apartment. Let's go find her."

What if he wasn't able to improve the apartment? I thought. Nothing could be done to increase the size, but a décor change was nonnegotiable. When we moved in that direction, I could see the door between the inn and our quarters was open and now we could move freely between the two places. Baker put Sarah down and stood behind me, covering my eyes with his hands. The four of us walked slowly into our living area.

"Steady, steady, let me turn you around. On the count of three, open your eyes. One, two, *three!*"

I opened my eyes to yellow. A bright, beautiful shade of my second favorite color (peach is my number one). The hideous burnt orange was gone and the doors and windows had changed from chocolate brown to white. The new tan Berber carpet, along with the fresh paint, drastically improved the aroma.

"What do you think? Do you like the yellow?"

"I do. It's beautiful, Baker, you've really been working hard." I threw my arms around him and gave him a big kiss.

Gracie came running up and pawed on the front of my calves. "Oh, Gracie, you've missed us, old girl." After putting Issie down, I picked up the dog and kissed the top of her head. She stunk to high heaven, but what could I expect? She'd been running around in a musty, BO-infested house for two weeks.

"Let me hold her," Issie said, and reached out for Gracie.

"Where's *my* room?" Sarah asked, and started toward one of the bedrooms.

"Hang on, let's go upstairs first," Baker told her. "I want y'all to see what I've done up there."

We ran up the steps to see the transformation. It, too, looked like a different place. The original character of the room stood out now, and the wooden beams made a lovely contrast to the freshly painted ecru walls. Logs in the Franklin stove popped, warming the room. The white kitchen cabinets Baker promised were gleaming from the fresh coat he had finished earlier in the day.

As it turns out, if it hadn't been for the two woodchucks he hired to help with the renovation, Baker would have never gotten it ready before we arrived. I learned that woodchuck is the nickname for a Vermonter equivalent to the Southern hick. They wear those lumberjack red plaid coats and hats with earflaps to match, like the ones my friends wore at the luncheon. (Sharp accents and lots of facial hair are two more characteristics of the woodchuck.)

Sarah tugged on my coat and pleaded with us. "*Now* can I see my room?"

"What are we waiting for?" Baker said, and grabbed her hand.

We all scurried back down the stairs. The doors to both of the bed-rooms, which sat side by side, were shut. With a big grin on his face, Baker slowly opened her door. Since it was the size of a postage stamp, joy was not the emotion I would use to describe the way Sarah felt when she first saw her new bedroom. The twin beds were unmade and boxes were every-where. But, the walls were pink, just like she wanted.

Sarah's smile drooped into a frown.

"We'll get it looking beautiful," I said, and caressed the top of her head. "Don't worry, sweetie, it'll only take a couple of days. You'll love it. I promise."

She shot Baker a sour look.

"It's pink, Sarah. Aren't you happy about that?" he said.

"I guess so." She hung her head and dropped her backpack on the floor.

Issie was happy to see Gracie and had no comment.

I felt bad for Sarah. She so loved her room back home. It's not like it was huge or anything, but her bedspreads matched and the area rug was pink and white. It was full of stuffed animals and there was plenty of room for her dollhouse. She spent hours playing in there and had plenty of friends from school to invite over anytime. Here in Vermont, the dollhouse would obviously have to go out in the hall.

I had no expectations of what *our* microscopic bedroom would look like, so when I opened the door and it barely missed the bedpost, I can't say I was surprised. Baker said it took all three guys two hours to get Great-grandmother's canopy bed to fit. After they finally got it in the room, there was no space left for another stick of furniture. I could sit on the bed, reach out my arm, and slide open the closet curtain. Baker said we could use the windowsills for nightstands but we had to put our dresser out in the hall. It gave new meaning to the word "*bed*room."

Even though I wasn't expecting much, I still had a hard time when I saw it. The letdown in my gut, that extreme feeling of disappointment, told me I should probably put my mind on something else. It was the kind of thing you had to flat forget about, or you might lose your mind. So I turned my thoughts to Vermont moose and diamond earrings and tried to con-vince myself to be excited about our new, adventurous life that lay ahead.

By now it was past dinnertime, the girls were hungry and cranky, and I was worn out from traveling with two children. It seemed the easiest thing to do at that point was order a pizza and Baker volunteered to go out and get it.

"They don't deliver here?" I asked, when I saw him grab his coat.

"Well, uh, not the kind I like." Baker ran out the door before I had a chance to say anything else.

Hmmm, I thought, and stored it—for future ammunition, if you know what I mean.

The Vermont Haus Inn was still closed down for Stick Season and we were gearing up for our grand opening in nine days. We had work ahead of us for sure. Apparently there are *two* downtimes per year: mid-October through mid-December, and April through Memorial Day. Let me try and explain. Stick Season is the time period between the leaves falling off the trees and the first snowfall. Nearly every day the sky is overcast and the landscape is drab and monochromatic. You'd never even know the sky had any color to it at all. The ski resorts open around Thanksgiving but don't really get cranking until Christmas. So most of the inns stay closed for Stick Season. (We'll get to the other interval later. But here's a hint for now—it's called *Mud* Season.) I'll go on record right now as saying no one ever told me about either of these seasons before I moved.

The Schloygins traveled back to their homeland for the first half of Stick Season. As far as I was concerned, this was the part of the Schloygin tradition I would definitely be carrying on—trips home!

The moment I opened my eyes, after our first night at the inn, I was determined to put my best foot on the floor. No more sulking, no more regret. I had a mission and I had chosen to accept it. The Vermont Haus Inn was my new home. I had arrived with every curtain, every bedspread, every stick of furniture, and even some of the light fixtures from Memphis and I was determined to stamp my fingerprints on this place within a few short weeks.

So, as I explored my new house, my first morning in Vermont, I had a new attitude. To make the unpacking more pleasurable, I carried the Beatles around with me from room to room, and cranked up the volume on my small, but powerful, pink boom box. I was peeking into drawers, examining the wall colors, even checking out the locations of the bathrooms for the first time. The one thing I had going for me was that I love to decorate, and this old place was the ultimate challenge. It was in desperate need of a face-lift and I couldn't wait to perform the surgery.

There was more charm than I had noticed when I was first there in the summer. A small dining room with a tremendous fireplace was the focal point of the house. The old wooden beams protruded from the ceiling and a big bay window brought the beauty of the snow-covered yard inside.

The wallpaper in that dining room, however, was horrific. It was red-and-white checked, just like a tablecloth, and resembled a cheap Italian eatery—at least I felt like it did. Now I don't profess to always have the final word on what's tacky, but trust me, it was *real* tacky. If any of my friends had seen the décor at that point, I'm afraid they would have told me to light a match and start over.

Baker told me that we were going to have to turn one of the guest rooms upstairs into a storage room due to all our extra furniture. And that was fine with me. There was no way I was getting rid of one thing that I had brought with me. (I couldn't bring myself to throw away the boxes, either. Once I had them unpacked, I stacked each one up, one inside the other, in a corner of the attic. The moving company charged me big bucks for those boxes. *Besides, I just might need them,* I thought.)

First order of business—get rid of the junk. Helga and Rolf were clutter keepers. Dozens of half-burned freestanding red (and only red) candles and hundreds of old paperback books were stacked up in the corners. The bookshelves were crammed full of garage sale knickknacks and cheap souvenirs, like the kind you find in airports with the name of the city imprinted on a shot glass or an ashtray. Helga must have thought she was doing me a favor by leaving her ceramic hippopotamus collection on the mantel, but that would have to go.

Each time I opened a new box, I found real joy in deciding where to place my stuff. My beautiful collection of Herend china looked perfect on the parlor bookshelves. My own crystal and silver made the rooms come

alive and I felt like the place looked more and more like home. I was having so much fun, I didn't even notice the time flying by. It was getting close
to lunchtime.

I never saw anyone come into the house, so when the cellar door in the
red-checked dining room swung open mysteriously, it scared the daylights
out of me. When I screamed, it made the man scream. Both of us had to sit
down at one of the dining tables to stop the adrenaline from rushing.

"Oh my gosh, you scared me to death. I didn't know anyone was down
there," I said, holding my hand to my heart.

"Well, I was scared myself," the man said, and nervously twirled the
end of his huge handlebar mustache. "I spend quite a bit of time down cellar. The name's Jeb Duggar. I'm the official handyman here. I also wash
dishes at night."

"For a minute there I thought you were a burglar."

"I'm no burglar, I'm your neighbor. I live right accrosst the street." He
pointed behind him and began whistling along with the Beatles in the
background.

"It's nice to meet you, Jeb. I'm Leelee, Baker's wife." I extended my hand
to shake his.

He stopped whistling for only a moment to ask, "You're not thinking of
changing the name, are you?" Then went right back to his habit, which
quite honestly was a little annoying.

"Pardon me?"

"The name of the inn. You're not thinking of changing it, are yous?"

"My husband doesn't want to change anything for a year. Why do you
ask?"

"I would have to redo my advertising."

I couldn't help the confused look that spread across my face. "What
advertising?"

"JCW's advertising. I took out an ad in the Yellow Pages. Them folks
charged me two hundred dollars, but Mom told me it was worth it as long
as they said it was right accrosst the street from the Vermont Haus Inn." He
hit the table with his fist and nodded with confidence.

I'm sure he could tell I was confused but he kept on jabbering. "How do you like my new sign? I just finished painting it yesterday." He puffed out his chest and combed his beard with his fingers; two of the many gestures I would learn were characteristically Jeb Duggar.

"I can't say I've seen it."

"If you look out the window in the front dining room, you can't miss it."

"Oh! Well, I'll go take a look." I stood up from the table, and thought about the girls back home. They would have killed to be sharing in this moment.

"I only work here on the side," Jeb said, while escorting me over to the window. "I'm really the solo proprietor over at JCW."

When I peered out the front window straight across the street I saw a modest old white clapboard home with a small front porch. A painted gray lean-to, about the size of an outhouse, sat about fifteen feet away from the house. It looked like half of a little hut, really, with a slanted roof on one side only. The whole other side of it appeared to be missing. The only sign I saw at all was a hand-painted job with red lettering that took up most of the wall of the lean-to. The words were stacked one on top of the other—JEB'S COMPUTER WORLD.

"Oh, so that's what you mean by JCW," I said, holding on to the window sash and peering through the pane. "Did you paint that yourself?"

"Why, sure." One could almost smell the pride exuding from his pores.

"I like the red." I turned to look at Jeb and smiled.

"Picked it out myself."

I glanced back out the window and looked around. "Where *is* Jeb's Computer World, Jeb?"

He was standing right behind me now, peeking through the same pane. "Right there."

"Right where?"

"*There*," he said, with an "are you blind?" tone, and pointed and tapped on the glass.

It took a moment to sink in. But I was looking dead at it. Jeb's Computer *World* was that tiny hut. And, as if that wasn't enough, pulled right in front was an old weather-rusted *pink* Chevy Chevette. JEB'S COMPUTER WORLD and the phone number were written in huge letters on the driver's side.

All I could think about was Alice Garrott's face upon her first glimpse of JCW. "Wow. I don't know what to say."

"You're not the first to lose their speech!"

"I'm sure I'm not. Where'd you find a pink car?" I just had to ask. "It's mighty cute."

"It's a hand-me-down from Mom," Jeb proudly fessed up. "She got it for all her years with Mary Kay. She don't drive that much no more, but we both use it for advertising. I've got the driver's side and she's got the other."

Rolf and Helga stopped by after lunch. As I have already mentioned, Helga has a strong personality. Very outspoken, very opinionated, and as I would find out, very set in her ways. She and Rolf weren't big fans of change. They didn't share in my enthusiasm for fixing up the place; they felt it was fine just the way it was. After all, they were the ones who decorated the inn in the first place.

Helga was a chain smoker and that bothered me a lot, since I was allergic to smoke. Even still, she sauntered around my house—her former house of thirty years—with an unflicked cigarette in her right hand, raised eyebrows, and pursed lips, eyeing my handiwork.

"You can't move these glasses out of ze cab-i-nets! How on earth vill the vaiters be able to get to them quickly?" she asked, from the red-checked dining room.

"Oh," she continued, with a real loud inflection on the O after she saw the way I had rearranged the fireplace mantel with my own things. "This vill *neva* vork—ze menus must stay right *here* behind ze hippo. Oh God . . . vhere's my hippo, vhat happen to my hippo?" She spied the beast sticking out of the box I had retired him in, snatched him up, and gingerly placed him back on the mantel. "There now," Helga said, petting her ceramic friend on the back. She dug out the rest of his siblings from the box and placed the entire collection back on the mantel.

Unfortunately for me, the front parlor was her next stop. "No. This vill not do, *either*," Helga said, peeved, when she spotted the bookshelves decorated with my Herend china. "We use ze shelves on ze right for condiments and ze shelves on ze left for tablecloths and napkins." And with that she proceeded to undo two hours' worth of careful thought and precise decorating.

I felt like a scolded child and couldn't say a word. She reminded me of an angry schoolmarm inflicting her personal misery upon a student simply because she was the authority figure. Those teachers always scared me to death and I was never at liberty to stand up to them. Now, standing next to Helga, I was transported back to grade school.

"Ve are opening this restaurant in nine days, you certainly have your vork cut out for you," she said. "You bought Vermont Haus Inn completely furnished. You should have sold all this extra furniture vhile you had ze chance in Memphis." She waved her hand across my cream-colored living room sofa and her ashes sprinkled onto the cushion. The woman never even paused to wipe them up. "You'll certainly need ze money for ze dry seasons," she continued, and kept on walking.

Dry seasons! I wondered. *What in the world did she mean by that?*

Helga had a stack of books in her arms when she arrived and had set them down on one of the tables. "Come vith me," she commanded. "Ve have vork to do."

Like a youngster minding the teacher, I followed her into the red-checked dining room, where she sat down at the table and lit another cig.

"Sit down here," she said, and patted the chair next to hers. (I couldn't help wondering if a tube of lipstick had ever glossed her lips or a mascara wand had ever swept through her eyelashes.) She had on the same preppy outfit she wore the first time I met her—white oxford cloth shirt and blue slacks. Her hair was pulled back so tightly it seemed to have a smoothing effect on her crow's-feet.

She lifted her glasses from the chain around her neck and placed them on the tip of her nose. "Let's see now, Baker vill be in charge of kitchen operations and you vill handle all ze bookvork. You must keep the vorkload equal vith your husband."

"I'm actually not much on bookwork," I told her. (I despise it.)

After peering at me over the top of her glasses for what seemed like a full minute, Helga remarked, "Not much on *bookvork*? Then how are you planning on running zis business?"

"Well, I . . . it's just that . . . bookwork's never been my responsibility—in Memphis, I mean."

She kept her stern gaze.

"But I suppose I could learn to do it here."

"Your husband vill not have time to operate this business all by himself. You must carry your own veight!" Her voice climbed.

"Oh, I plan on it, Helga. It's just that I have two daughters who need my full attention. In fact I should go—"

"You are a *vorking mother* now!" she declared loudly, and banged the table with her fist. "Let's get down to business."

Where was Baker when I needed him?

For the next two hours, my new hard-nosed boss instructed me on the accounting principles of the restaurant business while Sarah and Isabella played with Daddy. By the time Helga left, my job description had been laid out before me: preparing payroll, paying the bills, figuring the taxes and workers' compensation, hostessing, taking care of inn guests, *and* I was a bartender in training. *What about mother, Helga?*

When I climbed in bed that night, I couldn't hold in my feelings. I told Baker that Helga was mean and frightful. Instead of holding me in his arms and reassuring me that it would all be okay, he fluffed his pillow and turned off the light.

Baker and I were in the apartment unpacking early the next morning when I heard a door swing open in the inn. A woman had let herself in via the garden door that led in from the screened-in porch, which was now piled up with six cords of wood. No one knocked on the door, I would learn. It was like any business—no need to knock. The fact that it was also someone's personal residence had never stopped anyone before. After all, it was an inn.

I stopped what I was doing to greet her. "Hi there," I called out from the apartment.

At first she seemed a little startled—she wasn't used to seeing the door open between the apartment and the inn.

"You must be the Satterfields!" She moseyed over our way. I wasn't sure if she was talking to Baker or to me because her left eye wandered way off to the side. "I'm Roberta Abbott. Welcome to the Vermont Haus Inn and congratulations on becoming the new owners." She tugged on her underwear with her right hand and held a red down jacket in her left.

"Hi, I'm Leelee, Roberta. Have you met Baker yet?" I gestured toward him.

"Nuup, not yet, but I've heard about you." She gave him a big smile.

Baker shook her hand. "Nice to meet you."

A flame of bright orange set fire to her hair (all but an inch of gray that came off her scalp) and it was twisted in an unkempt bun on the top of her head. Black hairpins popped out every which-a-way. Her eternal smile disclosed her cheery disposition and I decided I liked her right away. Roberta was short and heavyset. (Mama always said that was the polite way to describe a person who is considerably overweight.) Her untucked flowery blouse had a hard time staying down and her huge bosoms made it hard for the blouse to stay buttoned. A plaid skirt hung just below Roberta's knees and brushed the tops of her clunky snow boots.

"Congratulations are in order for both of us. I have an anniversary coming up on the fifteenth day of this month. It marks twenty years of loyal employment right here at the Vermont Haus Inn."

"Congrats to you, too," I said.

"Why, thank you." Roberta beamed and took a bow. "I know every inch of this place. There's more of my elbow grease in it than anyone else's. I'll be happy to answer any questions you might have about anything that has to do with housekeeping—that's my specialty."

Thank you, Lord Jesus.

"I also help out in the kitchen at night, so I can show you the ropes there, too."

"I'll be the one needing help in the kitchen," Baker said. "Thanks, Roberta."

"You'rrre welcome."

Sarah and Issie heard Roberta's voice and peeked out of their bedroom.

"Hi there," Roberta said when she saw them. She leaned down to their level and put her hands on her knees. "What are your names?"

"Sarah."

"Hi, Sarah, is that your sister?"

"Yes, ma'am."

"What's your name, little sister?"

"Issie."

"Let me guess, are you six?"

Issie giggled. "No."

"Eight?"

"No." She giggled even harder.

"I'm five and Issie's almost three," Sarah told her.

"Well, you could have fooled me. You girls can help me anytime in the kitchen, would yous like that?"

Both Issie and Sarah nodded with a smile.

"Well, good. I better get a move on. Helga wants things cracking by eight sharp!"

"We'll be in soon," Baker told her.

"I'm really happy to know you, Roberta," I said. "I have a feeling I'll be leaning on you a lot." Leaning on her was one thing. Helping her in the bathrooms was another. I did not move to Vermont to scrub other people's toilets.

Rolf, Helga, Roberta, Baker, and I were in the kitchen talking when a tall brunette snow bunny bopped in the door. She was still bundled up from the cold and wore a pair of crocheted mittens with a ski hat to match, a darling white ski jacket, and a pair of lacy snow boots. The boots were to die for. They resembled Indian moccasins but they hit just under her knees and were lined with white fur. The thick laces crisscrossed up her shins and there was a pretty design stitched in the coffee-colored suede exterior of the boot. She looked vaguely familiar.

"Hi, everyone, merry Christmas." She took off her hat and mittens and unleashed her long brown ponytail.

Helga obviously liked her because she actually smiled when the woman came in. "Hello, Kerri, how vas your vacation?"

"Oh, I didn't end up going nowhere, I stayed right here in town." After hugging Rolf and Roberta, she gave Baker a side hug and extended her hand to me, like we were the only ones who weren't close. "Hi, I'm Kerri, we sort of met when you and Baker were here last summer."

Now I remembered who she was. The hostess who smiled incessantly at Baker.

"Oh yes, sure I remember. It's nice to see you again," I lied.

"Welcome to Vermont. I remembered Baker saying you and your daughters would be arriving sometime this week. How do you like it so far?"

"We just got in a couple of nights ago, and as you can probably tell we've got our work cut out for us."

"No joke. I saw all the boxes when I came in. Where are your girls?"

"Upstairs in our apartment watching *The Little Mermaid*," I said.

"For the fiftieth time," Baker added sarcastically. An awkward moment followed.

"I wanted to stop in and say hi, and also to say there are a bunch of us meeting at Donovan's tomorrow night. There's a great band playing. Do you like music, Leelee?"

I looked at Baker to step in and say: Leelee's been listening to music since she was yea high. And he only said, "Donovan's is a local hangout."

I said, "I love music. I haven't figured out the babysitter thing yet, but I'll keep that in mind. Thanks."

"Be happy to babysit anytime, all you have to do is ask," Roberta said. "I love children. Moe's got three but we never had any of our own. They're *like* mine though."

"Thank you, Roberta," I said. "I may take you up on that."

"Oh, and Monday is ski day. It's great fun." Kerri looked over at Baker for affirmation.

"Oh, yeah, Mondays are great."

"Well, I've got lots to do, I'll see you guys tomorrow night, maybe?" said the bunny.

"Yeah, we'll try," Baker replied.

"*Auf Wiedersehen*," she said to Helga and Rolf, and shot all of us a smile that revealed fluorescent white teeth. She flipped us a ta-ta wave and skipped out of the kitchen.

"*Auf Wiedersehen*," Rolf hollered after her from behind the line. (The line, I learned, is the place in front of the stove and behind the counter where the chef places the plates for the waiters to retrieve their orders.)

"Baker, would you mind checking on the girls?" I said. We had much to discuss.

"Sure." Baker told the kitchen staff he'd be back shortly and sprinted out of the kitchen.

I counted backward from one hundred and then hunted him down.

"Kerri seems like she already knows you," I said, when I found him in our bedroom. "What's the deal?"

"I was at Donovan's one night and she and her friends were there. The guys who helped with the painting took me out to get a beer—after working hard all day. Is that okay?"

"Sounds like fun," I said, sarcastically. I act that way sometimes when I'm threatened, and my head felt flushed with fear.

"Yeah, what's the big deal?"

"No *big deal*, I was just curious how Kerri already knows you so well."

"She works here, for God's sake. Was I supposed to be rude to her when I saw her?" He stood up from the bed and angrily yanked the curtain on our closet shut.

"No, I just felt funny back there. Plus, Helga obviously likes her and it's obvious she does not like me."

"Why would you say that?" Baker turned back around to face me. "That's not true, there's no way she couldn't like you. What's not to like?"

"I'm just telling you she doesn't like me. She changed everything I did in the inn back to her way of decorating. Our styles are completely different. I have to feel like it's my house if you ever want me to feel comfortable here." I sat down on the side of the bed.

"Helga will back off. Just give her a little time. Remember how you said Germans have strong personalities? That's just how she is."

"Everybody in Vermont has a strong personality."

Baker sat down next to me. "It's just different from the South. You'll get used to it, I promise." He put his arm around me from the side and kissed my cheek.

I wanted so badly to get a four-way conference call to Memphis going right then and there. But honestly, I didn't know what to tell the girls. I figured I'd better wait. They'd tell me to catch the next plane home.

One more full-time employee was included in the acquisition. Pierre Lebel, now *my* French maître d', had spent the break in France visiting relatives. He had returned from his travels a few days before, and spent most of the time since then sleeping off his jet lag.

Pierre lived in the little cottage with turquoise shutters that sat in the middle of the European garden. He lived alone and, as I would later come to find out, played solitaire and worked jigsaw puzzles for pleasure. He had a full head of jet-black hair, which he combed straight back, revealing a pronounced widow's peak. Pierre's hair was kept short and neat, and his slender frame made him appear younger than his sixty-two years. In the months to come, I always knew when he was mixing his Lady Clairol, because he'd turn out his light and pretend no one was home. Like Roberta, Pierre had been working at the Vermont Haus Inn for nearly twenty years.

When I met him again, early that same evening, Pierre greeted me with enthusiasm. His accent sure was thick. "*Bonjour, madame.*" He smiled and gave me a European kiss.

"Hi, Pierre. It's nice to meet you again."

"*Je suis enchanté de faire votre connaissance. Avez-vous passé un bon voyage?*"

"I beg your pardon," I said with a smile, "I don't speak French. Oh wait, let me try this, no poly vous Francais," I said, shaking my head.

Pierre repeated slowly, "Eh, eh, ple-zeer to see you, ta voyage, est vedy good, *oui?*"

I understood this time and proceeded to break into an oration about my day. "Oh yes, thank you for asking, we had a *great* trip. I'd like to apologize for the mess, Pierre. See, we had a large house full of furniture and I'm really not sure where I'm gonna put it all. Helga is scared to death it won't be cleared up before we open for the season but I promise you have nothing to worry about."

Pierre was smiling and nodding his head up and down as if he were in agreement with me.

"Helga tells me you've been working here nineteen years. Did you move here directly from France or have you lived somewhere else in America?"

Pierre still kept on smiling and nodding.

"Great! Do you still have family in France?"

More nodding.

"What part?" It was this last round of nodding that clued me in to the fact that he had not understood one word I had said. Just for the heck of it I asked one more question. This time I spoke a little louder and slower, something I inadvertently find myself doing when I speak with Chinese people at a Chinese restaurant. "WERE . . . YOU . . . BORN . . . IN . . . MEXICO, PIERRE?"

When his head kept nodding this time, I knew I was in trouble.

"Well, it's been great talking to you. I better get back to my girls." I backed out of the room waving. "*Adiós.*"

Before he met me, Pierre Lebel had never exchanged two words with a Southerner, bless his heart. I would discover that even though Pierre had lived in the States for twenty years, he still spoke French 90 percent of the time. Rolf and Helga were fluent, so they all conversed in French. In the dining room while he was taking orders, Pierre knew the English names of the food items by heart, so translating the menu was no problem.

Daddy always told me I'd regret it one day—taking the easy way out and signing up for Spanish instead of French.

Chapter Seven

After three solid days of unpacking, I couldn't stand being cooped up inside another second. I longed to get outside and check out my new surroundings. Willingham, my new city, was calling my name. Actually, "town" is the correct word. I would later learn that Northerners believe anywhere with less than one million people is only a town. City hall was town hall and the mayor was referred to as the town clerk.

I had a bona fide reason to meet our town clerk. A woman by the name of Betty Sweeney had called from his office early one morning to inform me that our liquor license was in. She went on to say I might as well register my dog and get sworn in while I was there, too, seeing as how I was a new citizen and all. Betty warned me they left by three o'clock most days, so if I wanted to be sure to get the license, I had better come before then.

When I arrived at the town clerk's office, around noon, a man was sitting behind the counter. I walked in, all smiles and eager to meet our town diplomat. He slowly rose to greet me. "Can I help you?"

"Hey there. I'm Leelee Satterfield. My husband and I just bought the

Vermont Haus Inn." I pointed in our direction up the street. "I'm here to pick up our liquor license."

Apparently, it's a big deal to obtain a liquor license. The state looks into your background and the town aldermen (we say councilmen) have to vote in unanimous agreement before they will issue one.

The man from behind the desk spoke with a thick Vermonter accent. "Yuup, I've gut it reet here. The name's Jack Sweeney." He laid the document on the counter.

"It's a pleasure to meet you, Mr. Sweeney. I spoke with your wife, Betty, on the phone this morning. She was so helpful. Is she here?"

He hesitated before answering. "Nuup. She's gun to lunch."

"Oh well, maybe next time. How long have you been the town clerk?" I asked, as I was signing the documents.

"Close to ten years now, I suppose."

"Is that right? Have you and Mrs. Sweeney been working together all that time?"

"Yuup."

"Have you really?"

"Yuup."

"Is this a full-time job for both of you?"

"Yuup."

For the life of me I couldn't imagine what could keep two full-time employees busy all day. The town hall had an office and a meeting room and one more small room. (A month later I rented the smaller room for Isabella's third birthday party and the cost for the afternoon was eight dollars. I got the resident rate.)

We chatted for about ten minutes, mostly about moose. When I asked if he'd ever seen one in person, he said, "Only once't. And that was somewhere close to the Canadian border. All the moose crossin' signs for Willingham and Fairhope are ordered through this office but it's pretty silly if you ask me. Moose are rarely seen around here."

I can't even tell you how disappointed I was to hear that. Even still, I was determined to beat the odds.

As I started to leave, I remembered Betty Sweeney's other requests. "Oh, I almost forgot, I'm supposed to register my dog. We get licenses back home in Tennessee, too. It proves they've had their rabies shot each year. Is that what your registration is for?"

"Nuup, we need to know how many dogs we've gut in town. Is yours a bitch or a stud?"

"Princess Grace Kelly is a girl," I told him, rather indignantly. "And she's up to date on all of her shots."

"That's good." He slid the registration papers and the liquor license across the counter, and handed me a pen.

"Oh, and Betty mentioned something about getting sworn in?"

"Raise your reet hand, please."

I obliged.

"Do you swear to support your town and vote faithfully and attend all town meetings?"

"I do."

With that I finished the paperwork and drove back to the inn to check on the girls. As soon as I walked through the door, our personal telephone line in the apartment started ringing.

"Hello," I answered.

"Mrs. Satterfield?"

"Yes."

"Jack Sweeney here, how are you?"

The same as I was forty-five seconds ago. "Fine, Mr. Sweeney, how are you?"

"I'm alreet, thanks for askin'. I thought I'd call and let you know something, 'fore you hear it from anyone else. Betty's not my wife."

"She's *not?*" I know I sounded shocked but I couldn't help it.

"Nuup, hasn't been for five years now."

I had no idea what to say. I wasn't sure if he was calling to cry on my shoulder or let me know he was available. Come to think of it, he did smile an awful lot while I was there. He may have even winked a time or two. I just thought he was being polite.

"Mr. Sweeney, I'm so sorry to hear that," I said, for lack of anything better to say.

"Well, I thought I should be the one to tell you. There's no doubt that damn George Clark would have told you as soon as he had the chance."

"I'm glad you told me. And who's George Clark, if you don't mind my asking?"

"The town gossip."

"*Oh my*. Well, have a nice day, Mr. Sweeney."

"Yuup."

I found out later from Roberta that Jack Sweeney had left Betty Sweeney for a much younger woman. Betty stayed on in her position as town secretary just to spite him. *Go, Betty!* I thought. What a wonderful day at the office that must be for ole Jack.

My next and most important order of business was to enroll the girls in preschool. Ed Baldwin had told me all about the Elfin Academy. Housed inside an old clapboard church and located two towns over in Shipley, the fifteen-year-old preschool used the Montessori method of teaching.

When I drove up to the building, around two o'clock, the children were just getting out of school. They were bundled up in winter garb from head to toe. Little tiny hats and snowsuits, boots and jackets—each one wore bright-colored mittens and gripped their prized artwork of the day. Their mothers held their other hands as they sloshed through the partly melted snow in the parking lot to their cars.

I met with the preschool director, Miss Susan, and she was delighted to accept both girls into the program. Since Issie would turn three in a few weeks, she could attend two days per week from nine until two. Sarah, having just turned five in November, missed the kindergarten cutoff, but the Elfin four-to-five-year-old program met every day. Personally, I thought it was a lot of school for a little girl, but Miss Susan assured me that the nurturing, hands-on Montessori approach kept the children relaxed and learning at their own pace. The school incorporated naps and lunch and she further contended that each child enrolled absolutely adored their teachers, Miss Penny and Miss Becky.

Sarah and Issie would love the school, I just knew it. As for me, I was glad we had the holidays to get used to the transition. I wanted them home. *Right after the New Year*, I thought, *I'll think about the book*vork, *as Helga called it.* But there was no way in hell I would so much as pick up a pen until my children were settled into their daily routine and my apartment was decorated the way I wanted it.

I spent the rest of the afternoon driving around exploring while Roberta babysat for Sarah and Issie. Willingham had a post office, a library, a hardware store, a tiny market that also rented a *few* videos, my inn, the town hall (used once a year for town meeting day), and that was about the extent of it. The population was about six hundred, so we were lucky to have as much as we did.

Fairhope, the next town over, was a metropolis in comparison. Fairhope had a grocery store, four restaurants, a drug store/card shop, and even a movie theater. There were two more inns, a couple of outlet stores, a combination beauty shop and Laundromat, and the other usual businesses any small town needs to survive.

The reason any business survived at all was because of the two ski resorts only five miles apart. It only took fifteen minutes to get from one to the other.

Sugartree is the largest with two hundred trails and full snow-making capacity. It's a four-season resort, with condominiums, a cobblestone village, restaurants, and health clubs. Without Sugartree, there would be no Vermont Haus Inn or most of the other businesses operating solely on tourist dollars. Dannon Mountain was the other popular resort and it appealed to the family crowd. It had the southern exposure and was considered the warmer of the two mountains. In the summer, Dannon had a three-course alpine slide, which was like sledding down the mountain on a bobsled. Dannon was the first place I skied when I moved to Vermont.

There were two gas stations in Fairhope, and Roberta told me the owners were mortal enemies. When I drove past George Clark's service station the cars were lined up to the street. Roberta explained that even though it was self-serve, George pumped the gas anyway. He did it so he could find out the latest gossip while it was hot off the rack. George Clark thought of gossip like he did a donut. First he craved it, then he devoured it, then he'd sit back full and happy while the sweetness lingered on his tongue. Everyone in town knew his gossip was the freshest, so they'd line up at his pumps even if it took twice as long. Little did I know the name Leelee Satterfield would become one of his tastiest treats.

Manchester was the town where I conducted all of my business. My bank was there, as was the large grocery store and the cleaners. The state of Vermont controlled the sale of alcohol, so I had to buy liquor for the restaurant at the state store in Manchester. If you wanted a decent haircut, you drove to Manchester. If you needed a dependable oil change, you drove to Manchester. If you had a craving for McDonald's french fries, you drove forty-five minutes to Manchester. If you wanted to buy birth control pills or condoms, you avoided the Fairhope Pharmacy and drove to Manchester. (If not, you ran the risk of George Clark spreading your most intimate business.)

Even though Manchester had a million designer outlets, there was not one department store. Back home, it was no big deal to run my stockings or break my blush compact fifteen minutes before I had to be at a party. I could run up to Goldsmith's and be back in ten. In Vermont, running out of Lancôme makeup meant I had two choices: I could drive to Albany, New York, or settle for CoverGirl or Coty at the Fairhope Pharmacy.

I suppose I felt a little better having ventured out and explored the places I would find essential to life in Vermont. However, I had an underlying fear that making friends would be a little more difficult for me than ever before. I was certainly atypical by Vermont standards. But the Vermonters, in my eyes anyway, were somewhat offbeat themselves. A peculiar incident, the next afternoon, left me wondering if and when I would ever really connect to those around me.

There was a faint rap on the apartment door. I opened it to find a man, a woman, and a little girl about Sarah's age. The woman was holding a cake encased in one of those disposable aluminum containers that you find in the grocery store.

He spoke first, in questions, and could hardly look at me. "Hello, um, we're the Grovers? I'm Fred and this is my wife, Pat? Oh, and our daughter,

Erica? We heard you have a little girl around our Erica's age, so we decided to welcome you to the neighborhood?"

"Well, thank you, that's so nice. Y'all come in. I'm Leelee Satterfield." I shook both of their hands. "My husband's upstairs with our daughters. Why don't y'all have a seat and I'll go find them." I motioned to the wicker sofa. The size of our apartment embarrassed me and I cringed when I realized our bedroom door was wide open. *Note to self: Must learn to keep the bedroom doors shut at all times.*

I bolted up the stairs calling Baker's name, and when I got to the top, I happened to look behind me and found myself nose-to-nose with Fred Grover. "Oh. Excuse me, I didn't realize you were behind me."

The man shrugged his shoulders and the rest of the Grover clan followed him into our upstairs den.

"Baker, girls, I'd like you to meet some of our neighbors. This is Fred and Pat Grover, and their daughter, Erica."

Baker stood up from the couch and shook Fred's hand. "Nice to meet y'all, have a seat. Meet our daughters, Sarah and Isabella." The children were playing with their Barbies, and eagerly welcomed young Erica to join them.

Fred Grover seemed a very timid man. He gestured, always with the same arm, and looked down at his feet when he spoke. His face was real shiny and his short dirty blond slicked-down hair had a perfect part on the left side of his oval-shaped head. A deep cleft in his chin made me wonder how he ever managed to shave it without cutting himself.

"Our Erica's in school at Elfin," Fred said. "Will Sarah be attending?"

"That's the plan," Baker said, all chipperlike. "And then next year we're on to Fairhope Elementary. Can't wait to get her on the slopes. Y'all ski, don't you?"

"Nuup. Pat's not too fond of heights." Fred gazed devotedly at his bride.

Pat Grover couldn't have been more than four-foot-ten if she was an inch. Her large frame loomed over her tiny feet and she looked as though she might teeter forward at any moment. These curly black hairs sprouted out of her chin—well, I'm sorry, but you'd have to be blind not to notice them, bless her heart.

Thirty minutes' worth of idle chitchat later, Pat was still clutching the cake, and after she made no gesture to give it to us, I sensed it was my responsibility to take it off her hands. *Maybe it's a Northern thing*, I thought. I forced myself to say, "Did y'all bring that to us?" And then I gestured toward the cake.

"Yes, we did," Fred gloated. "Pat made it last night."

"Thank you, that was so sweet of y'all."

When they still made no motion to hand it over, I took it upon myself to walk over to Pat and reach out for the interesting creation. The cake was iced with chocolate frosting and since it was uncovered, the top caught my eye. There was an odd pattern in the frosting that stretched horizontally across the rectangular sheet cake, bearing a strange resemblance to tracks of some sort. When I grasped one side of the pan and stared down to get a closer look Pat said, "I bet I know what you're looking at. After I iced the cake last night, I left it on the kitchen counter. One of those darned mice musta run right acrosst it."

Well, what do you say to someone after a statement like that? "Oh, don't worry about it; that happens to all my cakes"? Or, "Mice just love chocolate cake, don't they?" I couldn't *say* a thing. A rare speechless moment in the life—well, the new life—of Leelee Satterfield.

Then, to put icing on the cake (no pun intended—I swear), Fred Grover dropped his own bombshell. "I tried to cover it up."

Not knowing what in God's name to add to that I just stared at Pat's hands still clutching the other side of the pan. Once our eyes met again, it was then I heard myself saying, "Well, at least it wasn't a rat."

Out of the corner of my eye I caught a glimpse of Baker excusing himself. If our eyes met I knew the situation would have gone screaming downhill. It was all I could do to keep my shoulders from shaking and not bust into a full-blown laugh attack.

Now, I was left alone hoping Pat would just let go of the dang cake so we could move on with our conversation to something, *anything* else. Finally, I jerked the pan away from her and gazed at the Grovers with a forced smile.

Where in God's name am I? I thought to myself, a question that would pop up daily in the months ahead.

Chapter Eight

Opening night at the Vermont Haus Inn under the new Satterfield regime came and went, unnoticed. That's because nothing had changed. From the weathered VERMONT HAUS INN sign and the ancient menu to the severe houseitosis and the well-known staff, everything was exactly the same. Rolf was still at the helm and Helga was still "on the floor," working the front of the house. Baker had begun his training as Rolf's sous-chef, but none of the customers had any idea. During the first week, the customers rarely saw me, either. I was taking care of Sarah and Isabella at night and getting them acclimated to our new home and our new schedule.

Whenever I did make it into the kitchen, it was close to eight thirty—after the girls were asleep. I brought my portable baby monitor with me into the kitchen, so I could hear any little peep they made. The bad thing was when they did peep, customers were always seated at the six-top table Helga insisted on keeping in front of our apartment door. So to reach them I'd have to trample through the snow, in my heels, to the front door of the apartment. Then I'd fumble for my key to get inside. By that time, their peeps had usually turned into wails.

As fate would have it, Helga was serving drinks at the six-top table one night right before Christmas when Isabella woke up with a dirty diaper. Isabella stood in front of the door screaming her head off, mad as a hornet because she couldn't find me. It was making her even madder that the door was locked. She started yanking on the handle and pounding on the hollow door as hard as she could. I could hear her on the monitor, but I was on the phone with a New Yorker taking a reservation.

"MOMMY, I HAVE A STINKY!" Isabella shrieked loud and clear through the baby monitor for everyone in the kitchen, as well as the six-top table, to hear. "CHANGE ME, MOMMY."

Helga flipped. In a rage, she stormed into the kitchen and found me on the phone. She snatched the receiver out of my hand and handed it over to Pierre (I didn't know what good she thought that would do). "Your kid es screaming for her mother and ze area around table eight smells like a *cow pasture*. My customers are vedy upset. Go to her at once before zay leave and decide to neva come back!"

"I'm sorry, Helga, Issie never does this," I said, and scurried out of the kitchen.

When I finally made it inside the apartment, Isabella had stopped crying. She had decided to amuse herself instead by taking off her diaper and decorating the back of the door with her doo-doo. Sarah was awake by this time, running around the apartment singing: "Ooo, ooo, doo doo! Ooo, ooo, doo doo!" Gracie was barking up a storm at both of them.

"*Ssshhhh*, all three of you," I said in a hushed voice, and I scooped Isabella up—doo and all—and headed straight for the tub. I decided it was probably best to stay away from the restaurant for the rest of the night.

The phone rang around 9:30 P.M. I knew before I picked it up who the call was from. Mary Jule was over at Alice's, and Virginia was in her car headed out to the grocery store. All three of them were on the line.

"What's goin' on, girlfriend?" Alice, the boss, always initiated everything.

"Hey, Fiery," Virginia chimed in.

"It's me, too," was Mary Jule's response.

"Hi, y'all," I said wearily.

"What's the matter? You sound exhausted," Alice said.

"I am."

"Haven't heard from you in a few days, what's up?" she asked.

"That's because there's too much to report and I don't know where to start. Y'all are just gonna have to come up here to see what I mean."

"We're already planning a ski trip. I told Al exactly what ski suit I want from this gorgeous catalog I got in the mail." Mary Jule loves a good excuse for a new outfit.

"Are you serious? When are y'all coming?"

"I'm hoping for spring break," Virginia said. "Will there still be snow?"

"No problem there. I found out it stays around through April."

"*April!*" they all shrieked at the same time.

"That's what I'm told."

"Is everything okay, Leelee?" my sweet Mary Jule asked. She never ceased worrying about us.

"I guess. I just had a little run-in with Helga, though. I tell y'all what, I *can't stand* her."

"Who's Helga?" Mary Jule had obviously forgotten about my new nemesis.

"The bossy bitch who won't let Leelee decorate her own house," Alice said.

"Oh yeah, what'd Helga do this time?" asked Mary Jule.

I told them the whole story . . . and I didn't candy coat it at all.

"What is she still doing there, anyway? Why can't you ask her to leave?" Virginia wanted to know.

"Because Baker and Ed Baldwin said we have to keep everything exactly the same for a year."

"Easy for Baker to say. Personally, I don't know how you'll stand it eleven more months," said Alice.

"I'm just looking forward to April when they go to Germany for two months. I suppose I can make it until then. Here's another thing. We have had to spend so much money up here it's ridiculous."

I heard Baker's key turning in the front door. "Uh-oh, better go, here comes Baker," I whispered into the phone. "I don't want him to hear me ragging on Helga. I love y'all, call you later." I hung up just in time.

Not only did I not want him to hear me complaining about Helga, I sure didn't want him to hear me confiding to the girls about our finances. We were clearly in over our heads but there was no way Baker would admit it. We had written an awful lot of big checks for start-up costs. There was food and liquor and beer and wine to buy, propane gas *and* fuel oil to heat the place, and salaries and payroll taxes to pay. And that was just the beginning. Our mortgage to Helga and Rolf was nearly $2,000 per month.

Picking out the tree was our favorite holiday tradition. Baker and I always took pride in finding a perfect tree, a Fraser fir, and the bigger the better. So it was no surprise that the girls and I were counting the minutes until we could go in search of our first real live growing-in-the-wild Christmas tree. We learned that the Green Mountain National Forest, as long as you have a permit, lets people cut down one tree a year for free. And each one you come across is shaped more perfectly than the one before. Up north, you don't have to pull trees out from a huge stack and twirl them around 'til you've found the one you want; there are a million flawless ones growing wild in the woods.

After cutting it down, we had to put our Christmas tree in the parlor of the inn so our "houseguests" could enjoy it. (That was the term the Schloygins used when referring to the people spending the night in the inn.) I'd never shared my Christmas tree before; I felt a little funny leaving presents for my children underneath it during business hours. Of course, normal business hours were twenty-four hours a day, seven days a week. But my children wanted to see presents, naturally, so they saw presents. Baker and I got in a big fight over that one. I didn't understand why we couldn't put the tree in the "superb owners' quarters," but he insisted we had to keep everything just as it was for at least a year.

My present had been under the tree for a couple of days, and I had already picked up the box and shaken it two or three times. *Baker thinks he's so sneaky*, I thought. *He's hidden my diamond earrings in a big huge box and filled it with extra weight.* I just knew that after I agreed to move all the way to Vermont, he finally had bought them for me.

On Christmas Eve, the girls had been counting the minutes until the next morning and it took forever for them to fall asleep. We were huddled up together underneath blankets on the couch, and the Franklin stove blazed in front of us. As I read the poem "'Twas the Night Before Christmas," I thought back to the night before.

I had ventured out to Fairhope to pick up a pizza once the snow had stopped falling. The full moon beckoned to me from high in the clear star-lit sky. As I looked out over the flawless stretches of snow-covered pastures, I could have sworn it was daylight. The black-and-white colors of the cows were as vivid as if it were noon. Houses were illuminated by the lunar radiance, and even the details of the shutters were easily discernable. I wanted to drive and keep on driving; with every mile I was more fascinated than the one before.

Now, hidden in the lines of the famous poem, I stumbled upon a description of what I'd seen. I knew the words by heart, yet I had no insight into their true meaning until I experienced it myself. "The moon on the breast of the new-fallen snow gave the luster of midday to objects below."

After finally getting the girls to sleep, I drifted out front, looking forward to spending some alone time with my husband. Baker and I always opened our gifts to each other on Christmas Eve—alone, just the two of us—in front of our tree. But not this year. The staff was hanging around after the restaurant closed and seemed in no hurry to get home. Baker was busy passing out free liqueurs when I arrived. He was headed back to the kitchen for another round when I stopped him.

"Can we open our presents now?" I whispered. "Just the two of us?"

He looked down at the empty tray and then back up at me. "Sure, honey." I could tell he would rather keep partying but his better judgment told him not to.

We stole over to the tree but when Roberta spotted us she followed right behind and stood in front of the fireplace. I sat down in the tattered easy chair next to the tree and Baker knelt down right in front of it.

My husband seemed as excited as I was about my present. He scooped it up from underneath the tree, gazed at the shiny red paper tied up with a big gold bow, and passed it over to me. "Go ahead, honey, open it. You're gonna love it."

"What is it?" I asked him, gleaming with joy.

"I'm not gonna tell you, just open it."

"I'm excited," I said, turning the box over and shaking it. *That rascal,* I thought again, *he's hidden my earrings inside this big, heavy one.*

Roberta blurted out a clue as she reached around and tugged on her backside. "Oh, you're goin' to love 'em, alreet. You'll wonder how you ever lived without 'em, I tell you."

You're darn tootin' I'm gonna love 'em— Uh-oh, Roberta's acting like she has a personal connection with my Christmas present. My first rip into the paper revealed the word SOREL printed on the box. The second rip revealed a picture of a boot. *What in the world? . . .* I slowly lifted the top off the box, still thinking about which way I was going to wear my hair to show off my studs . . . only to find the most god-awful pair of . . . *rubber snow boots.* With horror written all over my face, I picked up the first one and peered inside before turning it upside down. When nothing fell out, I turned the other one over and frantically shook it as hard as I could. My entire right arm disappeared into the boot as I dug my hand all the way down to the stiff toe. Nothing. I frantically ruffled through the packing paper, still holding on to hope that a small package might be hiding in a corner of the box. No such luck.

I could feel Baker's eyes burning toward me but I refused to look at him. He knew dang well I was disappointed and tried back-pedaling his way out.

"They're *Sorels,* Leelee." He reached over and grabbed one of my Christmas galoshes out of the box. I watched as he fiddled with the laces and ran his hand over the toe. "The woman at the shoe store told me a Sorel is the warmest boot money can buy. It protects your feet in forty-below temps." He knocked on the sole. "Everyone wears them up here and yours are the top of the line."

Forty-below temps! It's not like we moved to Alaska.

"Try 'em on, honey!" Baker jammed the boot back into my hand.

Upon closer examination I realized they were even uglier than I thought: Number one, they were the biggest things I'd ever seen, and number two, they must've weighed ten pounds each. Reluctantly, I kicked off my kitten-heeled slingbacks and slipped the right one onto my foot. A thick black string laced up the front of the gray monster and a chunky rubber sole crept up from the bottom and almost covered the toe. The thermal liner stuck up a few inches from the top of the boot and came up to my mid-calf.

Roberta was about to bust. "My Sorels look no different now than they did the day I fought Buelah Mayweather for 'em five years ago at a tag sale. Yes sirree, the best money can buy." ("Tag sale" is Northern for yard sale.)

Interesting he didn't bother to buy me a pair that look more like the snow bunny's adorable ones. After Roberta's pronouncement all I could do was fake like I liked them. "Thanks, Baker," I said, with a phony smile. Really I was about to cry. Not so much because I didn't get the diamond earrings but that he would actually buy me *snow boots* for my Christmas present.

"You'rrrre welcome." He whispered out of the side of his mouth, "They were *real* expensive." As if that was going to make me like them.

"I like 'em," I lied. *It'll be a cold day in Cuba before I ever put those monsters on my feet. But how will I explain it to Roberta?*

Also in the boot box were four packages of something called toe heaters. I picked one up and examined the packaging. Supposedly, they provided eight hours of protection.

"I threw those in so your toes would stay *extra* toasty."

I had no comment.

Daddy would have told me to put the Sorels in my own tag sale, go out and buy the boots I wanted, and be sure and put them on Baker's American Express.

My husband seemed very excited about *his* presents. I wonder why? He got a ski jacket, a new sports coat, *and* a new tackle box.

I hated my Christmas Eve.

And my Christmas morning.

Breakfast for the inn guests had to come first. Of course, they wanted it during the time my children wanted to open their presents. Poor Baker spent the whole morning running back and forth from the kitchen to the parlor, lucky to even catch a bit of "Look what Santa brought me, Daddy!"

I couldn't hang out in my robe sipping coffee and munching on a danish, nor could I enjoy a nice, relaxing Christmas Day lounging around the house. It didn't stop me from putting on my favorite Christmas music, though. When Amy Grant's "Tender Tennessee Christmas" came on, I couldn't resist cranking up the volume, even if it was the parlor. At that one moment, I couldn't have cared less what Helga thought.

The Schloygins never closed for any holidays. Why on earth should they? Neither of them had children. And we were "keeping everything just the way it was," thanks to Ed Baldwin. "It's the key to success," he must have said a hundred times. Lesson number one about the restaurant business hit me like a cold shower: A holiday means business as usual. When most Americans take time off and hit the streets, those of us in the restaurant biz hit "the floor," as they say.

Later that afternoon, just before we geared up for dinner, we had a staff Christmas party in keeping with the Schloygin tradition. Helga had insisted we give everyone a Christmas bonus. Baker agreed with her that it wasn't the fault of anyone on the staff the Vermont Haus Inn had changed hands right before the holidays. So everyone received a Merry Christmas check of one week's salary from the Satterfields. *More money we didn't have.*

Everyone reciprocated, however, and we opened all kinds of gifts. Roberta brought Sarah and Isabella each a Beanie Baby. She brought Baker and me a little handcrafted HOME SWEET HOME sign. "I thought it would look nice on your apartment door," she said when I opened the gift. I imagined Roberta's whole house was filled with little objects like that.

Pierre actually went out and bought the girls Barbie clothes and gave Baker and me a bottle of wine. He even wrapped up a package of doggie treats for Gracie.

Helga and Rolf gave us a family gift. A fruit basket. It still had the price tag on the bottom—$8.99.

Jeb brought his mama over to join the gift swap, which embarrassed me to death because I had nothing for her. The only thing I knew to do was run back to the apartment and wrap up one of my own gifts. Since I wasn't sure of her style, I impulsively grabbed the tin of Dinstuhl's white chocolate that Virginia's parents had sent us for Christmas. Mrs. Murphey knew that white chocolate was my favorite so she sent Dinstuhl's biggest tin. I regretted it as soon as Jeb's mama opened it; she never even bothered to pass it around. To me, that takes gall.

Mrs. Duggar gave everyone a sample-size bottle of Avon Skin So Soft body oil. She had become an Avon rep, despite the controversy it caused at Mary Kay. According to Roberta, Mary Kay wanted Mrs. Duggar's pink car returned when they found out she was making Avon calls on the side. Roberta went on to explain that Doris Duggar paid for that pink Chevette with her own elbow grease and it didn't matter who she worked for in the future—it rightfully belonged to her. Jeb went out and bought her the Club, that red car lock thing that fits on the steering wheel. "Problem solved," Jeb said, and now his mama does whatever she pleases. When I opened my Skin So Soft bottle she made a comment about how handy it would be come spring. I was totally baffled by the comment but I didn't give it much thought.

Jeb wanted everyone to open his gifts at the same time. Talking about proud. When Jeb bought his floor model for JCW, he got a promotional bonus. Now, all of us had matching Jeb's Computer World mouse pads. Baker and I were the only ones who even owned a computer. Roberta just smiled and smiled and made Jeb think she was pleased as punch with hers. Later she told me that she had never before in her life owned a place mat for her coffee mug.

It was Kerri's gift to Baker that got the most oohs and aahs. She actually went to the trouble of tying flies for my husband. Turns out she is a flyfisherwoman herself, born and raised in Idaho. The rest of us received Sugartree coffee mugs. *How nice and thoughtful of you, Kerri.*

I'll tell you right now what Daddy would have said about Kerri. "Dahlin', any woman who would trudge through a stream in hip waders and extract hooks out of fish lips is no lady."

Chapter Nine

All the regulars wanted to meet us when the word got out that Helga and Rolf had sold the Vermont Haus Inn. The most important thing on their minds, however, was that their favorite chef was still at the helm and the prices were still the same. The menu had not changed for thirty years. I mean, *not one item* varied. Even the appetizers remained untouched.

We served eggplant caponata, roasted red peppers with anchovies, melon with prosciutto ham, pâté, escargot, herring in sour cream—and lastly, *head cheese*. The entrées were classics like beef Wellington, Dover sole, veal piccata, veal marsala, lamb, and duckling with cherry sauce.

Rolf was in the kitchen one morning preparing one of his infamous appetizers, when I bopped in with a basket full of dirty clothes and plopped them down on the washing machine. The washer and dryer were kept in the commercial kitchen, despite the fact that the health department counted off five points each time they made their routine inspections. As I was dumping the darks into the machine, I happened to glance over at Rolf. He was standing in front of his cutting board, holding a cow's head.

"AAAAAAHHHHHH! *Rolf! What are you doing with that?*" I screamed so loud I about scared the stew out of Roberta, who was standing in front of the sink, peeling potatoes.

"Making head cheese," he said, with a laugh. "There es no need to scream."

"I have been avoiding asking about head cheese and now I know why." I put my hand up in front of my face to try and block the grotesqueness.

"Head cheese is an old-fashion dish, one of my favorites. It es made from ze organs in a calf's head." When he pulled back the lips to expose the teeth, I felt the pit of my stomach start to churn.

Rolf smiled as he demonstrated. "First you clean ze teeth vif a stiff brush. Now—remove ze ears . . . ze brains . . . ze eyes . . . and ze snout . . . and most of ze fat. Soak it all about six hours in cold vater to extract ze blood."

Watching Rolf maneuver the cow head was the last thing I wanted to do, but I didn't want to appear rude. I kept watching, even though my belly begged for me to shut my eyes.

"Then, you wash and drain ze meat. Now put in cold vater and add onion and celery, and simmer ze meat until it falls off ze bones. Next, cut up your meat, remembering to reserve ze brains for later, and cover vith your stock. Now you are rready to season and cook a little more." He wiped his hands first together and then on his apron. "Then pour into a mold and cover. Be sure and serve it chilled and cut into nice thick slices." He glanced up at me before remembering one last piece of advice.

"Oh, ze most important part—cover vith a vinaigrette sauce that has ze brains that you saved all mixed in. Vedy easy and vedy good. Helga's favorite, too. Would you like to try a piece? Have it for lunch, vhy don't you?"

"I'm not really hungry right now. But thank you anyway." I slightly lifted the lid to the washer and peered at him over the top. "Now I know how to make head cheese!" *It would take a five-hour make-out session with Paul McCartney or Jon Bon Jovi to even get me to consider a bite of head cheese. Maybe I'll submit it to the next issue of the* Memphis Junior League Cookbook . . . Head Cheese from the kitchen of Mrs. Baker Satterfield.

Right after the New Year, Helga insisted it was time to hire an evening babysitter so I could start full time in the restaurant. More and more I was feeling like Helga's punching bag, dangling from the inn's dining room ceiling. And it seemed she felt it was her right to take a swing at me any time she passed by. The last thing I wanted to do was obey her but frankly I didn't need the trouble my resistance to her demands might cause.

Miss Becky at the Elfin Academy had a seventeen-year-old daughter who was a junior in high school and saving for college. The first night Mandy arrived, I was dressed and ready to head into the restaurant. I had been blue all day at the thought of spending most evenings away from my daughters.

But thankfully, Sarah and Issie fell in love with Mandy on the spot. Mandy's gentle yet playful spirit put me a little more at ease with having to abandon my daughters night after night. She told me her friends referred to her as "the bookworm" but as far as I was concerned, that was a big plus. We knew the Berenstain Bears books by heart and a week never went by that I didn't buy the girls another book to add to our at-home library.

Back home, I would have been thrilled to have a babysitter like Mandy. Don't get me wrong, I was thrilled to have her in Vermont, too, but in Memphis I only needed babysitters when I was going out for fun. Now, I had to desert my daughters six nights per week so I could apprentice under Sergeant Helga Schloygin.

My restaurant duties commenced with instruction by Helga, stationed at a makeshift service bar on top of the washing machine and dryer. Handwriting the dinner checks was my primary responsibility. Observing Helga while she mixed drinks was secondary and not a chore she was ready to pass down. Her cigarettes kept a steady burn in the ashtray right next to my allergic nose and a cloud of smoke always hovered over the light fixtures above. If her cig wasn't in the ashtray, it was hanging out of the right side of her mouth. She'd puff while vigorously shaking her martinis over to her left side. I'd sneeze and she'd smoke. One night she told me I needed to see an allergy doctor because my sneezing was irritating her. Now that's what I call *colossal* nerve.

Whenever Helga would allow me to make an appearance in the dining room, to deliver drinks or show a group of guests to their table, they all had the same question. Who were we and what brought us to Vermont? Even if a customer knew nothing about me, all I had to do was open my mouth. "What brings you to Vermont?" they would ask. "You must have family here." "Did you own a restaurant down south?" "This must be quite a change for you."

I would go into great detail about how we wanted to give our children the best life had to offer. I rambled on about my adventurous spirit, and the fact that Baker's job was allowing him no family flexibility. By the time I left their table, they knew my life history. But my long conversations with the customers used to bug the ever-loving fire out of Helga. That wasn't her style, so it need not be mine. On numerous occasions she would come up to the table, interrupt me, and tell me I was wanted in the kitchen.

When it got busy, Pierre would run around frantic, afraid of making a mistake. Helga insisted he be the only one to take every order and open every bottle of wine. One night I decided to help him by delivering a bottle of wine to a four-top table. I had completed only two turns of the cork-screw when I felt a hip knock me out of place. Before I knew it, the wine bottle was yanked from my hands and Helga muttered through gritted teeth and a phony smile, "I'll do it."

Silence loomed among the four people at the table. I'm sure they were afraid to say a word for fear the Sergeant would reprimand them, too. I managed to give them a weak smile as I sheepishly turned and walked away. That incident made me mad, but the situation with Helga was much too tense to make any waves. Of course, I complained to Baker, but his attitude was circumspect. "Just let it go," he said. "We need them. Let's not rock the boat."

Moving to Willingham, Vermont, was most definitely an avalanche of an adjustment. Topping the list for biggest adaptation was the climate. In thirty-two years of temperate Southern living, the coldest weather I had ever lived through was nineteen degrees. And on those very rare occasions in Memphis, pipes start bursting and animal safety warnings are broadcast. Everyone keeps their faucets dripping and the department stores sell out of electric blankets. Snow rarely sticks for more than a day or two. When it does snow, the mayor might as well put an Out of Order sign on Memphis. Even the banks close. People hurry out to put chains on their tires and the schools stay closed for days, until the last little bit of snow finally melts.

Snowfall up north, I learned, meant business as usual no matter how much snow happened to stick. Before you even noticed the snow falling, the town plows were on the scene. Their bellowing engines, mixed with the sound of the scraper on the front of the truck, could be heard a mile away. There's so much snow falling *and* sticking that it takes a monster machine with a tremendous shovel on the front to clear it out of the way. It gets pushed to the side of the road and there it sits until May. When it gets really deep, the town has to send in a backhoe. As the plows keep shoving the snow to the edges of the parking lots, the area for the cars keeps getting smaller and smaller. So it has to be removed and hauled off to a desolate area.

What the town was *not* responsible for was private driveways. In stepped the woodchuck. Every chuck living in the state of Vermont, even Jeb Duggar, attached a monster shovel to the front of his own truck in the winter. It took a total of two and a half minutes to plow our entire parking lot. (I know because I timed it once.) And for that I paid Jeb fifty-five dollars. During the heavy snowfalls, it had to be plowed two or three times in one day. Each chuck fought for his customers. It was not uncommon for one of them to take in over twelve hundred dollars within twenty-four hours. I would like to say "I'm in the wrong business." But for obvious reasons, I don't think I have what it takes to be a woman woodchuck.

Once, I went a week and a half without any mail deliveries. When I called the post office to find out why, the postmaster said, "Unless you keep the area in front of your mailbox free of snow, the postman will *not* stop."

"How was I supposed to know *that*?" I asked the postmaster. They should put out a newcomer's manual to educate poor unsuspecting souls on life in Vermont.

Ever heard of a roof rake? Me neither. People in Vermont have to *rake their roofs*! They have to clear the snow off before it turns into ice. Roof rakes come with telescope handles that can extend to thirty feet. They fly out of the hardware stores as soon as October approaches.

Jeb raked our roof. And sometimes he'd let it go too long, and would have to get up on the slate roof wearing these metal spiked shoes and chisel away at the ice. The fear is that the weight of the ice could cause extensive damage to the slate roof. Jeb scared me to death climbing on top of all that ice but it didn't seem to scare him in the least.

When I first arrived in Vermont, Roberta got a kick out of the contents of my suitcase. Talking about ill prepared for the elements. I had ten or twelve sundresses, four or five bathing suits, several pairs of sandals, silk cocktail dresses, shorts and T-shirts, skirts and blouses. Oh, and blue jeans, I had several pairs of blue jeans. Now, of course I had sweaters, the nice soft cotton kind. Even my nightgowns and socks were made of cotton. But I had never needed a heavy-duty wool sweater, until I moved to Vermont.

"Layer," people would tell me, but I had no idea what they meant. I *tried* shopping for the right clothes, but I couldn't seem to find my place in the fashion scene. In the same way that I'm not the Birkenstock type, I'm not the L.L.Bean type, either.

Consequently, I froze.

The little tiny bathroom in our apartment was the warmest room in the house because of the space heater. Each morning when I woke up I would grab my clothes out of the dresser in the hall, and head straight for the bathroom. I'd huddle in front of the space heater while I dressed; a habit that would become an everyday routine.

And I thank God for toe heaters. That extra little gift Baker added to my Christmas present. Once I discovered those, I wore them any time I ventured outdoors.

Roberta took great joy in taking on the role of my personal Vermont advisor, so I came to her with all my Northern questions.

"Black ice?" I asked, as I was getting ready to drive into Manchester for a liquor run. "What's that?"

"You better watch out for it, Leelee. There are deadly patches of ice hiding on them roads. Them are nearly impossible to see because they're the same color as the asphalt."

"Thanks for warning me, I'll be cautious," I told her.

As my luck would have it there were patches of black ice every quarter mile of the thirty miles between the inn and Manchester. The worst part is that I was going *down* the mountain. Every few seconds I was pumping my brakes (a trick Jeb taught me) and the line of cars behind me kept getting longer and longer. I shook my head at them in disgust every time a daredevil whizzed past me. I was driving close to thirty miles per hour, and everyone else was doing at least sixty. I didn't care what they thought about me, so I took my time and made it safely into Manchester.

Two weeks later, Baker and I were riding together and I was taking my time (moose-watching) and pumping my brakes the same way as before. He told me to either speed up or let him drive. "If you think, for one moment, I am going to be like one of those daredevils who speed over black ice, you are sadly mistaken," I told him.

"What black ice? There's no black ice today," Baker said, as if I had lost my mind.

"I beg your pardon, there's a spot right up there. Look." I pointed at a spot as we drove right past.

"What makes you think that's black ice?"

"Roberta told me. Black ice is dangerous and deceiving and this road is full of it."

"Leelee, I'm telling you *that is not black ice*. Those are tar patches."

"They are too black ice. Roberta described it to me in great detail."

"Here, pull over if you don't believe me and let all these cars pass us."

I pulled the Explorer over to the side of the road and waited 'til the coast was clear to get out and touch one of the spots. It was a tar patch all right.

I stormed back to the car and opened my door. "How was I supposed to know about *black ice*?" I slid back into the seat and slammed the car door. "I'd never even heard that term before we moved here. My God, I've never driven in this much snow and I've sure never *shoveled* it."

"Who's making you shovel snow? Have I asked you to pick up a snow shovel one time?" Baker raised his voice and glared at me.

"No, but I've had to make plenty of other adjustments about this snow.

It's pretty and all, but it sure is hard to live in." I looked behind me and eased back out onto the road. "We can't even run to the mailbox without bundling up. It takes a half hour to dress the girls to go outside. Every time they fall down they start crying. Then, they want to come back in ten minutes later because the snow's too deep. And Gracie, forget Gracie! Have you seen her scratch on the door to go out *one time*?"

"This is *the North*." He deliberately lowered his voice. Something he always does to make a point. "*Snow* is a way of life here."

"It's never been *my* way of life. No one ever told me any of this." Out of frustration, I clenched the steering wheel. Since I was trying to keep my eyes on the road, I could only steal looks at him.

"You'll be fine. Just toughen up and quit acting so helpless." Baker looked over at me. "Even Scarlett O'Hara learned to pick her own cotton."

Tears welled up in my eyes. "That is the stupidest, meanest thing I've ever heard. What's gotten into you, Baker?"

"I'm sorry, I was trying to make a joke," he said, and reached over and patted my leg. "I'm just tired. I'm working so many more hours than I ever have before."

Really? I longed to say. Why didn't you consider that before we moved? Much the same way you neglected to examine the finances this whole life change would require. Our hole had been getting deeper and the income from the inn wasn't filling it back up. We had no choice but to dip into what was left of Daddy's life insurance money. And once that was gone, we had no more reserve. Daddy, always the wise protector, had sheltered the rest of my inheritance. He left his money in trust and I couldn't touch another penny until I turned forty.

I was too upset to say another word so we rode in silence the rest of the way into Manchester.

I was in the commercial kitchen fixing an early dinner for the girls, sometime in the middle of February, when I felt my first Vermont sonic boom. It was a Monday—I lived for Mondays because the restaurant was *closed*. No customers, no employees, and *no Helga*. I was carrying their plates into the red-checked dining room when I heard a noise so deafening the whole house shook, like an earthquake had hit. It frightened me so that when I jumped back the chicken fingers on the plates flew up in the air and ended up on the floor. I squashed one running for cover. Since the girls and I were alone in the house, I yelled for them to jump into my arms and we all ran down cellar.

"What was *that*?" Isabella asked, as I was hurrying down the steps.

"Why are we hiding in the basement?" Sarah wanted to know.

"Mama's not sure, but everything's gonna be okay," I said, by this time out of breath and trying to keep them calm. As far as I knew, earthquakes never happened in Vermont. I distinctly remembered asking Ed Baldwin last summer.

After fifteen minutes went by and no more noises, we tiptoed up the stairs and peeked out the basement door into the red-checked dining room. Everything was perfectly still. Not wanting to take any chances, though, the girls and I bolted for the apartment. I locked us in until Baker came back from Manchester. He thought I was making the whole thing up until Sarah convinced him that I was really telling the truth.

It wasn't until Roberta came to work the next morning that I found out what really had happened. I waited until she had used the restroom before telling her about the noise I had heard. (The very first thing Roberta did when she got to work was slip right into the half bath in the kitchen. At first I wondered what her hurry was all about. Finally it dawned on me. Roberta saved her number two for the inn. Her woodchuck husband refused to install an indoor toilet at their house. Moe told her "pissers ain't nothing but a luxury." So poor round Roberta Abbott, nicest woman in Vermont, had to either squat over a bowl inside or traipse outside to an outhouse.) Before I had even finished describing the noise Roberta knew exactly what had happened.

"I'm happy to report you didn't hear an earthquake," she said confidently. "What you heard was roof ice."

"*Roof ice*?"

"Yuup. It makes an awful bang, when it finally drops."

"I don't get it," I told her.

"The first time the sun shines after a heavy snowfall, it melts the ice underneath the snow on the roof. When it cracks, the whole side slides off at once. It sounds like a bomb explodin', I tell you. And it comes with no warnin'."

"That could kill somebody!"

"It sure could. You better watch them girls, especially around the south side."

From that day on, the children and I only entered and exited by way of the front door of the inn, which had the pointy side of the roof's eave above it and no chance of our accidental death.

It should not come as a surprise that no one had bothered to forewarn me about Vermont's killer roofs.

One February morning Roberta told me a nor'easter was headed our way. She heard the weather forecast on her scanner before she came into work. She and Moe listened to a police scanner—religiously—every evening of their adult life. They even slept with it on in the background. Occasionally their scanner picked up cordless telephone conversations. I don't think Roberta meant to tell me that little detail; it just slipped out. Between Roberta Abbott and George Clark, privacy was a luxury, a downright precious commodity.

Nor'easter is slang for a Northeastern heavy storm. Before moving to Vermont, I had never even heard of a nor'easter. After Roberta's warning we all dashed out to the grocery store to stock up on food, candles, and bottled water. Jeb brought plenty of firewood in from the porch and placed it around all the fireplaces in case the power went out. "Fill your bathtubs up," he told me. "We could be without power for quite a while."

"Why do we need to do that?" I asked him."

"So you can flush your toilets and wash your clothes."

Lovely, I thought.

Snow started falling around lunchtime. When it came time for the restaurant to open, every one of our reservations had cancelled. Nor'easters are quite stressful in the restaurant biz. An overhead-only evening makes for a tense climate in the kitchen. Not only were the waitstaff upset over the loss of tips, Rolf would grumble and drop hints to Baker about getting his mortgage payment on time.

I, for one, was happy about the storm. It gave me a family night alone with my husband and daughters. We played Hi Ho Cherry-O together and then watched *Chitty Chitty Bang Bang* until the power went out, right as the magical car first took off in the air. Baker and the girls fell asleep on the couch. I sat alone in the dark listening to a branch scrape against the window and gazed out over the backyard. The snow was falling so heavily I couldn't see a thing. This must be the "whiteout" Roberta had warned me about.

Fortunately, the power came back on within an hour. Though once we crawled into bed the inside temperature had dropped dramatically.

"I'm gonna bring the girls in with us," I said to Baker, snuggling up behind him.

"No, there isn't enough room." He never even turned around.

"But they'll be scared. Just listen to the wind. *I'm* scared."

"They'll be fine. They're asleep."

"Issie wakes up during every thunderstorm at home and this one is ten times worse."

"Then go get in bed with her."

"Fine." I rolled off the bed and dashed into the girls' room.

Cuddled up next to my baby daughter, I listened while the house creaked and the crevices around the windows and doors whistled an eerie tune. It must have been after 2:00 A.M. by the time I fell asleep. *Something about Baker isn't right. He's a different man up here.*

The next morning, Baker and Pierre pitched in to help Jeb with the snow-blower. (Incidentally, a snowblower is another piece of equipment that was foreign to me.) It took them all day to clear the walkways. We had accumulated four feet of fresh snow and that was on top of the five feet we already had. By the time the guys finished, our dormant European garden had been transformed into a labyrinth of snow. The brick walkways leading to the doors were now hedged with pure white powder.

Inside we had a different problem; the pipes in our apartment froze. Instead of blowing snow, I spent the majority of the morning in the bathroom, blow-drying my pipes.

I physically survived my first nor'easter. Mentally surviving it was another matter altogether. My life had become a nor'easter.

Chapter Ten

Princess Grace Kelly had the hardest time adjusting of anyone. She only stood nine inches tall at the top of her ears. When it came to doing her business outside, I'll just say she wasn't up for the challenge. For fourteen years, Gracie was used to me opening the back door and letting her run outside. In Memphis, Gracie spent a lot of her time outside no matter the season.

The first time I opened the door in Vermont, the arctic wind blew the long hair around her face sideways and covered her eyes. She looked gorgeous, though, in her new faux mink coat. (I ordered it out of a doggie catalog before I left home.) "Go on, Gracie," I said. "Go potty." She just stared at me with a "you've got to be kidding" look on her face and never budged. I'll admit it—I didn't want to get out in the cold, either. So I pushed her out the door anyway. Gracie fell right off the steps and I watched in horror as my poor little senior citizen dog sunk into the middle of a four-foot snowdrift. Horrified, I went running outside in my socks to rescue her, screaming, "Gracie, Gracie, hold on, I'm sorry." I dug her out and frantically brushed off the snow. My lesson was learned after that. There was no way she was going to venture out alone, in the snow, ever again. My only choice was to bundle up myself and trudge on out with her.

Gracie hated putting her paws down on the snow because the hair around her feet always froze and she got little ice balls in between her toes. She'd just stand there three-legged with one foot up in the air like she couldn't bear to take another step.

Helga and Rolf insisted that I scoop her poop and cover up the yellow snow behind her. Before long, Gracie got back at all of us for making her freeze her little fanny off. Little did I know it, but Gracie had been escaping into the inn on a regular basis. During the day when our apartment door was open she'd slip under the six-top table, and once she knew the coast was clear she'd be on her merry way. Gracie's secret prowl remained undiscovered until one momentous night when she decided to leave the state of Vermont a small token of her appreciation.

The restaurant was in full swing; seventy-five reservations on the books. The front dining room was a favorite among the regulars. It was quite intimate with only four tables, hand-carved corner china cabinets, and a small fireplace. It was the only room with carpeting on the floor—forest green shag. There is no telling how long Gracie had gotten away with it, since number one was easy to conceal on a dark-colored rug.

What about the smell? Wasn't that a dead giveaway? Lest you have forgotten, the Vermont Haus Inn already stunk to high heaven. I tried eliminating the houseitosis by placing potpourri in bowls all over the inn. Downstairs, upstairs, and in every bathroom. When I ordered a case of magnolia-scented candles from home and scattered them around, Helga complained the place smelled too sweet. So I switched to lavender and she grumbled that the scent didn't go with the gourmet food. "People vant to smell the gah'lic—the aroma of the cuisine, not a flower shop!" What choice did I have but to give up the fight?

Anyway, Helga was expecting Mr. and Mrs. Richard Peabody that evening for the first seating; their dinner reservations were at 6:30 P.M. When a very proper couple opened the front door, exactly on time, I had a hunch it must be the Peabodys. I was standing in the foyer holding their menus when they stepped inside.

"Hi, are you the Peabodys?" I asked.

"We are indeed." The woman spoke for them both.

"I'm Leelee Satterfield, the new owner of the inn. It's nice to meet you. Helga's told me so much about you."

"Well, isn't that nice," the Missus said in a snooty way with her Northern aristocratic voice. "Is Helga here this evening?"

"Yes, ma'am, she's in the back mixing drinks. But I told her I really wanted to introduce myself. We've got the table you requested all ready."

"How nice. The rest of our dinner party, the Fikes, have they arrived?"

"No, ma'am, they have not."

"Well then, let's be seated anyway." She barreled right past me to get to her regular table. Mister didn't seem to be in as big a hurry, so he and I walked together.

As I approached their table, I happened to notice something small and brown poking out from underneath one of the chairs. As I got closer I realized it was no Tootsie Roll. In a panic and not knowing what else to do, I kicked it up under the table.

Now I was really in a pickle. I had to think fast. Mr. and Mrs. Peabody were seated at the table and someone's foot was only inches away from Gracie's poop piece.

I handed them both a menu and kept talking while my mind raced for a solution. "So, where are y'all from?"

"Connecticut," she said. No emotion. Mr. Peabody never even looked up from his menu.

"Really? Seems like there are lots of people here from Connecticut. Do y'all own a home here?"

"Why, yes. It's been in Richard's family for several generations." She closed her menu and placed it in front of her.

Just then Pierre walked in, followed by the Fikes, and as Pierre pulled the chair out for Mrs. Fike, I cringed at the thought of what might happen next.

My immediate concern was hiding it from Helga. I envisioned her as Elvira Gulch from *The Wizard of Oz*—wearing goggles, hunched over the handlebars of a snowmobile, and driving off with my Gracie locked in a basket on the back.

My only hope lay with Pierre. He seemed to really love Gracie. He would take her into his little cottage and the two of them would lie up on his bed watching the daytime soaps. Pierre started saving her the leftover pâté that came back on the dirty dishes. Thanks to Pierre, Gracie stopped eating anything but real goose liver pâté.

I excused myself from the Peabodys' table and when Pierre came out of the dining room, I pulled him off to the parlor where I was out of anyone's earshot or eyesight.

"It's Princess Grace Kelly," I said in a loud whisper, and made the shape of a little dog with my hands.

When he clearly had no clue, I said again: "Gracie," and barked, "Ruff-ruff."

This time his face lit up and he nodded and smiled.

Shaking my head, I said, "Gracie pooped at table four."

Pierre, of course, just shook his head in confusion.

"Gracie *doo-dooed* under table four," I said louder, holding up four fingers and pointing over to that dining room.

Still nothing. No comprehension whatsoever.

In desperation, I did the only thing I could do. I squatted down on the floor, on all fours, and grunted—like I was Gracie. I put my hand beneath my butt and made the shape of a small, Gracie-size, doo-doo log. Then I held my nose and pointed into the front dining room where the Peabodys and the Fikes were the only customers seated.

Pierre raised his eyes up in shock and stood there with his mouth open. "Aha! Puppy shit!"

"*Yesssss*," I squealed. "And I kicked it under the table." I got up and ran over to an empty table at the far side of the parlor and kicked my foot to show him how I did it.

"Oh my God," he said in English.

Finally, we understood each other loud and clear.

"Help, Pierre!" I pleaded with him.

"Eh, eh, come." He motioned to me to follow him into the dining room.

We both approached the table and Pierre greeted the Peabodys and the Fikes with his usual cheery manner. "*Bonjour.*"

"Helloooooo, Pierre," *Mr.* Peabody responded.

"*Messieurs, mesdames, comment allez-vous?*"

"*Très bien*," they said in unison. The customers loved to practice their limited French on Pierre.

"Ready to or-dare?" Pierre asked. That is one line from the English language he had down to a science.

Pierre Lebel is quick on his feet. As the party of four studied their menus, he extended his long leg under the table in search of the poop. I watched in amazement as he squatted ever so slightly and inched his foot slowly along, lightly scraping the carpet. If it weren't for accidentally brushing up against Mrs. Fike's foot and mistaking it for the table leg, his operation would have been flawless. She must have thought Mr. Peabody, who was seated right next to her, was playing footsie with her because she looked over at him and gave him a sultry grin. Then, she rubbed back. Pierre finished reciting the evening specials and continued his foot search for the log.

Somehow, some way, that piece of poop came rolling out from under the table. Without missing a beat, Pierre finished taking their order, bent down, and with the white linen napkin that he always had draped over his left wrist scooped the poop and placed it in the pocket of his jacket.

I knew from that moment on that Pierre Lebel was my friend.

Later, back in my apartment, I sat coloring with the girls. Sarah and Issie loved to make pictures for everyone who worked in the restaurant.

All of a sudden an angry pounding on our front door startled all of us. I opened the door to Sergeant Helga Schloygin with a nasty scowl upon her face. *Oh my God, my worst fears have come true*, I thought. *Pierre has turned me in. His true loyalty is to Helga. What was I thinking?*

"Ve have a problem. A vedy *big* problem. Your little mongrel has *rrreally* done it this time!" she said, with her hands pressed firmly into her hips.

"What do you mean, Helga?" I shrunk back and peeked out at her from behind the door.

"Mrs. Houston Norfleet vas seated at table seven in ze front dining room. Vhen she got up to use ze ladies' room, her husband noticed zat she had *dog shit* on ze bottom of her sandal. Pierre is busy cleaning her shoe and rinsing out her nylons. I vill not stand for zis. Vhat are you going to do about zat mutt?"

"What mutt?"

"Zat mutt," she said, and pointed at Princess Grace Kelly, who sat behind me, licking her privates.

"Princess Grace is not a *mutt*." I said, indignantly. "She is registered with the American Kennel Club as a pedigreed Yorkshire Terrier. As a matter of—"

"I don't care if she is the Grand Dam Vorld Champion! She is not velcome in this restaurant again. I had to apologize to Mrs. Norfleet and give her ze rest of her meals for free at Vermont Haus Inn *for ze rest of her life*! How do you expect to pay us ze mortgage if you have to give away meals for free?"

Well, let me just say my blood was rising up to my face. I had had it with Helga! I could either let her have it or keep it inside and let Baker have it.

"Helga, Gracie will never come into your *old, worn-out* restaurant again," was my way of letting her have it. After saying it I immediately felt bad, even though she was much ruder to me than I was to her. *Here I go again, letting people run all over me*.

"See that she doesn't," was the last thing Helga said before stomping through the snow back to the restaurant.

My poor little Gracie, she no more wanted to be outside than I did. "I don't blame you, old girl," I told her. "You're just as Southern as I am." From that point on I decided to cover every corner of the apartment floor with *The Sugartree Gazette*.

When Baker crawled in bed with me that twenty-below-zero night I asked him exactly what happened to Mrs. Norfleet. I thought he'd think it was funny. He just said he didn't want to talk about it and turned over on his side away from me. *That's it, just bury the problem. See if I care*. So I turned on my side facing the other way. I realized he had not reached for me in over a month. So not like him, I thought.

Money was tight and the belt around our bank account wouldn't be getting any looser. When bad weather hit, which was a weekly occurrence, all of our reservations would cancel, leaving us deeper and deeper in the hole. Baker never wanted to talk about it so I made at least one long-distance telephone call to Memphis every evening. The girls always listened for as long as I wanted to talk. I would hang up in a hurry though when Baker came into the room, not wanting to hear him complain about our large phone bill.

The winter wore long and my marriage wore thin. It seemed as though we weren't communicating anymore. Baker didn't want to share any of our free time together, either. He always wanted to go ice fishing or snow ski-ing on his days off. I *liked* to ski. I'd go with him, sometimes. But it was so cold on top of that mountain. I mean bitter cold. When we did ski together, Baker always wanted to go in a group, never just the two of us. The snow bunny and all her wild friends were always whooping it up at the base lodge every Monday. They'd be drunk as skunks by five o'clock that after-noon. Baker thought they were so much fun and that skiing wasn't skiing unless he was with their group. Without fail, he always wanted to stay on the mountain as long as they did. *What happened to all the hype about spending more time with Sarah and Isabella?*

"What's wrong?" I asked him one evening after the restaurant closed. The girls were asleep and we were upstairs in our apartment watching TV. We were on opposite ends of the couch, in front of the Franklin stove, and I waited until the commercial.

"Nothing's wrong." He stared straight at the TV and never bothered to look over.

"We've been married eight years. I know when something's wrong."

"I'm under a lot of stress . . . about money." He whipped his head around in my direction, threw up his arms, and went off in a tirade. "You obviously hate it here—you won't even keep an open mind. You don't get along with Helga. Rolf senses it, you know. I can tell because I work right next to him every night. He's always grumbling in German under his breath. I know he's pissed off about something."

"Do you even care about how I feel? What about me?" I felt myself shrinking under his brutal outburst as I pulled my legs against my chest.

"Sure I do, but I told you from the start that we had to keep the Schloygins around for a year. Can't you just get along with Helga?"

"Can't she just get along with me?"

"She's German, Leelee. She's different than you. Just accept her."

"I'm nice to her. She's the one who's nasty to me." I gritted my teeth to keep from crying. Helga was not worth it.

"She gets along with the other women working in the restaurant. I've never heard Kerri complain about her once. And she's in the restaurant way more than you are."

"You know what, Baker? I'm beginning to think you care more about Kerri than you do me." I parted my legs and leaned in toward him. "You ski with her almost every Monday."

"I don't ski with *just* Kerri, I ski with Kerri and *all* her friends. I ski with you, too, when you put forth the effort to come with us. Have you forgotten that?"

I tried to choose my words carefully, pausing before answering. "It's cold."

"I don't hear anyone else complaining about the cold."

"What about our daughters? You never spend time with them anymore."

"What are you talking about? I watch cartoons with them every morning before school."

"While you run back and forth to the kitchen meeting deliveries, ordering food, and unpacking beer."

"That's my job!" he yelled, and got up and walked out.

As usual, I turned to the girls. I'd sneak into the bathroom and whisper into the phone. As supportive as they always were it seemed every time I called home they were having a ball. I'd hear, "Mimi and Jim are having a huge party Saturday night, we'd give anything if you could be there." Or, "We played Spades at Alice's house last night until two in the morning."

But the worst was when Virginia broke this news to me: "Leelee, I hate to tell you this but Sting was in concert here last night."

"Where!" I screamed. "Why didn't y'all tell me?" All four of us have been in love with that gorgeous hunk of baby-blue-eyed burning love since we were twelve years old and we first heard the Police.

But they didn't have to explain. I knew. They never told me because they already knew it was pointless. I would not be coming home for the concert.

Travel, of course, cost money. Home was not the South anymore, I was reminded. "Home es Vermont now," Helga loved to say. "You betta get used to it."

Chapter Eleven

I woke up thanking God for Roberta Abbott around the first of April. It was the last day of the winter season and one of our houseguests had gotten sick in the middle of the night. Roberta was cleaning up the mess when I walked upstairs in the inn. She was leaning over the toilet and her backside was in full view, revealing a well-defined panty line. Roberta didn't seem like the type to wear string bikini underwear to me. No wonder they kept riding up. They were too small for her booty.

Roberta even smiled when she was scrubbing toilets. Now that really amazed me.

"Well, look at you, you're all dolled up," she said, when I poked my head in the bathroom. "What's the occasion?"

"Nothing really."

"No woman in Vermont looks like that in the wintertime. Are you going somewhere special?"

"No. Well, I mean not that I know of right now."

"Then what in the world?"

I figured I might as well go on and tell her. After all, Roberta was my only girlfriend in Vermont. "I want to look nice for Baker today. It's our anniversary."

Her eyes lit up. "Oh! Now I get it. Why didn't you say so in the first place?"

"I don't know, Baker hasn't mentioned it yet. I'm sure he just wants to surprise me. My legs haven't come out of long pants since I've been in Vermont. Do you think Baker will notice?"

"He'd have to be a bat not to. There aren't many women up here who go around in short skirts, nylons, and heels in the middle of winter," she said, and went right back to her scrubbing. I've got to point out something right here and now. Roberta considered April to be winter.

I took a seat on the edge of the tub. "Do I look silly? Maybe I should go change."

"Nuup. I say wear what you want. Who cares? I wear skirts all the time. I'm just not big on heels."

"I wonder what he's up to." I looked off in a daydream about the evening. "Last year, we went to dinner at Folk's Folly. Oh, Roberta, you would love Folk's Folly. It's a wonderful steak restaurant back home and it has the best creamed spinach you've ever put in your mouth." *I'd give my right baby toe to be back home at Folk's Folly tonight.* "After dinner, we came home and Baker had three presents for me to open. One was a bottle of my favorite bubble bath. The next was a bottle of our favorite champagne, and the last was this beautiful gown from Saks with matching panties to go underneath." I bent down and whispered in her ear. "Promise you won't tell anyone?"

Roberta smiled and held up only two fingers. "Girl Scout's honor."

"The panties are see-through."

Roberta got a huge smile on her face and for a split second it entered my mind she might let it slip to George Clark at the gas station. But it was too late; I had already revealed my secret.

"I bet I know what you two will be up to tonight after the restaurant closes. How about if I look after the girls and you and Baker can spend the night in one of the guest rooms? Would you like that?"

"Roberta! Do you mean it? Would you really spend the night here to-night? That would be wonderful." I reached over to hug her.

"Of course I would. Now, why don't you pick out the room you want and you can surprise the boss man with a bottle of champagne and something sexy for him to wear tonight. They make see-through undies for men, you know."

"Roberta Abbott! Aren't you the sly one?" I smiled at her and lightly pushed her shoulder. "Baker Satterfield would have to be at gunpoint to wear see-through undies, but still, if I know Baker, he's got something lovely planned."

"Well, you two lovebirds have a greet time and don't worry about the girls."

After hugging Roberta again I flew back down the stairs. I could hardly wait for the restaurant rush to be over. I could picture Baker now, fantasizing about me wearing the diamond earrings he was going to finally buy me . . . and nothing else.

I must have spent hours that day getting ready. After all the anguish we had endured over the last few months, I wanted this night to be special. I took a long hot bath, shaved my legs, took forever styling my hair, put on Baker's favorite perfume, and wore the slinkiest dress I had in my closet—even though I froze the whole time I was wearing it. It was black, of course, and the neckline veed in the front and in the back. The cap sleeves were slightly off the shoulder and made of black lace. It was fitted at the waist and the same lace that was on the sleeves was also on the bodice. I had worn the dress to Virginia's last cocktail party and Baker couldn't stop touching me.

When I walked in the kitchen that night everyone looked at me like I was an alien—especially Helga and Kerri. I shrugged it off, though. Number one, Helga would never own a dress like mine. Number two, Kerri would never have anywhere to wear a dress like mine. And number three, I didn't give a hoot what they thought. I knew Baker liked it and that's all that mattered.

Roberta winked at me when I walked in and I noticed Jeb look up from his dishes but then he looked right back down. A little later I caught him staring at me with his mouth open.

Here it was the last night before we closed for Mud Season and dinner was crazy busy. A party of eight local people called right as we were winding down to ask if they could still be served. There was no way we could turn down that kind of business, Baker said. Anniversary or not, it meant a high check and I knew we needed all the money we could get to sustain us through Mud Season.

Unfortunately it was eleven o'clock before that last table left. Baker hadn't mentioned our anniversary all day. But I knew him better than that. He did it on purpose so he could surprise me with a wonderful ending to the day. He called me his cherry on top. He said it was for all kinds of reasons, but I knew my red hair was the primary explanation.

So far, I had managed to keep my plans a secret. I had bananas for Baker and strawberries for me all ready to dip into my delectable homemade chocolate sauce. It was no easy task hiding it from Rolf and Helga, but I had managed to sneak a bottle of Dom Pérignon out of the basement and had it chilling in a bucket on the bedside table of the most beautiful bedroom in the inn. The bed was topped with a canopy, and a feather bed lay on top of the mattress. There was a fireplace in the room and I had asked Jeb to build a fire earlier in the day. All I had to do was light a match to it. This evening was going to be perfect and Lord knows we needed it.

Roberta knew to tell Baker I was waiting on him upstairs when he finished. While I was in *our room* I lit the fire and turned on *Cat Stevens—Greatest Hits* ever so softly. I sprayed lavender water all over the sheets and turned down the bed while singing along to "Wild World."

When midnight rolled around and Baker still had not joined me upstairs, I got anxious and went down to find him. Rolf, Helga, and Kerri were gone, thank goodness, and Jeb was mopping down the floor. Roberta was wiping the counters and Pierre was sipping from his white coffee cup that he always kept hidden away on top of the fridge. I discovered his little secret late one night when I accidentally "bussed" his coffee cup. Pierre drank red coffee that smelled just like our house merlot. No wonder he always slurred his words by the end of the night.

"Roberta, do you know where Baker is?" I peeked around the corner into the kitchen. "I've got something for him," I said with a big smile.

"I thought he was upstairs with you. I told him you were waiting." She gave me an impish wink.

"He's not upstairs. I'll check the apartment. He's probably freshening up."

The bathroom door in our apartment was open and the light was off. Our bedroom was empty and the girls were asleep in their beds. There was no sign of him in our apartment. I went back upstairs and searched every room in the entire inn. I even checked the attic, thinking maybe he had hidden my present up there. No Baker.

Lord God, this is strange. But . . . he'll be right back. Maybe he ran out to . . . to . . . pick up a pizza. That's it. We both love pizza. Okay, pizza and beer work, too. We'll save the champagne and strawberries until my birthday. It's right around the corner.

When I walked back into the kitchen, all three of my newfound comrades were huddled together. No one had seen Baker for at least thirty minutes. Reading the look of panic on my face, Roberta, Pierre, and Jeb helped me search every square inch of the Vermont Haus Inn. Jeb came up with the idea to check the barn where the garbage was kept and all four of us nearly trampled each other trying to make it out the screened porch door at the same time. *Maybe Baker had an accident while taking out the trash and is hollering for help without anyone hearing him,* I thought. Our barn search turned up the same result. No Baker.

Pierre started around back to make sure Baker's Explorer was still there, and the rest of us trailed right behind him. You could have heard snow falling when the three of them looked over at me—after discovering the only car parked behind the barn was my blue BMW.

When he still wasn't back by two o'clock in the morning I called the closest hospital. No Baker. There was no such thing as 911 in Willingham, Vermont, so I called the Manchester Police Department. I held out from calling as long as I could, since up until that moment I was convinced that this whole thing was nothing but a big misunderstanding. I was worried sick, but there had to be some kind of an explanation. Besides, I would be darned if I wanted all the police scanners in Vermont broadcasting the details of a disappearing Baker. We were talked about enough around this town.

The police told me that a person had to be missing for forty-eight hours before they'd investigate. I asked if there had been any wrecks reported around Willingham and the answer was no. The dispatcher let me know that ninety-nine times out of a hundred, the missing person turns up after no more than a domestic squabble. I asked if they could keep it off the scanner. The woman on the phone acted like she didn't know what I was talking about. (Roberta said that was a big fat lie and that more people have scanners around Vermont than they have satellite dishes and not to believe a word she said.)

The police said all I could do was wait. And wait I did. By the phone. By the door. In front of the window. Sometime around four in the morning I couldn't stand it anymore. Fortunately, Roberta had fallen asleep on my couch so I wouldn't have to wake up the girls if I wanted to go looking for Baker. I ran out to my car and took off toward all the local bars in town. I hadn't even been inside any of these places yet, but I knew where they were all the same. Baker's Explorer was nowhere in sight.

Kerri's house was on the way to the local all-nighter, the Moose Head Inn. As I approached her house an ominous feeling returned, one that I had fought over and over. And now, as I faced the possibility, I still had a hard time completing the thought. Could Baker, my one and only, actually be with Kerri? What was it about her that he preferred to me? I knew she was more of a sportswoman than me—that was obvious. And she had long, pretty *straight* hair. *Okay, her figure is amazing, but she cusses all the time and she drinks like a fish and she's not the mother of his children!* I slowed down as I drove past and stared up into her driveway. The house was pitch-dark without a car in sight. I thought about sneaking up and peeking in the windows. But to be honest, even if he was there, I wasn't so sure I was ready to know the truth. After an hour of aimless driving around I headed home, somewhat relieved but still devastated.

All the next day I waited for Baker to come home, and never closed my eyes. I explained to Sarah and Isabella that Daddy was out of town and he'd be back soon. If it weren't for having to keep it together for the girls, I don't know how I would have made it. I tried telling myself there was a logical explanation and he would be walking in the door at any moment.

Purely as a distraction, I stole away to the computer to prepare the payroll. Normally, I would wait until the last minute, but I decided to get it done early. When the computer was finished spitting out the checks, I flipped through each one making sure there were no errors. As soon as I caught sight of a certain name I finally lost all control. Tears welled in my eyes and I burst into sobs. *There's no way Baker would ever cheat on me. He's not that kind of guy. I don't care how pretty and sexy and fish-smart she is.*

Around noon the next day, twelve hours before I could call the police and report Baker missing, I called Roberta at home. She was disappointed to learn Baker wasn't back yet. I asked her if she would mind coming over.

When she arrived at the inn, I let her have her ten minutes to herself but I was waiting right outside the half bath in the kitchen when she finished.

"Roberta, if I ask you something, will you be honest with me?" She hadn't even closed the bathroom door behind her. "It's very hard for me to ask you what I'm about to ask you, but there's something I need to know."

"Why sure, Leelee, I'll be honest with you. What's on your mind?"

I'd rehearsed exactly how I was going to ask her a thousand times, but I just couldn't make myself be that direct. At the last second I chickened out. "Um, Roberta . . . what are you and Moe doing over the break? Got any big plans?"

"Let's see here, Moe's cousins over in White River Junction are having a big hoedown for Easter, and Moe's brother from Rutland will be there, so we're thinking of goin'. I'll probably make a broccoli casserole with Cheez Whiz in it, sprinkled with Ritz crackers on the top, and maybe a macaroni salad. Moe loves raisin pie so I'll—"

"Nice, that's nice, what's . . ." I looked around and twirled my hair, trying not to appear obvious. "What's Kerri doing?"

"Kerri? I think I heard her say she's goin' home to Idaho."

I knew it! No wonder her house was dark. They've run off together to fly-fishing heaven. I so wanted to say something more obvious to her, but I was afraid. "How long will she be gone?"

"She didn't say." I sensed she was catching on but I couldn't be sure. As Roberta strolled back into the kitchen, I followed behind and watched her pull on her panties.

"Say, Roberta, you don't happen to have her parents' number out in Idaho, do you?"

"Can't say as I do."

"What about Jeb? Do you think he knows the number?"

"You'll have to ask him." She turned to face me once she reached the sink. "What's up? Do you think Kerri knows anything about Baker?"

I was already dialing Jeb's home phone and never answered her question. When Jeb's mama picked up she told me he was at work. "No he isn't, Mrs. Duggar; he's not over here," I told her.

"I never said he was at your place. He's busy working at JCW."

Gosh, do you have to be so rude? "Oh, okay, would you mind having him call me right away, please?"

When ten minutes passed and I still hadn't heard from him, I couldn't stand it another second. Just as I was grabbing my coat to run across the street, he walked in the front door. "Jeb! I was just headed your way."

"Mom called me on the intercom at JCW and told me you needed me. What's up?" He was twisting that fool mustache again.

Before diving right into my inquisition, I needed a little clarification. "Wait a minute, y'all have an *intercom* at Jeb's Computer World?"

"Yuup, Mom picked it up for me at a tag sale a few weeks ago. The woman who sold 'em swore they could pick up reception over a mile away. She bought 'em for her kid for Christmas but he never liked 'em. Best pair of walkie-talkies I've ever seen."

"That's . . . that's . . . well, good for JCW," was all I knew to say until I forced out the words, "Jeb, I was wondering, do you by any chance know how to get in touch with Kerri in Idaho?"

"Nuup, can't say as I do. Why? Something wrong?"

"Oh no, no, no, nothing's wrong. Except the fact that I haven't seen my husband in almost forty-eight hours!"

"You don't think Kerri knows any—"

"Not at all, I just thought she might have overheard Baker talking on the phone making plans. Or something like that." Now I'd really done it. Jeb was definitely on to me. *Great, that's just* great, I thought.

Out of nowhere and right at that exact moment I could have sworn I heard the faint echo of Kerri's sickening cheery voice in the kitchen. I practically shoved Jeb to get around him and flew back to where I knew Roberta was fixing lunch for the girls.

"Roberta, I thought I heard Kerri."

"You did," answered the woman who had stolen my husband. She was standing there in the flesh and helping herself to a cup of *my* coffee. She must have slipped in through the back door. My competitor studied the stunned look upon my face and then had the audacity to say, "You look weird. Like you're surprised to see me." *Northerners are so blunt it makes me sick.*

I was dying to barrage her with questions, but how? "I just didn't expect to see you here, that's all." *I know she's hiding him.*

"Don't you think I need my paycheck? You know how it is up here. I need every penny I can get to make it through the next two months."

"Of course you do, don't mind me. When are you running off? For Idaho, I mean?" *Stay calm, Leelee. Get yourself together or she'll see right through you.*

"Probably not for another week."

That's odd, you would think they would want to get out of town immediately.

"Hey," Kerri had the nerve to ask, "are you and Baker coming to Sugartree tomorrow? This is the last weekend the slopes are open. Since the conditions are so icy, they're letting all the locals ski for free."

Stop trying to throw me off track. I couldn't hold back any longer. I had to say *something.* "I haven't seen Baker in two days."

Her hair was pulled straight back in a high ponytail. Brunette and gorgeous. *Baker loves brunettes.* "You have got to be kidding."

"Would I kid about that?"

"No, I mean, God no. Where do you think he is?"

"I don't know. I was thinking he might—" I wanted to scream at her but instead I burst out crying.

Kerri surprised me, I have to say. She put her hand on my back and drew me a little closer to her. "Leelee, I don't know what to say. I'm sorry. Do you have any idea where he could be?"

I wanted to say: I thought he was with you. "No, and I can't report him missing until tonight. I know you two had gotten close. Did he say anything you could share with me? I'm desperate for any information."

"No. He always acted like he was so together and had the restaurant thing down. He sure had me fooled."

Could she be telling the truth? Is there any way I can trust this Yankee broad? I bet she'd lie to me in a second to snag Baker. I was so confused my head was about to bust.

Pierre slipped into the kitchen with Gracie following right behind. Helga would have flipped if she had seen Gracie in the big kitchen, but thank the Lord she was in a foreign country by now.

I could tell Pierre was excited about his trip to France because his hair practically glowed from the jet-black Lady Clairol he must have freshly applied that morning. The black stain on the collar of his white shirt was more proof the amateur hairstylist had been hard at it.

"*Bonjour*, Leelee. Baker es back?"

"No, he's not," I said. I was wringing my hands and pacing back and forth in front of the coffeepot.

Jeb had slipped out to the mailbox and he wandered back into the kitchen whistling "Please Mr. Postman." I was ready to slap him. My nerves were raw enough without his annoying habit. Even Pierre glared at Jeb like he wanted to take his head off.

Our eyes met and Jeb shot me back a curious look. I thought it was because I had come too close to letting my true feelings about Kerri slip and he was letting me know that he was on to me.

Truth was he knew something I didn't. He had obviously nosed through my mail because lying right on top of the large stack of catalogs and bills was a letter intended for my eyes only. The word PERSONAL was hand-written next to my name. My kismet lay in the hands of Jeb Duggar. As he passed the stack of mail over to me his whistling got louder and more in-flective.

I clutched the mail to my chest and staggered out to the red-checked dining room, where I slinked down into a chair at one of the tables. There was no stamp; it had been hand-placed in my mailbox. My heart was beat-ing out of my chest as I slowly opened the white envelope with the inn's return address printed on the back. My small hands shook while I un-folded the one-page letter penned by the man I had loved since the tenth grade.

By now everyone had congregated around the table next to the one where I was sitting. They weren't even trying to hide their nosiness. I looked up at all of them and they all nodded their heads in unison, as if to say: Go on, get it over with. Each sat in silence as I read the letter to myself.

Dear Leelee,

By now I'm sure you're worried sick about me. I wish I could have found a better way to break this news to you, but I could not think of a better way to save my life. There's no easy way to say this but this whole thing with the inn—and us—is not working out.

I met someone. Actually, she's not just someone; she's amazing. I know what you're thinking. But you're wrong—you don't know her. Her name is Barb. She owns Powder Mountain and she believes I'm the guy to turn it around. It's not that the resort is in horrible shape but she wants to make it the premiere ski resort in Vermont. I won't be doing any cooking. I'll be the director of operations—a position I'm much more qualified for in the first place.

If you're honest with yourself, you'll be relieved when you get this letter. You hate Vermont. You hated it from the minute you got here. Now you can finally go home. If I were you, I'd use Ed Baldwin again to sell the place. Hey, he sold it once, he can do it again. Keep the money. It's all yours.

I'm not even sure what I want you to tell Sarah and Isabella at this point.

It's not like I don't love the three of you. I do. It's just that Barb makes me feel
like I've always wanted to feel. She loves sports, she loves the outdoors, and
best of all she thinks I hung the moon.

It's not you—it's me.

Baker

"She thinks I hung the moon." I echoed his words out loud before folding the letter and placing it back inside the envelope. *And no mention of*
our anniversary. When I looked up, everyone was leaning in toward me,
waiting for an answer. Here four strangers were sharing in the most devas-
tating moment of my life, instead of Kissie, Alice, Mary Jule, and Virginia. I barely even knew these quirky people but they were all I had. One
by one each of them came up and hugged me like they sincerely felt my
pain.

I knew they were dying to know what the letter said, but I didn't feel
like talking. "Y'all will have to excuse me. I think I need to lie down for a
while."

I honestly don't remember much of the next twenty-four hours. I do remember praying to God as hard as I could that it was all a dream and to
not let it be true. The faces of my precious little daughters peering at me
from my side of the bed are vivid in my mind. The voice of Roberta calling
to them from upstairs rings a bell. My soul felt like it had left my body and
I could no longer feel my flesh. When the nighttime came I remember
screaming out to God and Daddy, Mama and Kissie and anyone else who
would possibly listen to "get me out of here." I was weak, so weak that I lay
motionless in the bed. I began to fall into a tunnel that kept getting narrower and narrower, deeper and deeper. There seemed to be no end to the
tunnel. Only a dark, bottomless pit. I prayed to God for peace and slumber.
He answered and with His mercy I slept.

Roberta was upstairs in our apartment with the girls when I finally stumbled out of my fog.

"There's your mommy, girls. I told you she wouldn't sleep all day."

"What time is it?" I peered out the window at the gray, overcast April sky.

"Three thirty."

"*Three thirty!* My gosh, I've been asleep longer than I thought. I never ate lunch."

"Lunch, dinner, breakfast, and lunch again. Hon, you've been in a state of shock. Been in your room goin' on twenty-six hours now."

I sat down on the wicker sofa in the sitting room, outside the bedrooms.

"Are you okay, Mommy?" Issie jumped in my lap and covered me with kisses. "Me and Sarah tried to wake you up. You were sleeping tight."

"Yes, baby, I was sleeping tight. But I'm wide awake now." One look at Sarah's little face jolted me back to reality. "Sarah! How'd you get to school?"

"Roberta."

I glanced over at Roberta with both "thank you" and "I'm sorry" written all over my face.

"We're going over to Erica Grover's house," Sarah said, crawling up on my lap to join her sister. "Is that okay? Roberta said it was okay. Mrs. Grover will be here any minute."

"Pat called a little while ago, and I didn't think you'd mind," Roberta said, "seein' the state you're in. I thought you could probably use the break."

"Yeah, I guess so." I relented, but it wasn't without alarm. The thought of another mouse helping itself to my daughter's dinner was enough to push me on over the cliff.

Pat Grover was rapping on the door five minutes later. I thanked her for inviting the girls and told her I'd pick them up in a couple of hours. I watched from the window as they sloshed through the leftover snow and crawled into Pat's Subaru. Stay away from chocolate cake, I should have reminded them, but I couldn't say it.

While I was talking with Pat, Roberta must have slipped into my bedroom to make up the bed. When I saw what she had done, I gave her a huge hug and broke down crying all over again. She was taking care of me.

"Guess what, Roberta?" I reached across the bed to the windowsill and grabbed another Kleenex. "It doesn't look like Baker's coming home at all."

"I heard."

I whipped my head around. "You know about Baker? How? Is it on the scanner? Don't tell me it's been broadcast all over southern Vermont already."

"Oh, it's been broadcast alreet, but I didn't hear it on the scanner. Heard it from Betty Sweeney."

"*Betty Sweeney!* How does *she* know?" Upon hearing that, my tears stopped, and with arms flailing I thrashed out into the sitting room.

Roberta was on my heels. "Well, I'll tell you. Betty got an earful when she filled up her car at George's this mornin'. Called me as soon as she got to the town clerk's office."

"Don't tell me that. How in the world does George Clark know already?"

"George told Betty that a certain Ford Explorer with a Tennessee tag stopped for gas two days ago. Some buxom blonde was driving and paid for the gas with her own credit card. George recognized the name right away."

"Was her name Barb?"

"Yuup, Barb Thurmond."

"Does George know her?"

"Not personally, but he knows of her. She's a *rich* divorcée. Her ex is a powerful man on Wall Street and she got Powder Mountain in the settlement. Seems her and all her rich friends from New York City been skiing at Sugartree for years. George says she's got more money than God."

"Really? More money than God, huh?"

"Yuup. George also told Betty that Barb Thurmond looks amazing for fifty and—"

"Wait a minute, *she's fifty!*" I threw my arms up in the air and fell out on the sofa.

".Yuup, but George swore she looks closer to thirty-eight." Roberta put her hand aside her mouth, leaned down toward me, and whispered, "Thanks to a skilled surgeon in New York City."

"HOW WOULD HE KNOW THAT?" I shrieked.

"He's got his sources."

"I don't know what's worse. The fact that she's fifty or that I live in a town where the gas station owner is privy to the fact that she's had plastic surgery!" I held my face in my hands. "This can't be happening." *And what galaxy am I visiting again? My husband has just left me for a fifty-year-old Yankee divorcée with tons of money, counterfeit bosoms, and a fake face? Alice Garrott will never survive the phone call.* "Don't tell me anything else, Roberta, I don't think I've got the stomach for it right now." Roberta followed me as I stumbled back into my bedroom.

"Of course you don't," Roberta said, rubbing my shoulder with one hand and digging at her bottom with the other. "Say, I've been thinking. You don't need Baker. You're going to make it just fine. You've gut all of us; we'll help you make a go of the place."

"That's sweet of you, but I can't even think about making a go of the place. I just wanna go home. That's all I'm thinking about. It's the only peace I've got right now." I crawled back on top of my bed and turned around to face her. "Please understand. It has nothing to do with you, Jeb, or Pierre. Y'all have been very kind to me. It's just that I don't belong up here."

"Why, sure you do." Roberta could hardly fit in between the bed and the wall. Her right hip scraped against the footboard as she bent down to pick up my tennis shoes on the floor.

"This is not my home. I feel like an interloper trespassing on someone else's property. Surely Ed Baldwin, *the* real estate tycoon, can hang one more Sold sign in the yard by the time we open for the summer season." Just thinking about going home made the stress subside a little.

She stood back up and backed her way to the closet, placing my shoes on the floor behind the curtain. "Ed's the guy to make it happen."

"I might need your help with the girls over the next couple of days. I've got a lot of planning and packing to do. And so many phone calls to make. Are you busy?"

"Pooh. What are you talkin' about? It's Mud Season. I can use all the extra money I can get. Moe's not working during the Thaw, neither. You have to moonlight in Vermont or starve!"

Okay, who to call first? Virginia? Alice? Gosh no, I may never hear the end of the ranting and raving. It's Mary Jule. She won't be happy with Baker one bit, but she'll at least be sweet about it.

Then it dawned on me. Kissie was the person I really needed. Dialing her number, the sickness in my gut returned and the tears sprung up again as soon as I heard her soothing and familiar "Hello."

"Kissie." I struggled to get her name out.

"Is that you, baby?"

"Yes, ma'am."

"What's makin' you cry, baby? Tell ole Kissie what's wrong."

"It's Baker."

"Baker? He sick?"

"No, ma'am."

"Then what's wrong with him?"

"He's gone."

"Gone? Where to?"

"I don't know."

"You don't know?"

"No, but I know this. He's got a *girlfriend*," I wailed into the phone.

"A who?"

"A girlfriend," I cried.

"You don't mean it? Lawd have mercy alive, baby. Somebody need to kick his backside good and hawd 'til his brain start up again. Your po' daddy and mama be turning circles in their caskets if they knew what Baker be up to."

"Are you ready for the most unbelievable part? *She's fifty!*"

"Now I know you pullin' my leg."

"Nope." *Nope? What was I saying? One change of a vowel and I'd be sounding like a Vermonter. Get me outta here.*

"What could Baker want with a woman sixteen years older than him?"

"Money. She's filthy rich. You know what, Kissie? Daddy might have killed Baker if he were still alive. Can't you just see Daddy now, busting into Satterfield State Farm and letting Mr. Satterfield have it? As if Mr. Satterfield would have had anything to do with it. They'd be duking it out and rolling around on the floor."

Kissie let out one of her infectious, hearty belly laughs that I'd grown to love so much. It made me fall out laughing, too, and I felt a tiny bit better.

"Can't you just hear Daddy? 'Sattafield, that no count son of yours has messed with the wrong man.'"

"He'd be all talk. Your daddy wouldn't have the foggiest idea what to do in a fight."

We talked for more than an hour and as always Kissie made my spirits rise. But it wasn't until I was tucking the girls in that night that I had any real relief at all. Aurora borealis suddenly lit the way to my Southern world. *I could be home by Friday!* Why should I wait? There was no one to stop me. I could make all the listing arrangements with Ed Baldwin from home in Memphis just as easily as I could from Willingham.

*Now there's no need to phone my friends at all. I'll just surprise them instead. Let's see, if I hurry I can be home for Virginia's birthday. I'll show up, unannounced, at her birthday lunch at the club. Woohoo! The girls and I are out of here to*morrow.

I found my suitcases up in the attic. While I was packing I decided to call Kissie back to let her know I would be home in three days. I was practically singing this time when she answered.

"Guess what, Kissie." I didn't even stop to say hi.

"What is it, baby?"

"I'm coming home!"

"You don't mean it."

"I'll be there sometime on Friday."

"How long can you stay?"

"The rest of my life," I told her, dancing into the sitting room to empty out my drawers.

Kissie started to laugh all over again. I explained my plans about handling everything from Memphis. She let me blow off more steam and quietly listened to every word I said.

"I just can't wait to get home," I told her, certainly not expecting her next response.

"No, baby, you cain't come home yet. You not suppose to run off and leave things the way they are now. You suppose to get your business straight first. Your daddy done worked too hawd for you to run off and leave behind everything he lef' you. The time is not right."

"But *Kissie*," I pleaded, "I can always come back and get my furniture later. And besides, at this point, I don't care about the business. I just need you and Virginia and Mary Jule and Alice. I've got to come home, Kissie, I can't stand it here a day longer."

"My people always tol' me, 'You can stay in Hell a little while, long as you know you're gettin' out.' You won't be there forever, baby. But you cain't leave all your fine things up there in *Vermont*. Not your business, neither. Now don't you be feeling sorry for yourself. It don't help a thing. Your daddy always tol' you, you was a fighter. When you was a little girl, he used to say, 'Leelee be destined for greatness, she can do anything she puts her mind to' and you can! Now you go on and get your business straight first, Memphis ain't goin' nowhere."

We talked a little while longer and I finally told her good night. Somewhere, in a far-off corner of my mind, something told me she was right. I didn't want to hear it, though, least of all from her. I wanted to hear her say, Come on home, baby, you don't belong up there nohow. It'll be okay; Kissie take good care of you and your little girls. *Oh God, Kissie, I want you to take care of me, just like when I was a little girl. I need you now more than ever.*

I could hear Daddy's voice, too, somehow echoing Kissie's words of wisdom. "My baby's a fighter. Don't let anyone get the best of you. You can get through this, pull yourself up by your bootstraps and *be* somebody."

Chapter Twelve

"Surely nor'easters don't come in April." That's what I told Roberta when she called to report the weather forecast on April 22. She said, "Nor'easters *usually* don't come in April, but you never know."

Pierre was in France, Roberta was at home with Moe, and Jeb had ventured over to Maine to visit some relatives. The only people that were left at the Vermont Haus Inn were my little girls and me. And Princess Grace Kelly, of course.

When the four of us woke up Monday morning, I took one peep out the window and through the top left pane I could see only glimpses of life on the outside. Trees, rooftops, and telephone poles were my only proof that I wasn't living in Antarctica. There was at least four more feet of snow camped out at my doorstep. Thank God the door swung inside or I swear we would have all been housebound until May.

And with Jeb out of town, my driveway would not be getting plowed. I called his house anyway, hoping Mrs. Duggar would tell me that Jeb had come back from Maine early. Instead she gave me the number of a Bud Duke, another woodchuck in town, who "*might* be able to help yous."

I called immediately; my girls were hungry for breakfast. A woman answered the phone and tried to size up the situation. "Bud's been out since three this morning trying to keep up with the snow. If he had known you was out there, he would have plowed you two or three times already. Goin' to be quite a job to clear the snow for you now. But I'll get him on the radio and let him know he's gut a new customer."

"Thank you, I really appreciate this. Jeb Duggar usually plows for me but he's out of town."

"We require at least three foot of clearance around your car. Make sure it's done 'fore he gets there, Bud's on a tight schedule."

"Will do and thank you," I said, and hung up. I wasn't sure what she meant so I called her right back. "Hi, it's Leelee again, sorry to bother you, but I'm not really sure what you mean about making sure my car's got a three-foot clearance."

"Ain't it covered in snow?"

"Yes. Well, actually, it's buried in the snow."

"Then you'll need to shovel around it so the plow can get up to it, won't you?"

You don't have to be so rude about it. "That makes sense," I said. "I was wondering, though, do you think he'll be here any time soon? I have to feed my children breakfast, and I've run out of milk."

"Probably not 'fore noon. Lots more folks signed up 'fore you did. You're at the end of the list," she said, and hung up.

Shovel around the car? I never thought about it before now. Guess what, no one ever once mentioned that to me, either.

Even the schools were closed that day. After feeding the girls oatmeal for breakfast, minus the milk, I put *The Jungle Book* into the VCR. Keeping them occupied while I shoveled the "three foot of clearance" was crucial. I was guessing it might take me the full ninety minutes of the movie.

All dressed up in my ski suit, I set out to rescue my poor car. But I never made it that far. Think about it. When there's four new feet of snow on the ground, you can't just skip out the door. It's like wading through Jell-O. You have to lift your legs as high as they can go and stretch them out as far as they can reach to make any progress at all. After ten minutes of walking like that, trust me, you want to scream—especially when you look up and realize your car is still *forty feet away*. Once I even tried diving across the snow but all that did was add more ice pebbles to my hat.

During the last nor'easter, Jeb, Baker, and Pierre had stayed outside all day shoveling and snowblowing. I was inside making hot chocolate having no idea of the goings-on outside. Bitter truth was this: The only way over to my car was via a huge, red, rectangular-shaped shovel. Jeb always kept one propped up against each door. Looking back on it now, I guess it was a miracle that I'd made it four months without even touching a snow shovel.

So my luck had officially run out. I had no choice but to go for it. *This isn't so bad*, I thought—prematurely—when I shoved my first dent into the snow and lifted a huge load. It took both arms for me to dump a big pile off to the side. I had no idea snow was so heavy. Even so I was bound and determined and I began creating a maze with white walls on either side. Every few minutes I would stop to admire my handiwork.

But there was one big ole problem. It was approaching eleven forty-five, the snowplow was due to arrive in fifteen minutes, and when I looked behind I had only cleared a four-foot trail to my car, which was still over thirty feet away. Never mind the three-foot clearance that I had to shovel once I got to my car.

Totally frustrated, I returned to the house. Unfortunately my presence distracted the girls from their movie and they started begging to come out and play with me in the snow.

"I want to make a snow girl," Sarah began with a twinkle in her eye.

"Me too," said Isabella, jumping up and down.

I covered my hand over the receiver. "Just a second, girls, Mommy's on the phone. Hi, this is Leelee Satterfield again, I was wondering if Bud could push my appointment back an hour or so, I'm *still* shoveling!"

"He's so far behind, he probably won't be to your house 'fore four o'clock anyway."

"Oh. Well, hmmm, I have no bread or milk in the house, but I guess it can wait until then. I'll just see him around four. Thanks."

"Be sure and have that car shoveled out, he's on a tight schedule," the woman said.

"I will," I said, with a touch of irritation.

When I hung up the phone, Baloo the Bear was singing "The Bare Necessities" to an empty room and Sarah and Issie were by the back door tugging on their snowsuits. Every time the girls played outside I had them so bundled up they could hardly move. Their little arms stuck straight out due to all the extra layers.

"Mommy, will you make a snow girl with us?" Isabella pleaded, as she waddled outside along my path.

"No, first I want to go sledding. Then we'll make a snow girl. Where's my sled?" Sarah asked, tugging on my sleeve.

"Hold on a minute, girls, I've got to shovel out our car so the snowplow man can get our driveway all clean."

"No, I want you to make a snow girl." While Isabella begged and begged, I noticed her little freckled nose was already red.

"I know," Sarah said. "We can make a snow house. Come on, Isabella."

The situation went from grave to ghastly. The snow was way taller than Isabella and, in some spots, taller than Sarah's head. But my strong-minded daughters were determined, *at first*, to frolic in the snow. Glaring problem number two: The only place they could actually play was in the path I'd already cleared and it was getting filled up again from their attempts to build a snow house. Every time I'd get back to my shoveling, someone would start crying from getting stuck in the snow.

Let me stop right here and give all Southerners some headline news. Snow and little children *do not mix*. It's not a winning combination. There is nothing fun or the least bit enjoyable about it at all.

By this time my blood had reached the boiling point and I ended up raising my voice and demanding that Sarah and Isabella go back to their movie. Amid tears and drippy noses, they stomped back inside. "I'll be in soon, just finish your movie."

For the next *two hours* I shoveled my way to the car, amid various interruptions from my cranky little girls. They were hungry, they were bored, and they wanted me to read them a story. The longer I shoveled, the crankier they became. At one point I looked up to see Isabella in the window with big tears rolling down her cheeks and a wide-open mouth. "MOMMY" was all I could make out in between the long breaths she held in as she rapped on the window.

There was no telling what kind of mischief Sarah was up to, as I hadn't heard a peep out of her. Nanny Princess was keeping watch, I'm sure, safely inside where it was warm. She never even considered a stroll outdoors. *That's another reason I have to get to the store*, I thought. *More newspapers.*

Actually, it was a good thing I was working as hard as I was or I would have never made it through the frigid temperature. It never got above five degrees that day. My toes were completely numb (I was out of toe heaters), and my fingers felt like they were hiding somewhere in my gloves. With all the oomph I had left in my body, I heaved and hoed, pushed and pulled, trying my best to shovel an alleyway around my car—with three feet of clearance.

As I firmly gripped the shovel handle, my mind drifted to that familiar place. I started obsessing, for the one thousandth time, about *him*. Why is this my job? *I never asked for this. I had no desire to ever move up here. I DID IT FOR YOU*, my mind shrieked. *Alice has been right about you all these years. You do love people with money, and the fatter the wallet the better.*

There was no way around it. Husband or not, my life had to go on. Shoveling snow was only the beginning. I was going to have to operate a business, manage my money, *buy my own cars*, and raise my little girls all on my own.

"She's amazing, huh?" I finally screamed out to the frosty air. "I'll show you amazing. And she loves the outdoors! Oh, really? And does she still love the outdoors when the silicone in her huge, fake boobs *starts freezing*?"

I pushed my glove back to look at my watch. Four o'clock. At best, I could squeeze around the car with a half foot of room, *if* I was lucky. But, at least I had done it! Actually, when I leaned back and looked at it I was kind of proud of my handiwork. I wanted to pull up a chair and sit back and stare at it, to tell you the truth. But the more I stared at it, the more obvious it became that something wasn't right. On the hood, the trunk, and the top of my car, four feet of snow was still heaped up. That snow had to come off. And the only place it could go was straight down into my two-hours'-worth-of-labor alley!

I snapped. This wild woman took over my body. She started running around the car and cussing at the snow, waving the shovel above her head. "Get the hell away from my car," the wild woman screamed. "I want to go home. Do you hear me? *Home.* Somebody get me out of this godforsaken winter wasteland and back to civilization! Who's ever heard of snow falling in the dead of spring anyway?" Frantically, this crazy person started pushing the snow off the car, paying no mind to the fact that my alley was filling back up at a rate of speed ninety times faster than I had cleared it away!

Then the wild woman hurled the snow shovel as far as her strength could manage and stormed back down the narrow, barely passable, crooked path and into the house, kicking her snow boots off. One hit the sitting room ceiling and fell back down and clobbered her on the head. That made her even madder and she ripped off her snowsuit and flung her hat and gloves around the room. Without hesitation, she punched in the seven numbers to Duke Excavating and had the nerve to use my name.

"Mrs. Duke?" she said, when a woman answered.

"Yes."

"Leelee Satterfield calling."

"He's still backed up, Ms. Satterfield. I suspect now he won't get to your place b'fore five—"

"Here's the deal, Mrs. Duke. I presume you are Mrs. Duke, is that right?"

"I am."

"Good. I don't care what time he gets here. All I know is I'm not shoveling any more snow today. I've spent *hours* creating an alley around my car. And it took me four hours before that to even *reach* my car. And, when I finished, I realized that there was as much snow *on top* of my car as there was around it! Would you like to know what happened to all that snow on top of my car, Mrs. Duke?" The lunatic didn't even give Mrs. Duke a chance to get a word in edgewise. "I'll tell you. *It landed in my alley!* Now, I don't care what you have to do to get my car out of this driveway. You can bring in a backhoe if you like or you can send out an eighteen-wheeler tow truck.

BUT I AM NOT SHOVELING ANY MORE SNOW TODAY, THE NEXT DAY, OR THE DAY AFTER THAT! Please, just get this snow out of my life. Don't y'all realize that it's April, for God's sake?"

"We don't normally get out of the truck to shovel," the woman said in a monotone.

"Every job has a price tag. That's one thing I've learned for sure up here."

"Well, I'll see what we can do and get back with you."

"Thank you very much," the wild woman said. "You can call this your good deed *for life!*"

When Bud Duke finally arrived at 7:00 P.M., dusk had fallen over the Vermont Haus Inn. It was quiet as can be outside when his truck lights lit up my little car to free her at last. Another guy was in the truck with him and within twenty short minutes the two men had cleared a new three-foot alley around my car. His snowplow pushed the snow in my driveway to new heights, creating a snowy fort that made it impossible to see the road.

Much to my surprise, the man took pity on me. When he handed me a bill for his labor, it wasn't the two hundred dollars I had expected. He only charged me fifty.

"Gosh, if I had known it would only be fifty bucks, I would have had you here a long time ago, Bud," I said.

"Well, we don't normally do this, Mrs. Satterfield, but I could tell by your path and the way you slung your snow shovel you hadn't done much shovelin' b'fore today."

"You are extremely perceptive. I've never shoveled snow in my entire life. And I don't plan to ever do it again."

The look on his face told the story. He didn't say anything but I knew what he was thinking: *Yeah right, sister. Not if you're goin' to live around here.*

But I'm not, Bud Duke, I said to myself. *I'll never live through, nor will I ever visit, another Vermont winter again.*

Chapter Thirteen

Mud Season, as it is affectionately called, begins somewhere around mid-April or the first of May. The Thaw is another term the Vermonters use to portray this dreadful time of year. When the sun finally decides to shine, and the temperatures rise above freezing, the remainder of the snow starts melting and it seeps back into the ground. It creates one big slosh of a mess. Mud is absolutely everywhere and it covers everything—the yard, the car, the floors, the walls, your clothes. It's worse than kudzu.

To get from your house to your car, you have to walk tightrope style—across wooden boards stretched across the walkways—because of course, even the walkways are covered in mud. I broke down and ordered a pair of L.L.Bean duck boots and they never left my feet the months of April, May, and the better part of June. Every time I performed my circus act from the car to the house, and the boards wiggled and jiggled under my feet from the pressure of my weight in the mud, I was glad I had the boots.

The winter never seemed to want to disappear. The mounds of snow, piled up under the eaves of the roof, had the stubbornness of an old stain. They took forever to go away. And by this time of year the snow is filthy. What's left on the side of the road is black from the car exhaust and road grime. The Currier and Ives image of Vermont is replaced with dingy, dark, and depressing yuck. I decided to go on and unpack my shorts and sundresses anyway. I don't know, just looking at them in my closet gave me the hope that warm weather was on the way.

An even scarier thought than the treacherous winter weighed heavy on my mind. The idea of breaking the news about Baker to my mortgage holders was enough to make me sick. After all, they had handpicked the Satterfields themselves. They had chosen Baker and me to carry on their legacy. There was only one courageous way to handle the situation. I'd let Ed Baldwin do it. *You owe me that much . . . you asshole.*

I asked Ed to meet me for coffee at the only place in town to get a cheeseburger, JoJo's. Biggest problem with JoJo's was it was the hot spot, with George Clark and every local in town eating there almost every day. The booths and tables were close together, making it very difficult to carry on a confidential conversation. It was the kind of place where the people eating are so bored with one another that people-watching was the pastime of choice. Any time I walked into JoJo's everyone stopped and looked up at the same time. Blank stares from forty pairs of eyes, then all at once they'd drop back down to their meals.

Roberta came over to watch Issie while I stole away to JoJo's. Ed was already seated when I arrived. He stood up, offered me a phony hug, and then scooted back into a conspicuous middle booth. A cola drink was waiting for me on my side of the table. (Let me stop right here and say that everyone in Vermont refers to Cokes as sodas. It is only for clarification that I refer to my Coke as a cola drink.) My first sip let me know that Ed Baldwin still hadn't gotten my order right. Not only was it a Pepsi, this one was a diet. I hadn't seen ole Ed in nearly five months so when he opened his mouth to speak, I was taken aback all over again by his extra-thick veneers.

"You're looking well, Leelee. Vermont life must be agreeing with you," he said.

I wanted to say: Is that so? I'm as pale as a ghost. It's May, you know, and *May is still winter up here*. And, my husband has left me for another woman. But as usual I didn't confront him. "That's kind of you to say," I lied.

I made sure to keep my voice down, sometimes even whispering. After we ordered, I exposed the turmoil in my life, even though I was sure he already knew.

He *seemed* genuinely concerned. "I'm sorry to hear this. I thought Baker was gung ho about the restaurant business." Ed had to keep wiping his fingers on the napkin next to his plate due to slathering his french fries in ketchup.

"So did I." I sat glumly in the booth and stared down at my cheese-burger.

Obviously he didn't know how to handle my grief because his tone changed from disturbed to upbeat. "So you say he's the OM at Powder Mountain now, huh? How's it working out for him?"

"I . . . sshhh," I whispered, and pressed my hand up and down to let him know that I would appreciate him keeping his voice down. "I don't know and I don't really want to know." *Oh yes I do.* "How much do you know about Barb Thurmond?" I whispered, even lower.

"I only know what I've heard on the streets." He leaned in and whispered back. "She's divorced from a super-wealthy guy, a Wall Street mogul. They were real jet-setters from what I hear. Her ex still lives in New York and—I should pay her a visit sometime." He sounded like he had just come up with an idea of how to strike gold.

Talking about outrageous. Here I was in the middle of a disaster and this ne'er-do-well was planning his next commission check. Looking back on it now, I should have gotten up and walked out on the spot. But all I could think about was getting the place sold right away, and I thought surely Ed could find another sucker.

Ed, the slick wheeler-dealer, suggested a list price of $450,000. That was $65,000 more than we paid in the first place, a chance to recoup some of our expenses. Ed, of course, had a blank contract in his briefcase and filled out the listing agreement right there on the spot. I signed a contract giving him an exclusive on the property for one year. He reassured me it would never take that long to sell and that it was just a formality.

"May I ask you a favor?" I had just signed my name to the contract, so I felt like this was the time to get what *I* wanted.

"Of course, you may ask me a favor. What else can I do for you?"

"Would you mind breaking the news to Rolf and Helga for me, about the sale of the inn? I'm sure they'll hear about Baker as soon as they fill up their car, if they haven't already received a cross-Atlantic phone call by now. But I would so appreciate it if you told them that I'm gonna be selling the inn. Rolf is nice enough to me, but Helga's another story. She can't stand me for some reason."

"Huh," Ed said, seemingly confused. "I'm surprised to hear that. I've never heard of anyone else having problems with Helga. But, be that as it may, I'll go over to their home personally when they return from Germany. How's that?"

"That's perfect. Thank you. That's one mountain I don't want to climb."

"My pleasure." I knew it was his pleasure all right. He was going to make a fat commission on the same property twice in the same year. "I'll be contacting you soon with potential buyers. Keep the place in shipshape condition. You never know when I'll call with only a moment's notice."

I wanted to say: Don't forget to brag about the superb owners' quarters in your ad, but I knew I didn't have to.

The last thing I wanted was for it to appear to be a distress sale, even though everyone involved knew it absolutely, positively *was* a distress sale.

May was here and the girls were finally, *finally* able to play outside without snowsuits, hats, scarves, gloves, and boots. Actually, I take that back. We still had to wear jackets and boots and toe heaters but it was still wonderful to be outside.

Notwithstanding the fact that my departure was drawing near, the garden was still beckoning me. Crocuses were popping up and the peeping heads of the daffodil foliage were making their first show of the season. It looked like February back home instead of May to me, but I was elated to finally get a glimpse of color. White was the only color I'd seen in Vermont for months—white houses, white snow, white skies, white people, Rolf's white beard—I surely had had enough of white. Back home, the azaleas and dogwoods had finished blooming by this time and the leaves on the trees had long since popped out.

"Something's stinging me." Sarah ran toward me, crying. "Right here on my neck." When she pulled her hand away her little fingers were spotted with blood.

"What in the world?" I pulled up her dark wavy ponytail to see the back of her neck. Seconds later, Issie had the same complaint only she could hardly get a breath from crying so hard. Upon examination I learned that undeniably both the girls' little necks had been bitten. But by what? Mosquitoes don't draw blood, and neither do bees nor hornets. (The real reason for this unexpected disturbance, I would soon learn, would have been enough to put any relocated Southerner in bed for a week.)

"It's gonna be fine, sweet girls. Go on back to play. It was just a freak accident." The girls headed back to the swing set and I got back to digging.

I was daydreaming about my backyard in Memphis when something stung the back of *my* neck. I jerked my hand around almost as fast as it happened to try and catch the predator. No luck. It kept on hurting but I kept on digging—until it happened again. This time when I touched my neck, and blood stained my muddy fingers, I did the only thing I knew to do. I called the definitive authority on the state of Vermont herself, Roberta Abbott. She and Moe were to be spending the day chopping wood to store up for *next* winter. I told Roberta that it was still *this* winter as far as I was concerned. Lucky for me she was inside getting a drink of water and answered on the first ring.

"Roberta! Have y'all started chopping yet?"

"You bet we have. Me and Moe have chopped two cords already. What's wrong? You sound upset."

"I am upset. The girls and I were outside no less than five minutes when we were bitten by some vampire bugs. All three of us have blood dripping down our necks. Do you have them at your house?"

"Welcome to spring in Vermont."

"Hang on, Roberta, I must be hearing things. I could have sworn I just heard you say 'Welcome to spring in Vermont.'"

"I did! I'm talkin' about blackflies. Don't yous have blackflies in Tennessee?"

"Of course we have blackflies in Tennessee. But I've never in my life had one bite me, much less *draw blood*."

"Well, they draw blood here, and it hurts like a son of a gun."

"I'll say it hurts. Our flies back home hang out in the windows and around the food. Then, of course, there are the green ones that buzz around the dog . . . well, never mind, that's gross. They may drive you crazy by flying around your head but they don't *bite* you, for heaven's sake."

"You've gut the wrong fly. I'm talkin' about the blackflies that are nearly impossible to see."

"No-see-ums? We have those. They're annoying but they don't bite you. Tennessee doesn't have y'all's kinds of blackflies."

"Well, don't worry, you'll get used to them. Just make sure to use bug repellant every time you go outside and keep the rest of your body bundled up, too. They love kids. Moe's kids got covered in bites every year because their darn mother was too busy to wrap 'em up."

"You're not gonna tell me this goes on all summer, are you?" I said, just kidding around.

"Nuup, I'm happy to report they only last about seven or eight weeks."

"SEVEN OR EIGHT WEEKS?" I shrieked into the phone.

"Yuup. Them are usually gone by Fourth of July."

How much more could I possibly take? After we hung up I was ready to murder Ed Baldwin. I'd been dreaming of warm days and nights for five months. Here it was May and not only was it still chilly, with highs around fifty-five, we couldn't even go outside. The thought of keeping my girls back indoors until July because of a swarm of vampire bugs was my final straw.

When the bugs bite the back of the neck the lymph nodes swell up. It feels like little tumors back there. The first time I felt one on Isabella I nearly lost my mind. I called the doctor's office in a frenzy. "It's only the blackflies," they told me. "Their bites make the lymph nodes swell up for a while. Not to worry, they'll go away."

I learned a blackfly repellant trick from Jeb: Spray a bandanna really well with Skin So Soft and tie it around your neck and they won't come near. It finally occurred to me what Jeb's mama was talking about at the

Christmas party when she told me that Skin So Soft would really be handy come spring.

Here we go again, but I have to say, nobody ever told me about Vermont's kind of blackflies.

I don't think it had really sunk in to Sarah and Issie that Daddy wasn't coming home. They asked a few questions, about where he was and who he was with, but I managed to be evasive, trying to avoid the subject and divert their attention to other subjects. Like movies, books, or . . . actually, that's all there was for kids to do in Vermont around Mud Season. Read stories or watch movies. Period.

I was reading in bed, late one night, when Sarah slid into my room. A little sniffle alerted me that she was standing right next to the bed with her thumb in her mouth, rubbing what was left of her blankie under her nose.

"Can't sleep?" I asked her.

She shook her head. "Where's my daddy, Mommy?"

It killed me to hear her words and I reached out and pulled her up on the bed. She nestled in next to me and continued to fondle the corner of her blanket. "He's decided to live away from us, sweetie."

"Why?"

"Because he's found another job, and another . . ." I forced myself not to continue the sentence. "He wants to live on his own now." I looked lovingly into her sad little blue eyes.

"Is he coming home?"

"I don't think so. But I'm here with you. And you know what? I love you *this* much." I stretched my arms out as wide as I could. "And even though Daddy's not here, he loves you *this* much." Again, I stretched my arms.

She listened to what I was saying, but didn't speak. I seized the lag in the conversation and changed the subject. I didn't know what to tell her any more than she knew what to ask.

"Hey, we need a new movie. Why don't we drive to Rutland in the morning to pick out a new one?"

"Issie, too? Can she get one so we can have two?"

"Let's get three, why don't we?"

A big smile transformed her sullen face and she sat straight up. "Can we get four?"

I would have agreed to buy her ten movies that night, just to take her mind off the heaviness she felt from being separated from Baker.

My dreams of never working with Sergeant Helga Schloygin again were dying fast. The restaurant was due to reopen in only two weeks and I had no sale contract for the Vermont Haus Inn. Ed brought a couple of interested buyers traipsing through the inn but no one was ever interested in seeing it the second time. The price was too high. The chance of finding someone with a spare $450,000 who wanted to lose it in the restaurant business in Vermont was as remote as that of spotting a Vermont moose.

I went ahead and put an ad in *The Sugartree Gazette* for a sous-chef. But here's the hitch. I had never hired anyone before in my whole life. I knew myself well enough to know that it would not be easy, especially when it came to explaining my reasons for not offering someone the job. I didn't really know what to look for in a chef—but nice attitude and pleasant personality were numbers one and two. Cooking skills came third. (Just kidding.) I knew cooking skills were important but the former two requirements were paramount in my book nonetheless.

The first candidate I interviewed was a definite no. He showed up in his chef clothes, having come straight from his current job, stinking to high heaven with BO. I couldn't get past it. No more stinkiness needed around here, I told myself. But then again, what reason would I give for not hiring him? You stink, fella? I decided to worry about it later.

The second guy I talked to was better. He was dressed nicely and didn't smell bad at all *and* he was quite pleasant. Upon glancing at his résumé, I learned that he had tons of experience and was a chef at a smaller inn, two towns over. I was close to offering him the job when he told me he needed fifty thousand per year to make the switch. That was the end of that interview.

After interview number two, panic struck. What if I couldn't find any-one and Rolf came back to no assistant? What if I really had to pay some-one a ton of money? Let's not ignore the fact that I knew nothing about the restaurant business and now *I* was the one in charge. Who in the world could I trust at this point? Absolutely no one.

At straight up three o'clock on a Monday, exactly eleven days before we were due to reopen, I had scheduled my third interview. I was dreading this interview, too, because this particular guy was the sous-chef at a little restaurant called the Wild Duck down in Manchester. It had a great repu-tation although I had never eaten there before. I knew the food was pricey so my biggest fear was that he would want to be paid fifty thousand dollars like the last guy. I was embarrassed to be looking for an experienced sous-chef with no money to offer.

I never heard him come in. He didn't knock; no one did. He was stand-ing quietly in front of the fireplace in the red-checked dining room when I ambled in from our apartment.

"Oh! I didn't know you were here yet." Although I was startled I still thought to extend my hand. "Hi, I'm Leelee. I hope you haven't been wait-ing long."

"No, I haven't. I should have called out or knocked. I'm Peter." He made straight eye contact with me and smiled. *Perfect teeth.*

"Nice to meet you."

"Likewise. Great place you have here," he said, looking around.

"Oh, well, I appreciate you saying that." Embarrassed that this man might think the inn was a reflection of me I added, "Actually, I've lived here only five months and haven't been able to do anything to make it feel like home. We bought the place furnished and not one thing has changed." I cringed when I remembered the smell. "I'm terribly sorry about the odor." I waved my hand under my nose. "It was here before we moved in."

"No worries. I've never been here before, only heard about it. It's hard to eat out at other restaurants. Most of the good ones are closed on Mondays, and that's my only night off."

"Come to think of it, I haven't been out to eat anywhere else, either." An awkward moment followed, like neither of us knew what to say next. "Would you like a Coke or something?" I said, trying to push through the discomfort.

"No, thank you, but do you mind if I see the kitchen?"

"Of course not, it's right through here."

After a thorough tour of the kitchen we meandered back out to the dining room, having had a nice conversation. Peter took a seat at the table in the bay window. He had the classic little boy, all-American look—sandy blond hair, light blue eyes, and a cute nose. There was nothing little boy about his body at all. He must have been six feet tall and thanks to the T-shirt he was wearing I got to sneak peeks at his strong forearms.

We chitchatted for a few minutes longer, mostly about skiing and moose, and I found out that he loved to ski but, like me, had never seen a moose. Another awkward moment of silence followed. "Do you know Rolf and Helga?" I finally asked, getting back to the real reason he was sitting at my table.

"Never met either of them. I know Rolf's reputation, of course."

"I think everyone does." I wanted to say more but bit my tongue instead. I didn't even hint that we had . . . *issues*.

Something about this guy seemed right. He was pleasant and confident and easy to talk to. He stood out far above the other two guys I had interviewed. As a courtesy I felt I had to be up-front with him about the impending sale of the inn. Out of nervousness, I combed my hair behind my ears.

"Here's the situation, Peter. I'd like to hire you but I need to be up-front. The Vermont Haus Inn is for sale. Another chef could buy this place and then I'm not sure what'll happen to your job."

He thought for a moment before speaking. "I appreciate you telling me, but I'm not worried about it. I can find a job anywhere," he said. "I'm looking at this as another stepping-stone anyway. It's a great opportunity to apprentice under a renowned chef." He stared out the bay window for a second before adding, "Now here's my truth. I want my own fine-dining restaurant someday. I need to take advantage of any and all opportunities that lead me to that end."

This guy was the one, no doubt about it. "By any chance, could you start next Friday? I know it's soon, but we reopen for Memorial Day weekend and I'm kind of in a bind. The truth of the matter is, and you'll find this out soon enough, my husband *was* the sous-chef but he left."

"He left his job?"

"Yes."

"Will he be coming back?"

"I guess not, I mean . . . no, he won't." I glanced down at the table. My nerve endings had been set on fire.

He sat silently for a second like he was choosing his words carefully. "Are you saying he left *you*?"

I could feel the lump in my throat growing and I didn't want to cry in front of him. "That's what I'm saying, but . . . looking toward the future. Do you think you could start next week?" My eyes brimmed with tears but—oh well, I couldn't help it.

"I'm sure I can work something out," he said, *sooo* laid-back. I appreciated the calm yet confident way in which he spoke. He was quite the contrast to my fizzy self.

"Oh wait!" I suddenly remembered a vital interview question that I should have asked long before now. "Baker—that's my husband—wasn't getting paid, so I don't know how much to pay you?" *Leelee, interviewer extraordinaire.*

"What if you pay me what I'm getting now? Twelve dollars an hour?"

I couldn't believe it. "That sounds just right! It's a deal. Thank you." The fervor in my voice surely let him know how elated I was to have him.

"Thank *you*." He shook my hand and winked at me.

I escorted Peter to the door, and told him I'd see him next week. I stood behind the curtain and peered out one of the front windows, watching him walk to his truck. There was something about him. I couldn't put my finger on it but I felt good about hiring him. My only worry was a potential loyalty to Rolf birthed out of admiration for Rolf's culinary skills. *But I won't be here much longer anyway, and none of this will matter after I'm gone.*

Chapter Fourteen

There was only one good thing about Mud Season—well, two. Besides a two-month vacation from Helga, I got to spend all my time with my girls. Five days before the opening, we were inside (of course) baking cookies for Sarah's year-end party at preschool the next day. It was approaching 5:00 P.M. when the loveliest sound I'd heard in months emanated from the foyer.

"You-hoo, anybody home?"

Sarah and Isabella looked over at me and crawled down from their stools in the commercial kitchen. In an instant we tore off running. We met three beautiful Southern faces just as they were walking into the red-checked dining room, loaded down with suitcases and boxes. I almost fainted when I saw them.

"What are y'all doing here?" I shrieked when I saw them, amid long hugs and kisses.

"We figured you might need some help about now, you poor little thing," Mary Jule said while glancing about the room. Looks of astonishment transformed each of their smiling faces as they slowly pivoted around. My abandonment by Baker wasn't the only thing that blew their minds. The décor of the Vermont Haus Inn had them completely unnerved.

"How long can y'all stay?"

"About a week," Alice said, examining the red-checked wallpaper.

"We waited until the children got out of school so the guys wouldn't have to fool with all that," Virginia said.

"I can't believe y'all kept it a secret. Did you fly into Albany and rent a car?"

"Of course. And we're kidnapping you on the way back and taking you to New York for a wild girls' weekend!" Virginia said. Oh, how she loves New York City.

"Oooooh, I'd love that. But I don't know," I said, reconsidering when I thought of what lay ahead. "Opening night is in five days and there's so much to do here."

Virginia stood in front of the mantel, studying Helga's hippo collection. "You can say that again."

"You just calm your little self down. We're gonna help you do all of that and lots more, darlin'. What could it hurt to run off to New York for two little nights?" Mary Jule asked.

"Nothing, I suppose. I'll have to see. But right now, I'm just so glad y'all are here." I hugged all of them again. We each pulled out a chair at one of the tables in front of the bay window. Sarah climbed up in Alice's lap and Isabella hopped up with me.

"Girls, y'all look so pretty, but your mama sure seems a little pale. It's nearly June and you're still white as a ghost," Alice said, giving me a once-over.

"Does it feel like bikini weather here to you?" I asked her.

Virginia just had to comment on the interior design. "Fiery, I've got a great idea, we can help you decorate!"

"Fat chance. I told all y'all that Helga undid all my decorating on our second day here. Remember?"

They all nodded.

"She'll have a stroke if we move one pepper shaker out of its place."

"Pee-you, what's that smell?" Alice put Sarah down and marched over to the window to raise it.

I just shook my head. "Don't y'all remember anything I've told you about this place?"

"Oh yeah, now I remember. The houseitosis. We'll run up and get some potpourri in a little while."

"Forget it. I've already tried that. Helga poured it out. She said it made the inn smell like a flower shop."

"And what's wrong with that? It sure beats the BO."

"Tell me about it. *Shoot.* If I had known y'all were coming I'd have had you bring me some things from home."

"Speaking of that. Look what Mama sent you." Virginia dug into a big flowery tote bag and pulled out a box of Dinstuhl's white chocolate chunks. "I told her about you having to give that woman your Christmas present and how she didn't even offer to share. Mama went straight out and bought you another box."

"I'll have to write her a note, but in the meantime, please tell her thank you. I've been craving Dinstuhl's chocolates for five months." I opened up the box, crammed a piece in my mouth, and passed the rest around—like Jeb's mother should have.

"I noticed the side garden when we parked our car," Mary Jule said. "I can tell it's gonna be really pretty when it blooms. I'll help you with the pruning if you want."

"Don't bother. Unless you want your lymph nodes swollen and blood dripping down your neck, just stay inside. That reminds me, y'all have to bundle up your whole body when you go outside and wear Skin So Soft–soaked bandannas around your neck."

"What do you mean?" she asked, horrified and rightfully so.

"I haven't told y'all this yet but they have vampire bugs here that draw blood. Can you believe the lies these people tell you about living here? There have been heaps of strange things about Vermont that no one ever bothered telling me."

"Yankees," Alice said, and sat back down at the table again.

"There's a magazine here called *Vermont Life* and I'm starting to think it's my duty to take out an ad and list all of the things they don't want people to know, and prevent anybody else from making the same mistake I made."

"You could warn people about the gossipy gas station owner." Virginia laughed out loud. "John doesn't believe it."

"Is that a joke or what?" I said.

"Sorry to change the subject, but I just thought of this," Alice said. "Y'all don't let me forget about the moose souvenirs for the children. They'll kill me if I come home empty-handed. Plus, I'm dying to see one. I've still got the picture of you hugging that sign in full view on my fridge."

"That's the one thing I've looked forward to since I moved here. And to date, not only have I not seen a moose, but no one else has, either. For the first four months of living here, I never took my eyes off the side of the road. Now I don't bother. It's probably just another New England tall tale."

"Where's that Computer World place and the pink car?" Mary Jule asked. "Al wants me to take pictures; he doesn't believe *that* exists."

"Neither does John," Virginia added.

"I'm surprised y'all didn't see it when you walked in. Look out the window, you can't miss it." I pointed toward the front to show the girls where to look.

All three tried beating one another to the window to get their first glimpse.

"I don't believe it. That little hut is really *it?* Where's my camera?" Virginia said.

"I told you it's the kind of thing you have to see to believe."

"Can we go inside? Do you think he'd let us take pictures?" Alice had a shrill to her voice.

"I'm sure Jeb would absolutely love to take y'all on a tour."

"Right now?" Virginia asked.

"No, not right now," I told her. "Anyway, his car's gone, he must not be home."

"Why are we still in this room? I wanna see the rest of the place," said Mary Jule. "It's beautiful from the outside, Leelee. I'm dying to look around."

Gracie must have heard all the commotion because she came running through the door. God knows where she'd been. After two months of having free rein of the place, Gracie had no qualms about venturing anywhere in the inn she pleased. The mud kept her away from the outdoors so we were still in need of newspapers. Mary Jule loves Gracie (Alice and Virginia do not) so she picked her up and held her the whole time we toured the inn.

We explored the upstairs first and I showed Mary Jule and Alice which room they would be sleeping in. I asked Virginia to stay with me in my room. God knows I could use the company. They lingered in every guest room, giving each the once-over and doing their best not to make a negative comment. "I know, I know," I'd say whenever an eyebrow was raised. "I never said it wasn't tacky. But can't you see the potential?"

I even showed them the basement. Besides the massive amount of clutter down there, the girls were also intrigued by the wine cellar and the vast amount of wine. They promised to get to know that part of the inn better before the end of their visit, and I had no doubt they would.

When we finally made it to the superb owners' quarters, the unveiling didn't have quite the impact that it had had on me. After all, it was painted and new carpet replaced the old indoor-outdoor covering. Most of the stink was even gone. Our furniture from home made it look more familiar. But once they saw my bedroom, they couldn't hold back.

"Oh, Leelee. *Honey.* This is *pitiful,*" Alice said, placing her hands on either side of her cheeks. "I knew you said it was small, but seeing it in person is *tragic.*"

Mary Jule shook her head like she was in too much pain to speak. Virginia hopped up on Great-grandmother's bed, making herself comfortable, and announced, "I'm amazed you've made it this long." Seeing how there was nowhere else *but* the bed to sit, or stand for that matter, we all ended up lounging on top of it—and each other—to discuss.

"All I can say is, I can't wait to finally meet the Sergeant." Alice made little quote marks when she said "the Sergeant," and propped up a pillow behind her head.

"I can. I'm scared of her, just like Leelee," said Mary Jule, resting against a throw pillow on the footboard.

"Why are you scared of her, Mary Jule?" asked Virginia. "She can't hurt us. She needs to get the hell out of here anyway. Fiery, we've been talking and we think you need a new name for the inn. Paint the place peach and call it the Peach Tree Inn, or the Peach Blossom Inn." I could tell by the shrill in her voice how excited she was.

The idea sounded delicious to me, too, but I wasn't so sure I was up for it. "Peach *is* my favorite color . . . oh, I'd love to but I can't. Baker said we have to keep everything just as it is for a year. Besides, I'll be home soon anyway."

Alice immediately sprung up. "Wait just a minute. First of all, *Baker* has no more say-so in this whatsoever. Don't even get me started on that money-hungry son of a bitch." (Alice's always hated Baker.) "And second of all, who knows how long this place will take to sell. We want you to feel better in the meantime. If nothing else, changing the name will *help* you sell it. Vermont Haus Inn. If that isn't the coldest, most boring name for an inn I've ever heard."

"Wait 'til you see the woman who named it. You'll see why," I told her.

Virginia jumped off the bed and ran out to the sitting room. When she returned she was holding a roll of wallpaper. "All of us feel really bad about not sending you a housewarming gift." She looked around at the others for reassurance and they all nodded in agreement. "Remember that night we were talking on the phone and you were complaining about your tacky red-checked dining room? I asked you how big it was and you said about the same size as your dining room back home?"

"Yes, I remember."

"Well, that is coming down, and this"—she rolled out the paper in her hand—"is going up."

I was completely dumbfounded. It was my very favorite wallpaper in the world, the same exact pattern that had hung in my dining room back home. Even seeing it on the roll made my heart happy. "Where did you get it, how did you know how much to buy?"

"We asked the new owners of your old house if we could measure the dining room and then we ordered four more rolls just in case. We can return whatever we don't use—less something called a restocking fee," Alice explained. "No biggie."

"Y'all shouldn't have done that, it's too much money."

"Aren't you worth it?" Mary Jule piped up. "We wanna help you change this place up. It'll make you feel so much better, I promise."

"Hang on, there's more." Virginia crawled back on top of the bed. "We thought you could serve all kinds of peach desserts, and we'd make sure to send you the peaches from home. Peach preserves could always be on the tables for breakfast and each night in the summer you could feature a different fresh peach dessert. Peach cobbler, peach pie, homemade peach ice cream, peaches jubilee—now *I'm* gettin' excited."

"Wait, wait, wait. Here's the best part. Fresh peach daiquiris as the specialty of the house. You've got to *Southernize* this place, Lee," Alice said.

"I know I do. That was my original intention. But can we just get through the weekend first? When Helga and Rolf find out this place is for sale and that I've hired a new sous-chef, it's gonna be bad, really bad." Recalling what it was like to work with the Sergeant gave me a bad feeling in the pit of my stomach. "They liked Baker. I'm not so sure how they'll react to someone new."

"Leelee," Alice said, more seriously, "I know we've all talked about this hundreds of times on the phone already, but you're gonna make it without Baker. You don't need him. You'll run this place on your own just fine until it sells. I gotta tell you though, looking over at his clothes in your closet is making me sick."

"I was just gonna say the same thing," Virginia said. "Why are they still hanging there? Baker is such a damn coward."

"When was the last time you talked to him?" Mary Jule wanted to know.

"A couple of weeks ago but only for a second. He calls the girls though, and he's taken them to dinner a time or two." I shook my head and closed my eyes for a second. "You're right, Virgy; he is a coward. I can't believe he's done this to us," I said, as tears welled in my eyes.

My tears momentarily halted their jeers toward Baker. When they started rolling down my cheeks, Mary Jule scooted over and held me close. Her spontaneous grasp sprung forth a gush of agony, built up over months and months, and my spirit finally broke into a million tiny pieces. I cried the cry I had long needed, with heavy uncontrollable sobs. Mary Jule caressed my head while Virginia hooked her arm through mine and laid her head on my shoulder. Alice rubbed my legs and the three of them remained silent while I wept my way through a rite of passage, a transition from the only existence I'd known on to the uncharted trail of a new life without Baker.

Never one to remain serious for more than a few minutes, Virginia rolled off the bed and started shuffling through Baker's clothes. She pulled a hat off a hook and held it out, by its earflap, with just two fingers. "Wonder how much wood he's chucked in this thing—the woodchuck wannabe." She let it fall to the floor. "Let's get this crap *out of here*. Why should you have to look at it every day and be reminded of him?"

"He said he'd come for it all." I pulled myself up and wrapped my tear-soaked hair back into a ponytail and tied it in a knot.

"Too late. We're gonna take it to him. I've got a plan, an Agency assignment!" Virginia gets this great look on her face when she's got scheming on the brain. It appeared as if she had come up with a doozie. (The Agency, the *GK* Agency, was formed back in the seventh grade, to spy on Mary Jule's big brothers. It later came in handy when using the "drive-by" method to stake out the whereabouts of our boyfriends. GK stands for the one and only Gladys Kravitz. The nosy neighbor on *Bewitched*.)

"She's got that look in her eye," Alice said.

"Do tell," said Mary Jule.

"No, not yet. I'll tell ya later when I've thought it through more. Aren't y'all tired of lying here? Let's start decorating. I want people to know when they walk in the door that a Southern belle lives here and that she's the one in charge. Besides, I'm starving. Got any good food around this joint, Leelee?"

———

The first time my best friends met Jeb Duggar he had his head up a chimney. The inimitable sound of "Chim Chim Cher-ee" emerged from the
parlor early the next morning, and could be heard all the way from the big
kitchen. All of us were sitting around in our housecoats drinking coffee.

"I know that song. Jeb must be here," Sarah said.

"Oh, goody, maybe we'll get a peek into his Computer World today."
Virginia poured herself more coffee and headed out the door. "Come on,
Sarah, introduce us. I've been living for this."

"Okay," Sarah said, and all the rest of us grabbed our cups and followed
her out to the parlor.

Once she got to the hearth, Sarah started giggling and bent down for a
better look. "Jeb, somebody wants to meet you."

Jeb was on his knees in the fireplace. Upon hearing Sarah, he poked
out his head, which was covered in a dirty old top hat, and peered over at
all of us. With his giant handlebar mustache and big bushy beard, all covered in soot, and his big ole hairy stomach pushing out of a black long-
sleeved T-shirt that was made to look like the front of a tux, he was quite
the sight. I didn't even know chimney sweeping was one of his duties at my
inn. I didn't even know chimney sweeping was actually something that
needed to be done at all, to tell you the truth.

Before Sarah could make a formal introduction, Virginia started right
in. "So you must be Jay-eb." She overemphasized her Southern accent on
purpose.

"Yuup, how'd you know?" he said, arduously standing up and wiping his
hands on his pants.

"Leelee's told us all about you." Virginia moved in closer to him.

"I'd shake your hand but I won't." Jeb snickered and showed her his
covered-in-soot right hand.

Alice jumped right in with Virginia and laid the accent on thick. "Why,
Jayeb, you certainly are *quite* the entrepreneur. Aside from your work here,
I've heard all about your snow business and especially Jayeb's Computer
World. We sure would love a tour when you get a second," she said. Bless
Jeb's heart. He had no idea what he was in for.

A loud static noise interrupted their conversation and Jeb grabbed the walkie-talkie that was clipped to his belt and placed it right up to his ear. "Hang on a minute, would yous?" he said to the girls.

His mama's voluble voice boomed for all to hear. "I need a Three Musketeers," she said. "Go on up the street and get me one, would you? Over." Jeb kept that thing turned up so dang loud.

"Roger that, but it'll have to wait a while, I'm not finished here yet. Over."

"Then make it a large, and put a Mountain Dew with it. Over."

"Roger. Over and out. Now, what was you saying?" Jeb said, resuming his chat with Alice. "Oh yeah, you want a tour of JCW, that shouldn't be no problem to arrange." His slightly cool demeanor was just a cover-up for how thrilled he was inside.

"I can already see that this place would fall apart without you, Jayeb," Mary Jule said, buttering him up for the yet-to-be-tackled chores of the day.

I rolled my eyes and wondered how his head would ever fit back up the chimney.

"Jayeb, we're here to help Leelee," Mary Jule continued. "She's been having a hard time lately, as you know. We're gonna be changing things around a bit to make her feel better. We can count on your help, can't we, darlin'?"

"Sure, that's my job. I'm the official handyman of the Vermont Haus Inn." Jeb pulled nervously on his beard.

"Well, in that case, what are we waiting for?" Alice said. "Come on, sugar." She patted Jeb on the back, playfully yanked on his beard, and led him by his soot-covered hand out to the red-checked dining room.

The rest of us followed behind and Virginia whispered to Mary Jule and me under her breath, "Bless his heart, he's got a stenis."

"Shhh," I whispered back. "He might hear you."

"He's not listening to us. He's ga-ga over Alice."

Virginia made up the word "stenis" one day when we were all lying on the beach in Destin, Florida. This poor obese man strolled by and bent over to pick up a shell. He had one of those really big stomachs. Not the kind that spills out over the top of a man's belt, but the kind that seems to have another piece that hangs really low underneath. After studying him up and down she got the idea for a brand-new word that she fully intends to submit to Webster. She turned to all of us and said, "You see that low-hanging part of that man's gut? It's not his stomach, and it's not his penis, it's his stenis."

"Okay, first things first," said Virgy, clapping her hands. "Where's the boom box?"

"Back in my apartment," I said.

"Go get it. And bring plenty of fun tunes with you. I'm feeling like I need a little Mickey J. this morning."

"Which album?"

"Bring *Hot Rocks*. It's got everything on it."

"Got it!"

Next thing I knew, the place was hopping and Mick Jagger's voice was blaring "Gimme Shelter." We were having the best time. Dancing whenever we moved and singing at the top of our lungs while redoing this and changing that. Mary Jule and I hung pictures while Virginia bopped through the house with a big trash bag, throwing away the clutter. Alice, as the ringleader, was bossing everyone—in her nice Alice way—on what to do. It's not like she wasn't helping, she was—but someone had to be the director.

Seeing Virginia with that trash bag in her hand made me cringe. What would Helga say? But the dancing and singing took my mind off it and, for the moment anyway, I really couldn't have cared less.

There was one thing my friends didn't know about Jeb. Unless someone was watching over him and lighting a fire to his bottom, Jeb Duggar was as slow as a bottle of Heinz ketchup. He was used to taking work at his own pace with frequent breaks. Every time he'd take a seat, one of the girls would lean over him and say, "Can you please help me with this, Jayeb," or "Jayeb, darlin', these draperies need hanging over here."

Alice reached out her hand when he was sitting on the bottom step resting and pulled him up to be her dance partner when "Brown Sugar" came on. "Jitterbug with me, sugar."

When I saw Jeb step on her toe with his big ole foot, and she dropped his grip and boogied away from him, I couldn't help but laugh.

Virginia shimmied right on up to him and broke into a twist. Jeb tried as hard as he could to twist along with her, but when he tried squatting down to equal Virginia, the poor thing's feet spilled right out in front of him. He tottered over backward and, well, that was the end of that.

That man had never seen anything close to the likes of these three Tennessee girls. And I'd never seen anything like Jeb Duggar's sudden productivity. Beads of sweat trickled down his cheeks. He was a-heaving and a-hoeing as he carried the Schloygins' old, tattered furniture upstairs to the junk room, and hauled my antique furniture down to take its place.

"It's a good thing you don't live in Tennessee," Mary Jule told him, "we'd all be fighting over you."

At some point during the morning, Alice slipped out to the hardware store and came back with buckets of peach paint and plenty of drop cloths. The girls had talked Jeb into helping them paint both the parlor and the entrance hall a fabulous shade of pale peach.

He had to call in a helper though, when Virginia presented him with the new rolls of wallpaper. I caught him grumbling under his breath. Something about not seeing what was wrong with the old stuff, but with my best friends egging him on, he papered anyway. It took all of us two days to transform the dowdy red-checked dining room into a lovely Southern showplace.

Once the paint was dry, Virginia rearranged all the bookshelves and placed my knickknacks around the room. She could make any room look like it belonged on a page straight out of *Veranda*.

"Don't throw anything out," I reminded her. "Let's just repack Helga's castoffs inside my old boxes and we'll give it all back to her. Trust me, we'll never hear the end of it if we don't."

After three rigorous days of cosmetic surgery, my inn had a brand-new face. By the time we were finished, the Vermont Haus Inn was cute, cozy, comfy, and definitely Southernized. When you walked in the front door, you couldn't help but feel you were south of the Mason-Dixon Line. The draperies from my house in Memphis were hanging on the windows in the parlor. Sarah's and Isabella's portraits hung in the foyer and the rest of my paintings were scattered all over the place. The red checks on the dining room walls had disappeared and were replaced with parrots and toucans, palm trees and tropical plants on a peach background.

Antique books from my family's collection had replaced the twenty-year supply of *National Geographics*. The dozens of old, half-burned red candles were in the trash, and Helga's vast collection of gewgaws were finally out of the bookshelves and packed away.

My cushioned sofas and chintz easy chairs had taken the place of the old torn-up musty Schloygin furniture. My porcelain Herend animals replaced Helga's hippo collection on the mantel and that, I was sure, would be the final blow.

All the inn needed now was a fresh coat of peach paint on the outside and a brand-new sign that said PEACH BLOSSOM INN. Whether I would really change the name or not remained to be seen, but I loved the way it looked on the inside. And the new paint certainly helped the fusty smell, let me tell you.

With only two days left before the reopening, the four of us strolled around the downstairs admiring our feat of excellence. Jeb, still clad in an old one-piece work suit, was so worn out that he dragged behind hardly able to speak. We were pooped, too, but so ready to savor our new creation and revel in our achievement. Seeing my old things again gave me a huge lift and I couldn't stop smiling. Mary Jule and I ran our hands over the crisp peach walls and I even stuck my nose alongside, just to smell the fumes of the new paint. Jeb complained about the vapors but I told him he was crazy to wish for that rank odor back for even a second.

Alice, who had probably done the least amount of work, stood in the center of the freshly papered dining room and declared, "We are missing the boat, here, y'all. The Designing Women don't have a thing on us. I'm ready to start up our own interior design firm and hire Jeb to be our Anthony."

"And I'll be Suzanne Sugarbaker. Lord knows I've always wanted to be in a beauty pageant," Virginia said, and faked like she was fixing a crown on her head.

"Who's Anthony?" Jeb asked.

"The Vee Eye Pee!" Virginia told him, and went up to where he was flaked out in a chair and readjusted his mustache.

Jeb beamed with delight.

We had all changed out of our paint clothes—freshly bought from a tag sale just down the street—into jeans and light sweaters. As we lounged around in my comfy furniture in the parlor that now looked like my living room back home, Virginia got a devious look on her face.

She looked over at Jeb with her notorious impish grin, and upon seeing it I knew we were in trouble. "You look like you could use a drink, Mr. Duggar. How would you like for us to treat you to an ice-cold brewski for all your hard work? Surely, y'all have somewhere up here to get an ice-cold beer."

As worn out as he was, Jeb perked up like he had just been told he'd sold his first computer. "We sure do. Gut lots of places around here to get beer. How about the Moose Head? They have about twenty different kinds." He glanced over at me for assurance.

"That sounds *peachy* to me," Virginia said. (She had never said "that sounds peachy" about anything, but she was trying to act silly for Jeb's benefit.) "I've got another great idea, let's all go in *Jayeb's* car. You wouldn't mind taking us for a spin in your cute *pink* car, would you, Jayeb?"

Virginia Murphey loves an oddity more than anyone I know. And the quirkier the better. The idea of riding in a rusted-out pink Chevy Chevette with JEB'S COMPUTER WORLD on one side and MARY KAY on the other was as exhilarating to her as riding in an eighty-thousand-dollar Mercedes convertible would be to a normal person.

"I wouldn't mind at all, but I think you'd like my truck better. It's a newer model and it's gut two jump seats in my extended cab." He thought about it for a second and stroked his beard. "I haven't had a chance to remove the plow in the front, though."

"Oh, *no no no*," Virginia said. "We would much rather ride in your Jeb's Computer World *pink* car. Right, girls?"

Everyone nodded with glee. The pièce de résistance of the trip had arrived.

"Alreet. I'll go start her up. She seems to be a little slow on the take these days, but once I get her goin', look out!"

Before heading out to the Moose Head, the girls just *had* to tour Jeb's Computer World and get their pictures made out front. Jeb posed eagerly, arm in arm with each of my friends as I snapped the pictures they desperately wanted as souvenirs and would probably send out for Christmas cards.

"Can we take a quick peek inside, Jayeb darlin'?" Alice asked him.

"I suppose. Are you in the market for a computer?"

"I might be," Alice lied. "You'll have to show me your stuff and I'll call my husband."

"In that case, step into my showroom." Jeb gestured his right arm toward the door. "Only two people at a time, though."

We disregarded that last comment and all crammed in at once. I don't know what I thought I expected, but seeing the inside of Jeb's Computer World in person was a *lifer* moment for me. The lone, off-brand computer was set up on top of an old wooden desk. A space heater was in the corner and he couldn't close the door all the way because of the big orange extension cord that ran from his mama's house to the lean-to. A crinkly poster of Peter Fonda in *Easy Rider* was thumbtacked to one wall and on the back of the door hung a poster of a scantily clad girl in a bikini, which barely covered the girl's breasts. The only thing in the room related to computers at all was the computer. It looked more like the inside of a teenager's tree house, to tell you the truth.

Jeb started to give Alice the big sales pitch and after about a minute or two of that Alice waved her hand and cut him off. "I'm not interested in all that technical stuff, just tell me what colors they come in and I'll make my decision later."

"My computers only come in one color," he told her, "and you're looking at it."

"I'll have to think about it and get back with you, sugar. I'm not really a beige person. Hey, I'm ready for a cold one. Outta here, let's go, y'all," she said, and scooted us back out the door.

Once outside, I told everyone to go on to the Moose Head without me.

I had work-related phone calls to make and I sure wasn't going to bring Sarah and Issie to a bar. Mandy had been watching them for me while we decorated but couldn't stay the evening. I waved good-bye to all of them and crossed the street back to our apartment. *They are some kind of crazy*, I thought. Although, I'd be doing the same thing, I'm sure, if the situation had been reversed, and I was visiting one of them in a foreign corner of America.

Toot toot. The horn startled me as I was turning the doorknob to get inside. Pulled right up alongside the picket fence was the pink, weather-rusted Chevy Chevette with Jeb in the driver's seat, Virginia (wearing his top hat) in the passenger seat, and Alice and Mary Jule in the back.

"Leelee, what's the name of the gas station we wanna stop at?" Virginia yelled, and stuck her head way out the window. "We're gonna fill up Jeb's Mary Kay—I mean JCW—car for him as a treat." She shot me an "are you believing this" look.

"George Clark's," I yelled back across the yard. "Jeb knows where it is."

"Great," she said, and ducked back into the front seat. "First stop, George Clark's, next stop Moose Head."

"Toodeloo, Leelee," Alice hollered from the backseat, and leaned over Jeb's shoulder to crank up the radio.

"GUN IT, JAYEB!" Virginia screamed and Jeb Duggar sped off with my three best friends in tow, windows rolled down and the radio blasting.

A hot flash of terror screamed through my body as soon as I opened my eyes the next morning. It was official. My vacation from Helga was over. I was going to have to face her completely on my own with no more Baker as a barrier between us. I decided to put it out of my mind, for a few minutes anyway, as I huddled in front of the space heater and dressed for the day.

Alice and Mary Jule found their way down to the apartment about nine, despite their throbbing heads, all dressed up in their jogging suits and ready to explore the neighborhood on foot. When they walked into the apartment, Virginia threw on her tennis shoes to go with them and I soaked bandannas in Skin So Soft. Wanting to prolong my vacation as long as possible, and avoid any accidental collisions with Rolf or Helga, I was happy to stay behind with Issie and Sarah.

On their way out of the apartment door, all bundled up of course and armed with the toe heaters I had given them, I heard Alice saying hello to someone. When I peeked through the window, I was relieved to learn it was Roberta. She was returning from the backyard, clad in her Sorel snow boots, with a spade in one hand and a brown grocery bag in the other. I joined them outside.

"You must be Roberta," Alice said before I could make the introduction, and gave her a hug. "You have saved our Leelee from housework hell. I don't know how to thank you."

I was a little concerned that that might make Roberta feel bad, so I said, "Alice's just jealous, Roberta."

"Glad to be of service! You've gut quite a crew there, Leelee."

"Now don't I though? This is Virginia, Mary Jule, and you've just met Alice."

"Nice to meet all yous." Roberta smiled her smile, and her natural warmth enveloped us all.

"What's in your bag?" Virginia asked.

Roberta couldn't wait to show us her haul. "I've gut enough dandelion greens here to eat for Sunday lunch and have leftovers, too."

"Pardon me?" Mary Jule wanted to be extra polite to her but she was terribly confused all the same. "Are you talking about the kind of dandelions with a thingamajig that you pick, and blow the little fuzzy, fly-away things?"

"Yuup. Them are dandelions alreet."

"And y'all *eat them* up here?" Mary Jule asked, ever so gingerly.

"Why, sure. My husband's a green lover. He'll be happy tonight, I tell you."

Mary Jule looked over at me on the verge of tears. It all came home to her at that very moment. Her dear friend, Leelee Satterfield, was living in a place where people eat weeds.

Roberta was proud, as usual, to be the Vermont educator. She told each of them that she would be happy to give them any Vermont information they needed to know, all the while tugging on her undies with the spade still in her hand.

We chatted with her for a while, until she had to start her prep work. With the restaurant opening that night, Roberta had much to do and cordially shooed the girls on their way.

Once she thought about bumping into Helga *or* Rolf, Mary Jule decided to stay inside with me, and the other two took off down the lane.

Alice spotted Peter first. She and Virginia were returning from their walk when she saw him stepping out of his truck. They were beside themselves when they barged back inside the apartment.

"*Who* is that guy that just came in the restaurant door before us?" Alice ran right up to me with Virginia at her heels.

Since Mary Jule, my daughters, and I were hiding from Rolf and Helga in the apartment I wasn't sure which guy she was talking about. It could have been Pierre, Rolf, or Peter. They hadn't met any of them yet.

"Was he young or old?"

"Young*ish*," Alice said.

"Blond hair, kinda tall?"

"Yeah, that's the guy," Virginia said.

"Black truck?"

"Yes, Leelee, yes! Who is he?" Alice demanded to know.

"My new sous-chef."

"That's *Peter*. You have got to be kidding. Why didn't you tell us he was drop-dead gorgeous?"

"I don't know. Is he?"

"Naw, he's ugly," Virginia said.

"I guess he's cute, but I've always been attracted to dark-headed guys. I was just glad to notice he has good hygiene," I said.

"I wanna see him," said Mary Jule. "Come on, Fiery, introduce us."

"No, I don't want to see Rolf 'til I have to and if I take y'all in the kitchen, I'll have to talk to him. Besides, Helga could show up at any moment and I wanna avoid her as long as possible."

"Oh, come on, you scaredy-cat. What are you so afraid of? We'll be right with you," Alice said.

"*Okay.* But let's at least wait 'til Rolf has had a chance to get acquainted with Peter. I don't want to be the one to introduce the two of them."

Peter seemed confident to me, and perfectly capable of taking care of himself. I was sure his self-introduction to Rolf would go well and the two of them would ease on through the transition. *They are both professionals,* I thought. Ed had already broken the news to the Schloygins so there really was no need for me to say a word.

Twenty minutes was all my friends would give me. Knowing I had to face the kitchen people eventually, I white-knuckled it and with the other three trailing behind I crept out to the commercial kitchen for introductions.

"Hi, Peter," I said, and shyly waved at him from the door. My friends more or less pushed me from behind into the room.

He looked up from the veal stock he was preparing and smiled. "Well, hello there, Leelee."

"Hi, Rolf," I said, and waved at him, too.

"Hello," Rolf mumbled. No other comment. *Thank God.*

"Everyone, these are my best friends from home. Alice, Virginia, and Mary Jule. They've come to help me out."

All of my friends politely waved and said, "Hi."

Peter smiled again and simply said, "Hi, best friends."

Rolf was busy at the cutting board, slicing fillets. He said hello but never looked up again.

Alice went straight up to Peter and started chatting his head off. "Are you married, Peter?" I could have strangled her.

"Nope, not married."

Alice kept on. "Is that right? How about children, do you have any kids?"

"No children."

"That's good. Do you *like* children?" *What is she* doing? I kept thinking. I was dying to tell her to shut up.

"Sure, I have lots of nieces and nephews."

I couldn't take it any longer. I smashed my big toe on top of her big toe as hard as I could. She would have killed me if I had done that to her. "Excuse me, y'all, I don't mean to cut this short but I'm sure Peter's got a lot to do and Isabella is waiting on you to read her that story, remember, Alice?" I lied.

"Nice meeting you, Peter, hope you enjoy it here," Alice said, while I dragged her toward the door.

"Nice meeting you guys," he responded.

"Peter, I'm just curious," Mary Jule asked, right before we left the kitchen. "Where are you from?"

"Jersey."

"I knew it," she said. "You sound just like Bruce Springsteen."

"That's funny, I've been told Bruce sounds just like me."

Chapter Fifteen

"*Vhat* is going on here?" Helga demanded to know, in her commanding voice, as soon as she appeared in the kitchen after her two-month "holiday" as she called it.

Rolf looked up from his usual station behind the chef's line and answered, "Vhat do you mean, Helga? Everything es all right."

"*Nein!* Vermont Haus Inn has been changed. It looks one hundred percent different. My customaz vill never recognize dis place; they vill turn around and leave."

"I am unaware of dis," Rolf told her. "Nev'a mind!" For some reason he always said "never mind" when he was frustrated, upset, or angry.

My moment of truth had arrived. This was exactly what I had been dreading ever since Alice, Virginia, and Mary Jule insisted on revamping the Vermont Haus Inn. My body went limp at the thought of what she would say next. The day she screamed at me about Gracie pooping in the dining room was minor compared to this and all I wanted to do was sprint out of that kitchen. The fact that she spoke to Rolf in English instead of German told me that her comments were intended for all ears.

Mary Jule had been helping me with the seating chart for the evening when the embittered Sergeant stormed into the kitchen. Since it was a holiday weekend, Memorial Day, we had eighty dinner reservations already for each night. I had painstakingly mapped out both the 6:00 P.M. and 8:00 P.M. table sittings with regard to where each customer would sit, trying my best not to give Helga any other reason to be annoyed.

Mary Jule pinched me right above my elbow when she got her first look at Helga Schloygin. We'd been pinching each other since the third grade. I pinched her right back to acknowledge her uneasiness, and leaned in closer to her, pressing my arm against hers for protection. Helga marched right up to me, unflicked cigarette in her hand, never bothering to acknowledge Mary Jule.

"Hi, Helga, how was your trip?" I said, almost trembling. My tiny bit of hope, that she might consider the transformation a plus, had completely vanished.

"It *was* vedy good, but unfortunately all dat good is ov'a," she said, seething like a pot ready to explode. She lifted her reading glasses from the chain around her neck to her nose. That movement caused her ashes to drop and I watched as they splattered and then dissolved into the ice that was in a bucket on the floor next to the bar. "First things first. Vhat have you done vis my hippo collection?"

"My friend Virginia packed it up and she has it all ready for you. Just a minute and I'll go get it," I said, and hurried out the door. Mary Jule trailed right along behind me. There was no way she was going to be left behind to face that woman alone. *What must Peter think!* I had never warned him about the tension between Helga and me and now it was worse than before she left.

Mary Jule resembled a frightened teen in a Freddy Krueger movie as we pushed past the six-top table and ran for cover in my apartment. Sarah and Issie were upstairs with Mandy watching cartoons. Alice was in front of the mirror in the bathroom and Virginia had my makeup mirror propped up on my dresser in the sitting room with a chair pulled up to it. Both were primping for opening night.

"Virginia, where are Helga's hippos?" I cried. "She's having a stroke. I told y'all she would be furious. Now what am I gonna do?" I paced around the apartment, frantic.

"They're right there," she said, and pointed to a stack of boxes in the corner. H'S HIPS was scribbled in big black letters on the side of the box.

"She's scary," said Mary Jule. "Poor Fiery, I see exactly what she means; Helga is the Wicked Witch. Bless your heart, Leelee, I feel so sorry for you."

"Now wait just a second. Be calm, both of you. What can she really do to us?" Alice said, as she stepped out of the bathroom. "I'm not that scared of her—just give her back her stupid hippos! Follow me, Leelee." She grabbed the box of neatly packed away hippopotami and led the way to the kitchen.

Virginia and Mary Jule tagged along, too, not wanting to miss a potential showdown. If there is one thing my friends love, it's watching a confrontation, any confrontation, as long as it has nothing to do with them. Here's a secret about my friends. Not a one of them would have had the nerve to confront Helga alone. As a group, we'd always been able to do anything. Roll a teacher's house, back up a tall tale told to a parent, create an alibi for each other, or even assume each other's identities. I fired Mary Jule's housekeeper for her once over a three-way telephone call. I just said I was her. I'd never have been able to do that if Mary Jule hadn't been secretly on the phone with me or if I had had to say I was really Leelee.

Alice, chicken all of a sudden, made me go in first once we got to the kitchen door, claiming it was the least I could do since she was the one holding the hippos.

The two of us approached Helga, with great trepidation of course, while she was slicing lemons for her bar garnish. "Helga, I'd like for you to meet my best friends from home," I said as nice as I could, "Alice, Virginia, and Mary Jule."

"I'll take zat," Helga said, and snatched the box out of Alice's arms before she had a chance to hand it over.

"Sure," Alice said anxiously. The foreboding sight of Helga frightened even her.

Helga shoved the box under the sink and went straight back to her bar prep—never acknowledging my friends. All four of us slinked back to the apartment.

"I can't go back in there," I told my friends. "See how mean she is to me? I can't stand that woman!"

"I am totally in shock, is all I have to say," Virginia said, and handed a bottle of wine she had snuck out of the basement over to me to open. None of them had a clue how to properly open a wine bottle. They tried, but their efforts always ended in broken corks. *At least I've mastered this*, I thought, as I popped the cork right out.

"I say we should just ignore her. We don't have to speak to her, either. What can she do to us? Spank us? Scream at us? So what if she never talks to us, I couldn't care less," Virginia said. She took the bottle of chardonnay out of my hands and poured us each a glass.

"All *I* know is, I don't know what I'd do if y'all weren't here tonight," I said, and held my glass up to toast my closest friends.

All the rooms in the inn were full with guests from all over the New England area. The phone had been ringing feverishly for days. Many of the old customers were coming back in town for Memorial Day. *Why?* I wondered. *It's not the least bit warm. There are still no leaves on the trees and only crocuses and a daffodil or two have even started blooming. Why would anyone want to visit this time of year? To mud wrestle? Eat weeds?*

When my friends and I walked into the kitchen around 5:30 P.M. on opening night, ready to work and decked out to the nines, we looked more like we were arriving for a cocktail party. All of us wore heels and pretty cocktail dresses. The waitstaff at the Vermont Haus Inn wore black pants or skirts and white shirts. None of my friends thought to pack restaurant uniforms, but I'm sure they wouldn't have worn them anyway. Helga was on the phone next to the makeshift bar on top of the washing machine when we walked in. She looked up at us and sneered before returning to the reservation book.

Jeb took one look at the girls and about had a stroke. His mouth dropped open and his eyes followed them every step they took around the kitchen.

Virginia couldn't help herself. She had to get Jeb to show her how the big Hobart dishwasher worked.

She strolled right up to where he stood in front of the Hobart. "Look at you, Jayeb. If you aren't something else."

He just beamed, God bless him.

"Oooooh, Jayeb," Alice said, jumping in with Virginia, "I am mighty impressed with you, sugar. Just look at you with all those big pots and pans. We are all *fascinated* by the way that big machine runs. Can you show us how it works?"

"Yuup." Jeb proudly demonstrated for the girls how he arranged the dirty pots on the rack. He then slid the rack inside the washer and gave the big arm, which let down a door and started the cycle, a hardy push. "Not much to it," Jeb said, and wiped his hands together after the cycle had begun. The boy was wrapped around their baby fingers.

After that, every time the girls would come in the kitchen, Jeb would overemphasize the way he pressed down the big arm and look over at them, whistling "Whistle While You Work." Jeb was a brand-new man. He had three Southern belles making all over him. My friends justified their mercy flirting by saying, "We're only helping him. Think how popular he thinks he is now. We've changed his whole life."

Pierre Lebel can be one charming guy. When I introduced him to the girls it was obvious he, too, was goo-goo-eyed. I caught him out front in the fireplace room as he was filling a sugar jar.

"Pierre, my . . . best . . . friends . . . from . . . home . . . want . . . to . . . meet . . . you," I said slowly, and pointed at them and then back over to him.

"Ahhh, *bonjour, mesdames*," he said with a huge grin, and then got down on one knee. He kissed each of their right hands one at a time. As fate would have it, Helga happened to be rounding the corner at that very second. Once he caught sight of her his whole demeanor changed. He scrambled back up straight and his eyes filled with dread. "*Eh, pardon, mesdames.*" Pierre bowed, and scurried off to one of the dining rooms. Helga smirked at us in disgust but went on out front to rearrange the menus.

Pierre took great pride in his position as maître d', an honored profession in France. Before the customers arrived for the evening Pierre had quite a bit of "side work" to do. Making sure there was plenty of chilled white wine and cold beer for the evening was number one on Pierre's prep list. He and Kerri were in charge of setting the tables and making sure there were glasses for both red and white wine on each table. "That encourages wine sales," Baker once told me. Each table had to have fresh flowers and the salt and pepper shakers and sugar jars were to be filled to the top. The art of napkin folding was Pierre's pleasure. He painstakingly spent time designing a beautiful work of art that he twisted and folded into a creation that stood tall atop each plate.

The restaurant business was just as foreign to the girls as it had been to me, but they thought working there for a night or two would be a riot. They really wanted to help Pierre and take the orders but I assured them that Helga wouldn't stand for it. After our earlier confrontation, they could see why following her rules wasn't such a bad idea. Upon meeting the Sergeant in person, Alice had to let go of her dream of "fill-in bartender for a night."

The first dinner reservation of the evening was always at 6:00 and the restaurant was usually full by 6:30. Occasionally we would take a 5:30 "res" but that was rare. Most people didn't like to go out to eat that early anyway. Our second sitting was around 8:00 or 8:30. It's the period of time between the two sittings that can become quite hectic, even chaotic on the extremely busy weekends. That's when we had to "turn the tables," as they say in the restaurant business. The tablecloths had to be changed and the tables reset after the first party left and before the second party arrived.

We had it all planned. As hostess, I would be seating the customers and helping with turning the tables. Mary Jule would assist me, and Alice and Virginia were going to help Kerri and the other food runner, Jonathan. On a really busy night, we normally had to employ three extra people to deliver the food and bus (clear) the tables. The runners also filled water glasses and helped me with resetting the tables for the second sitting, so this job was most important.

We had a numbering system for each table. I drew out a seating chart for my friends and posted it in the wait station leading out into the restaurant so they would know exactly where to deliver each meal.

"Piece of cake," Virginia whispered to me early on in the evening as I walked by her on my way to table ten with four customers. "I'm not in the least bit worried. Pierre and I are like this," she said, and held up two fingers.

Virginia and Alice spent most of their time chatting with the customers instead of running food. Kerri and Jonathan ended up doing most of that. The girls loved filling the water glasses for people. When the customers would ask them about something on the menu, they interjected their two cents' worth, even though they hadn't the slightest idea. "The veal is to die for but the head cheese, I wouldn't touch that with a ten-foot pole," Virginia told one group of customers. When Alice delivered a bottle of wine to one of the tables and began opening it, she got so frustrated that she handed it to one of the men at the table and said, "I'm not that sure how to do this, would you be a love and show me how it's done?" If Helga had seen that, the earth may have split open.

Their accents opened the door for conversation about the new look of the Vermont Haus Inn. Many of the customers commented on the changes and how lovely the place looked. "Don't you think the inn looks so much better?" I heard Virginia say. "We're Leelee's best friends from home. We surprised her to help decorate and get this place *southernized*."

I knew Helga couldn't stand it that my friends were socializing with her customers, but what was she going to do? There were three of them and only one of her. Helga managed to hold her tongue but I suspected there was a storm brewing on the inside.

The restaurant was crazy busy that opening night. Pierre was running around as usual and before long I noticed that his coffee cup was back on top of the fridge. I never once saw him refill it. For the life of me I couldn't figure out how he did it when no one was watching. I expected the poor thing to be soused by the end of dinner. God knows I couldn't blame him. Twenty years of Helga would be enough to send anyone "down cellar."

At one point in the evening, I caught Roberta on her way to the dry storage room in the basement and followed her down. "What's going on? How is Helga treating Peter?" I asked her.

"Okay, I s'pose. She asked him who he was and when he told her 'the new sous-chef,' she didn't even seem surprised. Then she asked him where he had worked before. I'm sure she was impressed. The Wild Duck has quite a reputation."

"So she's being civil to him?"

"Why, sure she is. Why wouldn't she be? She can't blame Peter for Baker's mistake."

"I know, but she hasn't said a word to my friends. I was just curious. I'm worried she'll do something to make Peter want to quit."

"I wouldn't worry about a thing. Peter seems like he can handle just about anything. He and Rolf have been shooting the breeze all night. You concentrate on having fun with your girlfriends."

When the evening finally wound down, I felt a tremendous sense of relief. Peter was doing an excellent job and my friends certainly, if nothing else, livened up the place. I was feeling good, so good that I got up my nerve to venture into the kitchen, just as the staff was wiping down their stations. Mary Jule, who had been stuck like glue to my side all night, tagged right along with me. As soon as we walked in I heard Issie crying on the baby monitor. I told Mary Jule I'd be right back, and hurried off to the apartment.

Once inside, I saw Mandy had already gotten to Issie. She only wanted me though, so I held her in my arms and rocked her back to sleep. Just as I was sneaking out of her bedroom and closing the door behind me, the apartment door blasted open. Mary Jule was frantic.

"What is it? What's wrong?" I asked her.

"Stay right here and *don't move*." She grabbed me by the shoulders. "I'll be right back with Alice and Virginia."

Mary Jule never talks that way to me. She was so upset, for a moment she had me worried I'd done something wrong. Too anxious to sit, I walked around in circles wondering what in the world had happened. I slipped into the bathroom and nervously fluffed my hair in the mirror and put on some lipstick while I waited for my friends to show up.

When she finally made it back, Mary Jule was crazed. So were Virginia and Alice, who were not happy about being yanked away during the middle of a conversation with the last table of lingering guests. But the devastated look on Mary Jule's face told us all that the urgent news she had was dire.

"Y'all are gonna *die*," she said. "And I mean *die*."

"What in the world is it?" Alice asked impatiently.

"I gotta sit down." Mary Jule slowly steadied herself onto the wicker love seat outside my bedroom. Virginia and I crammed in on either side of her. Alice grabbed the floor and put her hand on Mary Jule's knee.

"Tell us," Alice commanded.

"*Okay.*" Mary Jule gets frustrated at Alice when she rushes her. "I'm trying to remember all this from the beginning." She let out a big sigh before continuing and held her face in her hands for a few seconds.

"I overheard Helga talking to Pierre in French." Mary Jule, the most intelligent of our group, spent her junior year abroad at the Sorbonne and is nearly fluent. "She spoke so fast it was hard to understand her, but I got the gist of it anyway."

"Go on," I said.

"She started out by saying that she thinks we all look like *idiots* working in a restaurant in our nice dresses and high heels."

All of us gasped for air on that statement alone.

"And she's mad as hell that there are three more just like you, Leelee."

I had that figured out already, but just imagine for a moment how disgusted we all felt at hearing it. We glanced at one another in outrage before urging Mary Jule to keep going.

"Then, she told Pierre that she never thought she'd come home and find you still here. She thought you would have gone home right away when Baker left you."

"She knew about Baker leaving?" I asked.

"It gets so much worse and I don't even know if I can say it, it's so bad." Mary Jule placed her hand on her heart, paused for a few seconds, and finally said, "Helga set you up."

"What do you mean, set me up?" I felt heat rising to my head and my heart starting to pound.

"She planned the whole thing with Baker and the fifty-year-old."

"*YOU'RE LYING!!*" Virginia yelled.

"Oh God, how do you know? What'd she say?" I felt the blood leaving my head.

"Helga told Pierre that she knew Barb Thurmond was looking for an operations manager for her resort and that she had told Barb all about Baker and that he'd be perfect for the job. Helga also told the fifty-year-old—and I hate, *hate* even repeating this—that Baker was married to a weak, mousy girl and that he was very unhappy." She said the last part really fast as if she couldn't even bear to hear herself repeat it.

Hearing her words made me shiver and that familiar sinking feeling returned to the pit of my stomach. I couldn't remember a time in my life when anything close to this had ever happened to me.

"Then what did she say?" Alice wanted to know.

"I'm thinking." Poor Mary Jule was so shaken up, it pained her to continue.

"Try and remember everything, Mary Jule, try," Virginia told her.

"I'm *trying*; I'm just so upset that I can hardly think straight. Oh yeah, Helga also said that she is furious about all the changes you made around here while she was gone. I'm sorry, Leelee, that's *our* fault." She glared over at the other two. Virginia and Alice rolled their eyes when Mary Jule tried to pass the buck.

"Helga wrapped it up by saying something like: 'She cannot make changes. If she does, there won't be any customers left and you won't have any tips.' Then she said: 'Trust me, Pierre, she will fail, and I'll get my inn back and you'll have your pension back. Then, we'll be free of her.' Or something to that effect."

Four hundred more collective gasps for air later, Alice spoke up. "It's a good thing we decided to come here and it was an even better decision to redecorate. It made her mad enough at you to dig her own grave."

"I thought Pierre was my friend. It really makes me sad to think he would turn on me like that."

"I guess Helga's his better friend. They must be good friends, Leelee. Why else would she confide in him?" Virginia said.

"I don't know, but it looks like you're right. God, when will this night-mare end? I'm going home with y'all. Can we leave right now?"

"I would love nothin' more than to take you home right now, seriously I would. I hate to tell you, friend, but it's showtime. You have no other choice but to fire the bitch," Virginia said.

"*Fire* her." I couldn't even imagine such a thing.

All three of them, in unison, yelled, "Yes!"

"I can't do that." I closed my eyes and jittered in my seat.

"Oh yes you can," Alice insisted.

"You can and you will. You have to, Leelee. There's no other way. This woman has not only thwarted everything you've tried to do over the last five months, but now she's responsible for introducing Baker to another *woman*!" Virginia's voice climbed ten decibels when she said "woman."

Anger started to rumble around in my stomach and I could feel the heat climbing up my insides and to my head. *Screw you, Baker, for leaving me to wipe up your nasty mess.*

Virginia leaned in closer to me. "I would do it now. Why would you want her to ever step a toe in your house again?"

"I don't *ever* want her back here. But . . . will you do it for me, Alice?" I said it half kidding, half serious.

"Yeah, will you do it for her?" Mary Jule asked Alice on my behalf.

"It's not that I would mind doing it for you. But that is not gonna work with her. You have to be the one to do it. Now's the perfect time. We'll be right there with you," Alice said. "If you put it off, you might lose your nerve."

As much as I dreaded it, I knew somewhere way, way down deep that they were right. "I know you're right, and I'm gonna do it, I swear. But I just don't know *how* to do it."

Mary Jule stood up. "Just tell her you won't be needing her services anymore, thank you very much."

"Tell her to get the hell out of your house *immediately*," Alice said.

"You are so full of it, Alice—like you'd really say that to anyone," Mary Jule teased.

"Rolf's gonna quit when I fire her. There's no way he'll work here anymore," I told them.

"So what? Peter can take over. He can handle it. I've been watching him; he's working much harder than Rolf anyway," Virginia said.

"Maybe I ought to warn him first."

"Forget it; he'll be fine," she said, and rubbed my knee.

Again, a flash of fury engulfed me and I tensed under its grip. Fear followed and I closed my eyes and leaned back in my seat. I didn't want to have to do it. "I am *so mad*. But even more I'm scared to face her."

"I know you're scared," Virginia said. "And I don't blame you, but we're with you, honey."

"The longer you put it off, the harder it'll be. You can do it." Alice took my hand and pulled me up out of the love seat.

"Okay. But can't we do it tomorrow?"

"Absolutely not," Alice said. "We have to do it right now."

All four of us took a deep breath and locked hands as we started toward the kitchen. I couldn't help falling behind as the caboose, relishing the final seconds before I had to face off with Helga. *Face off with Helga?* I'd never faced off with anyone, much less a six-foot-tall German woman with a strong personality.

It seemed like a mile-long walk from my apartment to the kitchen. Time slowed to a crawl as everything I had been through these last six months flooded my mind. I never wanted to move to Vermont in the first place. I just packed up my stuff and moved to a remote corner of the world because of a man—a man whom I had loved so long that I couldn't remember what it was like to kiss another. It struck me that for every time I had ever wondered how my life would've played out had I never met Baker Satterfield, nothing could've prepared me for this. No matter how much my life to this point was a result of his influence, his desires, his idea of how things should be (including me), it was changed forever in the brief time it took to read his letter.

I was trying to be a good wife and support my husband—and where did it get me? Absolutely nowhere. He wasn't supportive of *me*. He up and left me to run a Vermont inn and take care of our children all by myself while he ran off to ski seven days a week. And this witch of a German bitch, *my mortgage holder*, was responsible. It was Helga Schloygin who set the whole thing up. And furthermore, she'd been bossing me around in my own home ever since I arrived in Vermont. The more I thought about it all, the more furious I became until I was completely enraged . . . *at last*!

Out of nowhere, my anxiety vanished and a new resolve descended upon me, propelling me into the kitchen. Past Alice, past Mary Jule, and past Virginia I paraded—right up to Helga, who was wiping down the liquor bottles with a bar towel. Sensing the swiftness with which I made my beeline toward her, she chose not to look up.

"Helga Schloygin, who do you think you are?" *I* demanded to know.

She still refused to look at me. Her cig hung from the side of her mouth as she turned and feverishly stacked her liquor bottles back on the shelves above her.

"Did you hear me, Helga? I asked you who do you think you are? *How. Dare. You?*" I said, without one ounce of fear. (I'd always fantasized saying that to someone.) "How *dare you*," I repeated (just to hear myself say it again), "introduce my husband to another woman? What have I ever done to you that would make you stoop so low as to intentionally try and break up my marriage?" I was pointing my finger straight at her, now breaking a cardinal rule of Southern etiquette. "Maybe it never occurred to you, but you're not the only person here who can speak to Pierre. My dear friend Mary Jule spent a year at the Sorbonne!"

I didn't look behind me but that statement may have sent Mary Jule flying back to the apartment.

Still, Helga tried to ignore me. Once she finished with the liquor bottles she began busying herself on the calculator in an attempt to total the dinner checks. I continued to stare at her in silence.

Helga suddenly tried to escape but I stepped in her path. "Don't think for a minute you can walk away from me. What's wrong, Helga? Do you not want the whole world to know that you're the cause of my husband leaving? We have two little girls together."

At last she spoke, wryly, still not having the decency to look me in the eye. "I am not ze cause. You are your own cause." Her nasty cigarette still dangled from her lips.

The old Leelee would have run off in tears right about now but the new Leelee tore out of the corner of the boxing ring. "No, I am not! I have been a good wife to him. Maybe I've had a hard time adjusting to this freezing cold winter wasteland, but I have done nothing to you. Baker Satterfield may be a low-down dirty rotten jerk but you are worse. I've wanted to tell you what I think of you for five months and until five minutes ago I never thought I'd get the nerve. But you've plopped yourself on my *last* nerve for the *last* time, Helga Schloygin. YOU ARE FIRED." By now I was up on my tippy toes, shrieking like a banshee.

Absolute silence fell upon the room. Not a sound, not a movement, not a clink of a glass nor a clank of a plate could be heard—nothing except the pounding of my heart. Everyone in the kitchen was perfectly still. Mary Jule, Alice, and Virginia were on one side staring at me in utter disbelief and the people that I'd only known a few months were on the other side, equally shocked. I stood there in the middle, dumbfounded myself.

The furrow in between Helga's eyes deepened and because she wore her hair slicked back in a tight bun, her ears were in plain view. They looked as though they could blow steam at any moment, they were so red. Her face became even more crimson and she started shaking, as if she might spontaneously combust. But what could she say? She was caught and she knew it.

No one noticed Gracie slink into the kitchen. In our haste, one of us must have left the apartment door open by mistake, and upon hearing my voice, she snuck into the room while I was delivering my emancipation speech. She had a payback plan of her own.

Gracie slipped up to Helga and grabbed ahold of one of her pants legs with her tiny teeth. Breaking the silence, Gracie growled and shook her head from side to side while she tugged on the witch's navy trousers. That infuriated the Sergeant and she raised her leg and shook it, lifting Princess Grace up off the floor. Pierre, who had been nervously sipping on his coffee cup the whole time I was firing Helga, came to Gracie's rescue and bent down to get her loose.

Once he separated Gracie from Helga and put her safely back on the floor, Helga tried to kick her. But Princess Grace Kelly was too quick. She started racing around the kitchen, lickety-split, with Helga right behind her. After darting around, under the cooking line and in and out below the deep chrome sinks, my little Yorkie dashed back out of the kitchen.

In defeat, Helga grabbed her purse and muttered something in German to Rolf, who stood at the stove, flabbergasted. He tore off his apron, threw it down on the floor, and both of them stormed toward the back exit. Before the screened door had a chance to slam behind them, the Sergeant turned around and charged back inside with a ghastly scowl that would have frightened even her, had there been a mirror in the kitchen.

This is it, I thought, *she's gonna knock me down*. Instead she stormed over to the bar, slightly slipping on something, and bent down to grab her beloved hippos. The box had been pushed far enough under the bar that Helga had to crawl on all fours to scoot it back out. When she bent over it was clear Gracie must have left her a going-away present. The bottom of Helga's right navy flat had Princess poop smashed all over it. When she stood up she started sniffing the air and lifted each foot to get a look at the soles of her feet.

"Zat, zat, *mutt*, I vill kill it!" she yelled, as she took off her shoe. "Vhere is it?"

"NEVA MIND!" Rolf cried out from the back door in his booming voice. And Helga limped toward him, madder than a hornet, one shoe on and one shoe off.

When the door finally slammed behind them, the silence returned and hung thick in the air. Once again, all eyes were on me. My fear crept back in like an old demon returning to its roost. Overcome with angst and doubt, I wanted to run away and hide. I wanted to turn around and run as fast as my legs could carry me. I wanted to take my friends, my little girls, and my Gracie and hitchhike if I had to, all the way back to Memphis, Tennessee, right that instant.

"You fired her," Jeb said.

"She's gone," Roberta muttered, as though she, too, was in a state of shock.

Pierre made the sign of the cross on his heart and muttered, "Ay yi yi."

Kerri and Jonathan just stood there with their mouths hanging open. Peter stared at the floor and my best friends remained still, silent, stunned.

Maybe the Vermonters don't believe me, I thought. *Perhaps they think I made the whole thing up.* I knew all too well of their loyalty to Rolf and Helga. Pierre, Jeb, and Roberta were twenty-year veterans at the Vermont Haus Inn. They had pension plans and paid vacations. They even had their health insurance covered by the Schloygins.

"I'm sorry," I said, as sincerely as I could, turning around to face them. I'd held back my tears long enough, and they sprung forth like a bubbling brook. "But she left me no choice. She introduced Baker to Barb Thurmond on purpose."

An awkward moment of silence was followed by a miraculous turn. Everyone standing on the opposing side of the kitchen broke into applause. They cheered and whooped and they hollered paying homage to *me*! Each and every person wore a smile that could have lit the inn on fire. Jeb put two fingers up to his mouth and whistled in a high-pitched tone.

Roberta hooked arms with Jeb and the two began do-si-doing right in front of the Hobart. Pierre, happy to finally have a communicative comrade, grabbed Mary Jule's arm and waltzed her around the room. Virginia and Alice paired up to do-si-do, Kerri and Jonathan jumped in to jitterbug. And that left Peter and me. He shrugged his shoulders as if to say, I'm not sure what just happened here, but smiled and locked arms with me anyway. As we fumbled our way through an extemporaneous two-step, I felt so connected with Peter. He was cheery, easy to get along with, and, above all, fun.

A hoedown of happiness was going on in the kitchen of the newly named Peach Blossom Inn and I believe I was the happiest person of all.

Pierre escaped down cellar and emerged a jubilant man with as many bottles of champagne as he could carry. Alice popped open the first bottle and as it spilled onto the floor she exclaimed, "Hey, y'all, ding-dong the bitch is *gaawn!*" Jeb started right in with a whistling rendition of "Ding-Dong the Witch Is Dead," and for the first time since I'd first heard him whistle, I could have thrown my arms around his neck and kissed him. Corks were popping, glasses were toasting, and the champagne was bubbling.

The one and only problem with firing Helga was now I had no head chef. I was hoping Peter would want the position so once the partying died down, I motioned to him to follow me out to the dining room. I didn't even ask him to sit down, I started right in as soon as we entered the room. "You must be wondering what in the world you've gotten yourself into." By now, and thanks to the alcohol, I felt comfortable around him.

He got a cute look on his face and smiled. "Well, I won't need to browse the drama section at the video store any longer. That's for sure."

I reached out and touched him on the shoulder. "Was it that bad? That was not the normal me back there. I swear. But that woman deliberately broke up my marriage."

"Hey, I'm not criticizing you. You were great. I just wish I had it on tape to send to that Jerry Springer guy."

Right about then the girls rounded the corner, laughing, glowing, and more than just a little tipsy.

"Leelee Satterfield, I am speechless," Virginia said, and raised her glass. "You have blown my ever-loving mind." It would be a million years before Virginia would get over my new personality.

"I can't believe that was you talking back there. *Honey*. You have changed," Mary Jule said. "I'm so jealous." She looked over at Peter. "She's the best."

"There is no way in hell I could have ever done that. It was the performance of a lifetime. I am so proud of you." Alice reached over to hug me and when she did, a little of her drink spilled down my back.

"Y'all, hush," I said. "We might scare Peter away and I have something very important to ask him." I turned toward him. "So, it looks like I've got an opening for a head chef. How would you feel about taking over?" When I asked him I kind of openly winced like I was afraid of what he might say. "I can pay you what Rolf was getting. That's six hundred dollars per week."

"Are you kidding? I'm thrilled to have the opportunity." Peter genuinely seemed thrilled. I could tell by the way his nose flared slightly and the deep breath he took before exhaling what appeared to be a sigh of relief.

Alice took him by the hand and dragged him all around the down-stairs, pointing out all the glorious changes we had made. The rest of us followed right behind while Mary Jule explained our plans to change the name to the Peach Blossom Inn. Virginia told him all about the special peach desserts we wanted to add to the menu and Alice threw in her plan to make peach daiquiris the summer specialty of the house. I floated along with them, not really saying much, but feeling so fabulous and peaceful inside. Even if it were only temporary, my spirit seemed to be at rest.

"I've got a toast," Peter announced, once we had settled down at the round table in the palm tree dining room. He lifted his champagne glass and extended it right over to me. "To the boss. A real Dixie peach!"

Brassy cheers exploded from the other Dixie peaches and each clumsily leaned over from where she sat to make sure her own flute tapped Peter's.

Me, a boss? Before Peter left that night, we each took turns hugging him. When my turn came, I wanted to really embrace him to let him know how much I appreciated his help, but I gave him a light squeeze instead. *Peter is the nicest guy*, I thought. *God must have surely sent him to rescue me.*

I fell into bed that night going back over, again and again, what had happened in the hours before. Had I actually said "how dare you" to someone, much less *Helga*? And the hot fudge was I fired her! I really and truly had the nerve, on my own, to fire Helga Schloygin. *How great is that? I am not the same person I was five months ago*, I thought. I never, ever would have had the nerve to say any of the things I did if my daddy were still alive. He would have done it for me. And after that, Baker *kind of* did it for me. I knew one thing for sure. I liked the new me.

The Peach Blossom Inn might just have a chance. For the first time thoughts of home didn't engulf my mind before I fell asleep.

Chapter Sixteen

Best friends can and should be counted on for all kinds of things. Especially revenge. Most particularly in predicaments where a grief-stricken wife is incapable of eyeing her way through the dense amount of stuff that tends to clutter the mind—and the closet. In that case a best friend should have twenty-twenty vision.

"I can't look at this another minute," Virginia said as soon as she opened her eyes and caught another glimpse of my closet. "We're getting his crap out of here *today*." She jumped out of bed with far too much oomph for someone who had been drinking champagne the night before.

"I never doubted for a second that you would let it rest." I grabbed my head but never opened my eyes. "I have a horrible headache, Virginia. How can you be so gung ho this early?"

"Because, today's the day you are gonna finally wash Baker Satterfield out of your life altogether. Get up right this minute and let's go upstairs and wake up Alice and Mary Jule." She banged her toe trying to get around the bed, and yelled, "Ouch!"

"Uhhhhh. I hate this room." Reluctantly, I dragged myself out of bed and wearily pulled on my jeans and a sweater. After grabbing the baby monitor, Virginia and I headed up the stairs.

Once we had the other two awake, Virginia detailed for all of us her plan to get back at Baker. Mary Jule loved it. Alice really loved it and I—the new I—even thought it was Virginia's finest to date. Despite their throbbing heads, Alice and Mary Jule got so excited they sprung out of their beds.

"Coffee," Alice said, "I need, I need."

"What *I* need is at least three Cokes. And there better be plenty of cold ones," Virginia said, looking straight at me.

"You're wondering if *I* have cold Coca-Colas? Who do you think you're talking to?"

"Maybe Helga snuck in during the night and stole them from you, Fiery. I don't know," Virginia said. "Plus I'm starving. What's for breakfast?"

"Breakfast! *Aaaahhhhh*, I forgot all about breakfast. I fired Helga last night." Rolf was the breakfast chef, and it didn't take much to figure out that he probably wasn't in the kitchen flipping pancakes.

We all ran down the stairs and found Pierre behind the cooking line in the kitchen, frantically beating eggs for omelets. Little droplets of sweat made his upper lip glisten and his crimson face glowed next to the heat of the stove. I could only imagine the beating his head must have taken after all the alcohol he had consumed the night before. His smile let me know he was relieved to see us.

Here we had a house full of guests who had paid for bed and breakfast and the maître d' was cooking the food and delivering it to the tables. Pierre instructed Mary Jule to have us help with the orders out front and she could assist him with the cooking. So while the Frenchies held it together in the back, Virginia, Alice, and I took care of the front—*without* Helga breathing down our backs. For the first time since moving there, I actually enjoyed working at the inn.

Right after the breakfast rush was over and the kitchen was tidied up, Virginia enlisted Jeb, Pierre, and Roberta as temporary detectives of the GK Agency. She had all of us follow her into my apartment.

"Okay, everyone, here's the deal," Virginia said, gathering us around in the sitting room. "Baker's rotten clothes have been stinking up Leelee's closet long enough. I want everyone to grab as much as you can hold in your arms and head on out to Jeb's truck. We're gonna deliver this junk to Baker personally at his new job, which he obviously thinks is far more important than anything or anyone here." (It didn't take much for Virginia to sweet-talk Jeb into using his truck. I'm sure he'd have moved to Tennessee to become her personal houseboy if she'd have only asked.)

We loaded as much of Baker's junk as could fit into Jeb's truck and the girls' rental car. Both vehicles were filled to the brim with all of his clothes, shoes, UT stuff, trophies, fishing equipment, Bill Dance videos, yearbooks, old toiletries, and every bit of his stupid sports paraphernalia.

Powder Mountain was a forty-five-minute drive from Willingham. Jeb knew exactly how to get there so with Alice and Virginia seated right next to him, he led the way to the resort. Mary Jule, Roberta, Pierre, and I followed behind in the rental car with me at the wheel. For the first time, Pierre knew exactly what was going on, thanks to Mary Jule. It certainly felt nice to have an interpreter.

When we drove into Powder Resort, I saw immediately that it was by no means a Sugartree, or a Dannon Mountain for that matter. It was okay looking, but the 1960s, semi-modern exterior eluded the charm of most ski resorts. I was not impressed. Although snow could only be seen in patches on the mountain, the chairlifts were operating for sight-seeing.

As we pulled up in front of the base lodge, Virginia jumped out and dashed back to our car, motioning for me to roll down the window.

"Turn on your hazard lights. Let's leave the cars here while we unload." She tapped the door with her hand. "Hop out." Virginia hurried back to Jeb's truck and let down the tailgate. She jumped up and stood in the middle of the truck bed. Keeping her voice down she instructed all of us, "Pile up as much as you possibly can." She started scooping up Baker's clothes and dumping them, pile by pile, into everyone's arms. "Leelee, you carry the tackle box, and this big trash bag of his shoes."

When we were all loaded down in garb and barely able to see over the top, Virginia scooped up as much as she could hold herself and jumped down. Leading the way, she headed for the front door of the base lodge.

Virginia turned around backward once she got to the door, pushed it open with her butt, and held the door as the rest of us walked past her to the lobby inside.

"Which way to the chairlift, please?" Virginia stopped to ask someone wearing a green Powder Mountain T-shirt.

"Straight out that door," the young guy told us and pointed toward two heavy side-by-side metal doors. The bewildered look on his face was priceless.

"Thank you, darlin'," she said.

We passed tourists taking pictures, others simply strolling around enjoying the scenery, and several kids on skateboards. We passed all kinds of people who were staring us up and down. Virginia just pushed ahead, like she owned the joint.

Undaunted, she marched right up to the chairlift. "'Scuse us, 'scuse us." The few people standing in line to board obediently stepped back to let all from the GK Agency on through. She pushed her way right alongside where the next four-seater would pause, and as it rounded the base of the mountain she looked over at the rest of us and said, "Okay, y'all—one, two, *three!*" Then she leaned over and flung Baker's clothes into a big messy pile all over the seats. Proud as punch, she turned around to the rest of us and gestured back toward the lift. "Everybody, *let loose!*"

Everyone tossed the clothes they had been carrying onto the next few chairlifts and I dumped out the trash bag of shoes on one chair and placed Baker's tackle box on the next. Right beside it I placed my brand-new Christmas present from Baker. *They're all yours, Barb Thurmond.* All of us watched in triumph as the four chairs containing Baker's expensive suits, Brooks Brothers shirts, shoes, jeans, underwear, T-shirts, and my big ugly boots rode the incline up the mountain.

Items began to fall off as the chairs traveled all the way up. We stood there gloating in the thrill of it all as the first few T-shirts floated to the ground. Some of the hangers caught on the chair handles and Baker's clothes looked like they were hung out to dry. His freshly starched oxford cloth dress shirts blew in the wind before a few slowly cascaded down onto the muddy ground below.

"Just look at 'em go, woohoo," Virginia yelled. She shuffled her feet and snapped her fingers like she was doing a little jig. "Bet you wish you'd never left this stuff behind, don't you, Baker Satterfield?"

I had opened the top to Baker's new tackle box before placing it on the chairlift. One by one, Baker's beloved flies soared out. Caught by the wind, they floated through the air before disappearing altogether. I was caught up in the moment and excited along with everyone, but somewhere deep inside my heart zinged.

The other folks in line stopped getting on the lift. I suppose our show was much more exciting than the view atop Powder Mountain.

"Ooops. Guess you and your *old lady* will have to walk around picking all this stuff up. What's wrong, Baker? Embarrassed your underwear is flying through the air? I sure hope it's clean," Virginia yelled, having the time of her life.

"Hope your new Yankee life is worth every minute of it, Baker," Mary Jule said, and laughed out loud.

We all giggled hysterically, relishing the thrill of naughty revenge. Jeb just laughed and laughed right along with us, so incredibly happy to be "in" with our group.

"Payback's hell, idn't it, Baker Satterfield," Alice yelled, cupping her hands on the sides of her mouth.

Roberta even got into it and hollered, "Maybe this'll teach you!" After she said it she looked around at all of us for approval.

"Yeah! Oooooh, Roberta, I like your style." Alice reached over and took ahold of Roberta's hand and lifted both their arms up over their heads. "Go, Roberta."

By this time we had drawn a crowd. I saw one lady run up and start taking pictures of Baker's clothes riding up the mountain. I suppose the young employees running the chairlift were intimidated by us, because they never challenged our right to be there. It's not like we were destroying the property or anything. I suppose we were littering if you want to get technical about it, but we never actually defaced ol' fake face's property at all.

Once the last chair holding Baker's clothes disappeared from sight, we all turned around to leave. Just as we started to walk away, the crowd that had gathered to observe us broke into applause. Jeb soaked up the attention and held his arms up in a "check out my muscles" kind of way and bowed to the crowd. I overheard this one lady turn to her husband and say, "Now that's what I call payback, and don't think I wouldn't do the same thing to you, mister, if *you* ever try something stupid."

When we got back to our vehicles, we still had boxes, all the fishing gear, and other odds and ends left in the bed of Jeb's truck. Virginia's plan didn't stop at the chairlift, though. Oh no, there was plenty more up the girl's sleeve. She told us to get back in and move our cars over to the Powder Mountain welcome sign. Once again we followed Virginia's lead and started stacking the rest of Baker's junk up in front of the sign. Pierre jammed the handles of the fishing poles into the muddy ground so they all stood straight up. Jeb stacked all the boxes as high as he could stack them.

Once we had finished decorating with the new operations manager's stuff and what was left of his clothing, Virginia jumped in Jeb's truck and pulled out an old megaphone from Jeb's Computer World that she had spied during the tour.

"Baker Satterfield," she yelled through the megaphone, beginning to cackle all over again. "Ba-ker Sat-ter-field. You have a special delivery out front. Has anyone seen Ba-ker Sat-ter-field? Please tell him that he has a special de-li-ver-y." She could hardly get the words out she was laughing so hard. Of course Virginia's contagious laugh got the rest of us going again.

Alice had to have a turn and grabbed the megaphone away from Virginia. "Baker," she yelled, kind of sweet and singsongy, "you have company."

No one would have ever noticed the movement in a far-left upstairs window, if it hadn't been for that blessed, wandering eye of Roberta's. As all of the rest of us were staring toward the front door of the base lodge, waiting for Baker and the fifty-year-old to show their faces, Roberta's eye caught sight of someone's hand pushing down on the blind. "I'm happy to report that your master scheme is a success, Virginia. I would bet my soul Baker's the one peeking through them blinds upstairs there."

We all turned in the direction of Roberta's pointed finger.

"That's him, that's him," Alice said, getting excited and yelling through the megaphone again. "Come on down, Baker, and give us a *huug*. It's been too long."

Mary Jule leaned over and shouted through the megaphone, "Yeah, show us a little Yankee hospitality, why don't ya?"

Do you know that yellow sissy never had the guts to greet us face-to-face? We waited about fifteen minutes longer before finally giving up. "I'm not surprised," Alice said, as she stepped into Jeb's truck. "He walked out on you like a coward. He wasn't gonna meet us in person . . . the little chickenshit."

Maybe it wasn't him up there. After all, it was a Saturday and as rich as his new girlfriend was, they could have taken the holiday weekend off to *travel*. But then again who else would have *peeked* through the window?

On the way out of the resort, Jeb's truck slowed down in front of the window where Roberta had spied Baker. Next thing I knew, Virginia and Alice were climbing out of the passenger window. Virginia crawled up on the top of the truck. Alice handed her a large plastic cup before climbing up top herself.

I turned to Mary Jule, who had stopped her rental car behind them. "What in God's name are they doing?"

"I'm not sure, but this oughta be good."

"Pull the car up," I told her, "right alongside of Jeb's." I rolled my window down and motioned for Jeb to do the same. But he was all the way over on the passenger side holding something. "What are y'all doing up there?" I called to the girls.

"What does it look like we're doing?" Virginia answered. "We're poonin' him. Hand me another Tampax, Jayeb."

(Pooning is the act of ornamenting a glass surface with a surprise tampon. Instructions: Unwrap a super Tampax and dip in water. Once the tampon is bloated, hold it by the string and twirl, midair, in lasso rope fashion. Rear arm back and hurl at target. Optimum targets are large plate-glass windows, i.e., Waffle Houses or Krystal restaurants near college campuses at 2:00 A.M. when packed full of unsuspecting late-night diners. Element of surprise is crucial. College age–appropriate.)

Pooning on school nights provided the best entertainment for Virginia and me back at Ole Miss. Along with Genie and Mary Gaston, two more of our Chi Omega sisters, we'd drive through the Krystal, or the Greasetal as we called it, and order a sack of burgers. Just after the clerk handed over the bag, we'd pull the car up a little, have the poon dipped and ready, and the driver would slam it against the big plate-glass window. We'd watch the poon slide, slowly, down the glass. The surprise on the faces of the bookworms, who had been studying all night, was enough to make you wet your pants.

Jeb stuck a super out the window and handed it up to Virginia. She dipped and flung that thing as hard as she could. We all watched as it sailed through the air and missed the upstairs window completely. Alice had the second one already dipped and hers flew through the air and hit the window underneath.

"Aw, *hell*," Alice said. "You try it, Jayeb, you'll prob'ly have better luck."

Jeb opened his door and pompously stood up on the edge of the truck, holding a tampon. "Might as well take a shot."

Lying on her stomach, Virginia bent down from the roof with the cup of water and held it for Jeb. Just as if he was a veteran pooner, Jeb dipped the tampon in the cup, twirled it in the air, and flung it with all his might. He nailed the flying white mouse right in the middle of the upstairs window. It splattered on the pane and then slid down slowly before wedging into a groove on the window ledge.

"Throw another one, Jayeb. Get him good!" Virginia cried, and handed him a fresh Tampax.

Jeb took another shot and . . . *splat*, the second one hit the bull's-eye, too. (Knowing Baker, he was absolutely furious. He always said our shenanigans were *so* annoying and juvenile.)

"Way to go, Mr. JCW!" Alice squealed. The girls took a few more shots each before some guy came out the front of the lodge and walked briskly toward us.

"Get your butts down," I yelled. "Someone's coming."

Alice took one look at the guy and hollered, "What's your hurry, *shoog*?"

Virginia yanked Alice's jacket and they both scurried back down into the truck. "Haul ass, Jayeb," Virginia yelled. "Let's get the hell outta Dodge."

Jeb screeched out of Powder Mountain on two left wheels with Mary Jule flooring it right behind him.

Exception to pooning age-appropriate rule: Although originally intended as a college prank, sometimes life deems pooning necessary later in life. As in the case where estranged husband runs off with older (or more often younger) woman. In that instance one is never too old for pooning.

When we got back to the Peach Blossom Inn Roberta and Jeb went straight to work. Pierre disappeared into his cottage and the girls and I returned to my apartment. Once inside, all four of us climbed back up on Great-grandmother's bed.

Right then, eyeing the closet without Baker's clothes on one half, was the first time I had had to admit to myself that he was really gone: I'd cried so much about it, but I never thought about it being final. I knew he was gone on a subconscious level, but I think consciously I never believed for a second that he wouldn't have come back home by now. Somewhere in my mind I always thought he'd be back for Memorial Day weekend, and this nightmare would finally be over. But here I was staring into my closet, Baker-bare.

"All I can think about is the look that must have been on Baker's face when he saw his clothes riding up that mountain," Virginia said. "Wonder if he'll be the one to pick it all up."

"I doubt it," said Mary Jule.

Virginia stretched her legs out on top of Alice's. "I bet he is some kind of mortified about now."

"Furious is what he is," I told her.

"Good. Then maybe, just maybe, he'll get an idea of how furious we are at him. He makes me sick." Alice's always hated him.

Even though she was across from me on the bed, Mary Jule noticed something when I put my hand to my mouth. She sat straight up. "Leelee, look at your ring!"

I jerked my hand around to look and sure enough, the emerald-cut diamond at the center of my engagement ring was gone. The four lone platinum prongs and the two baguettes on either side were all that were left of my ring.

"It was there this morning," Alice said. "I remember distinctly because I was wondering when you were gonna finally take the damn thing off."

"It probably fell out on that mountain," I said, feeling depressed all over again. "It's up there with the rest of Baker's belongings."

"If you want to go look for it," Mary Jule said, "I'll help you."

My initial reaction was to jump back in the car and whiz off toward Powder Mountain, but my better judgment set me straight. "Oh, what's the point? We'll never find it. I'm not even gonna try. It doesn't mean anything to me anymore, anyway."

"It's no coincidence that you lost it up there," Mary Jule said. "Truth is, he'd already taken your heart with him up to that mountain."

"I, for one, am excited about it," Virginia said, looking me straight in the eye.

"Excited about it? How come?" I asked her, thinking of all that was lost today.

"Just thinking about how you're gonna spend the insurance money, that's how come. I'm thinking Tahiti." Her devilish smile returned.

"With whom? *Jeb?*"

"Yeah, right. I think you should take Jeb. *Me. I'll* go with you," Virginia said.

"So how do you get to be the one to go?" Alice bolted straight up. "Y'all are just gonna leave Mary Jule and me at home?"

"Did I say anything about leaving y'all at home? Y'all can go. We'll all go," Virginia said.

The only place I wanted to go was home to Memphis with my friends. Telling them good-bye on Monday was going to be excruciating, but I knew I was on the downhill stretch. I could "stay in hell a little while longer" as Kissie would say, because I knew I was getting out. I could practically taste Tennessee, *and* Tahiti for that matter. Time was so close now.

Chapter Seventeen

If, after Baker left, someone had told me that I'd still be living in Vermont in August, I'd have said, I think not. But it was most definitely August and I was most definitely still here. Hard to believe, but my friends had been gone two months already and Ed Baldwin hadn't darkened the doorway of the Peach Blossom Inn in three months. He hadn't brought a single soul through to show his listing that he told me would be "no problem whatsoever to move."

"People will be clamoring to buy it, you wait and see," he said at first. Then it went to "Folks like to wait until fall when the leaves are turning," and then to "Vermont is depressed right now. Nothing is selling at all."

Vermont is depressed *right now*! Why else would people drive around with a bumper sticker that says MOONLIGHT IN VERMONT OR STARVE? Or, WORKING VERMONTER: ENDANGERED SPECIES. It's beyond me how these Vermont real estate agents stay in business at all. The only thing I can come up with is that late July, August, and September in Vermont spell redemption. June gets off to a buggy start but by the time mid-July rolls around, Vermont is magnificent. Late summer is the payoff for the whole year. Now, make no mistake about it, it's fleeting. A six-week summer is all you get. But it is quite lovely.

The garden outside our apartment was stunning. Red and white hollyhocks reached up past the windowsills pointing to the sky and the lupines were big and bright. Butterfly bush, dianthus, foxglove, purple coneflowers, columbine, lavender, you name it—the perennials were vibrant and crisp. The lilac bushes were enormous and you could smell them from across the yard. And the roses. Oh my gosh, the roses had no yellow leaves or black spots at all. Granted they were short-lived but they were gorgeous and smelled oh so sweet. They hardly needed watering because of the cooler temperatures at night. To tell you the truth, that was my only gripe with the summer at all—the cold nights. And most people, even Southerners, might tell me I was crazy to wish for a hot August night.

"Hey, boss!" Peter shouted from his truck. He was driving up to work at the exact same time my girls and I were returning from our dip in the river. (FYI, there are very few outdoor swimming pools in Vermont and the few in existence are located at a select inn or two. What's the point, right?)

"How many reservations on the books tonight?" he asked as he grabbed his gym bag out of the back of his little black truck.

"Sixty-two so far."

"And the day is young. I predict we serve eighty dinners." Peter's smile really is something else. I couldn't help but wonder if he'd worn braces or if his teeth were naturally that straight.

"I sure hope so. I can't tell you how nice it is to have cash flow," I said, and rubbed my hands together.

"I knew we could do it."

Without warning, Peter threw me his bag, which I barely caught, and scooped up the girls. He sat Issie on top of his shoulders and let Sarah ride piggyback. Their little bathing suits were still wet but Peter didn't seem to mind. "We'll race ya, Leelee. Hold on tight, girls." They took off running toward the inn. I dropped his gym bag and ran with all my might. We both reached the gate under the arbor at the same time. That's where I got my edge. While Peter took the time to open the gate I decided to hop the little white picket fence instead. He's already six-foot-two and with Isabella on top he had to duck up under the arbor, and by the time he finally reached the apartment door I was propped against the post. I glanced at my wrist like I was checking out the time when he made it to the door.

"You cheated," he said, out of breath. "Right, girls?"

Sarah agreed with him. "Yeah, Mommy, you jumped over the fence."

"Cheated? I did not. You never said hopping fences was against the rules. I won fair and square."

Isabella squealed and clapped her hands. "Yay, Mommy!"

Suddenly, Peter's eyes dropped. My bathing suit wrap had fallen off while I was running and all I had on was my light green strapless bikini. I could feel his eyes on me as I ran over to the grass to pick up my sarong and wrap myself back up. Peter put the girls down in front of the door and opened it to let them run on through.

We stood there staring at each other for an uncomfortable moment. "I'll see you in the kitchen a little later," he said, and winked.

"See ya," I called from the yard, and watched him walk in through the porch.

We had become good friends over the summer. With a lively sense of humor, Peter had a great way about him. When he spoke to me he looked directly in my eyes. The edges of his mouth always curved up when I was speaking to him and he never glanced around the room or let anything distract him from giving me his undivided attention. Whenever I was in the restaurant, he made a point to find me and find out how things were going with the girls and me. Someone in Vermont actually cared how my day was going.

He never seemed to mind working late. When it came to breakfast though, he started out cooking for the first week or two and then he made sure I learned how to do it. I figured out real quick Peter was not a morning person, but he sure was a big help to me, anyway. Jumping in and handling all the restaurant duties, such as ordering the food and the wine, was only the beginning. Peter designed a new wine list and taught me about matching wine with food. One of the guys he had worked with at the Wild Duck, Jim, heard the news about Peter's new position and applied to be his sous-chef. Head chef Peter Owen was on his way.

Right after Helga and Rolf left, the two of us got to work on our new menu for the Peach Blossom Inn. The first thing I wanted to do was throw out that nasty head cheese. Next it was out with the canned eggplant caponata and a big sayonara to the pickled herring. Peter spent a great deal of time creating the new menu and both of us spent time designing it. We felt it was important to keep some of the old traditional favorites for which the Vermont Haus Inn had become famous. We needed a balance of old and new.

For starters, our new appetizers included smoked North Atlantic salmon, served in buckwheat crepes, with horseradish cream and golden caviar. We added a chilled jumbo shrimp cocktail, served with either traditional cocktail sauce or a creole remoulade sauce. We kept the house favorite from the old menu, escargot maison, as well as a soup of the evening and a European style pâté. Peter changed the pâté recipe a tad but since it was the only thing Princess Grace Kelly would eat now, thanks to Pierre, we couldn't change it all that much.

The final appetizer was created in honor of Daddy. His favorite first course came from an old famous restaurant in Memphis called Justine's. Lump crabmeat, lightly seasoned and topped with hollandaise, served over toast points. We named that one after him: Crabmeat Henry.

Our new entrées were equally as delicious. The first item on the menu was a roast Statler breast of chicken, served with sautéed seasonal fruits and a sauce supreme, which was a creamy yet light sauce made with crème fraîche. Veal scaloppini was next, prepared either classic way—marsala or piccata. Peter's filet mignon was always perfect, served with either a fresh béarnaise or sauce au poivre. Roast Long Island duckling was another old favorite that needed to stay on the menu; Peter just changed the sauces du jour more frequently.

A daily pasta was added, as pasta was Peter's specialty. He could conjure up the most beautiful creations with the most delicious flavors. Peter changed the lamb dish a little to a roasted rack of baby lamb. He served it

with roasted garlic and a port wine rosemary sauce. Another one of my favorites was the shrimp dijonaise. Jumbo shrimp were sautéed with shallots
and tarragon, flamed with cognac, and finished with a white wine and
grainy mustard cream sauce. The next item threw me for a loop when Peter
suggested it, though. Calf's liver was permanently added to my menu—
thinly sliced and sautéed with balsamic vinegar and red onions, topped
with apple-smoked bacon. Peter told me to trust him and that's exactly
what I did.

A grilled fillet of salmon topped with a mango chile salsa was added
and the sweet of the fruit mixed with the salmon formed a delicious sensation. Last but not least was a loin of pork, center cut, boneless, and grilled,
wrapped in apple-smoked bacon and glazed with apricot and curry.

Our desserts were finally something to boast about, too. I found a local
lady whose cakes were works of art. Instead of *canned* peach melba, I was
proud to offer homemade peach cobbler. Alice came through with her
promise of sending me fresh peaches from home, so I could remain true to
our name. And finally, my all-time favorite dessert was added—straight
from the kitchen of Kristine "Kissie" Johnson—Southern pecan pie.

All this delicious food aside, I still missed my good ole down-home
Southern cooking. You simply could not buy grits in the grocery store.
When I called the Smuckers 800 number to inquire about where to buy a
simple jar of cherry preserves, the guy on the phone told me that I'd have
to go down south to find them. Barbecue to Northerners meant "grilling
out" so if I wanted a barbecue sandwich I might as well set my taste buds
on a hamburger.

If you do find a restaurant that serves fried chicken, it's usually chicken
tenders, and you can flat forget about a decent glass of sweet tea to go
with it.

So, one night Peter surprised me by featuring Southern fare as his
"chef's special" for the evening. He made fried chicken, mashed potatoes
and gravy, green beans, corn pudding, and spoon bread, just like Kissie
would have made it. I had told him all about Kissie and her famous Southern cooking. I wondered why he wanted to know, in detail, my favorite
Kissie meal and how she made it. Now it made sense.

Right before the dinner rush, in late August, he knocked on the inside door to my apartment. His hands were behind his back when I opened the door. "I have a surprise for you. Okay if I come in?"

My hair was still wet, but I was dressed for work. "Of course. What's behind your back?"

"Close your eyes and open your mouth wide."

"What for?"

"Just *trust* me," he said, as he had numerous times before.

So I did. Even though I was embarrassed he would see my gold filling, I closed my eyes and opened my mouth. A spoon filled with the most delicious thing I had tasted in so long rested upon my tongue. White chocolate—creamy, rich, and so yummy—along with a whole, fresh raspberry. It created that bite, that salivating sensation I get on my tongue when tasting a perfect blend of tart and sweet.

I opened my eyes to his big, wide smile. "That's the most delicious thing I've ever tasted. What is it?"

"White chocolate mousse."

"How'd you know I love white chocolate?"

"Roberta told me. White chocolate, moose, and Leelee seem to go together, so I thought it was the perfect dessert—even though it's not peach."

"And who needs peach, when you can have this?" I threw my arms around his neck to hug him and when I did, he held on to me an extra second or two. Something curiously familiar shot through my body. I quickly pulled away. "Thank you, Peter. That was mighty sweet of you."

"Anytime, Leelee. I mean, boss."

Could it be that I was *enjoying* what I was doing? I was spending time in the dining room at night, getting to know the customers. I even made the bold step to convert the front parlor into a dining room and turn the back dining room, right off our apartment, into another sitting room and waiting area. Now I could go in and out of our quarters at will, without going outside during dinner to get to my children. Moving that table made life so much simpler. It was my second big step toward independence.

For the first time in ten months, I didn't wake up every morning dreading my day. Sure, I was still looking forward to going home, but at least the weather was nice, the Schloygins were gone, I had a little money in my pocket, and I had a new fun friend in Peter.

When Kerri got an offer to move back home to Idaho to work at a dude ranch, I would be lying if I said I was really all that sorry to see her go. I know she had nothing to do with Baker leaving and all, but she was still a big flirt and I don't know, that gets under my skin after a while. I'm not saying that I really cared all that much, but when she flirted with Peter it was truly nauseating. Even Roberta thought so.

She would steal behind the line every chance she could and offer to knead Peter's neck muscles. Then she'd work her way down his back. "You look beat," she said once. "I bet you could use a good rubdown. My neighbor's getting her masseuse license and she's been practicing on me. Here, sit down on this stool and I'll get your neck."

Roberta's face killed me. She raised her eyebrows and nodded her head up and down. As if she knew exactly what Kerri was doing. Peter let her knead his neck. I mean who in their right mind turns down a massage? I certainly wouldn't. Male or female—I love nothing more than having someone caress my flesh.

Sarah started kindergarten at Fairhope Elementary and I have to say it wasn't as bad as I thought. Her teacher, Miss Bev, was adorable and Sarah seemed to be crazy about her. The bus picked her up in front of the inn each morning and dropped her back off every afternoon around 3:30 P.M. Tears welled up in my eyes the first morning she boarded, proudly displaying her Barbie backpack and clutching her Little Mermaid lunch box. She hopped on eagerly, as Issie and I waved from the curb. Sarah never let on, but I was sure of the void inside her that must have ached without a daddy there to see her off. The idea of what it meant to be the child of a single mama had not yet taken root, but in the months to come, I was sure she would become more aware.

Since Issie's fourth birthday was approaching in January, the Elfin

Academy admitted her into their three-day-a-week program from nine to two. I had a few hours to myself in the morning, but I still hated all the time I had to spend away from them at night.

Fall arrived in a blaze of color. Leaf Season starts around the last week of September and lasts through the middle of October, with the peak occurring around October 5. I had heard about the fall foliage, but until you are there for Leaf Season there is no way to fully appreciate it. It's the maple trees that make all the difference. They take on a pink tint at first before turning into their full vibrant shade of crimson red. The birch and the aspen will glow yellow; and the oaks will become a warm purplish brown.

People come from all over the world to experience Vermont during the foliage. Leaf peepers they're called and the rooms in the area get booked a year in advance. My inn was no exception. Theoretically, we were supposed to make enough money during those three weeks to sustain us through Stick Season. We were serving on average ninety dinners per night, and every room we had was booked solid. We were right on track to get us back in the black.

Smack dab in the middle of Leaf Season, an older couple with heavy New York accents joined us for dinner, just as we were opening for the evening. We had been running an ad in *The Sugartree Gazette* that offered half-price entrées to anyone arriving by 5:00 P.M. That helped to stagger the seatings, easing the burden of the 8:00 turnover. We could even turn the tables three times per night if we were lucky, with seatings at 5:00, 7:00, and then 9:00 P.M.

Pierre could always tell by someone's drink order what kind of meal they would have. No drinks usually meant no appetizers, maybe one dessert to split. When Pierre gave me the order he immediately knew the type.

"No drinks, table nine. Cheap. Vedy, vedy cheap." As he said "cheap," Pierre pursed his lips, raised his eyebrows, and flipped his hand in the air. When he did that, he wasn't expecting much tip.

Pierre cynically announced table nine's order to Peter, "*Un* pork, *deux* plates. That's it. Sheet." I had figured out by now that "sheet" meant "shit." They ordered the cheapest item on the menu.

Pierre brought them two salads, even though they were only supposed to get one. Peter split their pork on two plates, but gave them each the regular amount of potato and green beans—even though they were only supposed to get enough for one. The amount of bread they ate was a meal by itself and they didn't order a dessert.

When it was time to total their check, I added in a three-dollar plate charge to cover the extra salad, vegetables, bread, and potatoes. The bill came to a whopping $14.81 including the plate charge, tax, and the half-price coupon.

Pierre returned to the kitchen with the bill and no money to go with it. "Ze man, table nine, es not happy. No pay three dollars."

"You've gotta be kidding," I said.

"No, ze man es outside ze kitchen. He wants you."

"Me? Okay. I can handle this," I said, out loud but to myself.

"Go get 'em, boss," Peter yelled from behind the line.

Confident on the outside, but scared to death on the inside, I fluffed my hair and meandered out to the waiting room to greet Mr. Cheap. He and his wife were standing just outside the kitchen door where four other people were waiting to be seated. As soon as he saw me, he started right in.

"I have a complaint, miss, uh, what's your name, miss?"

"Leelee Satterfield. I'm the innkeeper here. And what is your name, sir?" I shot him a big smile.

"No matter." The man was well dressed but quite short.

"Well, nice to meet you anyway, how can I help you?" I extended my hand, which he, by the way, did not shake.

"I demand that you take this three dollars off my bill. That's how you can help me. There is nothing on your menu that indicates that you have a plate charge and I refuse to pay it!" As he got to the "refuse to pay it" part, his heels came off the ground and he got right in my face. We were about the same height.

Here's the incredible part. Mr. No Matter was wearing Gucci loafers! That really bugged me. Wearing Gucci loafers and refusing to pay his three-dollar plate charge. What *nerve*. What *colossal* nerve.

"I see your point, sir," I said sweetly. "Even after the half-price coupon you still had a balance of ten dollars and fifty cents. I would venture to say that at all the four-star restaurants around here, a plate charge is pretty standard. But I don't want you to feel like you didn't get your money's worth."

"That has nothing to do with this hidden charge!" He looked over at his wife, dressed to the nines in a mink stroller and Ferragamo pumps. She was standing about five feet away with her head down, digging for something at the bottom of her Louis Vuitton pocketbook. At least *she* was used to this.

When I realized he was trying to make a scene and that customers like this simply were not worth the trouble, I said, as sweetly as I could, "You know, uh, sir, Friendly's doesn't have a plate charge. Perhaps you should try them sometime."

I thought his ears would start smoking when he blurted out, "Now that you mention it, we would have been better off going to Friendly's in the first place!" His voice climbed to a shout. "WE PROBABLY WOULD HAVE GOTTEN A BETTER MEAL."

That did it. He was deliberately trying to insult me so I'd take three measly dollars off his bill. "You know what?" I said, trying hard to remain calm. "You're absolutely right. Friendly's would have been a much better choice for you. The most expensive item on the menu is only eight dollars. In fact, the next time you go out to eat, be sure and call me. I know a couple of the waitresses down there and I'll hook you up with the best table in the house . . . facing the parking lot!"

I stunned him. More importantly, I stunned myself. *Who are you now, Leelee?* He slammed a ten and a five on the counter of the wait station and hurried off without saying another word. Mrs. No Matter tried to keep up his pace but the heels on her Ferragamos kept her a few steps behind.

The silence in the room startled me and when I looked around, four blank faces were staring my way. And now I was going to have to seat them and pretend nothing had ever happened.

Nervous and flustered, I led the way to their tables. Luckily, the first couple were regulars and already knew that the Peach Blossom Inn was a delectable experience. It was the other two gentlemen I was worried about. They were unfamiliar and the looks on their faces were hard to interpret.

When we got to their table (accidentally the best seat in the house, right in front of the fireplace) I attacked the situation head-on. "I have to tell you, I am so sorry for what happened back there. Normally I bend over backward for my customers, but that man was really hard to reason with." I was still shocked over the way I acted. Firing Helga was one thing and my response was way overdue, but now I was beginning to take on the persona of a tough Northern broad. *Daddy would absolutely flip if he could see me now.*

The older guy spoke up. He seemed to be about fortyish and his friend looked younger—maybe twenty-five or so.

"Personally, I thought it was great the way you handled it. He asked for it—comparing your restaurant to Friendly's. I've never eaten here before, but hey, even if the food stinks, the ambiance alone is well worth the drive up from Manchester. Even if the innkeeper is a bit fiery."

"That's my nickname!"

"I see why."

"It's not for this kind of thing, it's for the red in my hair— Oh, I don't know why I'm telling y'all this. In any case, I kind of lost it there for a minute. He brought a different person out of me. I'm Leelee Satterfield," I said, handing them each a menu. "What are y'all's names?"

"John Bergmann, and this is my cousin Ron Olson. We've heard a lot about your place and decided to check it out." He glanced at the menu. "What's your favorite dish?"

"Hmmm, that's hard to say, probably the lamb or the shrimp dijonaise. But truly, I like everything. Oops, I lied, I'm not a fan of calf's liver. I'm surprised to say it sells very well though."

"I can tell you're not from up here; what part of the South are you from?" John asked.

"Tennessee."

"Ah, yes, the Rocky Top State."

"Go Vols! Actually I didn't go to UT but my hus . . . band did." The word was halfway out and I couldn't go back. "I'm an Ole Miss girl. Where are y'all from?"

"I live in Manhattan and Ron's out on Long Island. Our family is having a reunion weekend here and we stole away to dine at a quaint Vermont inn."

"Actually, we saw your menu listed in the Sugartree Dining Guide and thought we'd check it out," Ron said.

"Great. I promise you won't be disappointed. That incident back there has never happened before. I am really very embarrassed."

"Don't be. It made it all the more intriguing. I'll let you know if we're displeased, you can count on it," John said, and winked at his cousin.

"Okay, but your first round of drinks is on me. I wouldn't want you to think I'm cheap. What are y'all drinking this evening?"

"I'll take a vodka and tonic with a twist," John said.

"How about a Jack and Coke?" Ron asked. "Talking to a Tennessee girl has put me in the mood for Jack Daniel's."

"I'll be back in a flash." When I came back with their drinks, the guys kept looking at each other and smiling. They were making me paranoid the way they kept at it. I had to know what in the world was so funny.

"What are y'all laughing at?" I set the drinks in front of them.

"You might as well go on and tell her, John, she'll find out soon enough," Ron said.

"What? I'll find out what? Were those people kin to y'all?"

"No. They have nothing to do with it," John responded, still smiling. "Normally I would get fired for telling you this but I just can't resist. I'm from *Food and Wine* magazine. I'm here to do a review on the Peach Blossom Inn."

I covered my eyes with my hand and shook my head before slumping down in one of the extra chairs at their table. "Of course you're from *Food and Wine* magazine. Why am I not surprised? Leave it to me to let a customer have it right in front of a reviewer from *Food and Wine* magazine." I shook my head and leaned back in the chair. "But here's the crazy part. It's only the second time in my life I've ever let anyone have it."

"Relax, everything is fine," John reassured me.

"I never even thought about having my restaurant reviewed by a magazine much less yours. I've got to tell Peter, he's my chef. That's okay, right?"

"Well, no, not normally, but this is not your average night," John said. "I'll never be allowed to review again, if the magazine finds out."

"I'll just give him a little hint. I promise not to ever breathe a word that you warned me. You secret's safe with me. But I so appreciate it. I hope you get *your* money's worth at least."

"I'm sure we will, and we'll start by making up for what you lost on the last check. Bring us a bottle of this Jordan cab to start."

"Pierre will be right out." I hurried into the kitchen to give everyone the news.

After a long evening of Murphy's Law mishaps I needed a beer. For the first time in a very long time I wanted a good, cold one. The last customers hadn't even left before I raided the fridge and pulled out a Corona Light. I went over to the bar, cut myself a big ole lime, squeezed it inside, and plopped down on the stool in front of the washing machine. I was totaling up the dinner checks and sipping away when Roberta came over to call Moe.

"Look at you. Long day, huh?"

"Yuup, Roberta, it has been and I deserve every sip of this." I held it up, took a big swig, and told her, "Go get one for yourself, in fact grab one for everybody. Want a beer, everyone?" I called out. "They're on me."

"Sure, make mine a Guinness," Peter yelled from the oven.

"Hey, I know, let's all go to the Moose Head," Jeb yelled with shrill excitement in his voice. "Right after we close."

"Sounds good to me," Roberta said, and hung up the phone. "I bet Moe's already there; there's no answer at home."

When the restaurant finally closed, I'd had two beers already and that's right at my limit. Everyone headed up to the Moose Head and Peter and I were the only two left to lock up.

Peter rapped on my apartment door just as I was getting ready to come out and tell him to go on without me.

"I'm not going to leave you here by yourself," he said.

"That's okay. Go on, I'll catch y'all another night," I said. "I've got stuff to do around here and besides, Mandy couldn't stay."

"I'm not leaving you alone. Here, I'll get you another beer. You still drinking Corona Lights?"

"I guess so." I grabbed my baby monitor and followed him back into the kitchen. "Are you sure you don't want to go with everyone else? The Moose Head will probably be more fun."

"Naah, I'll pass. It's no big deal to me. A Guinness is a Guinness whether I drink it here or there. Besides, when do I get a chance to party with the boss? I might just learn a thing or two."

Peter and I never left the commercial kitchen. I sat on the stool by the phone and he hopped up on the washing machine in front of me. He told stories about when he was little and how he had grown up an Irish Catholic in New Jersey. We talked about my childhood, too, and how I had been a ballerina. At one point I actually got up to show him a tour jeté and how I could still do the splits. I should have known right then and there that I was in trouble but for some reason I kept on drinking and got tipsier and tipsier.

I even hopped off the stool, went over to the bar, and poured myself a big ole snifter of Grand Marnier. What in the world was I thinking? I absolutely knew better than that but my God, I hadn't done anything fun since Baker left me. After pouring it, I handed the Grand Marnier over to Peter and instead of sitting back down on the stool I used it as a step up and scooted in next to him on top of the dryer. To make matters worse I proceeded to embarrass myself completely by saying stuff like, "Baker will never have it this good again." I held up my snifter and said, "Here's to Mud Season, blackflies, and black ice." Then I toasted "Tacky ski resorts, snow bunnies, and women who need face-lifts to attract younger men." Peter toasted and laughed right along with me.

"So, as long as we're talking dump stories, want to hear a really good one?"

"Sure, why not," I said, beginning to trip over my words.

"I got dumped for my little brother."

That stopped me dead in my tracks. It even seemed to sober me up a bit.

Peter stared ahead, expressionless, and avoided looking at me. It was quite uncomfortable.

Searching for the right words to say, I reached out and touched his leg. "That breaks my heart for you."

"Tell me about it." He still wouldn't meet my eyes. "That's the kind of shit you don't ever want to be a part of. It messes with your head in a way that stays with you. But . . . it's all in the past now." He turned to look at me. I could tell he was deeply hurt even though he was trying to hide behind his forced smile.

Our calves were touching, ever so slightly, and when I lifted my hand off his leg, he shifted in his seat and now our legs brushed against one another all the way down. My foot hit somewhere around the middle of his calf and I playfully kicked him. He responded by wrapping his leg over mine and lightly pinning my foot down.

"Owww."

"That doesn't hurt, you big baby."

"It does so." Not sure why I brought the subject back up but in a light-hearted way I asked, "So are they . . . is she still your brother's girlfriend?"

"Nope."

"Well, that's good. Right?" I tried in vain to unpin my foot.

"She's his wife." With that, Peter slid down off the washing machine and slowly walked over to the fridge, reached inside, and grabbed another beer.

I didn't know what to say; it was obvious he was still in great pain. I thought about how selfish I'd been to talk only about myself; I never once, all summer, inquired about his past loves. He never mentioned them but I never made it a point to ask. As cute as he was I guess I assumed he'd never had girl problems.

"Do you wanna talk about it? I'm a really good listener."

"I don't think so, but thanks. Hey, I'm hungry. Let's raid the walk-in." Peter strolled over and opened the handle of the huge refrigerator and waited for me. The two of us stepped inside. He handed me the container of jumbo shrimp, then grabbed the huge vat of cocktail sauce and, of course, the pâté. He knew by now to include Gracie, who had been curled up right underneath me, silently awaiting her own midnight snack.

Stuffing shrimp cocktail in my mouth as fast as I could get them in, you'd have thought I hadn't eaten in days. I knew I had no business drinking that Grand Marnier but it was too late now. When I saw two Peters spreading pâté on a Carr's wafer, I knew I was in big trouble. That was the last thing about the night I can remember.

When I opened my eyes the next morning I was in my bed but I wasn't sure how I'd gotten there. I tried to recount every last detail, but my mind came to a dead end when I got to our midnight snack.

I happened to glance over and notice that the shoes I had worn were perfectly placed in my closet. I never would have done that; I would have kicked them off out in the hall. I lay there a little longer imagining every possible scenario. Hard as I tried I couldn't remember a thing.

I jumped out of bed, and boom, lay right back down again. My head hurt worse than it had since I drank PGA punch at an SAE toga party at Ole Miss. The room twirled like it does after fifteen pirouettes. And here's the worst part—I was only wearing my panties. I grabbed the cordless phone that sits on the windowsill and called the inn, hoping like crazy that Roberta would answer.

After three rings Peter answered, "Peach Blossom Inn." I hung up, waited five more minutes, and called right back. Four rings and then the same voice. This time I had no choice but to disguise mine, and with my best Northern accent I said, "Hi-eeee, is Ro-birt-a there, please?"

"I'll get her for you. Roberta, phone's for you," Peter said.

A couple of minutes later she picked up. She must have had her hand in something. "Peach Blossom Inn, Roberta speaking."

"Roberta," I whispered, "can you come to my apartment?"

"Is that you, Le—"

"*Shhhhhhhhh*," I said, as loud as I could, before she got "Leelee" all the way out. "Don't say my *name*, for goodness' sakes."

Now she was completely silent. I scared the poor thing so badly that she couldn't say anything at all.

"Roberta. *Roberta*, can you hear me?"

This time all she could do was grunt.

"Good, come quick and hurry, *hurry*."

Within seconds Roberta was rapping on the inside door. I leaped out of bed this time, grabbed my housecoat, and ran over to open it, holding my head.

I scooped her in and shut the door quickly behind her. "You have to find out what I did last night."

"What *you did*? What do you mean?"

"I got drunk and passed out."

"Nuup, not you, Leelee."

"Oh yes I did. After y'all left for the Moose Head."

"I was wondering what happened to yous."

"Peter kept me company. We talked some, laughed some, drank *a lot*, and then we raided the walk-in. That's the last thing I remember—raiding the walk-in. Then I woke up this morning and my shoes were neatly placed in my closet."

"You wouldn't have done that."

"That's my point! You've got to find out for me."

"I'll give it a whirl but I don't know how much I can uncover."

"Just *try*, Roberta, please. Gladys Kravitz would be proud."

A nod of her head told me she was pleased with her assignment.

"But don't be obvious. And for goodness' sake, DON'T TELL GEORGE CLARK!" I gently nudged her out the door, and added, "One more favor. Please bring me lots of Coke."

A little while later Roberta came back into my apartment carrying a restaurant tray with a big glass of ice and three Cokes.

"Well?" I said, as I popped the top, poured my hangover tonic into the glass, and watched the fizz race to the top. "What'd ya find out?"

"Nothing. He just said you guys had a good time. That's all."

"How'd you put it to him?"

"I didn't have to bring it up. When I was fixing your tray, *he* asked how you were feeling. I told him you were a little under the weather and he just smiled. That's all. I'm sure it's fine, Leelee. I wouldn't worry if I was you," she said, tugging on those panties yet again.

"Roberta, can I ask you something?"

"Why, sure."

"I know this is none of my business and if you don't want to answer me you don't have to, I swear. I never would want to hurt your feelings but— you're always tugging on your panties, are you buying the right size?"

"Aw, sure. Moe's always wanted me to wear those sexy string under-pants so I bought 'em at Penney's in Rutland. Not too fond of 'em, to tell you the truth. But Moe likes 'em and I do it for him."

"Maybe you should try a thong."

"A who?"

"A thong. You know, panties with no butt at all."

"Too cold up here for that. I need to keep my cheeks warm," she said, and patted her wide little backside.

Once Sarah and Issie were awake I fed them breakfast and put them in the tub. Thank goodness it was Saturday. I honestly don't know what I would have done had I been hungover on a school day.

I stayed away from the kitchen for the next couple of hours but when I remembered my clothes in the dryer, I crept in, hoping no one would no-tice. Jeb spotted me though, and started whistling "Rocky Top." He had taken to doing that right after meeting my friends. He whistled it every time any of us came around. Anyway, when Peter heard my anthem, he immediately looked up and saw me slithering in behind the bar to get my laundry.

"Hi, boss," he yelled from behind the line. "How ya feeling this morn-ing?"

"Oh, pretty good," I sheepishly answered back. Meanwhile, I dumped my dried but much-wrinkled clothes into the basket, trying to get out of there as fast as I could.

"Need another Coke?" Peter called out.

"No, thank you, I'm just getting my laundry. Looks like I've waited too long to fold; they're mighty wrinkled." Just as I was slamming the dryer door shut, ready to make a run for it, I stood up straight and there he was, right next to me.

"Hi," he said.

"Oh, hi."

"What's your hurry? Where you going?"

"Back to my apartment to fold." I pushed past him and hurried out the door.

That didn't discourage Peter at all; he followed right behind me into the waiting area outside my apartment door. "Here, I'll help you." He took the basket out of my hands and placed it on the top of an easy chair, picked up a towel, and starting folding.

"You don't have to do that." I picked my basket back up and started for the door.

"Oh yes I do." He blocked me with his body and wouldn't let me pass.

I couldn't look him in the eye, but the more I avoided him the more he purposefully stared into my face.

"*All right.* I can't take it anymore. Go on and tell me. What did I do? What did I say?"

Peter let out this cute little laugh. "Nothing. You were great. I thoroughly enjoyed your company. And your ballerina moves."

"Ohhh," I said in horror. "I forgot about *dancing.* That is *so* embarrassing."

"You forgot about that?"

I closed my eyes and shook my head. "You don't understand, Peter. I never get that drunk. Go ahead and tell me what else I did."

"You were fine. We just had a fun conversation. I have to say I learned a lot about you though."

"How so?"

"Just stuff you told me."

"Like what?" There was no way to avoid the grimace on my face. I was about to die.

"Well, for starters you told me that you were a really good kisser and that Baker would never find anyone that could kiss as good as you."

"*Nooooo.* I *said* that? Tell me I didn't." I sat down in the easy chair, drew my legs up under me, and buried my face in the seat back.

"You said it. Then you went on to say, 'I guarantee you, Barb Thurmond can't kiss like me.'"

"I can't hear it. Stop. Don't tell me another thing." Covering my ears with my hands, I kicked my feet back and forth.

"Okay, I won't tell you anything else." He reached over and pulled my hands off my ears.

I thought about it for a second and knew I had to, at least, find out how I got into my bed.

"Did I *do* anything . . . unusual?" I couldn't bear to hear the answer.

"*Do* anything? What do you mean?"

"I woke up in my bed this morning. I don't remember getting into it and I was just wondering if you knew how I got there."

"I might have an idea."

This was excruciating. "Please tell me, Peter. I'm dying here."

"You have nothing to be ashamed of. I promise you that. So you say you can't remember anything?"

"No, the last thing I remember is watching you and your twin eat shrimp cocktail. I haven't done anything like this since my ten-year class reunion."

He shrugged his shoulders. "Well, in that case, I'm going to throw a class reunion for you here at the Peach Blossom Inn every week. In all seriousness, you were fine, *really fine*."

"Peter, stop it! Don't tease me anymore. I've got to know the truth." At this point I stood up again and looked him straight in the eye.

"The truth about what?"

"What I did, after we ate the shrimp cocktail. That's the last thing I remember."

"Okay, I'll put you out of your misery. You started talking about Baker after I told you about my brother and his wife. That's when you told me about being a good kisser and all. Pretty much right after that you started closing your eyes while you were eating shrimp so I knew you wouldn't last much longer."

"Then what?"

"I helped you to your bed and you climbed in and fell right to sleep. I took off your shoes and pulled the covers up over you. Turned out the light and left. I got to tell you though, your bedroom is small. I don't know how you got that bed in there."

"Don't even get me started."

"Anyway, I slept upstairs on your couch. I knew I shouldn't drive home and plus I thought if one of your girls woke up you'd never hear them. I did hear a lot of commotion in your bathroom in the middle of the night though."

"Gross. I'm sorry you had to hear that. You've got to believe me, I never ever do this."

"Seems to me it was long overdue."

"Maybe so; you're probably right. But thanks for taking care of me . . . and for watching out for the girls. I don't know what to say."

"It was no big deal. I was happy to do it," he said, and winked.

I swear that wink was confusing to me on so many levels. It was almost like he was holding back and not telling me something. Then there was the wink itself. It was so . . . so . . . tantalizing and mysterious. I could make myself crazy wondering about it if I wasn't careful. But, whatever it meant, didn't really *mean* anything. What meant something to me now was getting rid of this monster headache.

Chapter Eighteen

November in Vermont is downright dismal. No getting around it. It's as bad as April. We were closed down for Stick Season and I loved that, but there wasn't much to do. It's not like I could go home—the girls were in school. Pierre went back to France, Roberta hung around town, Jeb worked at JCW, and Peter went to New Jersey to help paint the house of one of his friends. The girls and I spent time together drawing, baking, and getting ready for Christmas.

Christmas number two in Vermont was not something I had ever planned on. But now that it was happening I made sure that this year was different. We had a family tree in our apartment. There was one for looks in the parlor of the inn but our main tree was in with us. The girls begged to go into the forest and cut down another tree. And since we had had so much fun last year I promised we could do it again.

Jeb said he would take us in his truck. I knew he was gonna charge me though, and when I asked him how much he thought about it for a second and then said, "Thirty bucks . . . plus gas."

Pierre would have taken me for free if he'd been in town.

The morning we were supposed to go with Jeb, Peter called to let me know he was back from New Jersey. As soon as I heard his voice I had an idea.

"I've got a huge favor to ask you," I said.

"Okay, shoot."

"Is there any way you might take the girls and me to cut down a Christmas tree this afternoon? Or tomorrow or whenever it works for you."

"Of course I'll take you guys. That'd be fun. Just bring your chain saw."

"I don't have one," I said, disappointed.

"I'm just kidding you, Leelee. I've got a chain saw. What time do you guys want to go?"

"Anytime."

"Okay, I'll pick you up around one thirty. That ought to give us enough time before it gets dark."

Peter arrived right on time and the girls and I were already bundled up (toe heaters and all) when he got there. He let himself in through the kitchen and hollered out our names. "Leelee, Sarah, Issie, are you guys ready?"

"Mr. Peter!" The girls ran right up to him and gave him a big hug. I hugged him, too. It was good to see him.

It only took fifteen minutes to get to the forest and once we arrived Peter hopped out and grabbed his chain saw out of the back. I have to admit, this is a cool thing about Vermont. You just park your car anywhere on the road, and wander into the forest to cut down any tree you like.

Every time I'd hear a noise though, I'd jump.

"What are you so nervous about?" Peter wanted to know, once we had ventured about ten minutes into the woods.

"Nothing, I'm fine."

"You don't act fine. You're peeking around the trees like you expect to see the boogeyman. What's up?"

"Actually, I was hoping we'd see a moose. But on the other hand, I'm kinda scared since I've heard they can be aggressive if you get too close. I know they live in the woods and every time I hear something, it just makes me jittery, that's all."

· "I'm scared, Mommy," Issie said, holding up her arms for me to pick her up. Now I'd really done it; I was going to have to carry Isabella through the forest. I picked her up and plopped her on my hip. "Don't be scared, baby, I'm only kidding. There are no moose in this forest. Right, Peter?" I said, and winked.

"I don't know so much about that, but I do know there are reindeer in this forest."

"Where!" both girls squealed at once.

"It's hard to see them, because they're magic. But Santa gets lots of his reindeer from Vermont."

"How about Rudolph?" Issie asked. "Is he from Vermont?"

"No, Isabella," Sarah told her, "Rudolph was born in the North Pole, don't you remember from the movie?"

"Oh yeah, I remember," Issie said.

Peter squatted down and motioned for Sarah to crawl up on his back. Somehow he was careful enough to carry her without getting her legs anywhere near the chain saw. Of course this made Issie want to be carried the same way so the four of us traipsed piggyback through the woods. It was only a few minutes longer before Sarah spotted the tree she wanted.

"That's it, that's the one." Sarah pointed to a beautiful fir tree, probably nine or ten feet tall, full-figured, and waxy green. "Can we have that one?"

"Looks great to me, okay with you, Issie?" Peter said.

Isabella nodded her head.

Peter had us all stand to one side while he crawled up under our perfect tree and made a small wedge-shaped cut into the trunk. He poked his head out through the bottom branches. "We may have to take some off the bottom. You don't mind, do you?"

"That's fine," I said. "Wait, Peter, can we yell timber? I know it sounds corny but I've always wanted to yell timber."

"Whatever you want. On the count of three. Are you ready, ladies?"

We backed up as Peter cut a little more into the trunk. He hastily rolled away from the tree and counted backward. "Three, two, *one*!"

"TIMBER," the girls and I shouted. Our Christmas tree gave way, slowly at first, then cracked and fell to the ground. The sawdust underneath clouded around it.

Peter effortlessly picked up the tree and all four of us found our way back to his truck.

"Thank you," I said, when he started the engine.

"For what?"

"What do you mean *for what?* For looking out for me. For . . . today."

"I wouldn't do it if I didn't want to."

"I'm glad you want to."

He never said anything else. He just shot me a perfect smile and a wink. *There goes that wink again. Dangit.*

This year's Christmas turned out much better, at least as far as the inn was concerned. I closed the restaurant for both Christmas Eve and Christmas Day and accepted no reservations for rooms. Everyone on the staff got a mini-vacation.

The night before we closed, though, while I was making my routine check on the girls during dinner, I got an unexpected surprise. Sarah was standing in front of the wall phone in our apartment when I strolled in a little after eight. "Bye, Daddy," she said, and put the phone back on the hook.

It caught me completely off guard and before I had time to purpose my words I heard myself say, "Wait, Sarah, let me talk to him."

"He hung up already. I'm sorry, Mommy."

"Didn't he ask to speak to me?"

She shook her head.

"Oh. Well, what did he have to say?"

"He left our presents on the screened-in porch. Come on, Isabella." She tugged on the front door and when she opened it a blast of frigid air whooshed inside.

"Sarah! Haven't I told you not to open this door? It's freezing enough in here without you letting more cold air in." I slammed the door behind her and bolted the lock. They both stared at me like I was the meanest snake on earth. Any mention of Baker turned me totally upside down. "I'm sorry.

Mama's just tired. Forgive me?" I squatted down and reached out for them. "Come on. Let's go through the restaurant."

I opened the inside door and the girls blasted past me, heading straight for the porch. Once we were outside, it looked like Christmas morning already. A pink Barbie jeep was in the center of a sea of silver and gold packages.

Sarah jumped up and down and squealed. "It's just what I wanted!"

"It's just what I wanted!" Isabella always copies Sarah. Bless her heart, she idolizes her sister.

The girls jumped into the jeep and tried starting it. Fortunately, Baker must have forgotten to charge the battery. *And where in the world does he think they'll be able to ride this? It sure is easy to waltz in and take credit for all the presents. What about Santa? Isn't he supposed to be the one that gets the glory? All my gifts, hidden upstairs in the attic, are from him.*

"Let's carry the gifts upstairs, y'all. It's cold out here."

Sarah started to push the jeep toward the door.

"No, honey, that's too heavy. Let's leave it outside."

"No, it's my favorite. I want it under the tree."

"Sarah, I can't carry it by myself. I'll get Mr. Peter or Jeb to bring it up after dinner."

"Need some help?" All three of us turned around at once at the sound of the voice emanating from the yard just outside the porch.

"Daddy!" they both screamed, and ran out the door.

"Girls, you don't have on your coats or boo—"

The street lamp illuminated the yard and I watched as Baker grabbed them both at once and lifted them up in his arms. My heart felt like it was speeding down a freeway and my stomach was about to drop out of the floorboard. I didn't know what to say or how to act. Should I go back in the house, or go outside and scream at him? The last thing I wanted was for my girls to be hurt even more, so I took a deep breath and said a prayer. Almost seven months had gone by since I'd laid eyes on him. Every time he picked the girls up for dinner I couldn't bring myself to come to the door. He'd called about sending money, but never wanted to talk long and I was always too hurt to ask many questions. He told me to get an attorney and he'd sign all the papers. Here it was going on seven months and I still hadn't done it. *Did he break up with fake-face?* I wondered. *Is that why he's here? Did* she *dump* him? I wanted to know and, then again, I didn't.

I picked up as many of the presents as I could carry and headed back upstairs into our apartment. Baker's flood of gifts would make the few I would put underneath look pitiful. But after all, Santa wasn't due to arrive until tomorrow night. Mandy was watching TV and jumped up to help me. Just as we finished placing the gifts under the tree, Baker reached the top of the stairs with the Barbie jeep. The girls were loaded down with presents behind him.

"Hello, Leelee."

"Hi, Baker." Oddly enough, I was calm when I said his name.

He looked exactly as he had seven months ago when I last saw him in this very room. The same eyes, the same black hair, and his familiar sleek slender body. Once my storybook prince—now all I could see were the stains and blemishes my friends had always known were there.

"You're looking well," he said.

"I am well." I couldn't return the compliment. "I need to get back to work. Are you gonna stay with the girls a while or do you need to rush right off?"

"No, I wanted to watch them open their gifts . . . if that's okay?" He turned around to Isabella and Sarah, who were diving into their presents. "I'll be right back, girls. Don't open anything 'til I get back. I want to tell your mommy something. Mandy, please don't let them open anything." Baker followed me down the stairs and into the sitting room. He looked off to the left and then down at his feet before his words finally spilled out. "Leelee, look, this is awkward as hell. I know you think I've been a dick. But things are much better for me now. I'm happy! For the first time in my life, I've got a job that I feel good about. I've raised the revenue this season at Powder Mountain by thirty-eight percent over this time last year. *My degree's in marketing.* I'm intelligent and I want to be successful. I was dying in insurance. You know that. Then, when we came here, the stress of the move and your reaction to it nearly killed me."

"*My* reaction?"

"You hated it from the minute we got here."

Instead of arguing, I just stood there—silent and indifferent.

"Why haven't you gone back home, anyway?"

I didn't want him knowing that I hadn't had a single offer on the inn. That was my business now. I didn't want him to know anything about me, actually. "I don't know. Maybe I will, maybe I won't. What's it to you, anyway?"

He didn't answer me. Instead he appeared quizzical. I could tell he was taken aback by my audacious approach.

"And what about our daughters? What's your plan for them, Baker?"

He hung his head, but only for a moment. "They're better off with you . . . in Memphis. I know that. They can spend their summers up here. I mean, shit, it's paradise in the summer. You have to admit that."

"All six weeks of it?"

"Whatever, Leelee." *It was always all about Baker. Whatever Baker wanted Baker got. Why hadn't I seen it before?* "The place looks nice. New name. New look. When'd you move the six-top table?"

"Right after I fired Helga."

"*You* fired Helga?"

"I certainly did."

"I heard she quit."

"Well, you heard wrong. Now if you'll excuse me I've got a business to run . . . with employees who are *counting on me*." With my hand on the doorknob, I turned around to face him. "Have a merry Christmas, Baker," I said in a cheery voice, and passed on through to the inn.

Moments later, I was walking back in the kitchen and right up to Peter. I even went behind the line (a no-no with most chefs) and gave him a hug, dirty apron and all.

He took a small step back and furrowed his brow. "What's that for?"

"For being my friend."

He seemed confused.

"Aren't you my friend?"

"Of course I'm your friend."

"Good." I went to grab the food for table four that he had just placed on the line, when he reached out and grasped my shoulder.

"Wait."

My head whipped around with a startled look to find his face close to mine.

Instead of words, his eyes dropped, but only for a moment.

"What?"

"Never mind."

"Don't *do* that to me," I said, and lightly stomped my foot. "I hate it when people change their mind about telling me something."

He went back to his stove and tried ignoring me, but I refused to budge. "I'm waiting."

Finally, with faltering words, he said in a kind, tender way, "I'm happy you're my friend." He looked right at me.

My face felt flushed. I couldn't tell if it was from the warmth of the stove or from him. "And I'm happy you're *my* friend."

He looked at me a second longer than normal. Not one for discomfort, no matter how brief, I grabbed the plates from the line. Smiling to myself, and happy for friend-boys, I sashayed back out to the dining room.

Chapter Nineteen

If there's a holiday that spells fun for me, it's New Year's Eve. Not because it's a drunk-fest, but because of the ambiance and the luscious feeling it evokes. I love the fact that everyone is happy, and looking forward to a new start. Hope is alive and resolutions have a chance. Kisses are brand-new and full of promise.

And for those who don't receive one, emptiness forms a hole in the heart and leaves it hungry.

It never crossed my mind, in thirty-three years, that I would ever have to spend this wonderful evening carrying a bar tray. But we had 106 reservations, we were completely sold out, and I was officially now a bartender with a bar tray.

Since Peter knew it was one of my favorite holidays, he helped me plan a midnight countdown with balloons, hats, shakers, and scads of confetti. We hired a piano player, ordered tons of booze, employed extra waitstaff, and really went all out to make the Peach Blossom Inn the site of a memorable evening for all who dined with us.

Our kitchen had to be the busiest place in all of southern Vermont that day. While Roberta cleaned the kitchen, Jim, the sous-chef, worked on the stock and chopped potatoes and veggies. Peter cut fillets, readied his soup, and prepared the pâté. I was helping out in the front of the house, arranging fresh flowers on the tables and replacing melted-down candles. Pierre was restocking the fridge.

Around noon, Peter came up from the dry storage room in the cellar with some bad news. "Something is leaking, you guys," he told all of us in the kitchen. Then he turned to me. "I think you better call a plumber. I have too much work up here in the kitchen to take time to stop. Hey, Jeb, help Leelee, would you? You can stop what you're doing."

Jeb was already hard at work. Peter drafted him, as well as another guy, Tim, to help with the prep work—washing veggies, deveining the shrimp, and anything else that didn't require a chef's expertise.

"This is why I'm the official handyman here. I've got my hand in everything," he muttered, in a semi-begrudging way. He untied his apron and laid it over the deep chrome sink. Jeb's laziness amazed me sometimes. I didn't make an issue out of it and waited for him to take his sweet time.

I led the way down cellar. Just off to the right, at the bottom of the stairs, a pool of water had collected. Jeb took one look at it and knew right away the source of the leak.

"That's a fine how-do-you-do. Now we really have a problem. It's the Hobart. And it's not for me to fix. Wouldn't touch it with a ten-foot pole, no siree, Bob. You better call Mountain Plumbing. They're your only hope."

Mountain Plumbing promised to make it sometime that day but couldn't guarantee me a time. And as the day went by, I sort of forgot about it, to tell you the truth. I spent the afternoon running to the phone—more New Year's Eve hopefuls. We had been booked solid for over a week, with a mile-long waiting list. I had John Bergmann to thank for that. When his review came out in *Food & Wine* the phone had hardly stopped ringing. "Superb cuisine. Warm ambiance with real Southern charm. Call well in advance for a fireside table."

I don't think there was one dinner reservation left in southern Vermont and I know there were no available rooms. Kathy at the Chamber told me there was absolutely nothing else left in the entire region.

Mandy arrived sometime around two and bundled up the girls for a romp in the snow. She had become indispensable to me by now. Although, as much as I appreciated her, I could never shake the feeling that I had abandoned my daughters.

About 4:00 P.M. my last four houseguests arrived from New York City. They had rented the two-bedroom suite and were in town to par*teee*. I had explained to the guy on the phone that the Peach Blossom Inn was not the party palace they were looking for, but he rented the room anyway, hoping to find the action elsewhere. He asked me lots of questions about the size of the suite. Their wives, the guy explained, did not want to be cramped. After informing him there were no TVs in the rooms, telephones, or honor bars, I suggested again that maybe they should think about staying somewhere else. He assured me the suite sounded fine and they were going to try something different for a change. Maybe the peace and quiet would do them good. Besides, he said, there was nothing left in town and he was tired of calling around.

"Hi, y'all," I said, when they walked in the front door. "I'm Leelee, the innkeeper here. Welcome and happy New Year."

"Same to ya," one of the guys said, with his arm around his girl, who was smacking her gum. "I'm Nick, this is Denise." He pointed to his friends. "Timmy and Cheryl."

They reeked of smoke, and I could smell the liquor on their breaths a mile away. I hated to have to break the news to them, but the minute I fired Helga I instituted a no-smoking policy in the kitchen and the guest rooms.

On the way up to their room, Denise, a short girl with a severe New York accent, remarked, "This is our first time at a B and B. We tried renting a place up at the ski resort but everything was booked. Thank gawd you guys had an opening."

"Wait 'til you have dinner. You're really gonna love that. Our chef is fantastic," I told her.

Once inside their suite, I pointed out the closet and the suitcase racks.

"Hey, where's the honor bar?" Denise asked. "*Just kidding.*"

Timmy and Cheryl were busy scouting out the bedrooms and the bath with solemn looks on their faces. "We won't be spending that much time in here, Timmy," Nick said. "When we're not on the slopes, we'll be in the bar. Lighten up, man, it'll be fine." He said it under his breath but I still heard him.

I could feel the tension growing. Tim and Cheryl were not happy. "I'm gonna go back downstairs, y'all, let me know if you need anything," I said, dying to get out of there.

Right as I had my hand on the doorknob, Denise glanced around the room. "How about an ashtray? I don't see one in here."

Uh-oh. Here it is. "I told Nick on the phone we're nonsmoking." I cringed when I said it. Denise immediately looked over at Nick, who merely shrugged his shoulders. "If y'all really need a puff, you'll find some ashtrays on the porches." *In the twenty-below temp.*

Dead silence.

"Well, I'll be on my way."

"It's co*w*old in here," the Cheryl girl slipped in before I could get out of their room.

"I feel your pain," I told her from the doorway. "I'm still not used to it. It's just life in Vermont. Feel free to turn on your space heaters though."

Now, no one was smiling.

"Oh, one more thing, do y'all prefer the first seating or the second seating?" I asked, trying to lighten up the mood.

They all looked at me, confused.

"For dinner? It comes with your room. All except the liquor."

"First seating. We'll be up at Sugartree when the New Year arrives," Nick said, and cracked his knuckles.

"Okay, we'll see y'all at six thirty." I gave them a quick wave and escaped.

When I got back downstairs, Gracie was barking her head off at the guy from Mountain Plumbing. The poor old thing had become possessive of everyone who worked at the inn and she was trying to protect Jeb from the stranger.

"Gracie, shhhhh." I scooped her up and tossed her into our apartment. "Hi, I'm Leelee."

He nodded his head and said, "Mountain Plumbing." EDDIE was mono-grammed on his shirt.

"Has Jeb already shown you the problem?"

"Yuup, and that's what it is. A problem."

"I know that. Is it bad?"

"The booster to your Hobart's got a leak."

"Soooo, is it gonna take a while to fix?"

"Nuup."

"Well, that's good."

"Only if you consider not fixing it good. The problem is I don't have the part. We can't get one until Monday due to the holiday weekend."

"Will it even make it through the weekend? I've got three more sold-out nights ahead of me."

"If I was you, I'd keep my fingers cross't. If she blows, your Hobart blows, and then you'll be washin' all your dishes by hand."

"And if that happens, I might just have to quit," Jeb said, twirling his handlebar.

"Come on, Jeb, you wouldn't do that to me. We're gonna think positive and pray it holds out on us. Out of curiosity, about how much do you esti-mate this costing?" I asked Eddie.

"It's hard to say, miss, but somewhere in the neighborhood of fifteen hundred dollars, I'd guess."

There went the weekend's profit.

That one mishap set the tone for the entire evening. Every staff member was on edge afterward. Pierre's coffee cup appeared on top of the fridge before the first customers even arrived. If we lost our Hobart, we might as well shut down. When we were busy, Jeb spent all night sliding the trays in and out of there nonstop. And now we were staring at the busiest weekend of the year.

On top of everything, it was the coldest night of the year. The tempera-ture outside plummeted way below the zero mark. My two-hundred-year-old inn with hardly any insulation was downright freezing. The heat was cranked up full blast in all the rooms, fires were going in all seven fireplaces, extra blankets were on all the beds, and I had space heaters in each room, yet it still felt like a meat locker to me. If I hadn't been moving all the time and running in and out of the warm kitchen, I would have had to wear my fur coat inside.

The first customers began arriving around 6:00 P.M. Knowing I'd never be able to get everyone seated *and* mix their drinks I decided to hire Sarah's kindergarten teacher, Bev. Whenever the restaurant had more than sixty reservations, I always hired Bev to help out. Bartending was Bev's other job—her moonlight.

The first seating went pretty well; Peter and Jim were cranking out the dinners in the kitchen and the "front of the house" seemed to be on top of things. About 9:00 P.M. though, around the time when all the tables started to turn over, holy hell broke loose.

Right as I was helping Jonathan change over a table from a party of ten *poof*, the lights went out! It wasn't pitch-dark inside, thanks to the candles on the tables and the fires in the fireplaces. But every light downstairs suddenly went black. I fled from the table and burst into the kitchen, which, thank God, was still lit.

"The lights are out in the restaurant," I yelled from the doorway. Not one person looked my way. "Everybody! Anybody? *Help!*"

Roberta finally looked up from the cake she was slicing and shrugged with an "I'm sorry but . . ." look on her face. Pierre was announcing table four's order to Peter, who was all but ignoring him. Peter had every pan in the place full, and since each meal was made to order his total concentration was required. There was not one soul willing to stop and help me.

"Jeb, the lights are out, I need your help!" I pleaded.

"What's going to happen to all these dishes if I leave the Hobart?" When Jeb gets busy, he loves to act like he's the VIP in the kitchen.

"But, what'll I do?"

"Go check the fuse box."

"Where *is* the fuse box?" I yelled back.

"Down cellar!"

"And then what?"

He just shrugged his shoulders.

"Ohhhh," I sighed in frustration, throwing up my arms, "just *forget it*." I ran back out of the kitchen, and noticed Nick motioning me over to the foyer, where thirty people, *at least*, were waiting to be seated.

"Look, I'm not sure what happened, but it's pitch-dark upstairs. All the electricity is out and my wife's freaking out, man. Can you do something about it?"

"THE LIGHTS ARE OUT UPSTAIRS, *TOO*?" I heard myself shrieking, even though the guests were within earshot.

"Yep. Do you got a flashlight?"

"I'm sure we have several, but I have no idea where one is!" Inside, my head was spinning and I felt like I couldn't get a deep breath. "Wait right here. I'll get a candle." I pushed through the growing crowd of people with nine o'clock reservations, grabbed a candle off the mantel, and hurried up the stairs with Nick.

"Hey, I'm sorry about all this," he said, as we dashed up the stairs.

"It's not your fault. This has never happened since *I've* lived here." Just thinking about the impatient customers in the foyer made my heart beat louder and harder until I was nearly out of breath.

Once I was upstairs, where the fire in the fireplace illuminated the sitting room, I caught sight of Cheryl sneaking out of their suite with a space heater in her arms.

"Where are you going with that space heater?" I barked.

"Uh, to the room across the hall."

"There is someone staying in that room, and they already have a space heater."

Something about the way she turned around and scurried back to her room with the space heater told me they were up to no good.

I peeked inside the room she was headed to, and the space heater that belonged there was gone. The sound of people scampering down the hall startled me, and when I turned around, Nick and company were breaking out of their room all bundled up.

"We'll see you later," Nick said, while the others giggled, and all four raced each other down the stairs to get out the front door.

The inside of their suite told the story. While all the other houseguests were downstairs at dinner, the frolicking foursome must have snuck into the other rooms and stole the space heaters. Six space heaters, two in each bedroom and two in the little sitting room, were plugged into the sockets. Even *I* know you can't do that.

I yanked the cords out of the sockets, grabbed the handles of two of the extra heaters, and stormed out of the suite. After placing each one back in the room where it belonged, I flew down the stairs, past the foyer full of antsy people. With no time to seat another single soul, I descended the cellar stairs in search of a black box, or a silver box, or any kind of box that looked like it might contain circuits. There were two big black circuit boxes at the bottom of the stairs and a flashlight hanging on the wall in between the two.

I threw open the door of the first one and scanned the labels on the inside. Cellar, kitchen, side porch, front porch, owners' quarters—not a one of them said a thing about the upstairs or the front dining room. I threw open the next box and my eyes made the same descent down the list. Furnace, dishwasher, walk-in, dryer, washing machine—again, *nothing* about upstairs or the dining rooms.

There must be another circuit box somewhere in this dungeon, I thought. I shined the flashlight in every nook and cranny in the basement (which by the way creeps me out just being down there alone). Down where the wine was kept, in a faraway corner, I spied a small gray box up on the wall. It was high above my head so I pulled up an old rickety chair. I climbed up, having to balance myself on top of the wobbly legs. Jerking open the door of the box, I found eight old-timey fuses. How in the world was I supposed to know which fuse was bad or if this was the right fuse box anyway? There was no itemized list.

So I shined the flashlight up and down the fuses until I discovered a little black mark. *Aha! This has to be the problem*, I thought. Carefully I unscrewed the bad fuse. Then it hit me. Yes, I had discovered the problem—but now I was faced with an even bigger one. It was after 9:00 P.M. on a Friday night—a holiday night—and I was in *Willingham, Vermont*, population twenty. I couldn't just run to Home Depot and pick up more fuses.

Just as I was considering throwing all the breakers, causing a full black-out in the place, and hiding until all the guests finally left, I noticed, among the cobwebs on a ledge at knee level, lots of old dusty fuses. Some were in boxes, others were not. But in keeping with the Schloygin tradition, noth-ing old was thrown away. I knew they never discarded anything but this was ridiculous. Every dead fuse they ever bought was on that ledge.

They were filthy. I had no choice but to use my dress as a rag to wipe away the thick layer of dust covering each glass top, in hopes of finding one good fuse. I must have wiped off fifty of them before I noticed, hidden among the used ones, a 30-amp fuse with a *clear glass top.* "Thank you, Jesus!" I screamed. I climbed back up on the chair to screw in the fuse with no black dot. *Please let this one work, God, please.*

I raced back up the stairs and when I reached the top and saw lights on in the dining room, I almost cried. I tore back through the foyer and could tell by looking up from the bottom of the stairs that all was back to normal up there, too. The only thing abnormal was that each and every foot-tapping person that had been waiting in the foyer miraculously had a seat.

I practically crawled back to the kitchen. Bev was busy mixing drinks and I forced myself to jump in and help her deliver the beverages out to the dining room. As I rounded the corner on the way back to the kitchen, Sarah opened the door from our apartment. I could tell that something was terribly wrong. She seemed horrified. Mandy and Isabella appeared right behind her and I knew for certain there was an emergency.

"There's something wrong with Gracie," Sarah said. "She won't get up and she's breathing funny."

"She's in your closet," said Isabella. "I found her when I went to try on your shoes."

Mandy's tortured face told the whole story.

Into my bedroom I flew, all dusty, frazzled, and red hair flying every which-a-way. There was my little Princess Grace Kelly, lying motionless in my closet with her head upon my slipper. I knelt down right next to her and put my face close to hers. The fur around her face brushed my cheek and I could hardly tell if she was breathing or not. Her eyes were barely open but she could sense me.

"Gracie," I said softly, as tears streamed down my cheeks, "what's wrong? Are you okay? Oh, sweetie, please get up." She moved not a muscle. *Oh God, please. I'm not ready for Gracie to go. Not tonight.*

"Gracie, Gracie please, please get up." I gently stroked her little head and cautiously moved my hand along her tiny body and onto her tail. Her breathing was labored and I knew in my heart Gracie wouldn't last long. Yet I couldn't imagine such a thing. She'd been my little companion since I was seventeen, long before the births of my daughters. Gracie was the last present Mama ever gave me before *she* died.

Ever so gently, I scooped Gracie up and placed her in the crook of my arm and caressed her tiny head. The girls knelt down beside me, stroking Gracie's body, and all of us watched our petite friend slipping away. Her shallow breaths came further and further apart until her belly heaved and she gasped for her last bit of air. I cradled her close to my chest and burst into heavy sobs. Naturally, Sarah and Isabella did, too, and Mandy's eyes welled up right along with ours.

Gracie's eyes finally closed all the way. I stared down at her tiny limp body, motionless in my arms. I felt the warmth leave her and I couldn't bear it. "Go get a towel from the bathroom for me, Sarah."

"Okay, Mommy, I will." Sarah went into the bathroom and brought back her most favorite towel, with the Little Mermaid on it, and knelt back down beside me.

"Here, baby," I said, "lay the towel down on the floor where Gracie was." Sarah stretched it out on the carpet. Isabella sat in Mandy's lap, still too young to fully comprehend.

"Put Princess Grace right next to Ariel. That's the best spot," Sarah said.

I laid her back down on top of the towel right next to the Little Mermaid. Then I covered her up, spreading one side of the towel over her at a time.

My mind drifted off to how much Gracie hated Vermont and I wondered if she might have lived longer if she hadn't had to deal with all this ridiculous weather. That thought made me angry and resentful—especially at Baker—and I loathed the day I ever agreed to move. *I hope you're happy, Baker Satterfield. Now look what you've done.*

I knew I had to get Gracie out of my closet. So I picked her back up, in the Little Mermaid towel, and carried her outside through the snow to the little garden shed just off the barn. It broke my heart to leave her there but I knew no stray animals could creep in uninvited and she would be safe inside.

The last thing I wanted was to go back out into that restaurant—my face was beet red—but we were short-staffed and they needed me. In a fog, I wandered back toward the kitchen.

Pierre was heading out to the dining room with a bottle of champagne when I opened the apartment door. One look at me told him something was dead wrong. "Leelee, *s'il vous plaît*, what es it?"

"Gracie passed, Pierre. Just now in my apartment." Of course as soon as I said it, I started crying again.

He gave me that familiar look of confusion and shook his head. I didn't have the energy to try and explain and I certainly wasn't going to hunt for my French dictionary. So, I collapsed down on the ground, put my arms and legs straight up in the air . . . and woofed.

Pierre about fell out. He put the champagne down on the wait station and grabbed the edge of a chair. Slowly, he walked around it and sat down, placing his hand on his heart. "Gracie," he whimpered and his bottom lip started quivering. That made me cry even harder, and both of us sat there weeping together—with an entire restaurant celebrating New Year's Eve all around us.

"Where es Gracie?"

I pointed outside.

"Come, *s'il vous plaît*."

Pierre stood up and headed immediately for the door. I grabbed my coat and both of us trailed out to the shed. He hurried inside, stood right next to where Gracie lay, and waited for me. All I could do was cry as he unwrapped the little towel and caressed poor ole Gracie. "*Petite amie. Bonne nuit, Gracie,*" he said, and kissed her little dead head.

On the way back into the kitchen, I grabbed a pair of sunglasses out of my room so no one could tell how hard I'd been crying. When I took a seat on the red stool next to the phone, I realized I hadn't sat down all day. I couldn't remember a day in my life when I felt this tired, and the New Year's countdown was still thirty minutes away. The phone next to me started ringing. I picked it up on the first ring with a stuffy resonance to my voice. "Peach Blossom Inn."

A female voice was on the other end of the line; background noises indicated it was a call from a cell phone. "Yes, hi, I'm looking for directions to the Peach Blossom Inn," the lady said. "Let's see, I'm on Route 21, passing the Gentry Farm?"

How about this caller, I thought. *Here it is right at eleven thirty and she thinks she can get a dinner reservation for New Year's Eve—now!*

"I am so sorry," I told her. "We are totally full for the night *and* we're booked solid for New Year's Day tomorrow, but I'd be happy to take your reservation for Sunday night."

"I don't need a reservation," she said, "I've already got one."

"Oh, my mistake, excuse me, I thought all the dinner guests had arrived already. I've been away from the phone actually. What's your name, please?"

"Emily Kay . . . for two."

I looked down my list and found no Emily Kay with a late dinner reservation, or an early one, for that matter. "I'm sorry, Emily, but I'm not finding your dinner reservation. When did you make it?"

"I don't have *dinner* reservations. I've got a room for tonight and I booked it two months ago."

"I beg your pardon?" The words squeaked out of my mouth. Every single one of my guests had long since checked in.

"A room, I'm staying there tonight and I'm lost."

"What did you say your last name was again? I'm sorry, it's been a long night."

"Kay. Emily Kay."

I ran my finger down the list of New Year's houseguests in my reservation book, still believing this woman was out of her mind, and there it was—bigger than life, right where it was supposed to be. Written in my own handwriting, with her MasterCard number to boot, was EMILY KAY PLUS ONE.

I had overbooked the inn.

Pressing the mute button on the telephone, I turned around to face Bev. Since I was officially in a state of shock, earned honestly from calamity hell, I could only stare at her with a blank, forlorn look.

She waved her hand in front of my face. "Leelee. Leelee. You look like you've just seen a ghost. What's wrong with you, gal?"

I didn't answer her right away. I just stared straight ahead, my head cocked to the side, resembling an intoxicated moron. "I've overbooked the inn." The voice I heard tumbling out of me didn't sound a thing like mine. A croaking toad was more like it.

"Are you sure?"

"Positive." In a trance, I lost the ability to blink.

"There's got to be some mistake," Bev said, snapping her fingers in front of my gaze.

"Look right here, see this name—Emily Kay?" I nervously pointed at the reservation book.

Bev just shook her head. "Crap, Leelee, what are you going to do?"

"I have no idea." I laid my head upon the book, my left hand still pressing the mute button, and barely opened my eyes to look over at her. "But I'm open to suggestions."

Bev pushed her hair behind her ears and shook her head. "I'm at a loss."

"*Help.*" The word barely made it out of my mouth.

The distinctive beeping of a receiver left off the hook gave us momentary hope that the woman had gone away. "She hung up . . . thank God!" I said to Bev. "Hopefully she'll never find us." Without a plan in place, I did the only thing I could do. I took the phone off the hook.

With only a short time left before the countdown, I hurried around to all the tables passing out hats and shakers, confetti and horns. I put on a hat, too, and flitted around from table to table. Fortunately most everyone had had enough to drink by now and my sunglasses just seemed to be part of my New Year's getup.

Three minutes and counting before the stroke of midnight, Pierre staggered around the restaurant holding a glass and tapping it with a spoon. "Midnight countdown, midnight countdown! Es almost midnight, *messieurs, mesdames,*" he slurred in his French dialect.

Victor, the pianist, got the countdown started by playing some dramatic piano chords, and yelled out, "Ten, nine, eight." One and all joined in, "Seven, six, five, four, three, two, one, happy New Year!" Horns started tooting and confetti was flying all over the place. Vic followed with "Auld Lang Syne," and it looked like every person was singing along with him. People kissed and they hugged each other and I . . . well, I didn't get to hug or kiss anyone. My favorite part of the night was happening without me. I turned away from the action to keep from another big boo-hoo and happened to catch sight of a young couple standing in the foyer with their coats on. I didn't remember seeing them before, but then again, I only seated four people from the second seating. I thought it an odd time to leave since the countdown was barely over.

I couldn't hear the conversation between them but my stomach suddenly fell to my feet. Now I knew exactly who they were. I ran toward the kitchen to buy myself a few more moments of clear thinking. I caught Bev on her way out and dragged her by the arm over to the front of my apartment door.

"They're here, Bev. What'll I do? I got my hopes up that they wouldn't show but they're here. Where am I gonna put them? Help me, Bev!" I grabbed my head and this time I really wanted to run and hide.

"*Your* room?" she said, as more of a question than a solution.

I opened the door and let her peek inside. Everything was still a big mess from Christmas. Toys all over the place, clothes strewn all over the floor—you could hardly make out the color of the carpet. Through another door, she could clearly see the huge bed in my bedroom.

"What about Pierre's cottage?"

I raised my eyebrows as if to say, be serious. Then, out of nowhere, lightning struck. The brainstorm of brainstorms shot down from heaven. "I've got it!" I squealed. "Now, you'll probably think I'm crazy but it's our only chance. Mr. and Mrs., uh, Follett, you know, the couple in their late fifties, early sixties?"

"I think so."

"The Folletts are sitting in the front dining room and they are already pretty tipsy. You go keep their drinks filled up, bring them free champagne, the best we have—or a pitcher of martinis if they want. Just stall 'em. Do whatever you have to. I'm going upstairs to move their suitcases out of their room. Then I'll check the Kays into that room. And put the Folletts into the junk room."

"Okay, now you've lost me. What and where is the junk room?"

"Right across the hall from the Folletts' room. It's really a guest room, but it has all of Helga's tacky furniture and my stuff from home that I couldn't fit up the narrow attic steps."

"And where exactly is it all going now? *On New Year's Eve?*"

"I'm still figuring that part out but I'm sure it'll come to me."

Bev looked at me like I had lost my mind.

"The junk room's my only hope. It's either that or I risk a huge scene."

"I guess we don't have a choice. But you better come up with a place to put everything from the junk room, and quick!"

"I'll go get Roberta, she'll know what to do. You go out and tell the couple it'll be a minute. And do whatever it takes. Make up a lie if you have to. Just don't let the Folletts go up to their room."

Without further ado, Bev proceeded out to the front dining room.

I flew to the kitchen and stood in the doorway motioning for Roberta to come quick. By now Roberta knows how to read panic on my face and she dropped what she was doing and followed me out the door.

"There's no time to give you the history but trust me, it's the worst night of my life," I told her. "I desperately need your help."

"I'm with you—at your service."

"Good, I knew you would be. Here's the sixty-four-thousand-dollar question. Where would we put two extra houseguests if we were already booked up solid for the night?"

I could see her mind drive into deep thought. She started mumbling under her breath and I couldn't make out any of the words. All of a sudden her face lit up. "Your apartment?"

"No, try again."

She paused before she spoke, even scratched her chin. "Pierre's cottage?"

"One more guess. Third time's a charm."

"The Willingham Inn down the street?"

"No, Roberta. *The junk room*. We could clean out the junk room!"

"Of course. The junk room! Sounds like a plan to me. Just let me know when you want to get started and we'll get her done."

"I knew I could count on you. Do you want to leave your apron here?"

"My apron? Why would you want me to leave my apron?"

"Because it's covered in flour and restaurant goo."

"You don't mean clean it out *tonight*, do you?"

"*I overbooked the inn, Roberta!* The Kays are standing in the foyer right now ready to check in." I pointed behind me in the direction of the front entrance.

"In that case, we better get cracking."

Right at that moment Pierre staggered past us completely smashed and all covered in confetti. His New Year's hat was a tad crooked.

"I've overbooked the inn, Pierre." When he never commented I turned to Roberta. "Why am I telling him? He can't understand me."

"He understands more than you think he does, I tell you. Pierre would rather you think his English is limited, so he can get away with more." She put her arm on my back and nudged me toward the door. "Let's go."

Bev was on her way over to the Folletts' table with a bottle of Perrier-Jouët chilling in an ice bucket when Roberta and I ran past her and flew up the stairs to the Folletts' room. I opened the door and barged right in. Stuff was all over the place. I quickly unzipped both suitcases and started stuffing anything I could see inside.

"Roberta, get some new linens," I whispered, as I carried the Folletts' suitcases out into the hall. The only place I could find to hide them was behind the couch in the sitting room. *Dear God, I must be out of my mind*, I thought. But what in the world else was I supposed to do?

Back inside the Folletts' room, I remembered to check the closet. Sure enough, more clothes were there, so I stuffed them inside their hanging bag and carried it back out to the sitting room to hide with the suitcases. Roberta rounded the corner with fresh linens and the two of us stripped the bed and made it up again in two minutes flat.

Within twenty-five minutes of their arrival at the Peach Blossom Inn, I showed the Kays to the Folletts' room.

"This is nice," Emily said, looking around. "Worth waiting for."

"Thank you, I'm glad you like it. Well, let us know if you need anything," I said, scooting backward out into the hall.

"Are you okay?" Mr. Kay asked. "You seem winded."

"Oh, no. I'm just busy, that's all, and the night's young. Why don't y'all go downstairs and toast the New Year? Have a glass of champagne . . . on me."

They looked at each other and shrugged, threw their coats on the bed, and followed me down the stairs.

"See Bev, the lady over there?" I pointed to where Bev was standing at the Folletts' table. "She'll take good care of you." I motioned over to Bev and pointed at them behind their backs. Bev gave me a wink and I was off—to hold a little impromptu waitstaff meeting.

I had no time to explain to the staff *why* we were doing what we were doing. "Just follow me," I instructed. Three people on my waitstaff trailed behind me upstairs to the junk room. Roberta was already inside pulling stuff out into the hall.

I took one peek into the room and thought, *Oh my gosh, no, there's no way.* I had all of Helga's tacky old furniture, every spare mattress, all my old clothes, old files, pictures, and lamps stored in that room. I even had Issie's old changing table set up in there. The junk room had become a rest stop for all my surplus goods when I didn't have the time to climb the attic stairs. The room was completely jam-packed and impassable. But I had no other choice.

I couldn't start making up beds until I could get to them, so all the other junk had to come out of the room first. Everyone carelessly banged this and that. "Shhhh, y'all, please, we have guests in these rooms," I told them. But how quiet can you be with six people moving furniture out of one room?

Jonathan and Vanessa carried the extra lamps, pictures, and other oddities down the stairs, through the restaurant, and back to my apartment. I can only imagine what my lingering dinner guests must have thought when they saw the staff that had been so attentive to their needs hustling through the restaurant carrying armloads of clothing, boxes, lamps, and files.

An hour later we had the room cleared out enough to uncover the double mattresses that had been propped up against the wall since the day I moved in. Still, the biggest dilemma was finding a home for all the unwanted pieces—another double mattress set, a twin set, a chest of drawers, an old twenty-inch Magnavox TV, all of our suitcases, a couch, and three ugly, oversized chairs that simply weren't going to fit anywhere. Obviously we couldn't store them in another guest room and we certainly couldn't carry them through the dining room to the apartment. Our only choice was to haul them down the stairs, straight out the front door, and down the street to the barn.

So at one o'clock in the morning, negative twenty degrees outside, and with a foot of fresh snow on the ground, all six of us began the long, frigid haul to the barn—five women and one guy in a furniture procession. I never had time to change out of my heels and cocktail dress. A little bolero was the only thing keeping me covered, and one can only imagine how warm that felt in the frigid air.

Just as Roberta and I rounded the corner with the double mattress, Peter, Jim, and Jeb were en route back from emptying the trash in the barn. Until that moment I had successfully kept the overbooking a secret from the guys in the kitchen. When they saw me, with my head propping up the weight of the mattress, Peter's mouth gaped open.

"Leelee. What. Are. You. *Doing*?"

"It's a long story. Don't ask."

"Give me that," he said, jerking the mattress away from me. He motioned to Jeb to help him and when Jeb didn't move fast enough Peter yelled, "Get the damn mattress! Where are we going with this?"

"The barn," I yelled, and scurried back to help Jonathan and Michelle with the heavy old TV they were helping each other carry. Jim took the weighty suitcase from Vanessa, who had had to take little tiny baby steps because of the way she was holding it in front of her with both hands.

After all the unwanted furniture had been dumped in the barn, Roberta and I dashed back to make up the bed and lay out fresh towels for the Folletts. Once inside, Roberta noticed all the goose bumps covering my arms and legs. "Look at you, Leelee, you're ice cold from head to toe. But it's no wonder, you're not as big as a minute."

"You don't have on a coat, either. Aren't you freezing?"

"Nuup, I'm fine. Besides, I've got plenty of padding to keep me warm," Roberta said, and grabbed ahold of her tummy.

"Let's keep our fingers crossed that the Folletts are drunk as skunks by now. Peek in the dining room and tell me what they're doing."

Roberta peeked around the corner and jerked her head back around. "Oh my, you've got to see this."

"What is it?"

"See for yourself."

I peered inside the dining room and there was Mrs. Follett running her hands through Pierre's thick, shoe-polish-black hair and tousling it all around. They were sitting next to each other at the table giggling, and the champagne flutes they carelessly held in their hands looked like they would topple over at any second. Meanwhile, Mr. Follett's head rested on the table next to them and he was fast asleep. Bev was nowhere in sight.

"Pierre's a charmer," I said. "Look at him—he's loving every second of it. He needs a honey, bless his heart."

"He very well may, but we've still got work to do," Roberta said.

"I'm ready to drop dead."

"You can do that later, but reet now we need to get cracking, missy."

Roberta and I dragged ourselves back up the steps, one more time, and while she made the bed I fetched the Folletts' suitcases. I unzipped them again, just as they had, and scattered their things around the room like before. I placed their hanging clothes exactly as they were in the other closet and messed up the bed. The two guest rooms were very similar. The bed coverings were different, but basically, it was the same furniture, lamps, and the old hardwood floors. True, it was still a bit Helga hideous, but hey, who's complaining at two in the morning?

With the hardest part behind us, now we had to get the Folletts to their new room. Bev was back at their table when Roberta and I made it downstairs. She'd been finishing the dinner checks and counting out the tips for the rest of the staff so they could go on home.

Drunker than two Cooter Browns, Pierre and Mrs. Follett paid no attention to anyone else. Mrs. Follett's speech was slurred and I heard her tell Pierre that he was wickedly handsome. Pierre uttered ne'er a word but he smiled and glowed back at her. Her husband was still sound asleep with his head resting on the table.

"Mr. Follett. Mr. Follett," I said, and gently patted him on the back. When that didn't rouse him I shook his arm and raised my voice a little. "Mr. Follett, it's time to go up to your room."

Mrs. Follett never even looked away from Pierre. Now she was stroking his widow's peak with her thumb.

I tried once more to rouse her husband and this time I really shook him. "*Mr. Follett, it's two o'clock in the morning.* Don't you want to get in your bed?"

"Huh?" He finally opened one eye, never moving his head from the table. "Take me to my room, would you?" He rose clumsily from his chair and I grabbed ahold of his arm.

"That's it, now put your arm around my neck and I'll lead you upstairs." I motioned to Roberta to get on his other side.

We walked the poor thing upstairs to his room. Once inside, I pulled back the covers and Roberta and I laid him down on the bed and took off his shoes. Suddenly, out of nowhere, Mr. Follett reached out for me and tried to pull me down on top of him. Somehow, I managed to duck my head under his reaching arms and squirm away. He rolled over and fell right to sleep.

"That was close," Roberta said, outside the door.

"I'll say."

"What should we do about the missus?"

"Here, we'll leave the door cracked open; she'll figure it out."

Roberta and I headed back down the stairs. "Even if Mrs. Follett does notice the change, she's not about to say anything after the way she's carrying on with Pierre."

We dragged ourselves into the kitchen, which had already been mopped down and cleaned for the next day. After changing into her Sorels, Roberta grabbed her coat and purse at the back door.

"I don't know what to say, Roberta. You've come through for me again. You must think I'm cuckoo by now. Maybe you're even starting to miss Helga around here, huh?"

"What are you talking about? I've started havin' fun since you took over the reins."

"Now that's the best compliment I've heard in a long time. You better get on home; Moe's probably waiting on his New Year's kiss."

"He's fast asleep by now. Moe never stays up past ten, even if it is New Year's Eve. But even still, I must say I'm ready for bed myself."

"Happy New Year." I hugged my Vermont friend extra tight and sent her on her way.

New Year's kiss. Where's mine? I stepped inside Roberta's little bathroom off the kitchen and studied my sulky face in the mirror. My eyes matched the color of my hair and they puffed out like two marshmallows. *No wonder I didn't get a kiss. I'm a fright!* My sunglasses still sat atop my head so I reached up and slid them back down onto my nose.

Dying to call Virginia, I stumbled back to my apartment and collapsed onto my bed. My cordless phone was not on its cradle in the windowsill, so I got up again and fumbled around for it in the mess out in the sitting room. When I couldn't find it there, it suddenly dawned on me that I had left it in the kitchen.

With just enough strength left, I trudged out to the inn one more time. Just as I rounded the corner to the kitchen, I happened to hear Jeb's voice out in the dining room. I thought about ignoring him altogether, but when I heard him talking to Peter, I changed my mind. The two of them had on their coats, ready to call it a night, when Peter caught me peeking in on them.

"Hi, boss! Are you pooped?"

I nodded my head and collapsed into the nearest chair.

Jeb made sure that I had heard about *his* night. "*I* washed a thousand dishes tonight, *with* the Hobart. Thank God I didn't lose her."

I was too tired to comment.

"Is it too bright in here for ya? What you got your sunglasses on for?" Peter asked.

"To hide my puffy eyes. Did you hear about Gracie?" My voice cracked when I said her name.

He came over and sat down next to me, patted my back, and pulled me close to him. "I did hear. I'm sorry."

When I felt his arm around me, my tears sprung forth again and streamed down from underneath my sunglasses.

Peter drew me even closer to him. "Hey, don't cry. It'll be all right."

When I pressed into his shoulder my sunglasses dug into my forehead. He must have sensed my discomfort because he pulled back and looked at me. "Why don't you take these off," he said, and tried to lift the glasses off my face.

I jerked my hand up to my face and held them on. "No, I'm too embarrassed. I don't want anyone to see me looking like this."

A sweet smile spread across his face, which was only inches away from mine, and his voice was filled with tenderness. "It's just Jeb and me, we don't care what you look like with swollen eyes. Do we, Jeb?"

"I don't care," Jeb said.

"But I do." I held my glasses in place and changed the subject. "Did y'all have a nice New Year's Eve, even if you did have to work?"

Peter scratched the back of his head and glanced at Jeb. "It was like every other year. I always work on New Year's Eve. And have for as long as I can remember."

"New Year's is a big night in the restaurant business," Jeb informed me.

You don't say. "So you never get New Year's kisses at midnight?" I said to both of them, before I had a chance to think about what I was saying.

Peter shook his head. "Not in a long time."

Jeb didn't comment. Poor thing. I wondered if he'd ever had a kiss at all.

They couldn't see the anguish in my eyes but perhaps Peter sensed it in my voice.

"You missed out on your New Year's kiss this year, didn't you, boss?"

My right hand lay resting next to his and I saw him eye it. I thought he was merely admiring my emerald dinner ring, when he slowly lifted my hand up off the table and brought it up to his mouth. Peter brushed the top of my hand with his lips and paused before giving it a soft, tender kiss.

For some reason, I tensed underneath his touch. I suppose I was startled—it came so unexpectedly—and a mixture of nervousness and exhilaration ran through me.

Peter pulled away and glanced over at Jeb. "Man, it's late. And we've got to do it all over again tomorrow. How many reservations do we have?"

"Ninety," I said.

"Woah." He backed his chair away from the table.

When he made his move to leave, I felt the disappointment creeping up and I so regretted the way I flinched underneath his touch.

"Hey, Jeb, let's walk Leelee to her door."

"Don't be silly. It's just a few feet away, I can—"

"I insist." He pulled me up from the chair. "Southern guys aren't the only gentlemen on earth."

Before they escorted me the thirty feet back to my apartment door, I ran into the kitchen to grab my phone. Once we had reached my door, Peter said, "Dixie peaches need rest to be ripe and sweet. You get some sleep." He patted me on the head and winked.

I smiled through my weariness. "'Night, guys." I waved and then shut the door.

When I fell out on my bed, I looked over at the windowsill. The backlight on the clock illuminated the dark room and read 2:30 A.M. Even still, I dialed Virginia's number. "Gracie's gone," I wailed into the phone, as soon as I heard her voice.

Chapter Twenty

We rang in the New Year and ushered out our little Gracie. Little did I know, I was in for the mother lode of all Yankee oddities. As I was planning the service, and writing her eulogy the next morning, Jeb had the nerve to tell me that all my planning would have to wait.

"No funerals this time of year," he told me, then took a big stretch and pulled out a seat at the table where I was sitting in the dining room, writing out my speech.

"What do you mean, no funerals this time of year?" I looked up at him like he'd lost his mind.

"Nuup, Princess Grace Kelly will have to stay laid out on the garden shed shelf until the Thaw."

"What in the world are you talking about, Jeb Duggar?"

"I'm trying to tell you. We don't bury our dead in the winter."

"You *what*! What do you mean y'all don't *bury people* in the winter?"

"Exactly what I said."

"Why not?"

"The ground's frozen."

"And what difference does that make?"

"A big difference. You'd never get a shovel in the ground," Jeb said matter-of-factly, and then took a loud slurp of his coffee.

"*Jeb.* This is not acceptable! I would never ever in a million years make Princess Grace Kelly lie on a shed shelf all winter. You're gonna have to come up with another solution."

"There isn't one."

"Jeb, please, this is not proper. I've never heard of such a thing." I've just got to say this right here and now. Not once, not one time, in my whole entire life did one person ever mention this to me before that day. I had no earthly idea that you can't bury people up north in the wintertime. "So what do *people* do? What happens to humans when they die in the winter?"

"They lie in a mausoleum until the Thaw. Then they get buried."

I was completely and utterly dumbfounded. "So let me get this straight. You mean when someone dies in the winter, their family can't even have their *funeral?* They have to grieve all over again months later?"

"Yuup."

"You know what, Jeb, this takes the cake," I told him, and stood up from the table. "This Yankee idiosyncrasy is my last straw. I've so had it with y'all's quirkiness up here. What else do I have left to discover?"

"That depends on what subject you're interested in."

If Daddy only knew.

Come hell or high water, I was determined to let Gracie rest in peace and no idiotic Yankee custom was going to stop me. I even went outside with my own shovel to make sure Jeb wasn't just being his usual lazy self. Sure enough, I couldn't get the dirt to budge even a sixteenth of an inch. But while I was standing there with a shovel in my hand the perfect solution dawned on me.

I wasn't sure what they were called, but I'd seen some road workers with those big, heavy tools that have the spirally point. It bobs up and down and digs a hole in concrete. I didn't see why one of those wouldn't dig Gracie's grave. On top of that, I figured I could get every pot in the kitchen and boil a whole bunch of water. Then I'd pour it all onto the gravesite while Jeb used the big, heavy bobber.

When I told him about my plan, Jeb bucked and hem-hawed around and did everything he knew to get out of burying poor old Princess Grace. But in the end, he finally relented.

Maybe it's just me, but I think there's always something that can be done to get through any situation. But that's not the case with Jeb Duggar. He ended up charging me an extra hundred dollars, even though he knew I was grieving, to break open the ground out back with what I found out was a jackhammer. Jeb made me hire his buddy to help him, too. When you add in Jeb's normal pay, the whole thing ended up costing me $325. But if you ask me, that was the littlest bit of nothing, when you consider the alternative.

First of all, Jeb had to use the snowblower to make a walking path over to the hill where I wanted to bury Gracie. That job alone took them a couple of hours. I watched periodically from the window. I could tell by Jeb's body language, though, that he was not enjoying himself.

After a long break, and two cups of coffee, the boys told me they were finally ready. Jeb moaned and groaned the whole way up the hill. It's not like it was a huge hill but it did take some work to get up there.

"Couldn't you have picked a spot closer to the house?" Jeb asked me. Beads of sweat trickled down his broad face, even though it couldn't have been more than two degrees outside.

"It's the prettiest spot in the yard. I want it to be nice for her," I said.

"She don't care, she's dead."

"Oh yes, she does. And even more, I care."

Jeb and his buddy, Frank, carried the jackhammer and I pulled a little wagon with two big stockpots of boiling water. Even though I had the lids on both pots, the water swished around and spilled all over the sides. Once we got to the base of the hill, the two guys had to come back down and carry the pots up to the top. They were way too heavy for me. Both of them murmured under their breath as they leaned forward on their way to the top. I don't know what they were complaining about, it's not like they weren't getting paid—and paid well.

At the top, Jeb cranked up the jackhammer. I tipped the first pot over and we all watched as the snow washed away and the water slowly seeped into the ground. Jeb helped me pick the second one up and both of us dripped the water little by little onto the spot until it made a muddy paste.

"Hurry up, Jeb, get the jackhammer going," I told him. "We don't want the ground to freeze back up."

"Alreet, already, I'm going as fast as I can."

Jeb and Frank picked up the jackhammer, put the spirally point right on the muddy spot, and cranked her up. All three of us had on ear protectors resembling headphones. They came with the rental. Even with those on I still heard that thing echoing in my ear for days.

Once they had the hole dug I asked Jeb if he thought he might like to moonlight as a wintertime gravedigger. I told him I thought people might pay big bucks to be able to get their grieving over with.

He let go of that jackhammer and Frank lurched for it just before it fell to the ground. Jeb's face was all sweaty and he looked over at me like I was out of my mind. "Have you forgotten about my number-one job? There is way too much going on at JCW for me to spend my precious time digging graves."

"It was only a suggestion," I said, holding my hand up. "Don't ever say I never tried to help you become a millionaire."

I watched Frank's eyes nearly pop out of his head as he picked up the jackhammer and held it close beside him. *That's right, Frank,* I thought to myself. *You're no fool; make your hay while the sun is shining, or in this case while the sky is snowing.*

The funeral started at 2:00 P.M. Sunday and in attendance were Pierre, Roberta, Peter, and Jeb. And of course, Sarah, Isabella, and me. The girls and I wore our dark colors when it came time for the service. We couldn't wear dresses, obviously, but we dressed up in our nicest long pants and sweaters.

We all gathered at the bottom of the hill and in single file made the trek up to the top. I led the way, carrying Princess Grace Kelly in an old Donald

J Pliner shoebox. It was the only thing I could find that was fitting for her. I certainly wasn't about to put her in a Sorel boot box. The only problem with the Donald J Pliner box was that I had to cut out a little hole on the side for Gracie's tail. When she was waiting on the garden shed shelf it must have frozen sticking straight out.

Sarah carried Gracie's grave marker. "Princess Grace Kelly (Gracie). Beloved pet of Leelee, Sarah & Isabella. We will 4ever miss you." The girls and I spent the better part of the day before the funeral painting the wooden cross and Jeb nailed a long piece of wood to the back to bury it into the ground.

Isabella carried Gracie's favorite old toy. She'd had it since she was a puppy, one of my old worn-out slippers, and she kept it hidden under my bed.

On the way up the hill Jeb whistled "Taps" and I had to bite my lip to keep from crying. I wanted to be able to get through the eulogy, at least, without sobbing. The tears could come later.

Once we all gathered on the top of the hill, I pulled out my carefully planned speech from my coat pocket and started the service. "I'd like to thank y'all for coming." I cleared my throat. "Princess Grace Kelly was fifteen, that's a hundred and five in doggie years. She was born in her beloved hometown of Memphis, Tennessee, to two registered AKC Yorkshire Terriers. And I can't remember their names. Sorry, Gracie," I said, and looked up at the sky.

"Princess Grace Kelly was a wonderful dog, the best any person could ask for. She was loyal and loving and watched over her owners at all times. Gracie loved everyone here. She really did." When I looked up and saw everyone smiling my voice cracked. "I can't say that she loved Vermont or all this ridiculous snow, but she appreciated everything each and every one of you did for her. As hard as it was for her here, there were some good things. She would have never tasted pâté if she had never made the move. And that's thanks to your marvelous cooking, Peter." I glanced over at Peter for reassurance. "She enjoyed a rich diet of goose liver pâté right until the day she died."

Peter winked and smiled back at me with an impish grin.

"Roberta. You always made sure that Gracie had fresh water both in the kitchen and upstairs in our apartment and you were always so good about keeping clean newspaper in every corner of our owners' quarters. She so appreciated that," I said, and looked straight at her.

Roberta gloated like she was family.

"Jeb. If Gracie were here, I know she would be thanking you for making this winter funeral possible. I know it was terribly hard work, but don't think for a second it's gone unnoticed. Gracie is up in heaven right now, with her little jeweled crown on her head, looking down on you and wanting to lick your face."

Jeb puffed out his chest and glanced around at everyone else for credit and appreciation.

"And Pierre. What can I say about you? You welcomed her into your cottage, gave her doggie treats out the wazoo, picked up her poop in the dining room, and protected her from Helga. You were a great friend to Gracie, Pierre, and she so loved you."

Pierre looked up at the sky, kissed his fingers, and threw Gracie a kiss.

"Sarah and Isabella." I squatted down to their level. "Gracie has been around your whole lives. Life will be much different now, but she will always live on in our hearts. Gracie protected you both from the minute you were born. She barked her head off any time someone unfamiliar came near you. She absolutely loved you from the bottom of her heart."

I stood back up, folded my piece of paper, and shoved it into the pocket of my coat. "Does anyone have anything else to say about Gracie? Don't be shy, say what you feel."

Nobody said anything for the longest time, and I was afraid they might let the moment pass, when Roberta raised her hand.

"Yes, Roberta, go ahead."

She stepped forward out of the group. "Princess Grace Kelly was a beautiful dog. I enjoyed being around her and I'm happy she moved here with yous." Roberta nodded her head, and took a giant step backward to rejoin the others.

"Thank you, Roberta. Anyone else?"

"I think we'll all miss Gracie," Peter said from where he stood, and then he smiled and held his hand over his mouth like he was trying to keep from laughing. Okay, it was a bit over the top, I know that. But still, it was Gracie and she deserved to be buried in the ground and said nice things about for goodness' sake!

It was when Pierre broke down in sobs and fell to the ground that Peter totally lost it. His shoulders started shaking and he grabbed his scarf and pulled it up over his mouth but that didn't work. Finally he turned around and tried not watching, but that didn't help, either. Nothing he tried made him stop laughing and it didn't take long for it to become contagious. Pretty soon I got tickled and couldn't stop for the life of me. My little copycats joined in, too. "Why are we laughing?" Sarah whispered, pulling on my sleeve.

"I'll tell you later," I tried to whisper back, but I was giggling so hard my stomach hurt and tears were rolling down my face.

A certain someone didn't share in our amusement. Jeb marched over to his shovel, yanked it up, and started tossing dirt on top of Gracie's makeshift casket. "You people are downright strange." One look at his dour face was all it took to get me going again.

Pierre was still on his hands and knees sobbing when Roberta decided to take matters into her own hands. She stepped up again and in a loud voice announced: "That concludes our service, thank you all for coming."

Chapter Twenty-one

The art of fire building, to a Southern girl anyway, is not innate. When I asked Jeb to teach me how, he puffed out his chest and said, "Jeb Duggar, expert fire constructor, at your service, ma'am," and saluted me.

When he started whistlin' "Light My Fire," I shooed him off and said, "I'm serious now, I don't want to build just any fire, I want a full, blazing, crackling, big one!"

"All you need is four logs, some kindling, a big wad of newspaper, and a match."

Bless his little heart. "I know *that*. But they always die out after a short while. I can't ever seem to keep one lit."

In his defense, it was his technique that made all the difference. All my previous attempts failed due to the way I stacked my logs. Jeb taught me how to lay the first two logs across the grate with about three inches in between the two. Then he laid two more on the diagonal on top of those logs, keeping a small parallelogram in between all four logs. Next came the kindling and the paper and he showed me how to put it in the parallelogram and stuff lots more up under the grate. The trick to the whole thing was not stacking all the logs on top of each other where no air could escape. "A fire's got to breathe," Jeb explained.

Sunday nights were fairly slow at the Peach Blossom Inn, especially during the winter. On this particular Sunday night, around the first of February, we only fed twenty customers and they were all gone by 9:00 P.M.

The girls were sound asleep and I had the inn all to myself. It seemed like a great time to try out my new Northerner skill and build a fire in the parlor. I had just put a match to it when I heard the floors creak in the main dining room.

"Leelee, are you in there?" a voice called out.

"Peter! You scared me for a second." I turned around as he walked in the room.

"I'm sorry. Didn't mean to."

"I thought you were gone." He walked up next to me and we watched the fire spread out over the newspaper and kindling.

"I got almost home and couldn't remember if I turned off the ovens, so I decided to come back and check. Am I interrupting anything?"

"No, no, no. I'm just trying out my new pyro technique. Jeb taught me how to build a fire. Woah." The logs caught and popped like a crisp fall bonfire. The radiance illuminated the otherwise dark room and I couldn't help but notice how cute Peter looked in the firelight. He wore an old pair of Levi's, an off-white corduroy shirt he had rolled up at the sleeves, and a white thermal underwear shirt underneath.

"You're a quick learner," he said.

"Thanks. I'm pretty proud of myself, actually. You might not even know I was from the South, huh?"

"The Souuuth? What would ever make me think thaaat?"

"Fine, would you rather I *tawok* more like a New Joysey girl to make you feel more at home?"

"As a matter of fact, I would not. I love the way you talk. And I also love this album." He pulled up a chair to the fire. Van Morrison's *Moondance* played softly in the background from the boom box I had nabbed out of the kitchen.

I turned to face him with my back warming to the fire. "It's one of my all-time favorite albums, ever."

"Looks like all you need now is a Grand Marnier."

"Oh, no." I shook my head and waved my hand. "I'm not going there again, I've learned my lesson. Besides, I might tell you more stuff I don't want you to know."

"You mean there's more stuff about you that you don't want me to know?"

"There might be."

"Now you've got me intrigued. I'm grabbing a beer. Can I at least get you a beer or a glass of wine?"

"I suppose so, surprise me."

Peter left for only a minute and came back with two beers. A Corona Light for me and a Guinness for him. He handed me the beer and sat down in the chair next to the fire.

I had been dying to know more about his past but after he told me about his little brother stealing his girlfriend I never really knew how to bring it back up again. But he knew so much about me. "Where'd you learn to cook so well?" I asked him. "You hardly seem like you would ever need to be someone's sous-chef. You're a much better chef than Rolf could ever be."

"That's kind of you to say, thanks. I've been around. Apprenticed under some amazing chefs in the city."

I sat down on the floor in front of the fire next to his chair. "So, now I know where you learned to cook; what about your love life? You're too cute to have never been married." Okay, it was out there. I told him he was cute.

"I never said I haven't been married." He took a long sip of his beer.

"Oh . . . you mean you *were* married? Once before?"

"Yep. It didn't work out."

"Well, I understand that. Just look at me. What happened to your marriage?" I pulled my legs up and rested my chin on my knees.

Peter turned his head and stared at the fire. I sensed he didn't want to talk about it.

"You don't have to tell me. Just forget I asked."

"No, actually I want to tell you. I've wanted to talk to you about it for a while now."

"I promise I won't bite." I gave him a big smile and giggled. He didn't smile back.

"My wife and I owned a restaurant together. Not much different than this place, but it was on the Jersey shore. We had a nice, loyal clientele. It had a great reputation and I was proud as hell of it. I worked hard to build it up, put in thousands of hours. As you know, it's nearly impossible to get time off in this business. We were always busy."

I noticed he was picking at the label on his beer bottle and then started throwing the little pieces into the fire. "My younger brother worked with me. He was my sous-chef. I'd always looked after him, made sure he kept out of trouble. My wife, Shelly—that's her name—worked as the hostess before the baby was born. But once he came along she liked to stay home and take care of him."

A child. He never mentioned that before. I watched him talk but he never took his eyes off the fire.

"One August night, we were slammed and she knew I needed her to come in. She left Jeremy with a sitter. I was the one who told her it was okay. I mean the lady had raised three kids of her own." He glanced at me briefly. I nodded in agreement with him.

"Once Shelly got to work that night, she loosened up. Like she kind of enjoyed the break. She even had a couple of beers once we closed and I could tell she was happy to be hanging out with her friends again. We always got a late bar crowd and we were friends with all the regulars. She was having so much fun, I told her I'd go home and let the babysitter go so she could stay."

He picked up his beer and finished it all at once. There was a long pause before he continued.

"On the way home, I could hardly keep my eyes open so when I got there I asked the babysitter if she would mind staying a little longer. I just needed a short nap before the baby woke up for his next feeding. All I wanted was a few minutes just to close my eyes." As he said that, Peter dropped his head. Something about his tone of voice shot a chill through my spine.

"I bet I hadn't been asleep ten minutes when I woke to the sound of the babysitter frantically calling my name. She couldn't get Jeremy to wake up. I *always* checked on him when I got home. *Always.* But that night I was beyond my exhaustion point and I . . . never even peeked in on him. Doctors later determined it was SIDS."

It took a moment for the reality of what he had told me to sink in. Wanting to let him know I was there for him, I reached out and touched his arm. I ached to hold him in my arms and tell him it was all right, but he never touched me back. He just kept staring straight ahead into the fire. "I am so sorry, Peter. I never should have asked you."

"Of course you should have. How would you have known? I'm trying to move on with my life, that's why I haven't mentioned it before now. She said she didn't blame me, but . . . we're no longer together. And here's the end of the story. Shelly fled into my brother's arms. Given the devastation, I guess he was in a better position to console her."

My heart was breaking for him. "Is there anything I can do for you?" I asked, after a minute or so. "I feel so bad for you."

"Nope, but it felt good to tell you about it. Let's change the subject, okay?" At last he turned around to face me. "I'm honestly trying to put it all behind me for good. Hey, I've got a toast but my bottle's empty. Can I get you another?"

"No, thank you. I've still got half of mine." I held up my bottle to show him.

When Peter came back from the kitchen, I was standing and my back was toward the fire. He raised his bottle in the air. "A toast. To new beginnings."

"I'd love to drink to that." I raised my bottle and each of us took a sip, holding each other's gaze long enough to be awkward. Right then, the familiar first chords of my favorite song on the record, "Into the Mystic," softly began.

"Ohhh, I love this song. It's my very favorite Van Morrison song." I started swaying to the music and held up my right arm with the Corona still in my hand. I had my eyes closed when Peter gently took the beer away from me and set it on a nearby table. My heart leaped out of my chest.

Van crooned and Peter moved in toward me, clasped his left hand around my right, and slowly wrapped his other arm around my waist. My body tingled under his touch in a way that I hadn't felt in much too long a time. At first it was hard for me to look at him but I could feel his eyes upon me and I raised my head and gazed up at him. His coy smile reassured me that he, too, was nervous. Somehow, even through the tension, it felt peaceful, and when he put his cheek just above mine, I could hear his breathing start to quicken. We moved very slowly, cautious with each step, gliding along with the music. *Oh my God, we're dancing!*

It felt quite lovely to be back in a man's arms. I closed my eyes and settled into his embrace, Van's lyrics transporting me into a world far across the sea. Ever so slowly, we inched along with the music. Peter and I almost made it around two full circles before the inn phone started to ring. Nervously, each of us looked up, waiting for the other to make a move toward the kitchen. *Please stop ringing*, I thought. But reservations are money in this business and to ignore a phone call is to kiss away cash. It kept ringing and ringing. And it wouldn't stop.

"I'll be right back," I said, letting go of his hand and moving away from his embrace.

"Wouldn't want to miss a reservation, right?"

"Right," I whispered, hoping he would stop me.

When he didn't, I hurried into the kitchen.

I answered the phone, "Peach Blossom Inn," and a man started right into the conversation.

"Leelee, you've got your wish!"

His voice sounded familiar but I couldn't place it. "Excuse me?"

"You're going home. You can be in Memphis as soon as you've got a moving van to pack up your things."

"Ed? Is that you?"

"Of course it's me. Who else would be calling you with great news? I've got a buyer who is ready, *with cash*, to close as soon as you can vacate."

I had to sit down on the red stool to steady myself. "You've got *a buyer*?

You've got to be kidding. I had no idea you'd even been by to show the inn."

"I haven't been by. These folks knew about the place the last time it was on the market. They don't need to see it again. They're ready to move forward immediately. Isn't this great? I told you I'd get it sold."

"I don't know what to say," I said, in a not-so-excited way.

"I thought you'd be thrilled."

"It's just that you caught me by surprise. I wasn't expecting your call." Peter was in the kitchen by this time, watching me curiously.

"Hey, I know it's late but I just wanted to give you the good news. I'll call tomorrow and we can iron out all the details. Good night, Leelee. And congratulations."

"Good night."

I slowly hung up the receiver and glanced down at the floor, searching for the right words, the right emotions . . . the right way to feel. I had longed for this moment from the minute I stepped foot onto the soil of the state of Vermont, fourteen months ago. Here it was, finally upon me, and I wasn't even sure how to react. Thoughts of home were no longer consuming me every single minute of the day.

"Who was that? Obviously not a reservation," Peter said.

"No. It wasn't."

"Then who was it?" The gleam in his eyes served as a reminder of the tender moments we had just shared.

I hesitated before answering him. "Ed Baldwin."

"The real estate guy?"

I slowly nodded. "Yeah." Peter could tell I was stalling, I'm sure, because I couldn't say anything for a few moments, creating an uncomfortable silence. Finally, it spilled out. "He's got a buyer."

Right away, Peter looked down at his feet, and then mustered a smile. "Well, what do you know? That's great, boss! You've got your wish. You're finally going home. Good for you. I'm happy for you. Give me five." He raised his hand and slapped mine, which I had barely raised at all. "What's wrong? Aren't you happy?"

"I don't know."

"You don't know?"

"I *don't know.*"

He felt my forehead. "You don't feel sick. What's wrong with you?"

"Nothing's *wrong* with me, it's just that . . ."

"It's just what? That you're afraid I'll be upset I'm losing my job?"

"Well, yeah, that's part of it."

"You don't need to be concerned with that. I can find another job in a heartbeat," he said defensively. "You'll give me a good recommendation, won't you, boss?"

"Of course I will, that goes without saying. But—"

"Hey, I've heard the Sugartree Inn is looking for a chef. I'll call them in the morning. No sweat. I'm cool."

He acted like he wasn't bothered at all, that replacing his job at the Peach Blossom Inn was all in a day's work. Next thing I knew, he was headed over to the back door and grabbing his coat off the hook. "It's getting late. I'm gonna head out. See ya Tuesday."

He never even gave me a chance to move off the stool he was in such a hurry. So I just waved.

He waved back, headed out the door, and was gone. And so was our dance.

Why did I answer that stupid phone call? Why, why, why? We could have at least finished our dance. And then . . . and then *what*? Did I think he would have *kissed* me? Did I even *want* him to kiss me? I sat on the stool all alone in the huge commercial kitchen of the Peach Blossom Inn and glanced around, ready to cry.

The big pots hung above the line and the dishwashing station was wiped clean. The floor was mopped down and the rubber mats hung over the sinks to dry. The liquor bottles were placed neatly one in front of the other and all the plates were stacked and in place. I rose to get a better view of the ovens and I glanced over to where Peter usually stood behind the line.

He really is drop-dead gorgeous. Over six feet tall, blond hair, blue eyes, and a body so red hot, I could melt anywhere near it. I pictured him standing there with his apron folded in half, tied around his waist, and wearing his black-and-white checked chef pants. A bandanna wrapped around his forehead instead of a big, billowy white hat. Why hadn't I noticed it before? And now, I learn he's been hiding unspeakable grief.

Somehow my pain seemed minuscule in comparison. If something happened to Sarah or Isabella I'd go out of my mind. I don't think I could breathe another day into my body if I tried. Here he finally gets up the nerve to talk to me about it and I finally get the call I spent the first six months praying for.

Another beer? *Why not.* I grabbed a Corona, opened it, and wandered back out to my fire in the parlor. Walking up to the boom box, I searched through the CD 'til I found track five again. I hit Play and slowly drifted back over to the front of my fire to savor every moment of Van's voice.

"We were born"—I closed my eyes and lifted up my right arm—"before the wind"—I clasped his invisible hand into mine and I wrapped my arm around his waist. Slowly, I started moving with him. The top of my head brushed just under his chin and I pressed in closer to him this time, less timid and more willing to feel his beautiful body next to mine. I moved my legs in between his so that our bodies were touching all the way from head to toe. Round and round we glided to the unhurried rhythm of the song. Ever so tenderly, he reached down and lifted my chin off his chest. With inviting eyes, he leaned in and gently placed his lips upon mine. Kissing me softly once, twice, thrice; he slowly opened my mouth with his. Now his arms were wrapped around me as he tenderly savored my kiss and held me 'til the ballad's end.

As the piano sounded its last chord, I let my arms drift back down to my side. Wanting to thank him for the dance, I slowly opened my eyes to smile at him.

Where'd you go? Please don't leave. Not yet. Just one more dance?

Not tonight. My partner had silently vanished into the mystic.

Chapter Twenty-two

Huge flakes cascaded down from the sky and landed one on top of the other, quickly covering any patch that had melted away from the previous snowfall. Neither of my little girls were awake so I walked around the inn, admiring its beauty, especially in contrast to that first day when I stepped foot in the foyer. The houseitosis was completely gone and the place looked like another inn altogether.

After bundling up, I ventured outside to take a look at the front of the place. There my beautiful new sign hung in place of the old Vermont Haus Inn rusted one. PEACH BLOSSOM INN was in beautiful script with perfect little peaches in place of the two Os in "Blossom." I remember when the man delivered it last July. Peter and I raced each other to the front door to watch the man hang it. Peter was so proud of the way it looked. I thought nothing of it at the time, but in looking back on it now, I remember he picked me up and twirled me around he was so happy. I was kind of happy, but I was thinking more about getting back to Memphis than my new sign.

Then there was the day the new menus arrived. We used the new logo on peach parchment and the lettering itself was exquisite. Peter beamed every time he picked one up. I always thought it was because I had added his name to the menu, along with mine, as a courtesy to him. *Your hosts, Leelee Satterfield—Innkeeper & Peter Owen—Chef.*

Now I was realizing that it was much more than that. Peter put time and thought into every single detail of that menu. It took him a solid week to finalize the entrées and he spent hours and hours searching through his vast collection of cookbooks to come up with the perfect bill of fare. In the last eight months, Peter Owen had never missed one hour of work, forgotten to place a food order, wasted one cut of meat, over-ordered a single time, or let me down in any way. He had been there for me, unconditionally and with a smile, every single, solitary day since Baker Satterfield left me to run that place all by myself. And now he was losing his job.

But I warned him in the initial interview that this could happen. I remember distinctly being honest and up-front about the possibility of the inn selling at any time. The more I thought about it though, guilt was not the emotion I was feeling. It was sorrow. Sorrow over the end of the song, the end of the adventure, the end of the dream. I wasn't quite sure whose dream I was mourning or which one, but it was a melancholy time nonetheless.

It was getting mighty cold outside and by now I was covered in snow. As I stepped back into the foyer for warmth I heard Roberta pull up in her little Ford Taurus and park just outside the kitchen in the side parking lot.

She seemed startled when she walked out of the bathroom. I was waiting right outside the door.

"Oops, you scared me," she said. "You're up mighty early."

"I couldn't sleep."

"Did you finally break down and buy a scanner?" Roberta giggled, amused with herself.

"No, Roberta, never."

"Follow me upstairs if you want to chat," she said, heading out of the kitchen. "I've got to make up the guest room in the front."

I followed her up to the linen closet and then into the unmade bedroom, where I sat down on a chair in the corner.

Roberta unfolded the sheets. "Now then, why ain't you sleepin'?"

"Ed Baldwin called last night. He's got a buyer."

"You don't say! Why, you must be as happy as a fly drowning in new, warm syrup."

"I don't know what's wrong with me. Sure, I'm happy. It's what I've been wanting for over a year. But I never would have imagined in a million years that my happiness would feel this *un*happy."

Roberta went about her business of tucking in the corners of the sheets, her little round body stretching over the bed as she flattened out the top sheet with her hand. "You know what I think?"

"What?"

"I know I'm no shrink, but I think you're a lot happier than you realize. Right here in Vermont."

I thought about what she said but I didn't answer her right away. I helped her spread the blanket out over the bed. "But Memphis is my *home*," I finally replied, "and I miss it."

"It seems to me that everything's falling in place right here in Willingham. The inn's makin' money, you've got it decorated awfully nice. Helga's gone, and you're not crying every day over Baker. And that's thanks to Peter." She stared right into my eyes.

"He stepped right into the chef's job, didn't he?" I picked up the bedspread from another chair and tossed it onto the bed. "That does help, I have to admit."

"I'm not talking about Peter helping out with the cooking, I mean he gives you something to smile about. You turn into a glowworm any time he comes around."

"I do?"

"Yuup, you do."

"When do I glow?"

"The minute he walks in the room. Why, the same goes for him. He lights up like a firefly whenever you get near him. Call me nuts if you want to, but that's my observance." She shook out the pillow and held it up under her chin. Then shook it down into a freshly laundered case.

"Hmmm."

"It's something to think about." Roberta's eyebrows popped up and she smiled a toothless grin as she plopped the pillow onto the bed.

I was in the big kitchen taking a reservation when Jeb showed up, apparently ready to spend his day off—and mine—talking. I didn't have to break the news to him. Roberta nabbed him before he even made it into the kitchen.

"When do you leave?" Jeb said, as soon as I hung up the phone.

"Ed said I could leave as soon as I pack up my stuff but I still have to hire a mover. Maybe in a couple of months or so."

"You want to stay two more months in this winter? Are you sure you're still Leelee?" Jeb walked up and knocked on my head.

"I was just thinking that all the moving vans are probably booked up, that's all."

"I doubt that. But what do I know about moving vans? I've never lived anywhere else in thirty-nine years, except right acrosst the street." Jeb combed his beard with his fingers and looked off to the side. "I might end up down south. You never know. I think I might like it down there."

"Really? Jeb Duggar, you mean to tell me that you would actually leave Vermont behind?"

"I might," he said, nodding his head, lips pursed.

"Well, the upside is there's hardly ever any snow, not that many chimneys to sweep, and you sure don't have to get up on the roof to chip ice. And you can be assured of this, you'll *never* find a roof rake in any hardware store, no matter how hard you look."

"Hmmm, I guess that means my plowing business might suffer." Nervously, he twirled the edges of his mustache.

"Oh, it would suffer all right. Try nonexistent."

"Then what could I do down south?"

"I guess you could still be a handyman; I mean houses need fixing there, too."

"Why, sure."

"And you could paint. And wallpaper and wash dishes in a restaurant. Or how about your own business? Jeb's Computer World shouldn't be *that* hard to move."

Jeb puffed out his chest and I could see the wheels turning in that head of his. He hadn't even thought about JCW. "I'll think about it." He said it like he thought I was trying to talk him into it. "Mom's pretty sold on Vermont. She's never lived anywhere else either. And, you're wrong about something. It *is* hard to move a business. Jeb's Computer World's got a reputation around here."

"Yes, it does. And not only in Willingham. JCW's reputation has spread all the way to Tennessee."

"I might give Alice and them a call," Jeb said, like they were thick. "They told me when they were here they'd all be fighting over me if I lived in Tennessee."

Bless his heart. "Any time you're ready for their numbers, just ask." I could just picture Alice now when Richard told her there was a Jeb Duggar on the phone for her.

"Mommeeeee," Isabella cried, reaching out her arms to me, and I squeezed in between the two of them. Sarah crawled up in my lap and Isabella nudged in next to her on my other leg. I kissed the tops of both of their heads and wrapped my arms around them. Their little bodies were warm even though the temperature outside was negative fifteen.

What am I doing to them? I thought as I held them tightly. *All they ever do now is watch TV. They don't go outside, except when they're at school, and the teachers make all the kids go out for recess, no matter how cold. I'm not about to take them out for longer than fifteen minutes at a time. There is absolutely nothing else to do here,* I thought. *We go into Manchester every now and then to get to McDonald's. That McDonald's has to be the only one in the country without a playground.*

Thank goodness for Sarah's kindergarten class. The school bus took them to ski on Tuesdays and that was kind of cool. In fact when I went up to the mountain to watch last week, the instructor had all the kids following behind him, snowplowing without any poles. It was quite the sight to see all those children, seven and under, twisting and turning single file down a green slope all bundled up in hats and snowsuits.

I tried skiing in Vermont, really I did, but the temperatures up on the mountain were always under zero, *always*. It was unbearable to me. My toe heaters helped, but I was still miserable being outside for any length of time.

I seriously considered exactly what there was to offer my little girls if we stayed. Kids ice skated on ponds around Willingham, but that scared me. Which reminded me of another thing. No swimming pools in Vermont. I could have either skiers or swimmers. That was my choice.

"Girls," I said softly, and leaned down in between their little faces. "What would y'all say if I told you we could be home soon?"

Sarah took her thumb out of her mouth, and held it up, wet, like she would go right back to it. "In Memphis?"

"Uh-huh," I said.

"To our old house with Daddy?"

"No, not to our old house, but we'd find another one."

"With Daddy?" Sarah asked once more.

"I don't think so, angel, but he could come visit."

"Doesn't he love us anymore?"

"Of course he loves you, he's just gotten a little sidetracked. He wanted to try something new. He'll come visit, I'm sure of it."

"I miss Kissie, I want to see her." Sarah changed the subject abruptly. Those two were joined at the hip from the minute Sarah was born.

"I miss her, too." I pictured sweet old Kissie leaned over the stove in her little kitchen in Memphis, just off Elvis Presley Boulevard, tasting whatever she had cooking with a long wooden spoon. "She'd be so happy to have us home."

Isabella didn't bother to take out her paci, she clenched it with her teeth and said, "I just want to be with you, Mommy," and nestled in closer to me.

I started dreaming of enrolling the girls in the Jamison School for the next school year. Only missing kindergarten, Sarah would still make it into the Jamison School Twelve Year Club after all. Isabella could start junior kindergarten in the fall.

Pretty soon the butterflies found their way back to my stomach. It was the first of February and the daffodils would be out any minute now back home. March was just around the corner and that meant I could see green within weeks—instead of three and a half months! No more snowplows waking me up every time their engines ground their way up the hill. My little girls would say "yes, ma'am" and "no, sir" and we could throw away the snow boots and neck warmers. Nor'easters would be a distant memory in no time flat.

I flew down the stairs in search of my cordless phone, which I had left in the commercial kitchen. It was right where I had left it next to the inn's black dial phone. As I punched in the numbers to Virginia's cell phone, I found myself with a little skip in my step.

"Hi, Fiery," she answered. "What in the world have you been up to?"

"Let's see, work, snow, and snow."

"Nobody's talked to you in over two weeks. Is everything okay?"

"Of course everything is okay. In fact it's great. Guess what? I've got news!" There was a little singsong to my voice.

"Let's hear it."

"Where are Alice and Mary Jule?"

"Alice's at home and Mary Jule had to go to a planning meeting for the Lenten Waffle Breakfast at the church. Al's mother is the chairman this year and Mary Jule felt like she had to volunteer to be on the committee. She's losing her mind, though. Al's mother calls her fifty times a day."

"Can we get her on her cell?"

"We can try," Virginia said.

I dialed Alice. "Alice, it's me, can you get a three-way with Mary Jule, she's on her cell."

"Well, if it isn't Miss I've-been-meaning-to-call," Alice said.

"Will you *hush*? I've got big news. Virginia's on with us and I need you to get Mary Jule on the phone."

Within twenty seconds, Mary Jule whispered, "Fiery, are you there? I had to fake like I needed to tee-tee and go into the bathroom to talk. I don't have long. Al's mother is about to drive me *crazy*."

"What are y'all doing for spring break?" I asked.

"Destin, Alice's parents' condo. Wish you could join us," Mary Jule said. "It's no husbands—just us and all the kids."

"I *can* join y'all!" I squealed.

"How?" Alice asked.

"I'M COMING HOME!"

"When?" they all blurted at once.

"As soon as a moving van can pack me up. Six weeks or so."

"You mean you're *moving* home?" Mary Jule said. "Are you kidding? What's going on?"

"The inn sold and the buyer wants to close right away."

"Tahiti, here we come! We should cancel Destin this year. Leelee, did you collect your insurance money from your ring yet?" Virginia asked.

"I forgot all about that," I said.

"Table the Tahiti talk, would y'all, please. Leelee, *what about Peter?*" Alice asked.

"What *about* Peter?" I answered.

"I thought y'all were getting close," Alice continued.

"Not any closer than I've gotten with Roberta, Pierre, and Jeb. I'm really gonna miss them."

"And you're not gonna miss Peter? Bullshit, I don't believe it," Alice argued.

"When I told him about the inn selling he acted like he could care less."

"You're reading him wrong. He cares all right." Now Alice was monopolizing the conversation.

"How do you know? You only met him that one weekend," I said.

"Yeah, but every time I talk to you you're always talking about him and what good *friends* y'all have become. I think you kissed him when you got drunk that night."

"I did not! So what are you saying, I should stay here 'cuz of Peter Owen and not sell the inn?"

"Absolutely not, I'm just saying he's gonna miss you."

"Oh crap, here comes my mother-in-law looking for me, y'all. Gotta go, bye," Mary Jule whispered, and hung up immediately.

"I'm so happy, Leelee. F*inally*, is all I have to say," Virginia said.

"Ditto that. I'll let y'all know when I have a moving date."

"Move in with me," Virginia said. "You and the girls are welcome here as long as it takes you to find another place to live."

"Five children under one small roof? Y'all are crazy, John will pull his hair out. Maybe you should stay with me, my house is bigger," Alice said.

"Not that much bigger," Virginia told her.

"Would y'all stop? Let's not worry about that right now. Thanks for the invitations—both of you. But I better let you go. I wanna get quotes from some moving companies. Plus I need to call Ed Baldwin back. I never even asked him how much the offer was for."

"Alrighty then, talk to you soon. Love you, Leelee," Virginia said.

"Yeah, I love you, girl," said Alice.

"Love you both," I said, and hung up.

I grabbed the Yellow Pages and called the first company on the list—Allied Van Lines. They gave me an initial quote over the phone. It was when they told me their first available opening that left my tongue hanging out.

"We can move you Monday week," the man on the phone said. "Will that work for you?"

"You mean a week from today?" I giggled after I asked him.

"That's what I mean."

"No, that won't work. I haven't even had a real estate closing. What's your next opening?"

"Not 'til the middle of March. We had a cancellation for next Monday."

"Gosh, that's in a week," I said. "I better think about this, sir, and call you back."

"That opening won't last long," he told me.

Right away, I called Ed Baldwin. I still remembered the number. I'll never forget how it was typed out on his brochure. 1-802-CALL-ED-B. His Vermonter receptionist answered the phone on the first ring. "The Ed Baldwin Agency, Doris speaking."

"Hi, Doris, this is Leelee Satterfield. I'm calling for Ed. Is he available, please?"

"I'll check, he stays awfully busy, you know."

"So he's told me."

After what seemed like five minutes, and purely for effect, I'm sure, Ed finally answered. "Ed Baldwin."

"Hi, Ed, it's Leelee."

"*Leelee!*" he practically yelled with excitement. "I was working down my list to get to you. So how about that sale? Told you I'd come through for you."

"You sure did. Hey, Ed, you didn't tell me how much the offer is for."

"Three thirty-five."

"*Three hundred thirty-five thousand*! That's fifty thousand less than we paid for it."

"We can counter, I plan on it. But remember, Vermont is in the middle of a real dry spell these days."

"Ed, if everything is so dry around here, then how is it that you stay so busy all the time?" Of course I had to come right back with, "I mean, I don't mean to be *mean* or anything, but I *am* curious."

"Well, uh, I've got several properties that I've listed—on the market right now—and they require my full attention. I'm working on several deals in New Hampshire as well. But in my expertise, Leelee, you should take the money and run."

"So, what do you suggest as a counter-offer?"

"Three fifty-five. I could make the call right away."

"I suppose that sounds reasonable." *I would give anything if Daddy were here right now. But he's not. You have to do this yourself, Leelee.* "On second thought," I told him, "let's counter at three sixty-five—after all, they're getting a heck of a deal. I've made drastic improvements to the place. I bought it smelling like *body odor*, Ed. These new people don't even have to deal with that."

"Three hundred sixty-five thousand it is. I'll call you when I know something."

I hung up the phone and headed into the bathroom to run my tub. When I saw the light brown water filling up the tea-stained porcelain tub, I reminded myself, once again, I had made the right decision. After turning on the space heater to make the room tolerable, I huddled in front of it waiting for the tub to finish filling. *Why would I want to keep living like this?* I thought. *Freezing my butt off ten months out of the year.*

But on the other hand, I'm thirty-three years old, I own my business, and I'm making money. Not much, but we're getting by. And I feel like, for the first time in my life, I can do something on my own. I don't need anyone to do it for me.

What on earth is wrong with me? Why am I so confused? What is it about Vermont that's making me doubt myself now? I've never liked it here. Or have I? I cautiously stepped in the tub, little by little, getting used to the hot water. Finally, I was able to lie down, and as I soaked in the warmth and closed my eyes, I let my mind drift back over the last fourteen months.

The portable phone startled me from my thoughts. I leaned over, dried my hand on the floor mat, and answered it. It was Ed—only fifteen minutes in between calls.

"They've countered back at three fifty-five," he started right in. "I think you ought to take it. I've got clients that would give their eyeteeth to have an offer like that—considering the economy."

The economy. Why is it that the economy never works in my favor? "Well, if you don't think they'll come up . . . I better think about it, Ed."

"Oh, they aren't coming up. They almost walked away when I told them you had countered. They know how things are around here. They've also seen my listing in Rutland and they're interested in that inn, too."

I almost told Ed to just let them buy that inn instead. But images of home flooded my mind. I could see my little girls in their bathing suits on the swim team, and our girls' lunch at the country club, and barbecue sandwiches from Little Pig's, and the azaleas and the dogwoods and the concerts down at Tom Lee Park on the Mississippi with the prettiest sunsets in America. I could see Kissie, her hair pulled back into one big "plat" as she called it. Her stockings all wrinkled at the ankles, inside her white lace-up shoes. At eighty-one, there's no telling how much longer she might be alive. As I began thinking about *that,* I panicked and all at once I had my answer. I had to get home. *Peter, Roberta, Pierre, and Jeb are not my fam-*

ily. Kissie, Virginia, Alice, and Mary Jule are my family. Now that I'll be a single mom I'll need them more than ever.

"I accept their offer," I said, definitively.

"You're making a wise decision. Strike while the iron's hot, if you know what I mean. Have you given any thought as to a moving date?"

"I called one moving company, Allied I think it was, and they aren't available until mid-March, except for one opening a week from today. I laughed when the man said that. As if a real estate closing could happen that soon."

"Don't underestimate our buyers. Like I told you on the phone, they almost bought it last time it was for sale. They told me they could close as soon as you're ready."

"That's *real* soon. One week? I couldn't be packed up by then."

"I know all kinds of packers and between Roberta and Jeb I don't think it should be a problem to get you packed up and on your way."

"I guess I could *try*."

"We'll set the closing date for late Monday morning, and you can be on the road by Tuesday."

"I have to say, Ed, when you put your mind to something, you get it done." I accidentally slapped the water with my left hand. The last thing I wanted to do was let Ed know I was talking to him from the bathtub.

"I bring results. That's how I stay in business."

"There's one more thing. I've been feeling bad for everyone here at the inn. Do you think they'll be able to keep their jobs?"

"I don't see why not, there's a restaurant to run."

"What about Peter? Will they need a chef?"

"I doubt that, but I'll be happy to look into a sous-chef position for him."

"I'm not sure he'll want that, but I'll let him know you offered."

"Good enough. Congratulations, once again. I'll speak with you soon, bye now."

"Bye."

So the decision was made. The girls and I were leaving one week from tomorrow. We would be living at Virginia's house in Memphis in less than two weeks. Let me say that again a little louder, and a little better. I'LL BE HOME IN TIME FOR SPRING! And when I say spring, I mean *spring*. Flowers, azaleas, dogwoods, and green, green, green.

I wanted to tell Pierre myself, before anyone else got to him. Since it was a Monday, his day off, I knew he'd be sleeping late. I kept an eye on the little café curtains that hung in the front window of his cottage. An open curtain was the sign that his day had begun and it was okay to disturb him.

About a quarter 'til eleven, I noticed the curtains were open and I rapped on his door. It took him a little while to answer and when he did, he cracked the door slightly and peeked outside.

"Hi, Pierre." I smiled and waved.

"Ohh, Leelee. *Bonjour, amie*." He opened the door fully and motioned for me to step inside.

"Whatcha working on?" His latest jigsaw puzzle was spread out over a little card table in front of his twelve-inch TV. I sat down and started fitting the pieces. One of Gracie's little chew toys was in the corner and I reached over and picked it up. "I miss Gracie."

"Gracie," he said, shaking his head. "Vedy good dog, vedy good dog."

"You loved her, didn't you, Pierre?" I said slowly and loudly.

"*Oui*." Pierre touched his heart.

"I need to tell you something. This is very hard for me, but—I'm going home to Memphis."

"Memphis?"

"I'm . . . moving, Pierre, I'm going back for good."

"No."

"I got a call from Ed Baldwin. You know, the real estate guy? He . . . sold . . . the . . . inn." I was speaking quite slowly although we had begun communicating fairly well.

His eyes opened wide.

"Don't worry, you'll still have your job."

"*Merci, merci*. Eh, are you happy?"

"Yes, I am very happy. It's time for me to go home, Pierre, I don't belong here. I'm cold all the time." I held my arms like I was shivering. "And I miss my friends . . . *amies*, you remember Virginia, Alice, and Mary Jule?"

"*Oui.*" He smiled when I said Mary Jule's name.

I touched my heart. "I miss them. Memphis is my home. Vermont is hard. It's very difficult for me here. In all kinds of ways."

"Eh, Peter is still chef at Peach Blossom Inn?"

"No, I don't think so. The new owner is a chef, I think."

He got a perplexed look on his face. Maybe he didn't understand me. "I am sad, when you go. Sarah and Isabella vedy sweet girls." He acted like he was sucking on a pacifier and smiled.

"They love you, Pierre." I thought about when Baker predicted he'd be a grandfather to the girls. He was right. As hard as it was to communicate with Pierre, I knew he loved us.

"Sarah and Issie and I will miss you."

"You vedy smart woman, Madame Leelee."

A very smart woman. That's what someone who could hardly communicate with me thought about who I was. With all that had happened over the last year, there were times when I doubted that very statement and wondered if I would actually be able to make it on my own. To think that Pierre, who could only *watch* my actions, and observe me by the way I conducted my business rather than what I said, thought that I was a very smart woman gave me a renewed confidence. I had no doubt that it would be tough to go forth as a single mother, but I knew for sure that I could make it.

Chapter Twenty-three

All week long, Peter had been acting standoffish, leaving immediately after he finished in the kitchen. He hadn't done that from day one so that's how I knew for sure he was mad or hurt or feeling just plain let down by me. The Sugartree Inn hired him on the spot, just as he predicted, so that was one large worry I could strike off my list. In fact, he said they were paying him a hundred more dollars a week. In my mind, that was a big plus, and I assumed he was happy for the raise.

But every time he walked through the inn, and saw all of us packing, he never once offered to help and I never once asked him for it. We hardly said two words to each other all week.

Actually, as it turned out, I didn't need his help. Roberta stayed by my side, assisting me the most, and Pierre ran a close second. Jeb played like he was helping, but every few minutes he'd act like he was needed at JCW.

Roberta put on like she was happy for me but I could tell she was struggling. Her perpetual smile was gone and the lilt in her voice had disappeared.

We truly had become buddies. In fact, she was my closest friend in the whole state. If anyone had told me last Christmas Eve, when Roberta Abbott bragged about her Sorels she fought for in a "tag" sale, that she would become my best girlfriend in Vermont I would have said, I *doubt* it. But now I found myself despondent over losing such a faithful friend.

"Will you visit me?" I asked her as we packed up the parlor.

"I'm not so sure about that," she said, with a bit of melancholy in her voice. "I've never been past New Hampshire. Moe went over to New York once't, to the racetrack at Saratoga. He's been promisin' to take me but he's been promisin' that for six years now. Tennessee's a long way away."

"I know, but you might enjoy it. I could take you to Graceland."

"Now you're talking." Joy temporarily returned to her face.

Jeb overheard me and jumped right in. "I'm coming for a visit. I'll be checking out Graceland, the Grand Ole Opry, and Dollywood, too."

"Now you've got me taking you all over the state."

"Might like it so much, I might decide to stay. You never know. Don't you flatlanders have Mary Kay or Avon down in Tennessee?"

"I think so."

"Your mother would never go for that, I can tell you that *reet* now, Jeb Duggar." Roberta and Jeb's mama were friends. Roberta thought that gave her license to boss Jeb around.

"I'm not saying I'll move for sure, *Roberta*, I'm just keeping my options open."

I quickly diverted the conversation. "All y'all are welcome anytime in Tennessee. I'd be happy to have you." Jeb went back to his chores and whistled "Hound Dog" while he replenished the firewood.

"I'm gonna miss you, Roberta." I felt a lump knotting in my throat.

"Well, missy, I think I'm the one who's goin' to miss you." She finished folding one of the drapery panels, which Jeb had taken down from the window, and glanced over at me. "It won't be the same around here without you. Now that Helga's gone, I actually look forward to coming to work. You've made everything nicer."

I watched her place the panel neatly in the box in front of her and grab up another. "At first, I wasn't so sure about you and how you would fit in up here. When you started making all the changes I got nervous but now I can see it's done a world of good. I've learned a lot from you."

I had been wrapping my china in newspaper, and I stopped abruptly. Her words took me by surprise. "I am so touched by that, thank you. But I can't help wondering what in the world you've learned from *me*?"

Her good eye gazed at me as if she was genuinely shocked that I had asked her that question. "How to be a survivor. I watched you hold yourself up, even when your husband walked out and left you for another woman. You kept it together for your little daughters' sakes. You could have run back to Memphis then, but you didn't. You kept on goin'. Then when Helga done you wrong, you still didn't give up. You fired her instead and I don't know anyone who could have done that. You had the guts to change up this place and give it a new look and a new name and a new menu, too."

"Actually, the menu was all Peter."

"It don't matter who did it, it was done under your leadership. You know what I think?"

"What?"

"I think that after watching you, I could do it, too. If anything ever happened to Moe, I'm sure I could make it on my own."

"That is the nicest thing anyone has ever said to me, Roberta." I reached out to hug her and when I wrapped my arms around her little, roly-poly back, I felt so much love for her. I truly would miss her so much. "Daddy always told me I could do anything I put my mind to, but until now I never believed it."

"Well, believe it. I wish I could've met your dad. You've talked about him so much I feel like I know the man."

"He may not have liked the cold weather, but he sure would have been proud of the Peach Blossom Inn."

"It's you he would have been proud of."

Baker will want to say good-bye to the girls. I'd been dreading making the phone call, and by Friday afternoon I could no longer silence the small voice in my head. What I really wanted to do was skip out of town. Just escape and leave the way he had—with no warning. *Maybe I'll just write him a note and tell him we've gone home. He did it to me.* Didn't he deserve to have a dose of his own selfishness? Maybe he did, but my girls did not deserve any of this and it wouldn't be fair to deprive them of one last visit. There was no telling how long it would be until they saw him again.

I dialed directory assistance to get the number of Powder Mountain. The switchboard operator put me through to his office and the lengthy wait seemed downright rude.

"Baker Satterfield," he answered at last.

"Hi. It's Leelee."

"*Oh*. Hey." Boy, did I take him by surprise.

"Were you busy?"

"No, I mean— Well, yeah, I'm always busy. Things are crazy around here. We're having a banner seas—"

"The girls and I are leaving. We're going home."

"When?"

"Tuesday at sunrise."

"And you're just now letting me know?"

"Please don't go there. Unless you want to discuss *your* definition of advance notice."

Silence.

"Would you like to see them?"

"Of course I want to see them. Are you kidding? Let me think a minute, here." I listened while he cleared his throat. "Tonight's out. I've got a dinner. Sunday *day* is Huega Ski Club—"

My blood boiled. "You are *un*believable, Baker."

"Wait a second. You're the one that's just now springing this on me. How long have you known about it?"

Forcing myself to tame the sword in my mouth, I softened my tone. "Only a couple of days. Can you work it out?"

"Yes, I'll pick them up Monday right after work."

"I'll have them ready." I paused a moment, thinking about what else I wanted to say. I hate confrontational conversations, even with him. "When I get to Memphis, I'll . . . figure everything out. About the divorce and all."

"Sure. Whatever works for you."

"Okay. Well. I'll talk to you sometime. Bye."

I hung up the phone and screamed out loud, "*I hate you.*" I climbed up on my unmade bed and buried myself under the covers. *You are so selfish. How could I have ever been so blind?*

Sunday was my very last night in the restaurant. We were slow, only serving fourteen dinners. Peter and Pierre, now steadfast buddies, were attempting to have a lucid conversation about wine at the end of the night. Peter was listening to Bob Dylan on the boom box and drinking a glass of Sonoma-Cutrer chardonnay from a bottle that a customer had left half full. Pierre had brought it into the kitchen and immediately offered it to Peter.

When Peter saw me with a tray full of coffee for the customers at the last table, he lifted his glass to make a toast before I left the kitchen. "Here's to Leelee, owner and now deserter of the Peach Blossom Inn. Best wishes." Then he let out this contrived laugh, like we were supposed to think what he said was funny. When no one else but Pierre giggled at all, he said, "It's a *joke.* Can't anybody take a joke around here?" And he threw his sauté pan into the sink. It banged loudly when it hit the chrome bottom.

I didn't comment. Neither did anyone else. Roberta looked straight at me and I motioned for her to follow me out the kitchen door.

"Is he drunk?" I whispered, when we got to the waiting room just outside the kitchen.

"*Ohhh,* yes. He had a glass of wine next to him all night. Pierre kept it filled to the top. Never seen him do *that* in all these months I've worked with him."

"That was mean, what he said back there. He is not the person I thought he was." That kind and gentle man, whom I thought I knew so well, had just slit my trusting heart wide open and filled it up with doubt. Doubt about his character, our friendship, and what's worse—doubt about my decision.

"He don't mean it, it's his *de*fense talking. He's just sad to see you go, that's all."

"Well, he sure has a strange way of showing it. He's barely spoken to me all week."

"Remember what I told you? About the way he lights up when you come into the room?"

I nodded.

"I watched him looking at you tonight when you didn't know. He's hurting on the inside. That's why he's acting that way. He's goin' to miss you."

"Now you sound like Alice. She says the same thing only she's just speculating. She's only been around him once."

"Aren't *you* goin' to miss *him*?"

"Well, sure I'm gonna miss him. Just like I'm gonna miss you, Jeb, and Pierre."

"The heart speaks louder than words, Leelee. Listen to yours."

After the last four people left the restaurant, I slipped into my apartment to check on the girls and fix my hair. I brightened my lips and even added a little perfume to my wrists.

When I made it back into the kitchen, it was pitch-dark—not a soul in sight. When I heard the cellar door creak open in the dining room, it gave me hope that a certain someone was still around. My heart started to race and I hesitated a second before moving in that direction. Mustering all my courage, I slowly walked out of the kitchen and into the dining room, only to find Jeb pouring a glass of water over the remaining embers in the fireplace.

"Is everyone gone?" I asked, looking around.

"Yuup."

"Didn't everyone leave sort of soon? I mean, it's only ten thirty. Usually, the kitchen doesn't go dark until after twelve."

"It was a slow night, and tomorrow's a day off."

"I wanted to tell everyone good-bye. You'll be here tomorrow, won't you?"

"Sure. I'll be here at some point. Things don't get cracking around JCW until midday. Might try to sleep in for a change."

"My moving van arrives around eight tomorrow morning but I'm not leaving until Tuesday. I'm hoping to get an early start."

"I'll be over tomorrow."

"In that case, I'll see you then. Have a good night's sleep, okay?"

"I will. Sleeping's never been a problem for me. I sleep like a log. Mom tells me she can hear me snoring down the hall. Funny thing is, I can hear her snoring down the hall."

"Well, you better beat her to bed tonight if you wanna get some rest. 'Night, Jeb," I said, and headed back to my superb owners' quarters. When I shut the door behind me my heart stung. Peter Owen blew out of the Peach Blossom Inn without even waving good-bye.

The movers pulled up to the inn at exactly 8:00 A.M. Aside from directing, there was very little for me to do, as it had all been done in the days before. Almost fourteen months to the day had passed since the last time I hired movers. Everything we brought from Tennessee was going back and every single thing we acquired from the Schloygins was remaining.

Roberta arrived in the middle of the chaos all concerned about the news she heard on the scanner. "Leelee, I don't mean to scare you, but a nor'easter's comin'. It's predicted to blow in here by late tomorrow morning. Make sure you get out of town early. If you stay ahead of it, you should be alreet."

Around noon, Ed stopped by. He almost had me fooled into thinking he was offering to help, but within seconds of his arrival the real reason he was there surfaced.

I offered him a Coke and invited him to join me at the table in front of the bay window.

"So, everything seems to be going well." Glancing around the room, he pulled out his chair and laid a manila envelope on the table.

"Not that much to it, really. All the packing is done. I told you I kept all my boxes, right?"

"Yuup. Bet you're happy about that. Hey, Leelee, the reason I'm here is we won't be able to close this afternoon. I've had to postpone it a few days but your leaving is not a problem. That's what FedEx is for."

"What happened?"

"A death in the family."

"Oh, I'm sorry. Well, I completely understand that. Please send my condolences."

"Right. I certainly will." He offered no other explanation.

"So . . . I can just leave?"

"Yuup." He picked up the envelope and slid out the papers that were inside. "To expedite, why don't you go ahead and sign the closing papers. I'll FedEx the fully executed documents to you in Memphis." He passed me the papers along with a pen.

He could sense my confusion by the bewildered look on my face.

"Your ten-thousand-dollar earnest money check is in escrow and I'll wire your Tennessee account with the balance, or send a cashier's check— whichever you prefer. I've done it many times before. With all the second-home owners here, it happens all the time."

"Well, if you think it's okay?"

"Of course it's okay, I'll take them to get Baker's signature this afternoon."

"Oh my gosh, I hadn't even thought about that."

"He's got to sign, too. I've taken the liberty of calling him and he's got no problem with it at all."

I closed my eyes and sighed. "What did *he* have to say?"

"Not much, strictly business. He'll sign a quitclaim deed, too, no problem."

"Well, he's said good-bye to the girls, he's signing the papers, and I guess that's that. Strictly business." I changed the subject. "What about the restaurant? We have reservations for next week. I only planned for this one week of downtime. That's what they asked for, remember? It's just that I don't want Jeb, Roberta, and Pierre to be without a job."

"I knew you'd be worried about that so I made sure to ask the new owners. They'll be up and running within the week."

"Oh, good. That's my main concern. I figure it'll take me three days to get home so you can send the money on Friday."

"Friday it is. To what address would you like me to send the check? Or like I said, I can wire the money into your account."

"I don't have an account yet, so just FedEx it to me at my friend Virginia's house. I'll write it down for you." In a flash, he whipped out one of his business cards and shoved it in front of me. I wrote down the address on the back and slid it across the table.

Ed moved over to the chair next to me and flipped through the papers, pointing to the lines that required my signature. As soon as I had signed my name on the last line, he rose from the table. "Well, I guess I'd better be getting along. I'd stay around to help but it looks like you're all set."

I walked him to the door and as he reached out his hand I gave him a hug instead. He tensed up a bit, but I chalked it up to his uptight demeanor. "Thanks for everything, Ed."

"You'rrre welcome. It's been great. Don't be a stranger," he said, and hurried on out the door.

Roberta's always right when it comes to the weather forecast. When my alarm went off at 6:00 A.M. on Tuesday morning, I peeked out the window at a snowy sky. The girls and I had slept in the largest bedroom of the inn, since the movers had already left with our own beds. Getting Great-grandmother's bed back out of my room was a sight to see. Dismantling it was something else. With only an inch between the ceiling and the canopy, removing it took the movers over an hour.

It was normally hard for me to get up that early, but knowing what lay ahead, and since the butterflies in my stomach wouldn't quit, I jumped out of bed. After brushing my teeth, I pulled my hair back into a ponytail, not bothering with a bath. I huddled in front of the space heater in the bathroom a few extra minutes, for the very last time.

I kissed the girls awake and when we made it downstairs into the fireplace room, Jeb, Roberta, and Pierre were waiting for us. "Surprise," they all yelled. Those sweet people had prepared a beautiful going-away breakfast for us. Pancakes with warm Vermont maple syrup, crispy bacon, fresh-squeezed orange juice, scrambled eggs, and ice-cold milk. The table in the bay window was set and a big, crackling fire warmed the room.

"Y'all are so sweet, thanks, you guys." I unfolded my napkin and placed it on my lap. "Hey, did you hear me? I said 'you guys.'"

"But you still said 'y'all,'" Jeb pointed out.

"We're rubbing off on you," Roberta seemed thrilled to say.

"Y'all sit down with us." I patted the table and motioned for them to come over.

"Where's *your* breakfast, Pierre?" Isabella wanted to know. Pierre just smiled.

"SHE . . . WANTS . . . TO . . . KNOW . . . IF . . . YOU'RE . . . GONNA . . . EAT BREAKFAST." I pointed to him with one hand and made an eating motion with the other.

"Ahhhh." His face lit up when he understood my hand signals. "No, no, Isabella."

"Can y'all come with us?" Sarah asked. When all three told her no, she seemed disappointed. "You can visit us, can't you?"

"Oh, I'll be down there," Jeb told her. "I've got places to go and people to see."

"How 'bout you, Roberta?" Sarah said, with her sweet little angelic voice. "You'll come, won't you?"

"I don't know about that, missy. I'm not much on traveling. We'll have to see." Roberta leaned in toward her and put her hand up to the side of her mouth. "But I never say never."

"That's right, Roberta, never say never. We'll get you down south. I'm not letting you out of our lives that easy." When I eyed Roberta's little half smile, it broke my heart.

The pancakes were delicious, always cooked with drawn butter at my inn and somewhat crispy on the edges. While the three of us ate our breakfast, Jeb rambled on and on about the different cities and attractions around the country that he planned to someday visit.

I watched Sarah eyeing him and every time he paused, she'd start to speak but couldn't quite get a word in edgewise. Finally, she seized an extra-long lull in Jeb's babble. "Mommy says I'm going to a new school with just girls in my class. And that makes me so happy."

"Just girls, huh?" Roberta's eyes lit up and she bobbed her head in approval. "No boy cooties to bother you?"

Sarah scrunched up her nose. "That's right."

Isabella laughed out loud and then pointed to a little white stuffed kitty with blue eyes sitting on the table in front of her plate. "Mommy, who's that for?"

Sweet Pierre smiled the biggest smile I'd ever seen come across his face. He had gone out and bought us each a little going-away present.

"I think it's for you," I said to Issie. "From Pierre."

Isabella picked it up and hugged the kitty to her chest. "Thank you, Pierre."

At Sarah's place was another stuffed animal—a white dog about the size of Gracie. And at my place, a small snow globe with a moose inside. I picked it up and shook it. Isabella wanted to hold it, too.

"Careful, Issie, it's breakable," I said. "Hold it gently. *Merci*, Pierre."

"Es your moose," Pierre said. "No more looking."

I was *really* looking for Peter. In fact, I couldn't stand it another second. "Have y'all seen Peter by any chance?"

They all looked at one another as if to inquire but I knew they had to be wondering the same thing.

"I was hoping he might stop in . . . to say good-bye." I might as well have shined a flashlight into my heart.

"He's probably restin' before he starts his new job at the Sugartree," Roberta said. "I'm sure he'll call you once you get to Memphis."

"Maybe he drove over to New Jersey to see family. He's got a week off before he starts," Jeb said, and gave me an overemphasized wink.

"You're right. I'm sure he'll call." I feigned a smile.

Jeb glanced at his watch. "It's almost seven, you better get on the road if you want to stay ahead of the nor'easter. Take a look outside, it's gettin' goin' out there."

Sure enough, snow was beginning to fall. In a few hours my friends would become shut-ins. "Let's get our coats on, girls. We've got a long drive ahead of us, hurry, hurry."

Everyone bundled up and we all walked out together. Halfway to my car, I turned back around and studied the back side of my inn, the beautiful garden—now a winter wonderland—and the front door of the superb owners' quarters. Pierre's little cottage with the turquoise shutters and the big barn that still housed all the extra furniture and stuff from the junk room. Instead of melancholy, an unexplained peace suddenly washed over me. I glanced up at the snow, opened my mouth, and stuck out my tongue. A big fat snowflake landed right in the center and at that moment I felt an overwhelming sense of triumph and contentment. *What an incredible adventure*, I thought. How many Southerners in this world can actually say that they moved 1,473 miles away from home, due north to *Vermont* to operate an inn? And *survived*. I spent countless days and nights dying to get home but it wasn't the right time. Now I was going home a different woman—a better woman—a mother my girls would admire and respect.

I looked at my Vermont friends standing underneath the cascading snow. Roberta with her wild red hair sticking out of her knit hat, wearing her plaid skirt and her used Sorels. Jeb, with his lumberjack hat and his stomach poking so far out that his coat couldn't cover his middle. And Pierre with his dyed jet-black hair and no hat. I felt like the wealthiest woman in America for having earned their friendships.

One by one, and clutching their new stuffed animals, Sarah and Isabella hugged each of them good-bye. I reached out to hug Jeb, who was standing closest to me, and as soon as my cheek brushed his bushy beard I started to cry. "I never thought I'd say this, but I sure am gonna miss you twisting your mustache, Jeb. The next time I see you, I hope Jeb's Computer World has gotten so big that you've had to relocate to the shopping center." I reached up and kissed him on the forehead. His eyes moistened and I watched a tear roll down his cheek and disappear into his handlebar.

Pierre stood right next to Jeb and by the time I reached out for him, he was already crying. "*Au revoir,* Leelee," he said, and sniffed. "Vermont never same without you."

"We love you, Pierre." I put my hand over my heart and then touched his. Without a doubt, Pierre Lebel was one of the kindest men I had ever known.

"Oh, Roberta, I'm gonna miss you most of all." I whispered in her ear so no one else would feel bad. "You've been the best friend any Southern girl could hope for. What would I have done without you?"

"Aw, you'd have made it just fine. Remember what I told you. You're a survivor. You can start another Peach Blossom Inn down south if you want to. Go back to Tennessee and knock 'em dead, missy."

"I'm not so sure about another inn."

"Never say never."

"Okay, I'll keep my options open." I gave her one last long hug. "Take care of yourself. And write to me. Promise?"

"Of course I will. I'll catch you up on what all you're missin'."

"Look at all of us, crying like we'll never see each other again. I'll be back for a visit. And y'all can come to Tennessee."

"Be careful," Jeb said, "especially in that car. You need to stay ahead of the storm."

"I will. Hey, I'm part Yankee now. You don't need to worry about me."

Caution guided our steps as the girls and I fought the brawling wind over to our car, amid snow swirling frantically all around us. Still, I detected the faint harmony of Jeb's familiar whistle serenading us on our journey home. Although it had been years since I'd heard it, maybe even elementary school, I recognized the tune right away. "I wish I was in the land of cotton, old times there are not forgotten, look away . . . away down south in Dixie."

My little BMW was packed to the brim with only little slivers of space remaining for us to sit. I strapped the girls in and looked back at my friends. Before sliding down into my seat, I blew them a kiss from the door. I watched them slip away through my rearview mirror as I pulled down the street for the very last time.

Chapter Twenty-four

"Bye-bye Peach Blossom Inn, bye-bye Jeb's Computer World, bye-bye little store, bye-bye river, bye-bye our school." Everything we drove past, the girls would wave and tell it good-bye.

"Bye-bye grocery store, bye-bye pizza place, bye-bye George Clark," I said, as we pulled into Fairhope. *Oh, what the heck, I'll just make his day with one last tank of gas. He'll see my car all loaded up and by noon, the whole town will know that the "Southern gal" has moved away.*

The line for gas was only two cars deep and while I was waiting all I thought about was Peter. What would have prevented him from saying good-bye? I thought we were friends. Not just casual friends but dear friends. We hung out together six nights and six days a week for eight months.

"Hello. How are you?" George said, when I pulled up to the pump.

"I'm fine, thanks. Will you fill'er up, please?"

"Why sure." After he placed the pump in my gas tank, I saw him glance through the car windows. He even leaned in to get a better view. "Looks like you're goin' on a trip. Where to?"

"Tennessee."

"How long will you be gone?"

"Forever."

George's eyes about popped out of his skull.

"We're going home, George. I thought I'd stop in to say good-bye."

"You've made my day."

"That was my intention." I grinned at him and almost laughed out loud. I couldn't help it.

"So, did you sell the old inn?" he asked.

"I sure did."

"Who's takin' over the place?"

"Actually, I've not met the new owners. We had to delay the closing a couple of days. But I'm leaving anyway. The girls and I are anxious to get home to the *warm weather.*"

My comment went right over his head. "What about Roberta and Jeb and Frenchie? Will they keep their jobs?"

"Oh yeah, their jobs are safe and secure."

"And how about your new chef? What's he goin' to do now?" His face almost glowed when he asked that question. Fortunately, the gas line popped and George had to put it back on the pump. The man was aching for more dirt but I was not about to give it to him. "That'll be thirty-one dollars, Mrs. Satterfield," he finally said, after I ignored his question.

I handed George the exact change. "I don't want to waste a second more of your time, Mr. Clark. Something tells me you've got your work cut out for you today."

"Well, nice knowing you, and be careful there, Mrs. Satterfield. That car of yours ain't the best in this kind of weather. A nor'easter's headed this way."

"Nor'easter, pooh. I'm not afraid of a little ole nor'easter. I can drive in the snow as well as anyone else can now. Good-bye, George and hey, *stay warm!*" I rolled up the window and giggled to myself. *There's a choice, you Eskimos. You don't have to freeze your fannies off.*

I started my engine before I noticed someone heading in my direction. I pulled away from the pump and the person kept on walking—straight up in front of my car. He stood in my way so I couldn't drive another inch. His hands were shoved in his pockets and the collar on the red jacket he wore was turned up to protect his neck. A navy blue skullcap was pulled down over his head, covering his ears and all of his hair. Still, I knew the face.

I rammed the gearshift into park, right in the middle of George Clark's gas station parking lot, and flew out of the car. We stood there in front of the left headlight, two feet apart, lost somewhere between embarrassment and grief, neither of us confident enough to expose our hearts. We spoke over each other rushing to get the words out.

"I'm sorry," he said, at the same time I was saying, "Memphis is home."

"I never meant to hurt you," he said.

"I thought you were mad at me." Again our words fell on top of each other's.

"I could never be mad at you, Leelee. For Christ's sake, you're the nicest person I've ever known. When I walked out the door that night, I regretted it—immediately—but I couldn't make myself turn back around."

I started to speak and he waved his hand to stop me.

"Wait, let me finish. It's just that I'm . . . sad you're leaving. I've wanted to tell you for so long how special you are, and how beautiful I think you are, inside and out. I've never met anyone like you before, Leelee. And when I knew you would be leaving and going back home to Memphis, I started freaking out and I reacted like a jerk. I'm sorry." He dropped his head and stared at the ground.

"It's okay. I understand." I reached out and touched him on the sleeve. "You've got to hear me on this. This has been a very hard decision for me. Oddly enough, I've grown to like it here. And I didn't even realize it. When Ed presented me with an offer, I didn't know what to do. I *agonized* over it, Peter." A tear started rolling down my cheek. Then another and another.

He reached up, stroked my cheek, and wiped each tear away with his thumb. "Sweetheart, Vermont is not you. I know that. It wouldn't be fair of me to expect you to stay here. I always knew you'd eventually leave. You told me the day you hired me that it wouldn't last. I took that chance. I'm happy for the time I did spend with you."

By now huge snowflakes were collecting all over us. I was dying to say: Peter, I'm the one that thinks you're beautiful and you're the nicest guy *I've* ever known. But I couldn't say it. I don't know why, I just couldn't bring myself to say it. I was packed up and headed home.

The clumsy pause in our conversation grew longer. I wasn't sure whether to say good-bye and get in the car or wait for him to continue.

"What's in your CD player?" he asked, a random change of subject to say the least.

"I'm not sure, why?"

"Will you check for me?"

I opened the door, sat down inside, and turned up the volume. Only radio commercials—no CD in the player. I pushed on the eject button to make sure. "Nothing."

"You must have your CDs in the car for the long trip, right?"

"Yeah, they're right here." I patted the case next to me.

"Good. Hop out a second. Hi, girls," he said as he sat down in my seat.

What in the world is he up to? I wondered. Peter fished through my CD case until he came to the one he wanted. He glanced at the label. I watched him push in the CD and skip through the tracks. He turned the heat on full blast, cranked up the volume, and rolled down the driver's-side window. "You owe me a dance." He stepped out of the car and reached for my hand.

"Right now? *Here?*"

"Right now, right here, right in front of everybody." His mouth curved up and his eyes lit up his boyish face.

He ripped off his gloves and shoved them in his pocket. I wasn't wearing any so when Peter took my hand in his, it felt nice and warm. He slipped his other arm into the back of my coat and gently pulled me toward him.

Van's voice rang out loud and clear. Right in front of George Clark, my daughters, and all of Fairhope, Peter Owen and I slowly glided along with the music, underneath the cascading snow. This time no one stopped us. I buried my head in his chest and snuggled up next to him.

"Tell me what you're thinking." He peered down at me a couple of minutes into the song. *His smile kills me. His perfect teeth and perfect lips are intoxicating.*

I gazed up at him for a moment and hesitated before saying anything. "I was wondering if you might visit me. It'll be spring soon. Memphis is so pretty—"

He put his finger over my lips. "Do you *want* me to visit you?"

I nodded.

Peter let go of my hand and wrapped both of his arms around me. We danced in silence "and magnificently we floated into the mystic."

I had never been so sorry to hear a song fade away.

"You better get your butt on the road, young lady. The weather's not getting any better." He patted my bottom and slowly pulled away.

No, don't let me go. Let's dance the next one and the one after that. I was tempted to reach out for him again and pull him back toward me. I didn't care who was watching. But the awkwardness returned and we stood there in silence. "I can't say good-bye to you," I finally said. "Let's just say see you soon."

He turned toward my car, opened the back door, and leaned in to kiss the girls' cheeks. Then he turned to me. "See you soon, boss." He drew me close and this time he kissed the top of my head. When I looked up at him he cradled my freezing-cold face in his hands. "I'll miss you, and that's another promise." After beholding the thirst in my eyes, he leaned down and tenderly kissed my lips. "Trust me."

I never took my eyes off of him as he walked to his truck and stepped inside. *Should I stop him? Go running after him? No, I've made my decision already. God, this is torture. My head is about to explode.*

He backed up his truck and slowly inched his way out of the parking lot. Tears rolled down my face so fast and furious and all I had to wipe them on was my coat sleeve. I watched his car roll down the road until it disappeared.

Before I pulled onto the highway, I peeked back at the gas station in my rearview mirror. I could have sworn good ole George had a little skip in his step.

"How much longer?" Sarah asked, only thirty minutes into the trip.

"A lot longer," I said.

"I'm bored," Isabella cried.

"Me, too," answered her sister.

"All right, y'all, we can't start this early into the trip. Let's play a car game."

"Yay!" Issie squealed.

"Okay. Let's play the animal game. Think of different kinds of animals that live in Vermont."

"I call first," Sarah yelled.

"No fair, I wanna be first."

"Issie, going second is better, honey, just wait. Go ahead, Sarah."

"How about a moose!"

"That's what I was gonna say," Isabella said, with a pout.

"Moose are only legends around here, anyway. It's okay, Issie, now it's your turn. Go ahead."

She thought for a second but as hard as she tried she couldn't come up with one. "You go next, Mommy."

"Okay . . . how about a deer?"

"That's a good one," Sarah said. "Now you go, Issie."

I could see Issie in the rearview mirror trying her best to come up with an animal. "I know," she squealed, kicking her feet in her car seat. "Princess Grace!"

"Princess Grace? Oh my God. WE FORGOT PRINCESS GRACE KELLY!"

I swerved over to the shoulder, glanced quickly behind me to make sure the coast was clear, pulled a U-turn, and headed straight back to Willingham.

"But Gracie's dead," Sarah, the only one with any sense, exclaimed.

"No, she's in heaven," Isabella told her.

"Her spirit is in heaven but her body is still frozen under that ground! And she would never want to be left there without us." It was completely absurd, I realize that, but *still*. "People dig up bodies and move them all the time," I said, glancing back at the girls. "Look at Elvis. He was dug up from Forest Hill Cemetery and moved to Graceland."

"Who's Elvis?" Sarah asked.

"*Who's Elvis?* Another reason to go home. My own daughter doesn't even know who Elvis is."

Nor'easter or not, there was no way in hell I'd leave my precious Gracie in Vermont, as bad as she hated that state. My guilt would never allow me to leave her body there for the rest of eternity. What's another three hundred dollars to dig her back up? Nothing, in the scheme of Gracie's life, I rationalized.

So here we were, headed back down Route 12, thirty more minutes down the road in the *opposite* direction of Memphis. The whole way back to Willingham I kept thinking about Gracie and how I could have possibly left her behind. Then the most horrifying thought hit me. Jeb might guess wrong about her exact burial location and put that jackhammer right through her. "IT'S NOT WORTH IT!" I screamed.

"What's not worth it?" Sarah asked.

"Renting the jackhammer."

"Are we going to dig up Gracie?" she wanted to know.

"No, I've changed my mind. But we're going back for her cross."

When we drove back up to the inn at 8:30 A.M., I noticed the Peach Blossom Inn sign had fallen down. I made a mental note to hang it back up on my way back out of town but for now I was focused solely on Gracie. More new snow had accumulated in the hour and a half since we left. I pulled alongside the fence in front of the gate.

"I won't be long," I told the girls. "Wait for me in the apartment where it's warm."

"Is Roberta here?" Isabella wanted to know.

"I don't see her car, but it's okay, baby. I'll be back in a second. Go on inside. Sarah, hold your sister's hand, please."

I parked in my regular spot behind the barn and ran in to grab a saucer sled. The snow was really coming down now and the wind was blowing like a son of a gun. I hurried as fast as I could but it was quite a workout by the time I lifted my legs and high-stepped up to the top. What I really needed were snowshoes, but I had only found out about their existence a few weeks prior.

I spotted it right away. Only the top peeked out of the snow. I cleared away the powder from around it and tugged. It wouldn't budge. As hard as I tried I couldn't pull it up. By now the ground around it was, of course, frozen solid. All I could do was break off the stick and take the cross, so I pushed and pushed on it with my boot until I heard it snap.

Kneeling down over her for the last time, I bent down and kissed the snow. "I'm sorry, Gracie, but this is for the best. I couldn't take a chance on Jeb cutting you in two. Please forgive me. You'll always live in my heart no matter where you are."

I sat down on the saucer, put Gracie's tombstone in my lap, and grabbed the handles on either side. I scooted myself to the edge and leaned forward. Down the hill I flew, right into the base of the barn. I threw the sled inside, put the cross in my car, and ran back to the apartment.

"Sarah? Issie? Where are y'all?" I called from the base of the apartment steps. When they didn't answer I started up the stairs. "Girls, it's time to go. No hide-and-seek, please."

They were nowhere to be found. Back down the steps I dashed and into the big kitchen. Again, I called their names. "Sarah, Isabella, *let's go.*" They weren't in there, either. I was beginning to get a little nervous but when I got to the dining room, I saw a chair pulled up in front of the fireplace. Atop were both of my daughters. Sarah was reaching up on the mantel and Isabella had something in her hand.

"What on earth are you two doing?"

Sarah picked up something small and instantly recognizable off the mantel. Issie played with a similar one, only larger.

"Look what we found. Helga's hippos. She must have left them for us."

There, spread out on top of the mantel of my Peach Blossom Inn, resided Helga Schloygin's cherished hippopotamus collection—in its entirety.

It took a moment for the horror to sink in. "I'll . . . be . . . *damned!*" I cried.

"Mama. You said not to cuss," Sarah scolded.

"I sure did. But that rule does not apply to now. That double-crossing, no good, dirty rotten slimeball. Ed Baldwin, you duped me. And for the second time. I can't believe it." I paced around the room flailing my arms all over the place.

"What do you mean?"

"Don't you worry about it, Sarah, everything's going to be fine. No wonder the sign was gone."

My first thoughts were about Pierre, Roberta, and Jeb. Peter was taken care of, but what about them? Did they know? Or worse, were they in on it? *No way.* Should I stop this sale? I could, no problem. But then what?

"Ughhhh, how could he *do* this to me?" I sat down at one of the tables to think for a moment, with my head in my hands and my heart blasting out of my chest. Helga was nowhere to be seen. I never once even considered that Helga and Rolf were the buyers. A death in the family . . . yeah, right. So, what was I supposed to do now? Stop the moving van somewhere in the middle of Pennsylvania? Rent a storage unit in Memphis for my stuff and in the meantime move back in again with Helga's horrible furnishings?

Then it occurred to me. Why on God's green earth would I want to allow Helga Schloygin to occupy one more moment of space in my on-the-mend mind and heart? Sure, I could stop the sale, but why would I want to ever be around her again? I'd more than likely have to spend another year living here, *at least*, while I searched for another buyer. As much as I wanted to take care of Roberta, Jeb, and Pierre I knew it was not my responsibility. If I could survive—surely they could.

Roberta told me herself that she had learned to be a survivor from watching me. Jeb had plenty of work on his own, and any restaurant owner would be thrilled to hire Pierre. Peter already had a new job with a nice raise. As tempting as it was to change my mind and go running after him, something deeper tugged at my core.

I knew my heart's desire all along. Even though I was a different person now—how could I not be, I'd finally fled my cocoon and encountered life on its jagged edge—my heart never changed.

"Okay, girls, let's go," I said, rising up from the table. "Hurry, hurry."

Sarah and Isabella jumped down off the chair, each still holding a hippo in her hand.

"Oh no, we won't be taking those home with us. Hand 'em over."

"But Helga left them for us. Can't we just take one?" Sarah pleaded.

"Not even one."

I took the would-be souvenirs from the girls and put them back on the mantel. "Scoot," I said, and brushed them both on the fanny.

Sarah and Issie stomped out the door but quit their pouting once outside. Snow was falling faster than I'd seen it all season and they lifted their arms and spun around in circles.

If it hadn't been for a dog howling in the distance, I would have never thought about it again. But as I glanced over my shoulder toward the sound, I noticed the barren pole where my Peach Blossom Inn sign once hung. It hadn't fallen down like I originally thought. Someone had deliberately removed it. The question was: Where would she put it?

I headed straight toward the back of the barn. Sure enough, amid the debris, it had been tossed into the middle of the brush pile. My car had very little room but I'd have sooner thrown out one of my suitcases than leave my sign with her. There was no way I was going to give her the satisfaction of thinking she would burn my beautiful sign. So after cramming it in the car next to Gracie's cross, I ran back inside the house and scribbled out a note: *Thanks for the sign!* I propped it up in front of the big fat head hippo and ran out the door.

Just past the entrance to Sugartree the snow picked up even more and in what seemed like seconds turned into half-dollar-size flakes. No matter how long you live, I don't think you ever grow tired of watching snow fall.

"The snow is pretty," Sarah said.

"Yes it is, baby."

"Will it snow in Memphis?" she wanted to know.

"Sometimes, but not like this. Are you watching, Issie?"

"Mmhmm," she said, through her paci.

I was careful to take my time and we inched along at only twenty miles per hour. The city snowplows hadn't made it back around this stretch yet.

Just beyond the next curve I noticed something in the distance in front of the right side of the thicket. Large and black—I wasn't sure what it was—but it was motionless. Perhaps a vehicle had lost control and slammed into the embankment ahead. After all, the street was overly treacherous. I couldn't be sure, but in an effort to be extra cautious, I lightly tapped my brakes. And as my car slowed down to a roll, I recognized him.

Majestic and virile, he was just as I had imagined. After waiting for him all this time, I wasn't about to simply drive past, so I slowly pulled off onto the shoulder, making sure to keep twenty yards or so between us.

"Look, girls. I don't believe it. A moose!"

"Where?" Issie squealed.

"I can't see him," Sarah cried.

Ever so slowly I inched up toward him, hoping with all my heart that he wouldn't dash away. The closer we got the more his distinguishing features came into view. His antlers were gigantic and I couldn't help but wonder how in the world he could keep his head held so high. His tail was much smaller than I would've thought. Seeing it up close, it was more like a cow's tail. In awe, the girls and I gaped at him. He was covered in snow but didn't seem to mind.

Now we were only thirty feet away and as I was eager to get as close to him as I could, I guess the engine startled him. He turned and looked at us dead-on. I noticed his face and his big, round nose.

"What took you so long?" I whispered.

I know we sat there staring at each other for a full sixty seconds before he gradually turned and started walking away. His gait changed and he trotted several feet ahead. As he picked up his pace, I edged onto the road. Before long and almost miraculously, we were gliding along, the moose and

I, at the same rate of speed. Only a few feet ahead of us, it seemed as if the moose was escorting us away from Vermont.

Just at the edge of town the road curved off to the left. As my little car veered off toward home, our bull moose disappeared back into the thicket.

Epilogue

A Lovely Warm Autumn Day

MEMPHIS, TENNESSEE

"I'm so proud of her. Who would have actually thought she'd have the courage to do it?" Virginia said.

Mary Jule piped up from the backseat. "I couldn't do it. No way."

"Personally, I think I could. But we're not talking about me," said Alice, who was sitting in the passenger seat of Virginia's car. "Let's get down to Agency business. Mary Jule," she said, turning around to face her, "did you sneak into Leelee's address book?"

"Yes, I did. No address, only a phone number."

"No *address*? That's odd, how are we gonna find it?"

"We can call Roberta," Virginia said. "Who knows her last name?"

"I don't remember. Do you, Alice?" Mary Jule asked.

"Heck no."

"How about Jeb? What's his last name?" Virginia asked.

The other two shrugged.

"Don't tell me we've hit a dead end."

"I've got it!" Alice squealed. "Mary Jule, what's his phone number?"

"You're not gonna call *him*, are you?"

"Just give me the phone number and watch the master at work."

"I don't know about this but, *okay*: 802-555-9998."

"Thank you very much, may I have total quiet, please?" Alice pulled out a Virginia Slim, cracked the window, and took a puff before punching in the numbers. "I did a star-sixty-seven, just in case." Alice put a finger to her lips. "Shhh, it's ringing. Still ringing. Hi-eee," she said in her best Yankee voice, "is this Sam?"

"You've got the wrong number."

Alice held the phone out from her ear so Virginia and Mary Jule, who were huddled toward the phone, could hear every word. "This isn't Sam Owen?"

"Nope. You've got the right last name, but my first name's not Sam."

"Oh, well. That operator must have given me the wrong Owen. I'm looking for my old college boyfriend. He lives in Vermont on Acklen Road and I'm desperate to find him. Do you have a *cousin* named Sam Owen?"

"No, I don't have a cousin named Sam."

"Is your middle name Sam?"

"No, Sam isn't my middle name."

"Are you sure you're not pulling my leg? Sam, this really is you, isn't it?" Alice pinched her two fingers together and glided her hand through the air, pretending to be writing. Mary Jule quickly dug in her purse and handed her a pen.

"It's not Sam," he said with a chuckle. "And I'm not your old boyfriend. What's your name anyway?"

"Shauna."

"Nice to meet you, *Shauna*."

"You too, Sam, I mean, whatever your name is."

"Peter."

"Okay, nice to meet you, *Peter*. Listen, would you please do me a favor?"

"I'll try."

"If you ever meet Sam Owen up there, will you tell him I'm trying to find him?"

"You bet."

"Thanks. Hey, what's your address? Maybe I'll send Sam a letter in care of you."

"It's 415 Forrest Drive, but I doubt I'll ever meet him."

"In Willingham?"

"No, Dover."

"And that zip?"

"05356."

"Alrighty then. Thanks, Peter Owen. Good talking to you and have a *greet* day." When she got to the day part she accidentally lost her accent. She recovered, though, when she said good-bye. "Byeeee." She closed her cell phone and blew two smoke rings. "And that's how it's done."

"I gotta say. You never cease to amaze me," Virginia told her.

"All in a day's work of a good detective at the Gladys Kravitz Agency. I can't believe we actually caught him at home. What are the odds of that?"

"Oooooh, I'm getting excited," squealed Mary Jule.

"Who's got the letter?" Alice asked.

"It's in my purse," said Virginia.

Alice ruffled through Virginia's pocketbook and opened the unsealed envelope. She took out the newspaper clipping, which had one of the want ads circled with a black Sharpie, and read aloud:

CHEF NEEDED *Peach Blossom Inn—small, gourmet restaurant in mint condition. Must have nice attitude, pleasing personality, GOOD HYGIENE, and expertise in classic and nouvelle cuisine. Historic Germantown, 462 Old Poplar Pike, Memphis, Tennessee 38108. Call 901-555-8912 or apply in person.*

"Leelee's left us no choice but to take matters into our own hands, and we're all in agreement, right?" After nods from the other two, Alice folded up the ad and stuck it back inside the envelope. She gave it a lick and under Peter Owen's name she copied down his address.

"Here's a stamp," Mary Jule said, leaning over the front seat. "I've only got a love stamp. Do y'all think that's too obvious?"

"So what if it is?" With a quick lick, Alice placed the stamp on the letter and handed the envelope to Virginia.

They pulled into the post office and got in line for the drop box. Virginia rolled down the window and reached out to place the letter on the edge of the mail slot. "Okay. It's worth a shot."

She gently let go of the envelope and let it slide down, deep into the mailbox.

Acknowledgments

There are many people I want to acknowledge and thank from the bottom of my heart. This book has been my dream for more years than I care to count. The people I mention here have all contributed to the fruition of that dream, and I want each of you to know how much you mean to me.

My sincerest gratitude to all of the lovely people at Thomas Dunne Books/St. Martin's Press. Katie Gilligan, editor extraordinaire, who laughs her way through the day. You have greatly enhanced the lines on these pages. Not only did you fall in love with my book, you went to bat for me over and over. You got the vision, and for that I am deeply grateful. Sally Richardson, you did also—I am one fortunate woman. Thomas Dunne, Matthew Shear, and Peter Wolverton, I'm thrilled to have you all on my side. Thank you to Matthew Baldacci, Courtney Fischer, Lisa Senz, and Sarah Goldstein for your phenomenal marketing skills, and to Michael Storrings and Ervin Serrano for your creativity and *brilliance* with the cover design. In production, thanks to Julie Gutin and Christina MacDonald for your razor-sharp eyes. And in publicity, Rachel Ekstrom, Joe Rinaldi, and Jessica Rotondi.

Huge thanks to my wonderful, witty, super-smart agent, a real fireball,

Holly Root at Waxman Literary. You plucked me out of oblivion and believed in me. It's an honor to have you on my team.

Michael and Will, thank you for hanging in there with Mom all these years. I wanted to show you what can happen when you want something so badly and are willing to invest all the sweat equity you've got. Roll up your sleeves and go for it, no matter how long it may take or what struggles life may throw your way. I love you with all my heart.

My sisters, Laurie, Leslie, and Melanie. Thank you for your love and encouragement. They mean so much to me. I love you.

There are a few dear friends of mine who have not only lent me an unyielding ear, but have encouraged and edified me for years. Kathy "G" Peabody, you have gone way beyond the call of duty with all the drafts you have read, the help you have given me, and all the *Whistlin' Dixie* news you've listened to. Thank you, my dear friend, for your love and always being there. Penny Preston, your friendship and love mean everything to me. You are truly my blessing. Gail Donovan, without your love and reassurance I might not have done this. Becky Barkley, old movie buff, Princess Grace and I thank you. Sarah Berger, Steve Berger, Kim Carnes, Gail Chiaravalle, Jan Cross, Emily Kay, Scarlett McDonald, Robin Morrison, Anne Marie Norton, Ron Olson, Vicki Olson, LeAnn Phelan, and Margie Thessin, thank you all for investing your time into my dream. Mike McDonald, you believed in me from day one. Because of you, I actually started to believe I might have what it takes. Thank you.

Jeff Bridges, Christopher Cross, Karin Gillespie, Linda Francis Lee, Tracy McArdle, Michael McDonald, T. Lynn Ocean, Lee Smith, and Adriana Trigiani, thank you for taking time out of your insane schedules to read *my* book and offer up your praise. My head's still reeling.

Thanks to Mary Helen Clarke, an early editor who gave me a crash course in novel writing. You are fantastic. Wes Yoder, thank you for lending me your publishing expertise and guidance. Thanks to Linda Yoder, cussing coach, your much-needed consulting was invaluable.

I have been blessed to have lifelong friends from childhood. We wore the needles out on hundreds of albums and got into our share of teenage trouble. You have been the inspiration for some of the characters in this book. Lisa Murphey Blakley, Cary Coors Brown, Katy Collier Creech, Elise Norfleet Crockett, Wilda Weaver Hudson, Emily Freeburg Kay, Mimi Hall Taylor, and Lisa Earp Wilder. All of you have deposited more fun and laughter into my life account than one should be allowed. I love you.

Four of my dearest friends from college, Alice Davis Blake, Mary Gaston Long Catmur, Genie McCown, and Leelee Thomas Walter, have also contributed to hours of belly laughter, and I thank you for the inspiration that came out of it.

My gratitude and love to others who have labored through the reading of drafts or offered up encouragement, help, and inspiration: Kathy Aicher, Stephanie Alexander, Tasha Alexander, Allison Allen, all at Backspace the Writer's Place, Bill Barkley, Clemé Barkley, Tammy Baskin, Matraca Berg, Heather Berger, Josiah Berger, Mel Berger, Jim Bergmann, Julia Black, Mildred Bonner, Genie Buchanon, Chris Burke, Angela Calhoun, Teasi Cannon, Sherry Carr, Beth Nielsen Chapman, Bernie Chiaravalle, Pat Clonts, Hilda and Wayne Collett, Margaret Connelly, Kayleen Cox, Bill Crew, Gigi Crichton, the late Jenny C. Crumbaugh, Laura Elkin, Dave Ellingson, Maureen Ferguson, Denise Foster, Lark Foster, Ben Fowler, Helen Freeburg, Tara Gero, Dawn Goldman, Jennifer Hart, Matt Huesmann, Debbie Ingram, Eric Jacobson, Kim Jamison, Tammy Jensen, Dr. David Johnson, Harvey Kay, Lisa Kloepfer, Candy Kopald, Linda Abston Larsen, Dan Mann, John Marx, Jodie McCarthy, Amy McDonald, Susie Meeks, John Moore, Sherrie Moore, Penny Nelms, Mary Norman, Jessica Olson, Oxbow School, the Pastiche Girls, Rick Peabody, Michele Place, Terry Robbins, Molly Robinson, Emily Roley, Linda Roley, Scott Roley, Dick Runyan, Ed Ryan, Andrea Santee, Melissa Sarver, Gigi Steele, Joanna Stephens, Elizabeth Stout, Barbara Swan, Roger Thorn-Thompson, Grady Walker, Kathy Walker, Treat Williams, and Lisa Winters.

Mama, Daddy, and Chris—I know you're up there wishing like crazy you could be in the front row. All three had contagious laughs and wonderful senses of humor. Thank goodness they rubbed off on me.

And to you, dear reader, thank you for buying my book. Part of the proceeds will benefit struggling single mothers and their children in Williamson County, Tennessee.

Above all, I owe this book to God, my Redeemer. Without Him, I would have never been able to write it in the first place.

Reading
Group
Gold

WHISTLIN' DIXIE
IN A NOR'EASTER

by Lisa Patton

About the Author
- A Conversation with Lisa Patton

Food for Thought
- Recipes from the Peach Blossom Inn

Keep on Reading
- Recommended Reading
- Reading Group Questions

A
Reading
Group Gold
Selection

For more reading group suggestions,
visit www.readinggroupgold.com.

🦁 ST. MARTIN'S GRIFFIN

A Conversation with Lisa Patton

What was the inspiration for *Whistlin' Dixie in a Nor'easter*?

I really was an innkeeper in Vermont. Even better, a Southern innkeeper in Vermont! After surviving three sub-zero winters, discovering Vermonters don't bury their dead in the winter, suffering from vampire bug bites on the back of my neck, and enjoying a four-week summer where I still had to wear a coat at night, I knew I had a story to write.

How has your personal life experience influenced this book? What similarities do you have with Leelee Satterfield?

The first thing that comes to my mind is the way Southern girls are brought up, at least in my era. We were taught to be agreeable and polite. I've heard people criticize Southern women for not saying what's on their mind. That's because we are taught from a young age to be great hostesses and make everyone feel comfortable. It might not be the best way, but it's what we've learned. Sure, there's a bit of me in Leelee. I get caught up in the same trap of sacrificing my needs for everyone else's and wanting people to like me. Like Leelee, I'm a work in progress. Then again, so are most of my closest friends.

The best thing about Leelee is her fun side. Leelee gets herself into all kinds of messes—largely because of the choices she makes. She's Lucy Ricardoish. I'm the same way and while that sometimes makes for a crazy personal life, it sure produces some rich scenarios for writing.

Are any of those crazy characters (such as Helga) based on people you know?

No doubt the characters in *Whistlin' Dixie* are amalgams of all kinds of people I've known—Leelee's three best friends from Memphis in particular. I named all of

> *"Like Leelee, I'm a work in progress."*

them, Leelee included, after sorority sisters of mine from Kappa Delta at the University of Alabama. Helga is fashioned a little bit after an old spinster piano teacher I had in grammar school. She's also part Wicked Witch from *The Wizard of Oz* and a lot Cruella de Vil from *101 Dalmatians*. I just love a villain, especially a funny villain. Glenn Close is my dream choice to someday play Helga. And I'm dang good at dreaming; it's gotten me this far!

Whistlin' Dixie is a fish-out-of-water story. You mentioned *The Wizard of Oz*. Helga and Leelee are obvious parallels to Dorothy and the witch. Are there others?

Many. If you are an "Ozzy," the likenesses are easy to spot. If not, they might be subtler. Instead of a tornado, Leelee gets caught up in a nor'easter. Leelee befriends three unlikely characters in her own Land of Oz. There are even a couple of lines of dialogue very similar to the movie. Of course there's Leelee's beloved dog, Gracie. The only thing missing from *Whistlin' Dixie* is an actual wizard. But Leelee's survival symbolizes the wizard inside her. I wasn't intentional with the obvious similarities, it just happened that way.

What other strange things happen in Yankee territory, and how is that different from life in the South?

Oh my. To be Southern and living in Yankee territory is quite an ordeal. Not only does one experience culture shock, but the thermal shock is brutal. Southerners have this idyllic image of the Currier and Ives winter up North. We have no idea what it's like to actually exist in it. We see heaps of snow and think, "How perfectly beautiful!" Actually, shoveling snow and rearranging your life to exist in it is another thing all together—for a Dixie chick anyway.

I remember having to see a counselor four months into living in Vermont. He sympathized with my inability to connect right away and explained how the subtle cultural differences would make it hard for me. He was right. Southern women are generally bubbly and very friendly. Certainly, the people up North are more direct and they take longer to get to know, but once a friendship is formed it's there for life—without pretense.

What would you say are some of the positive things that Leelee experiences in the North?

Leelee is forced way out of her comfort zone. The nor'easter is a metaphor for the storm in Leelee's life. While living in Vermont, she learns that she can survive any storm, physical or mental. Leelee develops self-confidence in her ability to earn her own living (without the help of her husband). Several real friendships develop for Leelee in Vermont—unlikely ones at that. She gets to experience some Northern wildlife that she's only dreamed about in the South.

How does Leelee grow and change in your novel? What is a "Southern Belle"—a good thing? Or a detriment?

When someone first reads *Whistlin' Dixie*, they might be perplexed at Leelee's inability to consider her own needs. As the book develops, though, Leelee's metamorphosis becomes evident to everyone. Her girlfriends from home are shocked by her newfound ability to say no and stand up for what she needs. Even Roberta, her housekeeper in Vermont, has been secretly watching Leelee's inner strength and true grit develop.

Leelee is a Southern Belle, but that's a good thing. The dictionary.com definition of a "Southern Belle" is "a beautiful and charming woman from the southern US." Leelee is beautiful, inside and out, but her charm is the most endearing thing about her.

"Leelee is beautiful, inside and out, but her charm is the most endearing thing about her."

Can you explain the significance of the song "Into the Mystic" in your book?

First of all, it's my favorite Van Morrison song, bar none. Romance oozes from each note. Leelee declares it's her favorite song, too, so there's another similarity between the two of us. When romance finally touches Leelee again, I thought it would be the perfect song to set the mood for this climactic moment in the story.

I was working for Michael McDonald around the time I wrote the scene with "Into the Mystic" and when he read it he was inspired to record the song on his next CD. He covered it on his 2007 Soul Speak record in honor of Leelee's romantic dance. Michael's version is quite dreamy, by the way.

Can you discuss the role of friendship in *Whistlin' Dixie*?

Friendship equals family to Leelee. Having lost her parents at an early age, and as an only child, Leelee relies on her friends to be a substitute for that sense of belonging and love. Despite her insistence to the contrary, Leelee is definitely naïve. Her entire life, prior to Vermont, has been spent inside a reinforced bubble. Her friends from home, including her childhood nanny, are not only her family but also her advisors. Much to her surprise, Leelee's time in Vermont produces three more dear friends who become her Vermont kinfolk.

How did you find the time to write this novel, as a single mom of two boys? Is there any message you'd like to give to the single mothers out there who may read this book?

Single motherhood is an enormous job and it leaves very little free time. Stolen moments are responsible for the writing of this book. Late at night, early in the

About the Author

morning before work, halftime on the soccer field, and waiting in the carpool line for the boys—I grabbed all the spare time I could find. That's why it took me years and years to finish. I dedicate the book to my sons but I also have a dedication to single mothers. They need encouragement and it's crucial to have hope in difficult situations. My message is to find your heart's desire and never give up, no matter how impossible it might seem. I know because it happened to me. I have a testimony.

"Find your heart's desire and never give up, no matter how impossible it might seem."

Recipes from the Peach Blossom Inn

> *I'm a sucker for fine gourmet food and I get many of my recipes and ideas from* Fine Cooking *magazine. Most of the menu items in the book were taken from my own restaurant in Vermont. One of the appetizers, Crabmeat Henry, came from an old historic restaurant in Memphis called Justine's. Readers are invited to visit www.lisapatton.com to learn more!*
>
> —Lisa Patton

White Chocolate Mousse with Raspberry Purée

Ingredients:

Mousse

16 ounces high-quality white chocolate, chopped

½ cup unsalted butter

2 cups chilled heavy cream

6 large egg yolks

½ cup sugar

2 tbsp Kirsch

Raspberry Purée

2 cups raspberries

1 tbsp Grand Marnier

1 tbsp sugar

Garnish

White chocolate shavings, mint sprigs, whole raspberries.

White Chocolate Mousse with Raspberry Purée

Directions:

Mousse:

Separate eggs into two bowls. Melt chocolate in a double boiler (a metal bowl set over a pan of simmering water, or a glass bowl in a microwave at 50 percent power for 3 to 5 minutes), stirring frequently until smooth. Whisk in butter. Remove from heat and add egg yolks, whipping until smooth. Add Kirsch and mix.

In a separate bowl beat egg whites, slowly adding sugar, until soft peaks form. In another bowl (preferably metal) whip cream until stiff and slowly fold into egg white/sugar mixture.

Fold $1/3$ of the egg white and whip cream mixture into the chocolate. Then fold that new mixture back into remaining egg white and whip cream mixture. DO NOT OVERMIX. Cover and chill.

Raspberry Purée:

Puree $3/4$ cup berries with sugar and Grand Marnier in a food processor. Strain into small bowl, pressing on solids. Mix in 1 cup berries.

Spoon mousse halfway into 8 (6-ounce) stemmed glasses. Add some berry mixture. Gently spoon remainder of the mousse. Chill, covered, for at least 6 hours. Let stand at room temperature about 20 minutes before serving.

Garnish with whole raspberries, white chocolate shavings, and mint sprigs.

Serves 1–12 depending on indulgence.

Recipe compliments of Chef Paul Kropp

Peach Daiquiris: A House Specialty

1 fresh Southern peach, peeled, pitted, and sliced

1/4 cup lime juice

1 jigger (1 ½ ounces) light rum

1 ounce apricot brandy

dash of vanilla

1 tbsp superfine granulated sugar (or to taste)

1 cup cracked ice

twist of lime

In a blender, blend peach, lime juice, light rum, apricot brandy, vanilla, and, if desired, sugar for 10 seconds. Add the cracked ice and blend for 15 seconds. Pour into a chilled 12-ounce glass. Garnish with lime.

Crabmeat Henry

This one comes from Memphis's iconic culinary jewel, Justine's restaurant. Although it's no longer around, Justine's lives on in the hearts and taste buds of many Southerners from Memphis and way beyond.

6 tbsp butter

¼ cup sherry

dash of Tabasco

dash of lemon juice

dash of Worcestershire sauce

½ lb. of the freshest possible lump crabmeat, rinsed and pieces of shell removed

3 pieces French bread toast

¾ cup Hollandaise sauce

Food for Thought

Put butter, sherry, Tabasco sauce, Worcestershire sauce, and lemon juice together in a pan and simmer over low heat. When mixture is hot, add crabmeat and lightly fold over with a spoon. Heat. Be careful not to burn or boil.

Put slices of toast in bottom of 3 small ramekins. Cover with drained crabmeat mixture (use a slotted spoon). Top with Hollandaise sauce and place in a preheated 450-degree oven. Bake until Hollandaise begins to brown, 8–10 minutes. Serve bubbling hot.
Serves 3.

Hollandaise Sauce

1 lb. butter

4 egg yolks

¼ tsp cayenne pepper

4 tsp cider vinegar

Melt the butter. In a separate bowl, whisk together egg yolks, cayenne, and vinegar until yolks are fluffy and light. Add a small amount of melted butter at a time, while beating, until all is used. For added thickness, place pan over boiling water and beat until desired consistency. Served with just about everything.

For an easier version, use a mixer and beat egg yoks, vinegar, and cayenne together until thick and fluffy. Reduce mixer speed and slowly add the melted butter.

Makes 2 cups.

Recommended Reading

*The lovely people at St. Martin's Press asked me for some
comments about my all-time favorite books. This is just a
sampling, but each will forever hold a special place in my heart.*

To Kill a Mockingbird

What can I say that hasn't already been said? I'll just reiter-
ate the words of many. Literary genius—*Southern* literary
genius. If only I could be Harper Lee!

The Prince of Tides

Intrigue, mystery, dysfunction, compassion, and pain, all
blended together with a sardonic sense of humor. That's
what I'm looking for when I crack open the pages of a
generational saga. It's hard to call yourself a writer when
Pat Conroy claims the same profession. I'll just call myself
one of his interns.

Can't Wait to Get to Heaven

Fannie Flagg accomplishes the ultimate—at least she does
for me! She has written a novel that makes me laugh out
loud so hard that tears are tumbling down my face for a
solid five minutes. When Aunt Elner is wheeled through the
hospital on the gurney as a dead person and suddenly
speaks to the shyster hospital admin man, I threw the book
across the room. Thank you, Fannie, thank you. You are my
literary comedic hero.

The Notebook

Okay, I admit it. I'm a sucker for romance. Nicholas Sparks
gets me every time. I remember reading this one on a short
airplane jaunt between Boston and New York and almost
tripping down the steps of the plane because I couldn't bear
not to finish the scene. My face was a slobbery mess when I
turned the final page. Oh . . . I also wish I was Nicholas
Sparks.

The Great Gatsby

I've finally gotten to the point where I'm grateful to my high school English teachers for insisting that we read the classics. F. Scott Fitzgerald was the first writer to truly grab my attention, probably due to his portrayal of decadence and the insincerity of aristocracy. He introduced me to Long Island and the Plaza Hotel, the Rolls-Royce and gigantic mansions, not to mention that he gave me my first glimpse into an intriguing blend of characters so rich in dysfunction, opulence, and mystery that I was hooked on reading. The relationship between Jay Gatsby and Daisy Buchanan still intrigues me to this day and inspires me, as a writer, to reach for the stars.

Charlotte's Web

Breaks my heart. I was only a third grader when I first learned of Fern, Wilbur, Templeton, and Charlotte but the book still resonates with me today. An innocent portrayal of maternal love, loyalty, and friendship, it inspires me toward greatness and to try my hand at a children's book. Did I mention I suffer from author envy? E. B. White takes the cake.

Divine Secrets of the Ya-Ya Sisterhood

I read *Ya-Ya* when I was just starting to write *Whistlin' Dixie* and it served as one of my greatest inspirations. Identifying with Siddalee was a no-brainer, having grown up with loads of family dysfunction. (Are we beginning to see a familiar theme here in my favorite books?) I laughed, I cried, and I screamed out loud, "I get it Sidda, I truly do." Rebecca Wells is a treasure and her ingenious portrayal of Southern, life-long friendships is spot-on.

Reading Group Questions

1. Alice, Virginia, and Mary Jule try talking Leelee out of moving to Vermont. How blunt should you be with your friends if you see them potentially making a big mistake? Were you frustrated with Leelee when she made her decision to follow Baker up North?

2. Would you move across the country or even out of the country for the person you love? Ponder the thought. If your spouse wanted to pursue a dream that would uproot the family, would you actually leave your comfort zone and move far away from all things familiar?

*Keep on
Reading*

3. Friendship is vastly important to Leelee. Why do you think this is true? Virginia, Alice, and Mary Jule surprise Leelee by coming to Vermont to help her through her toughest time. What is the most selfless thing you've done for a friend in need? How far would you travel to help a friend?

4. Leelee is surprised by her growing camaraderie with Roberta. Have you ever become close with someone who at first seemed an unlikely friend? Do you make a point to diversify your friendships?

5. How much influence do your friends have over your life? Do you consult them or your spouse first when making big decisions?

6. When Baker deserts Leelee, all she wants to do is come home to Memphis but Kissie talks her into staying put. She tells Leelee, "You can stay in Hell a little while, long as you know you're getting out." What does she mean by this? Would you have left at that point or stayed put?

7. Why do you think Leelee decided to go back home to Memphis instead of staying in Vermont with Peter?

8. Although grown, Leelee and her friends still enjoy their shenanigans together. What is the craziest thing you've ever done with your adult girlfriends? Are you ever too old for pranks?

9. Leelee's friends think she is a doormat because she has a hard time saying no. Do you agree? Are you able to tell someone no and be okay with it?

10. Southerners are often criticized for not saying what's on their mind, and Northerners are often accused of being too blunt. Do you agree with this? What are the pros and cons of both sides?